Peter Watt has spent time as a soldier, articled clerk, prawn trawler deckhand, builder's labourer, pipe layer, real estate salesman, private investigator, police sergeant and adviser to the Royal Papua New Guinea Constabulary. He speaks, reads and writes Vietnamese and Pidgin. He now lives at Maclean, on the Clarence River in northern New South Wales. Fishing and the vast open spaces of outback Queensland are his main interests in life.

Peter Watt can be contacted at www.peterwatt.com

Excerpts from emails sent to Peter Watt since his first novel was published:

'I must congratulate you on your very fine series of books, which I have found to be of the highest calibre. Do keep on writing as I for one look forward to each new offering.'

'I have just completed *Cry of the Curlew* – I loved it. The characters you create become so real, each with their own definite personalities . . . I love reading and learning about history, and I thank you for your writing and for opening up my eyes to the reality of early Australia.'

'Your books are so well written. They actually transport you right on that page. They make you feel that it is you there. I felt every pain, cried every tear, laughed every laugh, and smiled and loved every minute of it. A writer who can transport you in that way is definitely in my book *the best* and you are that person.'

'Your books give us some insight into a part of the world we will likely never get to see . . . Keep up the fine work.'

'I just wanted to let you know how much I have enjoyed your books . . . I really loved the complexity of the plot and the development of the characters as they aged – although I must say that we felt quite a loss when [one of the characters] died!'

'Your books are just the greatest I have ever read.'

'I have just finished reading the fifth book in the Duffy series, *To Touch the Clouds*, and as always I find your writing compelling and wonderful.'

'I was captivated [by *The Silent Frontier*], I couldn't put it down, and when I had to I was thinking about it and I wanted to pick it up and continue reading.'

'I can't get over how good your books are . . . they are amazing and the history is very insightful for a young bloke like me.'

'We loved [*Cry of the Curlew*] and everything that followed . . . The top bookshelf in our living room is all Peter Watt! Thank you so much for your writings.'

'Your stories are edgy, a bit sexy, with adventure, history, strong and marvellous characters and some great Australian towns and villains. Can't wait for your next novel to arrive.'

'I am hooked on your writing. When reading *Papua*, the characters came alive.'

'As usual I loved *The Frozen Circle*. The worst thing is that everything else that needs doing gets left until I have finished reading.'

'[*Cry of the Curlew*] is gut-grabbing. I found myself clenched with trepidation as I was not able to foresee the outcome of each twist and turn of character and event.'

PETER WATT

TO RIDE THE WIND

PAN
Pan Macmillan Australia

First published 2010 in Macmillan by Pan Macmillan Australia Pty Limited
This Pan edition published in 2011 by Pan Macmillan Australia Pty Limited
1 Market Street, Sydney

National Library of Australia
Cataloguing-in-Publication data:

Watt, Peter, 1949–.
To ride the wind / Peter Watt.

ISBN 978 0 3304 0415 0 (pbk.).

A823.3

Set in Bembo by Post Pre-press Group
Printed by IVE

For two special women,
my cousin, Virginia, and sister, Kerry.

Will he go in his sleep from these desolate lands,
Like a chief, to the rest of his race,
With the honey-voiced woman who beckons and stands,
And gleams like a dream in his face –
Like a marvellous dream in his face?

'The Last of His Tribe', Henry Kendall

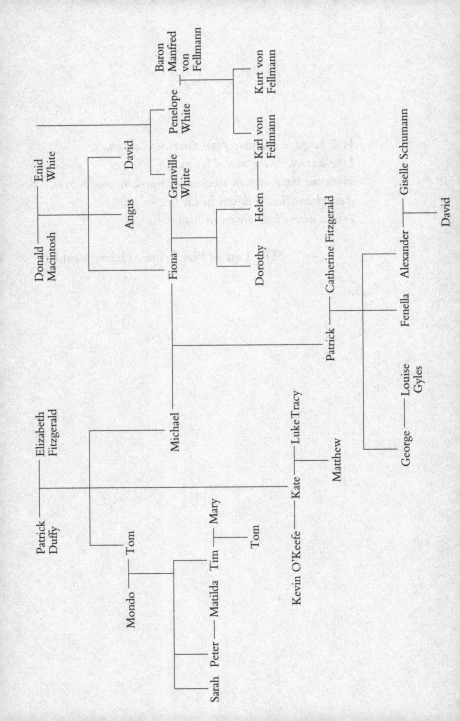

PROLOGUE

Central Queensland
Late Summer
1916

Leaning forward over the horse's neck the young man slid his hand to the rifle bucket. The searing air around him held a sinister silence he had experienced before when working as a stockman in the Gulf country of northern Australia. In those places the Aboriginal people still resisted the incursion of the white man and his cattle on their lands. He knew he was being watched – maybe some mysterious inheritance of his own Aboriginal blood had brought on his feelings of unease.

The Winchester repeating rifle was in his right hand but he was careful not to make it obvious that he was aware he was being observed from somewhere out in the arid brigalow scrub all around him. His mount snorted, raising her head with ears twitching. She had never let him down before and her actions only intensified his sense of potential danger.

Tom Duffy had ridden many hundreds of miles south

to be here. In his mid twenties, the young man was handsome by the standards of any race with his fine looks, olive skin and slightly crooked nose – the latter the result of a fistfight. His deep brown eyes reflected keen intelligence and he had the lean but muscled look of a man used to hard manual work on the vast cattle properties of the north. At first glance he might be mistaken as having Latin blood but on closer inspection it could be seen that he carried the blood of this new race of Australians who had emerged on an ancient continent. Half-caste, the white men called him, but still they envied his handsome features and proud bearing. Although reared in the white man's world, Duffy still suffered the snide remarks of his European workmates even though they grudgingly agreed on his skills around cattle and horses. Almost a whitefella, they would often comment behind his back.

Tom Duffy scanned the haze of the surrounding low, prickly trees, forcing his focus beyond the immediate stunted trees before him; there was nothing but a seemingly endless view of more scrub. The horse beneath him shifted sideways; she sensed the object of danger before her rider did.

'You can put the gun away,' the voice behind him said. 'If I wanted to kill you I would have done so before you even knew I was here.'

Tom slid the rifle back into its scabbard and turned his horse around to see an old Aboriginal propped against his deadly twelve-foot-long hardwood spear. He had a long grey beard, tribal scars and wore nothing more than a human hair belt with a couple of hardwood clubs tucked in the back.

As the two men's eyes met Tom noticed a sudden change in the warrior's demeanour. There was a hint of confusion and, at the same time, recognition.

'Tom!' the old man gasped.

The young stockman frowned. This had to be the legendary Wallarie. When his father had told him as a child of the kinsman he had not quite believed the stories. Men did not turn into eagles and fly. They were not able to become ghosts and hunt their enemies.

'Wallarie?' Tom slid from his mount to approach the old man. As he strode towards him he could see more gnarled scars on the old man which he took for marks made by bullets.

Wallarie dropped his spear and stepped forward to grip Tom by the shoulders. 'You have come back to me from the Dreaming, my brother,' he said, tears appearing in the corners of his eyes. 'It has been a long time since we hunted together.'

It was obvious that the old Aboriginal had confused him for someone else, Tom thought, although he had used his name correctly. He had been named after his grandfather, the infamous bushranger who had sired three children to his love, the Nerambura woman Mondo.

'I am the son of Tim Duffy, grandson of Tom Duffy and his woman, Mondo,' Tom said, realising the old Aboriginal was mistaking him for his grandfather. Wallarie had been as close to the white man as he could be to any of his own people.

'You are my whitefella brother's spirit come back to me in this body,' Wallarie answered.

Tom wanted to shrug off the mad blackfella's belief but felt it was best to humour him. After all, he had traversed a lot of hostile country to be here in the place of the dreams that haunted him – dreams about a hill and the sacred cave his father had often told him about before he died. His white mother, Mary, a cook in a hotel at Cloncurry, had dismissed

3

the stories as superstition. But now she was also dead. She had ensured that he received a European education and the young boy proved to be an excellent student, devouring his school work with such enthusiasm that he always came first in his class. But there was little opportunity for an educated, highly intelligent mixed-race boy and Tom found himself employed as a stockman in the Gulf of Carpentaria.

Without a word, Wallarie scooped up his spear and turned to walk through the haze of the scrub. Tom sensed that he should follow and led his horse, walking behind Wallarie. Before long he could see the top of a hill covered in sparse patches of stunted trees. Tom could have sworn that his feet had lost their power to move as the figure of the old Aboriginal was suddenly that of a young warrior, smeared with animal fat and strong muscles rippling on a lithe frame.

'Jesus, Mary and Joseph!' Tom swore, suddenly frightened by the apparition a few yards from him. But when he blinked he only saw Wallarie as he truly was – an old man with long, greying hair.

'You tie horse here and come with me,' Wallarie said, turning to look back at Tom, who removed hobbles from the horse to allow her to move about and graze on any sparse native grasses she could find.

Wallarie led Tom to the foot of the craggy hill that in the fading light had a strange, blood-like appearance about it. Tom followed him up a well-beaten, winding track to the peak from where he could look over a sweeping plain of scrub and red earth that stretched far beyond the limits of Glen View station. The sun was a red ball touching the horizon with a hot kiss.

'You come inside,' Wallarie said, gesturing to a half-hidden entrance to a dark place beyond. Tom hesitated and

Wallarie noticed his fear. 'Not going into your whitefella's hell,' he chuckled. 'Pastor Karl tell me about the Christian hell. He say it under the earth but I know that the good spirits live under the earth, not the debil.'

Tom stepped into the cave. A tiny fire still smouldered at its heart, throwing a dim light into the corners of the spacious opening upon whose walls he could see the ochre paintings of the Nerambura people, relating the story of ancient times as stick figures hunted giant kangaroos and warriors fought warriors.

'You sit here with me,' Wallarie said, gesturing to a place by the fire which he now stacked with a bundle of dry wood, causing it to flare into a gentle flame as smoke curled towards the rock ceiling. The old man produced a battered pipe and tamped down a plug of precious tobacco. Lighting the pipe he puffed contentedly away while Tom remained silent.

'You more whitefella spirit than blackfella,' Wallarie finally said, gazing at Tom across the fire. 'The last fella who come to the cave was a whitefella but he have more blackfella spirit than you. He fly with the great eagles in a place far, far from here.'

The accusation stung. Tom had long lived with the slurs against his mixed parentage. 'Why did you bring me here?' he asked.

'You have dream of this place?' Wallarie said.

'You could say that,' Tom retorted, still feeling wounded by the old man's blunt observation of him.

'Me think you my spirit brother who I rode with a long time ago,' Wallarie sighed. 'Me think he come back to take me to the sky where we hunt together and run away from the black crows of the Native Mounted Police. But they all gone now.'

'My father told me about you when I was a kid,' Tom said. 'I think he put the dreams in my head.'

'Mebbe.' Wallarie nodded. 'Mebbe not. Mebbe you meant to come here and see the Dreaming.'

'What do you know?' Tom asked, leaning forward in an attempt to see into the old man's eyes. Tom did not believe in the superstition of his Aboriginal ancestors, having become cynical when exposed to the great philosophical works of the European world and having seen the power of Western civilisation.

'I know that you do not believe in the ancestor spirits and their power over the world,' Wallarie answered. 'But the ancestor spirits believe in you.'

Tom shook his head, doubting the old man's observation.

'The ancestor spirits say that one day you become big boss of the whitefella,' Wallarie said. 'They say that first you must prove yourself as a warrior and kill more men than can be counted, and one day you be big boss. Many man and woman look up to you as their chief.'

Now Tom was convinced that the old Aboriginal was some kind of charlatan. No doubt he could fool uneducated stockmen and wild blackfellas with hints of supernatural powers. But the man who sat on the other side of the fire was nothing more than an aging Aboriginal – the last of his clan – who spun wild stories from a vivid imagination brought on by too many hours living alone in this landscape.

'But first you must stay alive in a white man's war far away from here,' Wallarie chuckled. 'Mebbe the ancestor spirits have fun with old Wallarie and tell him lies about you.'

'The white man's war is in Europe and they do not allow blackfellas to sign up,' Tom scoffed. 'No chance of me enlisting.'

Wallarie tapped his pipe on the log beside him. 'There is one who you must ride to. The ancestor spirits call her auntie and she will help you. She lives in a place called Townsville and her son believes in the curse that came to this place many seasons ago. The woman is my spirit sister. She has roamed all the lands of the north and has the soul of a warrior. Her name is Kate Tracy.'

'Kate Tracy,' Tom mused. 'I have heard of her. She was my grandfather's sister.'

Wallarie nodded. 'You must find her and listen to her words. The ancestor spirits do not tell me all, but I know she has the power to set you on the great hunt for your true place in this world.'

Tom smiled. 'Old man, your words are good but I am not some superstitious blackfella. I wish your thoughts were true but to the white man I am just another Abo – a boong, a half-caste.'

'Be proud of your blood,' Wallarie said softly. 'You are of the new people who come from the earth of this land. One day you will see that ol' Wallarie know because he listens to the sounds in the dark. Now it is time for you to go and ride to my spirit sister and listen to her words. The ancestors have told me that you will find the fiery stars in a land far from here and they will give you much power. You will be the man who will return our clan's blood to this land. Now I am tired and must sleep.'

Realising that he was being dismissed, Tom rose stiffly to his feet. 'I brought this,' he said, taking from his pocket a tin of pipe tobacco and placing it on the earth. 'My father said you had a liking for it.'

Wallarie looked up at the young man and smiled. 'You are a cheeky bugger – but your father was right. Mebbe there is hope for you if you listen to your Nerambura blood.'

'Maybe we will meet again,' Tom said, turning towards the entrance of the cave.

'Mebbe,' Wallarie answered, reaching for the round tin.

Tom left the cave just as the last light flickered on the horizon to the west. 'Matches,' he muttered, remembering that he had meant to leave Wallarie a packet. Quickly he returned but was stunned to see that Wallarie was gone. He searched in every part of the cave's interior but there was no trace of the old Aboriginal.

Mystified, Tom stood at the head of the track back down to where he'd left his horse. Suddenly the shadow of a huge wedge-tailed eagle rose up behind him from an old gum tree. The flutter of its wings caused Tom to jump as the great bird of the inland plains rose into the air to fly towards the sinking sun.

Tom shook his head. It was impossible. The unexpected appearance of the bird was nothing more than a coincidence and yet he remembered Wallarie's last words about listening to his Nerambura blood. Had the old warrior flown from the hill as an eagle? As Tom stumbled down the track he attempted to tell himself the great bird was nothing more than just that. But still . . .

After Wallarie watched the young man walk away, he closed his eyes to dream. He could see the plains below drenched in the blood of the current owners but the image was not of this time. He knew that he was seeing the death of many of the Macintosh and Duffy clans. He had not assured his visitor that he would live when he went as a warrior to fight in the whitefella war. Only the ancestors knew a man's fate, but Wallarie suspected that Tom's ability to stay alive would depend on his skills as a warrior. He did know that the good would die with the bad and Glen View would become a place of grieving. Just as it had a half century before when his people had been slaughtered by the whitefellas who came to seize the lands he still roamed.

PART ONE

1916

I

Lieutenant Colonel Patrick Duffy was approaching his fiftieth year, having served in three colonial wars for the British Empire. Tall with broad shoulders, he still had the patrician appearance of a man who inspired confidence in those he led. As a battalion commander, he had brought his men off the beaches at Gallipoli a few months earlier and his competence and concern for his men there earned their respect.

Now, as he leaned against the damp parapet of the trench, scanning the no-man's-land before him with a pair of field glasses, he wondered if they would continue to respect him after hearing the insane orders he must deliver to his company commanders. Briefed by the brigade commander at a gathering of battalion COs, he had raised the question of adequate artillery support for the planned assault on the formidable German entrenchments a mere 500 yards away.

The answer he received made the tactic appear suicidal, although he as an officer could not reveal his personal opinions to the men he would lead in the attack.

He could see a plain of knee-high grasses, nurtured by the rain and sun of the northern summer, sweeping towards a gentle rise etched with the outline of entrenchments along the high ground in front of him. The sea of grass covered the scars of battles from the year before when the British army had suffered terrible casualties on the German-held ground. Now it was the Australians' turn to assault the German trenches.

Only hours earlier Patrick had been behind the Australian lines, basking in the warmth of a beautiful summer's day, listening to the lazy hum of bees as they buzzed around fields of red poppies and watching butterflies flitting among pastures of blue wild flowers. The lush green grass dotted between neatly defined fields clearly impressed those men of his battalion who had worked the harsh lands of Australia, while the cleanliness of this countryside paradise was a sharp rebuke to his Gallipoli veterans, who were still living with the memory of flies, dust and, when the dust had gone, the biting cold of the peninsular winter.

As Patrick stepped back into the trench, his boots squelched in the glutinous clay. The stench of wet soil, cordite, decomposing flesh and human waste permeated the muggy air. Now he was away from the land behind the lines and had gone from heaven to hell in a matter of a few short miles.

'What do you reckon, sir?' Patrick's second-in-command asked. Major Fred Higgins had once been a solicitor practising with a well-known Melbourne firm before being commissioned into the army. Like Patrick, he had served with his local militia before the outbreak of war and, like all the men waiting that day, he was a volunteer.

'It's bloody flat terrain and the Huns have the only high ground worth a pinch of anything,' Patrick said, rubbing his eyes with the back of his hand. 'If we cross that bit of ground without a truly devastating bombardment from our guns then we can expect the worst.'

'They must know that at divvie level,' Major Higgins said, glancing around to ensure that their conversation was not being overheard by any of the soldiers near them in the trench.

'They don't ask the opinions of mere battalion commanders,' Patrick sighed. 'It's time to call in the company commanders for a final briefing.'

'Righto,' Major Higgins replied. 'I will have them report within the hour.'

'Good show.'

For a moment Patrick was alone in the trench, a rare moment to reflect. How different this time and place were to what they had known fighting the Turkish troops of the Ottoman Empire. His men had rejoiced in the country-side so wonderfully different from what they had known on the narrow beach and rugged gullies of the peninsula. Unlike Patrick, they did not dwell on the fact that, since 1914, this very land had seen the death and maiming of men on a scale far beyond their experiences in the Dardanelles campaign. Here was massed artillery capable of smashing whole divisions in a day, and barbed wire entanglements that stretched from the cobblestoned beaches of Belgium to the snow-capped mountains of Switzerland. No, this campaign was huge. Patrick felt some nostalgia for the trenches he left behind at Anzac Cove but well knew that the extent of a soldier's world on the battlefield was limited to the bit of earth that he could see and walk over; all else mattered little to the soldier with rifle and bayonet. He only knew terms like flanks, fronts and sectors. They had no bearing on his personal survival on that patch of ground that lay before him and which he must cross. Within the hour, Battalion Commander Patrick Duffy would be briefing his younger company commanders on their roles in the attack to be launched against what Patrick suspected was a well-entrenched and armed enemy. He fully knew that after the attack there would likely be many faces missing from his debrief – maybe even his own.

The company commanders assembled in battalion headquarters behind the lines. It was a sharp contrast to the trench line only a mere couple of miles away where Patrick had his forward tactical HQ. Young girls were selling gingerbread to his soldiers scattered about in their companies and the blue of the cornflowers in the fields contrasted sharply with the red geraniums in the windows of the picturesque stone cottages of the local farmers. He issued his orders which in turn would be filtered down to the platoon commanders and, finally, to the section commanders. Each and every soldier would be aware of his role in the upcoming attack on the German lines, and quartermasters set about issuing the extra equipment of shovels, hand grenades, bullets, sandbags and bandages needed in the operation.

'Mr Duffy,' Patrick said as his company commanders rose from around the earthen model that had been constructed to scale to display what was known of the enemy's fortifications. 'A word with you before you rejoin your lads.'

Sean Duffy, a young good-looking man in his late twenties, paused. He had been a solicitor in Sydney before being commissioned into the Australian Imperial Forces and was also a distant relative of Patrick. He had first served as a platoon commander at Gallipoli before taking over the dead company commander's position as acting OC. Patrick was supposed to replace him with a major from reinforcements but had been deliberately remiss in doing so. After Gallipoli the former solicitor had been decorated for bravery with a Military Cross and the men followed him for his competent leadership. He had been outstanding in his role as acting company commander, although he wore the rank of a lowly lieutenant.

'Sir,' he acknowledged with just the slightest frown.

Patrick looked him up and down with an expression of annoyance. 'I see that you have reported to my O group not properly dressed,' he said sternly, forcing himself to suppress a smile.

'Sir?' Sean replied, puzzled by the remonstration.

'You are not wearing the rank that has been gazetted and which was received in orders at my headquarters yesterday.'

Confused, Sean stared as Patrick reached into his trouser pocket to produce two star-like pips. 'Congratulations, Captain Duffy.'

Sean accepted the pips that would now make three on each of his epaulets but glanced up at Patrick with concern. 'These do not mean that I lose my company?' he asked.

'No, Captain Duffy,' Patrick replied. 'You remain to lead your men until those up top decide to send a replacement company commander.'

The position was normally held with the rank of major and Sean was still one rank below. Patrick not only respected his subordinate but was also very fond of him. A couple of years earlier Sean had acted in his legal capacity to assist Patrick's estranged daughter, Fenella, in matters concerning the murder of a well-known Australian actor. Patrick also suspected that Sean had fallen in love with his daughter but the two men had never spoken directly of his feelings. Now a bond had been forged between the two men separated by age and rank but united by a common blood in the rugged hills and ravines of the Gallipoli peninsula.

Patrick's beloved daughter was now making a name for herself as an actress in the American film industry. He had two other children – sons, but so very unalike. His youngest son, Alexander, was a major posted to a training battalion in Australia, while his eldest son, George, remained a civilian managing the vast financial empire of the Macintosh family of which Patrick was the head, despite retaining his family birth name. 'I am also sending one of the reinforcements from Brigade to your company HQ,' he added. 'His name is Jack Kelly and he is a South Australian who, I believe, had a colourful life in and around Papua and German New Guinea before he enlisted. Corporal Kelly is fluent in German, as it appears his mother was one of those many Germans we have at home. He has not seen any action yet, but his record is very good and I am sure he will prove useful if we take any prisoners.'

Sean would have liked to ask his commander his opinions on the forthcoming battle but refrained from doing so as he knew it would be inappropriate. 'Sir, thank you for the promotion,' he said instead. 'I have a feeling that you had something to do with it.'

'Not at all,' Patrick lied with a smile. 'You well and truly earned it but it will not get you out of further officer training at Staff College in Blighty. But that won't be until we finish our job in the stunt tomorrow. Now, go and join your company, Captain Duffy, and good luck.'

'Thank you, boss,' Sean replied, saluting his CO in the relative safety of the HQ. It was not a practice done in the field since it would inevitably draw attention to officers, who could be marked for elimination by enemy snipers.

As Patrick watched the departing back of his acting company commander, he wondered why he had not shared the news that came in the same set of orders delivered to his HQ, informing him that he had been gazetted to the rank of full colonel. Although it was an honour, he also knew that the promotion probably meant that he was slotted for a staff job in the divisional headquarters. Leaving his battalion was akin to being forced to relinquish his family. At least he still had command of his men in this attack on the formidable German lines.

That night the skies burst and the deluge pummelled all below. As the artillery could not register its targets on account of the lack of visibility, the attack was delayed. For soldiers waiting to 'hop the sandbags' this only meant more time to dwell on what lay before them. They shivered and cursed the soaking they were receiving in the forward trenches.

When the next day dawned a heavy mist lay across no-man's-land. From the high ground overlooking the Allied lines a senior German officer scanned the ground to the trenches where he knew the Australians were located.

'Will they come today?' a subordinate but still senior officer from the German regimental staff asked.

'No,' General Major Kurt von Fellmann replied. 'The mist obscures their gunners' means of observation. But they will come when the mist clears. I think tomorrow.'

He stepped off the fire step and into a deep, well-constructed trench to speak with his intelligence staff. They had been thorough in their battlefield assessments, observing the extra ammunition being brought forward as well as sandbags, scaling ladders, duckboards, shovels and picks – all activities that warned of an attack.

'We can expect a preliminary bombardment that will alert us to the attack,' he said wearily. 'Then they will come.'

All the staff officers clustered about the brigade commander nodded in agreement before he dismissed them.

'I believe a distant relative of your family commands a battalion in the English lines, sir,' the German colonel said quietly.

'Yes, Colonel Patrick Duffy,' Kurt replied. 'I met him a couple of years ago when I was on a visit to our Pacific territories. He is a good man.'

Kurt had learned from an intelligence briefing by his staff of some of the names of opposing commanders, and was startled to see Patrick's name among the enemy. Had it come to this when relatives, albeit distant, should try to kill each other? Almost two years of war and the butcher's bill was beyond the imagination of even the most pessimistic commanders. But he knew the answer. On both sides of the barbed wire military leaders were caught off guard by the development of weapons beyond their experiences fighting colonial wars against native peoples. The tactics used then were obsolete now.

'Do you think that we can hold our ground?' his assistant, a junior officer whose family lived in the province of Saxony, asked only to receive a reproving look from his commander.

'We will hold and I daresay the British will suffer terrible losses crossing no-man's-land,' Kurt answered. 'All we have to do is keep our heads during their inevitable artillery bombardment and man the parapets when the first of the enemy emerge from their trenches. The rest will result in the usual bloody list of dead – more their side than our own.'

Satisfied, the subordinate officer did not ask any more

questions and both men made their way down the trench. Kurt found himself reflecting on the next twenty-four hours and hoped that Patrick would not be killed leading his men. Despite the fact that they were sworn enemies, he was still a man he liked and respected.

On the other side of the world a former German consulate staff member sat playing chess in a cold and draughty tent. Maynard Bosch had been detained by the Australian government just after the declaration of war in 1914 and interned in a camp west of Sydney at a place called Holdsworthy. Over time, the small town of ramshackle structures and tents surrounded by wires and wooden towers had settled into a civilian community of men, women and children deemed to be enemy aliens. Although the German-descended civilians and nationals were not ill-treated, the conditions they lived under were spartan. To relieve their monotonous lives under the barrels of the tower-mounted machine guns the internees soon organised social groups and even shops to cater to their needs.

It was winter in the southern hemisphere and yet the cold was not as bad as might be found in faraway Europe when that season descended in snow and sleet. Maynard Bosch had befriended a Lutheran pastor, Karl von Fellmann, whose parish lay in central Queensland on a property called Glen View. The pastor had buried his dead wife in the red earth of his mission station and, from what Maynard could discern, the Lutheran man of God had no intentions of ever returning to the Fatherland. This was surprising to Maynard as he knew the pastor had a twin brother who was a highly placed officer in the Kaiser's army. But von Fellmann seemed content to sit out the war until the day he could return to his mission station, where sometimes lived an old Aboriginal the pastor often spoke about as his spiritual brother.

But Maynard Bosch had no intentions of sitting out the war while the Fatherland was struggling to win in Europe. Prior to 1914 he had been active in intelligence gathering and now vowed to do as much as he could to help his country – even from the confines of an internment camp.

'Your move, Pastor,' he said, bent over the slab of wooden plank they had marked up as a chessboard in an improvised carpentry shop. The pieces had been carved from local timbers by a skilled craftsman and were a work of art. They could have been sold to the guards for a good price but were more valuable helping pass the time in the camp.

'You have checkmated me, my friend,' Karl replied, glancing up from the pieces still left on the board. 'I think it is time that I should retire.'

Bosch rearranged the chess pieces as the Lutheran pastor stood with a sigh and stretched his weary limbs. Karl bid his chess opponent a good night and left the tent for his own at the end of the row, passing the pinched faces of women and children sitting quietly outside their abodes to take in the startling display of stars on this still, cold night. He greeted them warmly and they returned the salutations to the man they all respected for his gentle ministering to their spiritual and temporal needs.

Maynard Bosch waited for his friend to leave and when he was satisfied that Karl was well away, slid open a false bottom in the chessboard, revealing a thin compartment containing sheaves of paper. The papers each were scrawled in fine copperplate – information gleaned by Bosch's contact on the other side of the wire. He read carefully through the notes he had been delivered and immediately started making notes of his own, turning what looked like random observations into strategic intelligence. The information on Australian politics had been gleaned from a source beyond that available to the newspapers and touched on some very sensitive areas.

Bosch would need to distil the copious observations into succinct briefings for his superiors in faraway Berlin. While he could do this very competently, transferring the information halfway across the world was a different matter. But he already had in place a clever means of delivery. As a spymaster he had established his network and felt well pleased with himself for his foresight and skill. Although he was seemingly impotent to alter the course of the war, sitting in his tent within the wire fencing of a prison camp, he was still fighting for his country and some pieces of his intelligence could help kill Australian troops, allies of the English, on the distant battlefields. Von Fellmann's regular visitor acted as a liaison between him and the outside world, bringing in the collected intelligence and taking out the encoded reports. Bosch wondered what the man with the strong convictions would say if he knew his friend was using him to carry out espionage activities. Bosch shrugged. He was also acutely aware that if he was discovered in his present capacity as an intelligence gatherer – a spy – he would surely be executed by the Australian government, and so too would anyone proved working with him.

By the dim light of a kerosene lantern he worked alone in the cold, making his notes in a code that he hoped would not be broken if intercepted. The next stage was to transfer his coded message to Berlin and for that he would have to use his Australian-born civilian contact – a man who was the most unlikely of German sympathisers as he had a brother serving in the army and a father fighting on the battlefields of France.

★

George Macintosh gazed across the candlelit, polished dining room table at those surrounding him. The dinner was a regular Sunday night gathering at his mansion overlooking Sydney Harbour, a family tradition. George loathed these Sunday evening meals but his beautiful wife, Louise, insisted on the tradition being continued despite the fact that the family head, Patrick Duffy, could not be present. Talk of war was forbidden at the table at the insistence of George, who now ruled his family's vast financial empire to the extent that he actually paid his father and brother an allowance.

Sitting opposite him was his younger brother, Alexander, wearing his army uniform, a shiny Sam Browne belt across his chest. George was in his early thirties, his younger brother in his late twenties. They were a matching pair, having inherited their handsome Irish looks from their father. Beside George sat his brother's wife, Giselle, equally as beautiful as his own wife. It was ironic, George mused, that his younger brother should be married to a German Jewess who should by all means be interned at Holdsworthy – along with her mother.

The two seats left vacant at the table were meant for Fenella, who they all knew was living in California and working in the American film industry but under the assumed name of Fiona Owen. The second vacant place at the table was set for his father, anticipating his safe return from the war. The layout of the chairs had been insisted upon by Louise although George considered the tradition she was establishing to be complete sentimental nonsense. Secretly, he hoped that both places would not be filled; he wanted his father, brother and sister all dead, leaving him with complete power over the family business. He had used his managerial skills as an excuse to remain out of uniform mostly because he was afraid he might be killed in a war. But he dismissed his cowardly action with the rationale that by managing the company's links with the booming war production he was more important to Australia's strategic needs.

The fact that he had been able to secure very lucrative contracts with the government, supplying products on a grand scale, had helped the Macintosh family expand their already overflowing coffers, and George had voted himself a generous salary rise for his efforts while his brother insisted on living on his army pay. But Alex was a fool, and even more of a threat to all that George's ancestors had struggled for in their Protestant world after promising to raise his newly born son in the Jewish faith. That alone was enough to want his stupid brother dead. George cursed the fact that the military powers had not satisfied his brother's request to be sent off to war instead of leaving him at home in a training unit. After all, had not Alex proved his bravery in the covert operation against the Germans in the Pacific before the outbreak of war? Given time and good luck George might yet see the demise of his family in this time of war. He could only pray to the devil for such to eventuate.

'To those not with us tonight,' Alex said, raising his glass of wine. 'Hear, hear,' echoed from those gathered around the table. Even George responded to the toast. He did not want to be seen in his true colours although secretly he was toasting the prospect of his father's death.

'We are not to speak of the war,' George cautioned, placing his crystal goblet on the table before him. 'That was a rule we agreed on.'

'What should we talk about?' Alex asked. 'How the family business is booming when so many of my friends have already lost their lives in this war?'

'I know that you would like to join them,' George retorted.

'You mean – die,' Alex countered with a grim smile.

'No, no . . . I did not mean that,' George hurriedly said. 'I meant join them on the battlefield, where you belong.'

'I think that we can find a more pleasant subject of conversation than battlefields and business profits,' Louise said, attempting to defuse what she could see was a dangerous tension. She received a grateful look from Giselle, who also knew of the brothers' mutual animosity. 'Now that the table will be cleared I suggest we retire to the drawing room for coffee,' she continued, rising to lead the way, but her example quickly followed only by Giselle.

'I am sorry for that,' Giselle said to Louise as they made their way to stand beside the warm, glowing open fire. 'Alex is frustrated by the fact the army will not send him overseas. He becomes melancholy.'

'But I suspect that you are pleased he has been forced to remain home and can be with you and the baby,' Louise said, gently squeezing her best friend's elbow.

Giselle looked guilty. 'What woman wants to remain behind knowing that the man she most loves in this world might be killed? I pray that the war will be over before Alex can be sent to fight.'

'But you do not tell him of your fears,' Louise said gently, guiding her to a table where a decanter sat beside a tray of tiny crystal goblets set out by their house maid. 'Men are absolute fools if they think they can impress us with their heroic gestures of riding off to war.'

'You are fortunate,' Giselle said, accepting a glass of sweet sherry. 'At least George had the sense to remain out of uniform.' For a moment she could have sworn she saw a scowl cross her friend's face.

'Do you ever hear from Alex's cousin, Mr Matthew Duffy?' Louise asked, changing the subject.

Giselle glanced at her friend and replied with a mischievous tone. 'Alex still receives his letters but it is strange that you should so unexpectedly ask about him. Although he is rather handsome, dashing and single . . . as far as I know. Matthew is in England awaiting transfer with his squadron. At least, that is the last Alex heard.'

'Don't get any wrong ideas,' Louise chuckled. 'I was merely making idle conversation.'

'But he is rather dashing, is he not?' Giselle persisted, enjoying this game of teasing her friend who was more like a sister to her than a former schoolmate from the posh ladies' college they'd attended years earlier in Sydney.

'Oh, I wish I'd had the opportunity to accept his offer to fly up into the sky in his aeroplane before the war,' Louise sighed, taking a sip of her drink. 'It is so boring being married with little to do – except occupy George's bed, host his fat business acquaintances and supervise the servants. I wish I could do something that has meaning. At least your mother is doing something for the war cause, albeit for the other side, by visiting the internment camp and liaising with our authorities to help those poor women and children behind the wire. One has to admire Karolina for her selfless acts of charity.'

'I think that she has met someone at the camp she may be romantically interested in,' Giselle said, moving a short distance away from the fire gently flickering in the hearth.

'Oh, do tell!' Louise exclaimed.

'He is actually a distant relative of our family,' Giselle replied, wondering if she should indulge in gossip about her mother's affairs of the heart. For a long time her mother had been bitter about the death of Giselle's father in New Guinea. A native uprising had taken his life and she had blamed the Australian government, stating that if the natives had not known of the Australians seizing German territory they may have never rebelled, and her husband would still be alive. Giselle had disagreed, saying that they had no proof of this and that the natives at the end of the valley were always skirmishing with them. 'His name is Karl von Fellmann and he is a Lutheran pastor.'

'I know him,' Louise said thoughtfully. 'I met him at the regimental ball back in '14. He was with his twin brother, Kurt, at the time and I thought that they were a very handsome pair. Your mother has good taste in men. I remember how handsome your father was.' Louise could see the pain in her friend's face at the mention of her dead father and chose to change the course of the conversation. 'Well, I have been meaning to ask you if you would like to join me at the theatre this Tuesday to see Nellie's latest film.'

'That would be grand,' Giselle answered. 'We could do some shopping as well.'

As the two women continued to chatter about matters important to the family, Alex and George sat at the table with a bottle of good port between them. George had uncharacteristically taken to imbibing strong spirits since the outbreak of the war and Alex thought that at least this made him a little more human.

'George,' he said, taking a long sip. 'You and I may not have seen eye to eye on a lot of matters but I am going to ask a great favour of you.'

George stiffened. 'What would that be, old boy?'

'You know how much it means to me to join Father in France on the front,' Alex said, swallowing not only the port but his pride. 'And I know how close you are to people in the government. I was wondering if you could put in a word to those in the war department to have me transferred overseas.'

The tension in George flowed away. His brother was the fool he took him for, wanting to rush off to be killed. He would be more than happy to help him do so. Alex could not have asked a more pleasing favour. 'I must admit that I do have some highly placed contacts and it would be my pleasure to help you realise a dream,' he answered. 'I promise you that I will call on every favour owed me and get you transferred overseas to join Father.'

'I thought that my request might please you,' Alex replied, raising his glass in mock salute.

No other words were said about the matter between the two brothers and Alex soon rose to join the ladies in the drawing room, leaving his brother at the table to consider how he could satisfy Alex's request and at the same time see one of his own dreams come true. With any luck Alex would die a hero's death and bring glory on the Macintosh family name for the generations yet to be born in the dynasty.

2

'Cut!'
Randolph Gates could still feel the ringing in his ears and taste the Californian dirt in his mouth. The six gun on his hip had left a throbbing pain in his side which he guessed would produce a huge bruise. He lay face down and could hear the snorting of the horse that had thrown him a few feet away.

'You okay, pal?' a male voice asked above him.

He felt a pair of hands attempt to roll him over and hoist him into a sitting position. Randolph spat dirt from his mouth and gazed around the film lot. He focused on the cumbersome cameras and the men standing around while the director stood holding a cone-shaped megaphone at his side and watching him.

'They get the shot?' Randolph asked, clambering to his feet clumsily with the assistance of one of the film crew.

'Yeah, but I don't think your horse throwing you was in the script.'

Randolph dusted off the heavy cowboy chaps he was wearing with his huge Stetson hat and rubbed his hip. He recognised the man who had helped him as the assistant director, Joe Oblachinski. He had shown at least some concern for Randolph's welfare even if the young man holding the megaphone had not. It was the last day of the project and Randolph had been able to get a part in the cowboy film supporting the main actor, an Italian immigrant with oily dark looks and equally slimy charm. At least that was Randolph's opinion of him – though not that of the adoring female fans or, it would seem, Fenella Macintosh's.

Fenella was now known as Fiona Owens and was already a big name on the screen. She was touted by the film industry of California as an Irish woman although the surname was obviously Welsh, but this did not seem to matter to the movie studio's publicity department. When Randolph cast about to find her he noticed that she was deep in conversation with the up-and-coming Italian actor off to one side of the set. She had paid hardly any attention to his nearly fatal fall when his mount had suddenly baulked at the sound of an explosion on a nearby set where they were filming a Western using explosives to simulate a blown bank safe.

'You look like you could do with a shot,' Joe Oblachinski said, helping Randolph off the centre of the set to a folding canvas chair. 'We will keep the last bit of you being thrown in the can for a future film. Nothing gets wasted around here.'

Randolph nodded, watching Fenella break into soft laughter and lean forward to the Italian actor. It was obvious that he had her complete attention. Randolph shook his head in an attempt to clear the ringing in his ears and was satisfied to note he was not as hurt as he might have been. 'Thanks, Joe,' he said when the assistant director passed him a hip flask containing a shot of good bourbon to ease his pain. The American film man was of solid build and in his early thirties. Prior to drifting into the flourishing film industry he had managed a company making cameras and, on a whim, decided to stake his career using the cameras to make films for the entertainment industry. Randolph liked Joe and they often would drink together at the end of the day and have a game of pool in the newly opened hall constructed by Louis B Mayer on the corner of Hollywood and Western streets. It was a dingy smoke-filled basement in the movie producer's building but a place where Randolph could forget his troubles with Fenella.

'Fiona seems a bit distracted by that Dago,' Joe said, sensing that his friend was more upset by what he was observing than the heavy fall from the horse.

Randolph shook his head as if to dismiss Joe's comment. He had now lived in California for almost two years. At first his arrival had been welcomed by an overjoyed Fenella. She had been able to get him employment as a stunt man on the sets and he had proved very good at his job. The strict moral code of her studio bosses forbade her living with Randolph and marriage was a subject she avoided whenever Randolph hinted at their future. He was quickly learning how ambitious the daughter of Patrick Duffy was. Fenella would often rage at some other actress being given a role she felt should have been hers. Randolph was slowly learning too that he was not the centre of her universe, despite the fact that she had the ability to throw him off balance with her declarations of love for him alone. But California's seedy past had not been left behind. Randolph knew of the studio parties where sex, hootch and drugs were a heady part of the entertainment for those in the film industry. The town of Los Angeles was rapidly becoming a movie-dominated place of dirty secrets. The big studios ruled local politics and scandals were quickly suppressed by the specialists hired to do so by the movie moguls. Although, as a mere stuntman, Randolph was not invited to the parties in the rich suburbs of LA, he knew that Fenella attended. She did not attempt to hide the fact that she had been at rumoured sex orgies but denied she had ever let herself get involved, calming Randolph with the excuse that she had to be at the parties to garner favours for better roles from the movie executives.

Despite Fenella's declarations of love and her reasons for getting mixed up in the rumour mill, Randolph was beginning to consider moving on without her. His pride was severely hurt by the stories he would hear of what Fenella did behind his back. It was obvious to him that her words of endearment rang hollow. How could he compete against the younger, more handsome and suave men of the movie industry in California? He would have to confront Fenella at some time to save the little of his pride that still remained. He had survived years in dangerous places with his best friend, Matthew Duffy, who was now flying air-craft somewhere over Egypt or Palestine. He realised that he missed Matthew's company. Maybe it was time to join his old buddy.

Randolph glanced over at Fenella and saw her bend back her head in laughter at something the Italian actor said.

Turning his back, Randolph strode off the set with Joe.

Across the Pacific Ocean in Sydney, George Macintosh sat in his well-furnished office of the Macintosh companies in

Kent Street. He was not alone. Across the room sat a very attractive woman in her early forties. The presence of this woman, Karolina Schumann, made George very uneasy despite the fact that she was the mother-in-law of his brother, Alexander. Not only was she a German national released from the internment camp outside Sydney on his father's word, but she had in her hands a sheaf of papers for him that were as deadly as the poison gas now being used by both sides on the Western Front.

'How is Herr Bosch?' George hoped against hope that Karolina might say he was dying.

'He is well,' she replied. 'He sends his compliments.'

'Do you have much contact with him?' he asked, aware of the tension between them.

'Very little,' Karolina said. 'The guards observe me in the company of Pastor von Fellmann, whom they do not suspect. He has the respect of the commandant of the camp and their trust.'

George knew that the Lutheran minister was not a part of Karolina's espionage but simply a pawn in her danger-ous game. Karolina was a patriot prepared to die for the Fatherland. The former assistant German consul to Syd-ney, Maynard Bosch, was Karolina's contact in the camp and the puppet master for spying activities. George had deluded himself before the outbreak of war that he'd been an innocent contact, but now he was being blackmailed into reluctantly helping the spymaster transfer intelligence.

'My wife commented that you may have feelings for the pastor,' George said, taking the normally composed woman by surprise.

'Why would Louise say that?' she countered.

'Oh, I suspect idle gossip with your daughter,' George answered.

An expression of concern crossed Karolina's face. Giselle was completely unaware of her role in espionage and Karolina wanted it to stay that way to protect her daughter and grandson. That Giselle had paid so much interest in her comings and goings from the camp was disturbing. Karolina did not want to consider the consequences of her own discovery if things went wrong.

'Well, it is not true,' Karolina lied. She was, in fact, growing more than fond of the widower. 'But I am not here for gossip. I have the papers that we wish to send to Sweden.'

Karolina rose, walked over to George's desk and placed the sheaf on the ink blotter on his highly polished teak desk. George scanned the first page and noted that it was in the code he had seen before but been unable to decipher. The papers would be posted to an address in Stockholm linked to the Macintosh companies, and from there spirited to Berlin. To the casual observer they were lists of notes on commercial matters concerning wheat and sheep. International commerce went on, despite naval blockades, and Sweden was a neutral country, profiting from the madness of warring Europe.

'It will be done,' George said, placing the papers in a drawer of his desk, locking it with a key he always carried on his person. He knew that by complying with her wishes the Macintosh commercial interests in the German chemical industry were being secretly protected by the Kaiser's government. Still, George was uncomfortably aware that his brother had once mentioned in casual conversation that entering into correspondence with the enemy amounted to treason, one of the few capital offences under Australian army law. Unlike British military law, an Australian soldier could not be executed for running in the face of the enemy or desertion – something that British commanders, and some Australian commanders, bridled at.

'I have a request,' Karolina said, preparing to leave George's office.

'What is that?' he replied suspiciously.

'I believe that you are attending a garden party next weekend at Sir Keith Gyles' house,' Karolina said. 'I would like you to organise an invitation for me.'

'That can be arranged,' George said in a tired voice. He knew full well that many highly placed government civil servants would also be there – along with some front-bench politicians – and it was obvious to him why Karolina wanted to be present.

Captain Matthew Duffy's neck was stiff from continuously scanning the pale blue sky around him. The noise of the V8 engine of his BE2c twin-seat biplane deafened him and his gunner/observer, who was sitting in the forward cockpit swivelling his two Lewis guns, searching for a target. Matthew prayed they would not be intercepted by any of the superior German fighter planes en route to their targets near the Egyptian village of Romani. His aircraft was much slower and less manoeuvrable than the German Fokker fighters, as the British-built aeroplane was designed as an observation aircraft to be stable rather than nimble.

Below him were the ever-present arid deserts around the Suez Canal. At low altitude the heat given off by the hot sands would wash over him and the New Zealand–born Sergeant Bruce Forsyth. Sergeant Forsyth had once represented his nation as a rugby player and it took some effort to squeeze his solid build into the forward cockpit. He had enlisted in the Australian army on the first day of war as he had been working as a sales representative in the country and had met Matthew in England before their squadron was posted to Egypt. Matthew had bridled at his transfer as he had hoped for action on the Western Front with a squadron in the latest designed fighter planes. But his previous experience with the Half Flight in Mesopotamia had got him assigned to the ancient Biblical lands of the Middle East once again. There he had found himself flying photo recon missions as well as undertaking the occasional strafing and bombing of Turkish troops, airfields and infantry columns. It was dangerous but not glamorous work for an airman hoping for the honour of being called an ace. To reach the five enemy aircraft downed needed for the title of ace, he found himself five short of the total required. He was, however, seeing his dream of aerial warfare put into practice. Since the outbreak of war in 1914 aeroplanes were now being used as offensive weapons over the battlefields instead of simply passive collectors of intelligence.

His gunner suddenly gestured down to the starboard side of their aircraft. Matthew craned his neck to gaze at the flat desert below them and as he did so he could see his gunner swivel his twin machine guns. Then Matthew saw what had attracted Sergeant Forsyth's attention. Below them was a Turkish patrol of soldiers. Around platoon strength, Matthew calculated. They were closely clumped together and had seen the low flying aircraft, and were already desperately setting up a machine gun on a tall tripod constructed for anti-aircraft defence.

Bruce turned to grin at Matthew, his face smeared black by engine oil and only his goggles cleaned to provide vision. Matthew nodded vigorously and flipped the aircraft into a banking motion. What had first appeared as little dots now took on the form of uniformed men as Matthew guided his aircraft into a shallow dive. Bruce was already firing, the sound of the machine guns merging with the roar of the engine. Spent cartridge cases glittered in the sun as the New Zealand gunner poured a stream of .303 bullets into the enemy scattering below. Matthew saw men fall as the bullets found their targets on the first sweep. He pulled up, aware that his little biplane was lucky to make 70 knots of speed and was alarmed to feel the frame of his aeroplane shudder. The enemy were returning fire and some of their bullets were ripping through the flimsy canvas of his wings. Matthew jerked on the controls to take him off a straight course. The aircraft responded, reassuring him that his ailerons were undamaged by the Turkish fire. Bruce was occupied replacing the empty ammunition drums on his twin Lewis guns with two more full cases. He turned to glance at Matthew, the big grin still on his broad face. Matthew made a sweeping turn and Bruce swivelled his guns to the portside for another strafing run on the patrol. When Matthew took in the desert below he could see at least five men sprawled in bloody rings while the remainder were firing upwards with their rifles and machine gun. The Lewis rattled into life again, spraying the scattered force with bullets. Two more men fell as the dust kicked up by the bullets hitting the ground swamped them. With the pass complete, Matthew pulled on the controls to roll to make a figure eight pass on the Ottoman troops taking casualties from his gunner. It was then that he felt a real shudder of impacting rounds close to his feet and was alarmed to see the New Zealand sergeant let go of his guns and slump back into his cockpit. Matthew did not have to be told that Bruce had been hit. How bad, he did not know. Matthew's only concern for now was to return to his airfield and get the New Zealander medical treatment – that was, if he were still alive. He aborted his pass and flung the little biplane over, to track back to base.

Bruce struggled to get to his feet. He looked over his shoulder and gave Matthew a thumbs-up signal but his face was twisted into a pain-filled attempt at a smile. He pointed down into the cockpit to indicate that his wound was below his waist somewhere and held up a blood-soaked flying glove. Matthew returned his gesture by pointing to the south, indicating they were returning home. Bruce nodded his understanding and collapsed back into the sitting position in his forward cockpit. Matthew prayed that they would make it to the Regimental Aid Post before his fellow crewman and friend bled to death.

Matthew glanced over his shoulder at the rapidly disappearing troop of Turkish soldiers and could just make out that they also were attending to their wounded. He forced himself not to think about what they had just done. Somewhere in far off Constantinople or some little Turkish village, mothers, wives and children would soon learn of the death of their loved ones. Matthew only hoped that the same would not be repeated in Bruce's home town of Christchurch. But mostly he was glad that it was not his cobber, Randolph Gates, manning the Lewis guns in the forward cockpit. Last he had heard was that Randolph was enjoying the high life of California far from the world war on the other side of the Atlantic Ocean.

Kate Tracy had reached her seventieth year yet she had the appearance and demeanour of a woman much younger than her actual age. She sat on the front verandah of her sprawling, high-set timber and corrugated iron-roofed home on the outskirts of Townsville in Queensland's far north, reading a selection of poetry from a slim leather-bound book in the late afternoon. Below her, two gardeners (old men she employed so they would have a home and three meals a day) pruned a hedge of rambling tropical shrubs. Her house reflected a modest affluence, belying the vast financial empire she had acquired through hard work and wise investment. Kate had outlived two husbands and survived life as a young woman on the wild frontier of the Palmer River goldfields where she had gained her first fortune walking beside the great bullock teams heaving supplies to the miners. She had given birth to her son, Matthew, in the arid lands of central Queensland under one such bullock wagon and lost her beloved husband, an American gold prospector, somewhere on that same frontier. He had simply disappeared.

'Missus, a man come on a horse,' Mary, her young Aboriginal housemaid, said as she brought afternoon tea for her employer.

Kate glanced over her reading glasses to look down the long avenue of gum trees now rapidly filling with raucous white cockatoos. She loved the big white birds despite their destructive and mischievous ways. She focused on a tall, young man who sat astride his mount as if he were part centaur.

'Tom!' she gasped, but quickly checked herself. She knew that was impossible. Her brother had died almost a half century before in the wild country of Burkesland from a trooper's bullet. But the man was the image of her long-lost brother, albeit with a darker skin.

The rider reached the house, dismounted near the bottom of the stairs and hitched his horse. Kate was already on her feet, staring down at the stranger.

'Mrs Tracy?' the young man asked, looking up at her.

'Yes,' she replied, still amazed at the uncanny resemblance the visitor had to Tom Duffy, the bushranger who had once roamed the north of Australia, in company with Wallarie.

'I am Tom Duffy,' he said, removing his broad-brimmed hat.

'Oh my God!' Kate exclaimed. 'You must be Tim's son!'

'Yes, Mrs Tracy, my father was Tim Duffy,' Tom answered, pleased to note that this woman he had only heard about knew his place in the family. 'But he is dead now.'

Instinctively, Kate took the steps down the verandah and wrapped her arms around the startled young man, who stiffened at her embrace. 'You have come back to us. You must join me for afternoon tea and tell me all that you remember of your father,' Kate said, taking Tom's arm and leading him up the stairs. 'Mary, fetch another cup and saucer for our guest.'

With some confusion, Mary, who was fifteen years of age, stared at the tall and handsome young man she knew to be part-Aboriginal.

'Yes, Mrs Tracy,' she finally responded, disappearing inside the house to bring an extra cup for the visitor.

Kate sat Tom down in a chair beside her and continued to hold his hand. Tom suddenly felt a sense of belonging and, before he knew it, he was answering Kate's many questions. The sun was well on the horizon before he paused. He had told her how his father had met his mother and how Tim had died from a snake bite while mustering cattle. He explained how his mother had raised him and insisted that he get an education.

'I will have the gardeners stable your horse and have Mary prepare a room for you,' Kate said firmly, quelling any protest from Tom. 'It is not every day that I have a prodigal son return from the wilderness.'

Kate had warmed to her long-lost relative as she observed the obviously highly intelligent young man. Dinner was served and afterwards Kate arranged for a bottle of good quality rum to be taken to the verandah where they could continue talking in the warmth of the tropical night. Tom was stunned to see that Kate poured herself a liberal nip of the dark liquid, rather than tea or coffee. She chuckled at his surprise. 'I found that it was a great comfort on the Palmer track at nights,' she said to answer his unasked question. 'Much better then sherry. And now, I must ask you why you are here.'

Tom accepted the tumbler of rum from Kate. For a moment he stared out into the night. 'I was sent by Wallarie,' he said. 'I don't really know why. He just said that it was important that I meet you.'

At the mention of the old Aboriginal warrior, Kate felt a lump in her throat. Throughout her life he had always been a presence, both physical and spiritual. 'How is my old friend?' she asked softly, unconsciously raising her glass to salute him.

'He was well when I last saw him at Glen View,' Tom answered. 'Just a cranky, crazy old blackfella.'

'Oh, Wallarie is more than that, young man,' Kate said with a smile, sipping her rum. 'He is the link between heaven and earth for two families. Do you have any idea *why* Wallarie sent you to me?'

'Not really,' Tom answered. 'As I don't know how you could help me enlist in the army.'

Kate glanced sharply at the young man beside her. 'Why would you want to join up, when the Aboriginal part of you makes you exempt from service?'

Tom glared at the dark sky. 'Maybe it is because the white man tells me that as a blackfella I am not good enough to fight in his army. I just want a chance to prove them all wrong.'

Kate could hear the anger and pain in his voice. 'Or is it because of your fighting Irish blood that you want to enlist?'

Tom took a long swallow of his drink. 'I have heard about my Irish family – and the other mob, the Macintoshes.'

'My son, Matthew, is somewhere flying his aeroplane in this damned war,' Kate said with a sigh. 'I dread the sight of the post office boy every time he pedals his bicycle out here to deliver a telegram. I fear that one day I will be informed that Matthew is not coming home.'

'I am sorry to hear that,' Tom said.

For a long time Kate did not reply but remained absorbed in her thoughts about Matthew. Finally she turned to Tom. 'If you truly feel that your destiny is to join the army and go overseas then I will help you. God knows why Wallarie would support your ambitions, considering what Europeans have done to his people in the past. Tonight, sleep well and tomorrow you and I will go into town to meet someone I know who can help you.'

After breakfast, Kate arranged for her car to be chauffeured by one of the gardeners for a trip to town. Tom had bathed and made himself look presentable after the long trek from central Queensland, and as he sat beside her in the rear seat Kate could not help but think how much the boy reminded her of his grandfather, Tom Duffy.

They reached the centre of Townsville where Kate ordered the car to be parked in front of a building with a sign outside declaring that Australia needed men to volunteer. They alighted and Kate strode forward through the doors of the building followed by Tom, hat in hand. They marched up to a desk where a sergeant in the uniform of the Light Horse sat reading a paper. He was in his sixties and from the ribands on his uniform jacket had served in the Victorian days of the Queen's colonial army. He put down the paper, glanced up at Kate and immediately rose to his feet.

'Mrs Tracy, how are you?' he asked respectfully, as if somewhat in awe of Kate. 'How is young Matthew?'

'I am well, Clarence,' Kate replied. 'And I believe my son is still well.'

'What can I do for you, Mrs Tracy?' the sergeant asked, remaining on his feet.

'My nephew Tom Duffy wishes to enlist in the Light Horse,' Kate said without further small talk. 'I expect you to sign him on.'

The recruiting sergeant eyed Tom up and down with a sceptical look. 'Mrs Tracy, as well as I know you, I am afraid we cannot sign on blackfellas.'

'I don't see any great lines of volunteers here today,' Kate retorted.

'The bloody . . . my apologies, Mrs Tracy,' the sergeant said. 'What I meant to say is that the casualty lists the newspapers publish seem to put a dampener on recruiting. All the boys from around here are already in uniform.'

'Well, I am sure that you would be more than pleased to have a fine, strapping young man who can ride like the devil and shoot just as well in your ranks.'

'We do, Mrs Tracy, but I cannot sign on blackfellas.'

'My nephew is not of Aboriginal blood, Clarence,' Kate said with just the hint of a smile. 'He is of Indian heritage.'

'With a name like Duffy!' the sergeant blurted.

'Of the Irish–Indian side of the family,' Kate replied with a smirk. 'I believe that those of Indian heritage may enlist. Did I not read an article about a sharp shooter at Gallipoli with the name of Billy Sing?'

'Yes, Mrs Tracy, but Billy is not an Indian,' the sergeant answered, shrugging his shoulders in defeat. 'I will sign on your nephew, and record him as non-Aboriginal.'

He sat down and rummaged in a drawer for the relevant enlistment papers, which he retrieved and pushed across the desk to Tom. The recruiting sergeant was fully aware that the formidable woman who claimed the half-caste across the desk from him was her nephew not only had a vast financial empire but her power reached to the highest levels of government. If the blackfella wanted to die for his country then so be it.

'I will leave you with my nephew, Clarence, and bid you a good day,' Kate said. 'Please pass on my regards to your family. Tom, I will meet you at the milliners when you have finished your business here.'

'Thank you, Aunt Kate,' Tom said with a cheeky grin. 'I will not be long.'

The recruiting sergeant sighed, passing a pen to Tom. 'Can you read and write?' he asked in a tired voice, accepting defeat.

'Somewhat well, old chap,' Tom answered in an affectation of a foppish English gentleman, causing the older man to look sharply at his new recruit. Bloody uppity blackfellas, he wanted to say, but wisely kept his mouth shut. Soon Tom Duffy would be Trooper Duffy, of Irish-Indian heritage in the Light Horse Division.

It was a place of death Wallarie had avoided for over a half century. But in his dreaming hours the ancestor spirits had bid him return to the creek where the Native Mounted Police under Lieutenant Morrison Mort had slaughtered his clan, riding down and trampling old men, mothers and children. Shooting, stabbing and clubbing those too slow to flee the massacre.

This was a place of spirits best avoided and now Wallarie sat under the night sky filled with a myriad of stars. In this forbidden place by the once-sparkling river course, the waters were now muddy from the hooves of the Glen View cattle, and the bleached bones of the slaughtered trampled into the red earth hid the horror of the atrocity ordered by the long-dead Scottish squatter Donald Macintosh.

Uneasy, Wallarie had lit a camp fire. He waited in the flickering light for another sign from the ancestor spirits. In the moonless night a curlew wailed its eerie song, causing the old Aboriginal warrior to clutch his hardwood nulla for protection.

He waited but nothing happened. He heard only the splash of a fish in the muddy waters and the night sounds of the bush creatures all around him.

Wallarie began to sing in a low chant, words in a language that only he now knew. When he was gone the language would disappear forever from the earth. As he sang his trance-like song, he was aware that the stars had cast a light on the creek and when he gazed into the waters he saw what the ancient peoples who had roamed the land wanted him to see. Wallarie smiled, just as the stars above turned in a slow circle overhead to herald the coming dawn. An act had been played out in the great wheel of life. A young man of mixed blood related to his own was on the path to close the circle. Wallarie knew that Tom Duffy could not see his future but through the eyes of the ancestor spirits Wallarie could. Little did the Macintosh and Duffy clans know it but the young man in far-off Townsville was being guided by the ancient ones.

3

Captain Sean Duffy huddled beside the shrapnel-torn body of a young Australian soldier at the bottom of the forward trench. They had not even commenced their assault on the German lines and already the casualties were piling up as both enemy and their own artillery shells ripped through the heavily congested jumping off trenches occupied by the Australians. He had experienced artillery bombardments before at Gallipoli but nothing to the extent he was now enduring. The sound was deafening, muffling the screams of helpless men being torn apart by red-hot shrapnel balls and shards of exploding shells.

Beside him crouched Corporal Jack Kelly, clutching his bayonet-tipped rifle. Sean had forgotten the itch of lice and the ever-present stench of the clay trench. He realised that he was terrified, and fought with the last of his sanity to retain control. He was aware that he had wet himself and was close to defecating with fear. His hands shook when he removed his fob watch to check the time. It was 1530 hours but, in the European summer, a long way from nightfall.

'Over the bags in ten minutes.' The order was shouted in Sean's ear and when he glanced up from his huddle he saw the face of his commanding officer, Patrick Duffy, who placed his hand on Sean's shoulder reassuringly.

An artillery shell exploded on the lip of the trench, showering the men below with clods of earth. Men fell back screaming in agony as the shrapnel shredded their bodies. Sean was aware that Patrick was staring down at him with an expression of concern. 'Get your company ready, Captain Duffy,' he yelled. 'They need you.'

Sean shook off his fear for the moment. He could see a corporal watching him, ashen-faced, and understood that he was not the only one experiencing the crippling fear as they huddled helplessly under the terrible barrage. Despite his terror he knew that three young platoon commanders and their respective men looked to him for leadership. This alone forced Sean to rise to his feet. 'Ten minutes before we go over the bags,' he yelled at the top of his voice, and the word was passed down the trench, amid the earth shaking of the barrage on their lines.

And then it was time.

'Over you go!' Sean bellowed, and his men rose from crouching positions to scramble over the sandbags with bayonets fixed. Between them, his men carried sacks full of hand grenades, picks, shovels and even scaling ladders for the assault on the heavily entrenched enemy. Sean found himself on his feet, gripping his revolver at the end of its lanyard and glancing to either side to ensure his men had come out of the trenches. They had. 'Follow me!' he called out.

He had placed himself with his forward platoon and was accompanied by his company sergeant major and Jack Kelly. Corporal Jack Kelly was still beside him as he had the task of remaining with company headquarters to act as an interpreter for any Germans they may capture. Now there was no going back, Sean thought grimly. They had a job to do and it lay a mere 200 yards away across a field of tall grasses being thrashed by bullet and shrapnel. If hell had a French name it must be Fromelles, Sean thought as he staggered forward.

From the dominating feature known to his enemies as the Aubers Ridge, General Major von Fellmann watched the Australian and British troops spill out of their trenches. From intelligence reports, he knew that his distant relative Lieutenant Colonel Patrick Duffy would be leading one of the battalions. The major scanned the churned-up no-man's-land between the lines. He could see tiny figures advancing bravely through shell and machine-gun fire.

'Australians,' he murmured, but loud enough for the clutch of officers beside him to hear.

'How will they perform?' he was asked by the less senior officer who was also watching the advance.

'I suspect as well as the Canadians and South Africans we have faced in the past,' Kurt von Fellmann replied. 'The British colonials are all volunteers and have a character that makes them adapt to war very well.'

Kurt turned to the officer. 'Ensure that communications with our reserves is kept intact at all costs,' he said, knowing that they may be critical in any possible breakthrough of his forward defensive trenches. 'Even if you have to crawl out there and check the telephone wires yourself.'

The officer saluted and hurried away to organise a party to check the buried telephone lines had not been cut by artillery fire from the enemy positions, leaving Kurt alone to resume surveying the assault on his lines.

'Colonel Duffy,' he whispered under his breath. 'I pray that God will spare you in your foolish venture.'

But God was asleep that day and the carnage had begun as if orchestrated by the devil.

The German staff officer located the regimental runner behind the lines and passed on the message to their signalmen to keep a check on the lines, ensuring that they remained intact. The staff officer did not know the runner but history would one day record him as the devil incarnate. His name was Adolf Hitler and although many of his countrymen were soon to die, he would survive the terrible battle of Fromelles.

The machine gun firing from high ground tore through the ranks of Sean's company. His company sergeant major, a former British army NCO, had bullets rip through his legs, chest and jaw only a few yards from Sean. In the blink of an eye the CSM shuddered, fell and remained still. The loss of the man who had survived the Dardanelles campaign came as a shock to Sean, who had convinced himself the strong, solid professional soldier could never die. All around him others fell; some screamed, some died silently as bullets cut through them. The 200 yards might well have been two miles. Time lost meaning and the rapid beat of his heart and laboured breathing of his lungs were the only sounds Sean could hear as they advanced at a rapid walk.

He could now actually see the enemy standing at their parapets, firing rifles and tossing the long-handled grenades in swirling arcs through the air towards the clusters of soldiers attacking them, and he felt numb from the tension of waiting for the bullet or shrapnel meant to kill or maim him. His company headquarters was now reduced to himself, Corporal Kelly and a private who was also his runner. In a brief lucid moment he attempted to assess the situation and became aware that he could no longer see the platoon that he had attached his company HQ to. Even his runner seemed to have disappeared, leaving him and the South Australian corporal alone, facing the zigzag of German forward trenches. Sean was hardly aware that he had not fired his revolver although he could hear and see Corporal Kelly stopping to aim and fire at the head and shoulders of the German infantry on the parapets before them. His accurate fire appeared to be telling as men disappeared whenever Jack Kelly fired.

The artillery bombardment had succeeded in tearing apart barbed wire directly in front of Sean's company and those of his men who survived were able to clamber into the German forward dugouts where savage hand-to-hand fighting ensued. Both Sean and Jack found themselves tumbling into a trench and when they were on their feet realised that they had become well and truly separated from the rest of the company. Bodies of German soldiers lay in heaps around them, mutilated by the explosive artillery shells that had fallen among them. One or two were still alive but not in any position to pose a threat. Jack laid down his rifle and immediately hefted out two hand grenades from the bag he carried. The primed bombs were in his hands as he sought about for enemy troops. The dugout had a right angle turn at its end and suddenly a German appeared, wielding a wicked-looking medieval club with nails embedded along its length. He was a huge man and charged at Jack and Sean.

Jack had placed his rifle on the bottom of the trench to arm himself with bombs, and was now virtually helpless against the huge German.

Sean flung out his arm and emptied his revolver into the charging German, who fell dead at Jack's feet. Without hesitating, Jack pulled the pins from the grenades and hurled them around the corner of the trench. Screams of wounded men followed the twin explosions. Jack snatched up his rifle and advanced along the trench to peer cautiously around the corner where he saw the victims of the grenades either dead or badly wounded. The scent of blood filled the air along with the acrid smell of cordite. A section of German soldiers spilled from a dugout doorway that led down to concrete-reinforced shelters. Jack let out a roar and charged the Germans emerging from their bunker. He caught the first in the chest with the end of his bayonet and pushed him back into the entrance, forcing the men following him to reel back. Heaving with all his might, Jack extracted the bloody bayonet and stepped back as a volley of rifle fire ripped from the bunker door.

Before Jack could react, three determined soldiers rushed through the entrance to confront him. Without hesitation, he charged them, skewering a second soldier through the throat. The falling man caused the rifle to be pulled from his hands and the Australian immediately picked up an entrenching tool that lay close by. Using it as part-club, part-axe, he fell on the two remaining German soldiers, who had been unable to bring their rifles to bear on him in the enclosed space. The edge of the swinging shovel caught one of the enemy in the arm, eliciting a howl of pain from the soldier, whose arm had been partly severed. The man behind him had been able to bring up his rifle and thrust at Jack with his own bayonet, forcing Jack to trip. He dropped the shovel and fell onto his back. For a moment he could clearly see the features of the man about to kill him and noticed that he was not young. Maybe in his forties, Jack thought, as he waited helplessly for the bayonet to take his life. But suddenly the German crumpled as the top of his head was smashed, despite the protection of his helmet. A stray bullet – friend or foe – had saved Jack, who scrambled to his feet, retrieving his rifle from the dead soldier with a grunt and extracting the bayonet from the man's throat. He was aware of a Maxim machine gun rattling off long bursts only feet away, around another corner of the trench. Jack fumbled in the bomb bag for another grenade, pulled the pin and hurled it through the air. It exploded but the machine gun only hesitated for a moment before pouring more death into the ranks of still advancing Australians. Jack knew that the only way to silence the deadly gun was to personally kill the crew that manned it. Once again he advanced down the trench, stepping over the bodies of the men he had killed. When he rounded the corner, he saw two Germans crouched behind the belt-fed machine gun, focused on spraying the advancing Australian infantry. Jack charged, this time using his rifle like a club, and fell on the machine-gun crew with adrenaline-pumped savagery. He smashed at the helmeted heads and then reversed the rifle to slash and stab with the already bloody bayonet.

Gasping for air, Jack stood back to see that he had killed both men who now lay in their own blood at the foot of the trench. He yanked the heavy weapon off its tripod and placed a grenade under it. Jack knew that he did not have time to strip the weapon to render it useless and hoped that the grenade would damage it enough to make it inoperable. After pulling the pin, he retreated quickly before the bomb exploded. He peeked around the corner of the trench and could see that the explosion had partially twisted the weapon. Satisfied he had put the weapon out of action, he retreated further down the trench to see Captain Sean Duffy sitting with his back against the earthen walls of the trench, weeping like a child. Jack Kelly had only heard about so-called shell shock and guessed that Captain Duffy had been broken by the terrible slaughter of his company.

'Sir,' he said softly, reaching down to help Sean to his feet. 'Sir, you have to get a grip of yourself.'

Sean did not respond, his empty pistol still clasped in his hand. He buried his head between his legs and continued sobbing.

It was unnerving to Corporal Kelly, who glanced up and down the short trench for any signs of an immediate threat, but for the moment they were alone among the dead and badly wounded German soldiers. 'Sir, you have to snap out of it.'

Sean looked up at Jack with a grimy tear-stained face and blank eyes. Only a few feet away a German soldier groaned in his agony from the shrapnel wounds to his face, chest and stomach. A soldier tumbled over the lip of the trench and fell down beside Jack and Sean. He was Australian and had the rank of sergeant. Jack recognised him as the sergeant from one of Captain Duffy's platoons.

'We have cleared about twenty yards of the trench next to this,' he gasped, his eyes wide with adrenaline and fear. 'What do we do, skipper?' he asked Sean who stared at him blankly.

'The boss is recovering from a bomb blast,' Jack said, hurrying to explain the apparent lack of response from his company commander. 'His last words were for us to hold any ground we take until reinforcements come up.'

The platoon sergeant glanced at Sean and then with a questioning look at Jack.

'You sure, Corp?' he asked suspiciously, eyeing the tears streaming down Sean's face.

'Bloody right, Sarge,' Jack answered. 'Just let the skipper get his breath, and he will tell you himself.'

The sergeant accepted Jack's explanation but was not totally convinced. He slithered over the edge of the trench and returned to his platoon commander to relay the company commander's order to hold their ground.

Jack turned his attention back to Sean who had stopped crying and even had a serene expression on his face. 'You know where you are?' Jack asked, crouching in front of Sean.

'Not home,' Sean replied. 'I think that I have been asleep and have gone to hell. How long have I been like this, Corporal Kelly?'

Jack was relieved to hear his commander actually philosophising on their predicament. It meant that he was slowly coming out of his almost catatonic state. 'Not long, sir,' Jack replied. 'I think you got a bit of a bump on your head.'

Sean slowly focused the reality around him, vaguely remembering firing off his revolver into a giant of a man in a grey uniform who had been intent on clubbing them to death. He flipped open his revolver, removing the spent cartridges to reload with fresh rounds. 'I am sorry that I let you all down,' he said. 'I don't think there is much of the company left to apologise to anyway.'

Jack did not reply. From what he remembered of the advance he knew the company commander was correct. It had been a disaster despite the fact that the survivors had actually been able to get into the German forward trenches. Even a lowly corporal knew that a half-hearted counter-attack from the enemy would easily drive them out of the trenches they had captured. It had all been for nothing, he thought bitterly.

'I think that we should join the rest of the company in the trench next to us,' Jack prompted gently.

'Good idea, corporal,' Sean responded, getting unsteadily to his feet.

Machine-gun and rifle fire still cracked all around them mixed with the earth-shaking explosions of the occasional deadly artillery round landing nearby. They were far from safe despite their minor victory. Cautiously they eased themselves over the edge of the trench and slithered along the ground now devoid of vegetation and into a trench filled with the remains of his company mixed among the dead of the enemy.

The platoon sergeant who had received the order from Jack greeted them, looking hard at Sean when he did so. 'Good to see that you have recovered, skipper,' he said. 'I guess it was you who knocked out that Hun machine gun that was doing us so much grief.'

Sean did not reply as he was confused as to what the sergeant was telling him. Before he could gather his wits one of his platoon commanders, Lieutenant Wilberforce, made his way along the captured trench to report. The matter was dropped as Sean was more interested in assessing their current situation. Around him, his men lay against the sides of the trench, smoking, attempting to nap or just staring with a faraway look at the darkening sky above, while the battle continued to rage around them along the front between the two armies. For Sean's remaining men the only war they knew was the immediate earth and sky they could see. The strategy of generals was of little interest to their thoughts of immediate survival.

It soon appeared obvious that there would be no reinforcements to bolster the trenches they had captured and to remain where they were would only mean certain death or capture. In the dark of the night Sean Duffy led his handful of men back across the grassy plain to the relative safety of the trenches they had left only hours earlier.

Colonel Patrick Duffy had been given a corner room in a Flemish farm house to lodge his HQ. He had pored through the post battle reports and grasped the magnitude of losses his battalion had absorbed in the futile attack against the better-entrenched German forces. He contemplated the letters he would have to write to the families of the officers he had lost from the battalion and knew he would be busy. Down the chain of command similar letters would be composed by junior officers for the men that they had lost.

But now he was reading through the reports by his few surviving company and platoon commanders detailing what they had experienced. One matter caught his eye when he read of a machine gun that had wrought havoc on one of the companies and how it had been knocked out, thus saving many Australian lives. Other reports corroborated that the machine gun appeared to have been neutralised by Captain Sean Duffy. Patrick was not surprised. Already the young former solicitor from Sydney had earned a Military Cross for his courage at Gallipoli, so why wouldn't he risk his life to save his men by attacking and killing the German machine-gun crew? Although the act had not been witnessed by a fellow officer, Patrick felt the incident worthy of a recommendation for a further medal of bravery for his newly promoted captain on the strength of what he was able to assemble from the different reports.

He flicked through the reports to find Sean's and was surprised that it was so sketchy – just a report on the ground captured and the casualties his company had sustained with a short note on his withdrawal. He mentioned that he had been temporarily cut off from his men during the assault on the forward lines but nothing else. If he had alone cleared the trench and silenced the German machine gun then his act was worthy of a Victoria Cross. Patrick commenced drafting his recommendation for the medal to his superiors. The matter would have to be investigated but Patrick felt Sean had been too modest in his report. He realised that the recommendation would be his final act as battalion CO before being moved to Divisional HQ in a staff officer's appointment. It was a fitting way to say goodbye to the man whom he loved as much as his own sons.

Corporal Jack Kelly lay on his back in a field of wild flowers under a hot summer sun. His company had been pulled back behind the lines for a rest and a chance to recover from the horror that had been Fromelles, and it was a rare opportunity to do nothing but sleep and dream among the vivid colours of the Flemish countryside. The remaining men of the battalion had been stood down and they also sat around smoking, chatting or sleeping in the tiny oasis of peace away from the war despite the distant thump of artillery and the faint sound of small-arms fire occasionally drifting to them on a gentle breeze.

Jack closed his eyes and tried to imagine what his infant son looked like. He had received a letter from his wife but as yet had not had a photograph of young Lukas Kelly. He was aware that a shadow had fallen over him.

'I hope that I am not disturbing you, Corporal Kelly,' Captain Sean Duffy said, sitting down beside Jack before he was able to stand and salute. Sean was in full dress uniform and wore his shiny Sam Browne belt across his chest as well as the distinctive white and purple riband of the Military

Cross decoration on his left breast. 'I noticed that you were alone in the field and felt that this might be a good time for us to have a small talk.'

Jack sat up, brushing away grass from his flannel singlet and adjusting the braces to his trousers. He was not wearing full uniform because of the heat of the day and reached for his jacket. 'Not necessary,' Sean said, observing how Jack was attempting to make himself look respectable. 'This is just an informal chat.'

'What can I do for you, sir?' Jack asked, sensing that something was playing on his company commander's mind.

'I just wanted to ask your forgiveness for what happened to me back there,' Sean explained.

Jack was taken aback by the frank apology. A commissioned officer apologising to or confiding in a junior NCO was not something usually experienced.

'Nothing happened,' Jack said, shrugging his shoulders. 'I have seen men go troppo in New Guinea when I was prospecting and know that it is usually a temporary thing. You saved my life when that big Hun was about to brain me.'

'I don't even remember that,' Sean said, squinting against the bright sunlight. 'I hardly remember anything after I saw the CSM cop it.'

'Well, sir, you did not disgrace yourself,' Jack said gently. 'So, that is it.'

'I have just returned from seeing the CO,' Sean continued. 'He had the happy news that I was being recommended for another gong for neutralising a German machine-gun crew and damned if I can remember doing so. I have racked my mind but cannot recall anything – except that you were with me before we joined the rest of the company for the withdrawal. But if the reports are to be believed I must have killed the Huns manning the gun.'

The mention of the machine gun had been something Jack was trying to put out of his mind. 'Then it must be true,' Jack said, refusing to push himself forward as some kind of hero. 'Congratulations, skipper,' he said, looking away to the end of the field, where he could see cows grazing and an old farmer hoeing weeds oblivious to the war raging a few miles away.

'Well, I just wanted to have this chat and apologise for the temporary loss of my reason,' Sean said, rising from the grass. 'Don't get up, Corp,' he continued when he saw Jack about to rise to his feet. 'Stay here and take your rest. I will be parading the company at 0600 tomorrow morning. I have recommended you to temporary sergeant's posting in Mr Wilberforce's platoon. His sergeant is being sent to Blighty for senior NCO training.'

Jack was stunned by the casually delivered announcement of his sudden promotion and watched as the officer strolled through the field, idly hacking at the plants with his swagger stick. He wondered what sort of man Sean really was. Did the captain really remember all that had eventuated when they were alone and was now attempting to take credit for another man's act of bravery? Was the promotion a pay-off to ensure Jack stayed quiet as to who really killed the machine-gun crew? Or was his senior officer really suffering the after-effects of shell shock and did not remember? Jack scowled. No matter what the reason, he did not care. All that mattered was that he survived the war to return to his beloved wife and child and eventually go back to the jungles of New Guinea and Papua to prospect for gold. Medals were simply cheap metal and cloth to attach to a uniform. Jack Kelly preferred to see the end of the war in one piece.

★

Sean Duffy did not return to his company straightaway. He had completed all his military duties and chose to stroll down a leafy lane to sit under a beautiful old tree with branches that hung to the ground as if the tree were weeping. He sat down with his back against the trunk and, out of sight of any living human, he began to cry softly. The shell shock had not gone away and he knew that his sanity was hanging by a fragile thread. Only the fact that so many depended on him kept him from the edge of madness. How was it that he could remember very little of what had happened in the trench when he was with Corporal Kelly? Had he killed all the men that had been reported dead by personally inflicting their fatal wounds? All he could remember was the soothing voice of the corporal pleading with him to snap out of his stricken state. Colonel Duffy had been beaming when he announced to him at BHQ that he had submitted the recommendation and would not be surprised if he did not receive a Victoria Cross for his actions. How could he tell his distant cousin and man he most admired in the world that he, Captain Sean Duffy MC, was actually a craven coward who had relinquished his command in the middle of the attack on the German lines?

4

With the first buds of the spring of 1916 appearing in the trees, the balmy day could not be better for an outdoor garden party overlooking the city's harbour. George had sent out invitations to the most influential people he knew, wanting them all to hear his most important announcement since his marriage to Sir Keith Gyles' daughter, the very attractive and charming Louise Gyles.

To most of the guests the war raging in far-off Europe was of little interest, apart from how it impacted on their commercial or social interests. There would be no European holidays this year as the tedious war continued, interrupting their social plans. The slice of society George had invited comprised people much like himself – men interested in company profits and concerned about the restrictions to trade caused by the threat of German U-boats and surface raiders interdicting the sea lanes between Europe and

Australia. The tiresome casualty lists mostly consisted of working-class names, and these human losses did not impact on the lavish lifestyles of the better-heeled, although there was the occasional comment from one of their own, usually some foolish, patriotic officer who was 'going west' somewhere on the Western Front or in the Palestine campaign.

Louise dutifully welcomed each guest with a bright smile and the offer to help themselves from the lavish spread of food set out on the tables in the garden. White-coated waiters carried silver platters, carefully balancing crystal glasses of expensive French champagne. There were one or two men in uniform, usually with red tabs at their collars denoting staff officer appointments. Although Captain Alex Macintosh was the most junior officer among the guests, his wife Giselle looked most elegant and turned one or two heads from the men present.

'Oh, Giselle,' Louise said, giving her long-time friend and sister-in-law a peck on the cheek. 'I am so glad that you and Alex could make it today.'

'Is my brother going to announce that our companies are making record profits?' Alex asked sarcastically.

'Stop it, Alex,' Giselle rebuked. 'I am sure that he is not going to do any such thing.'

'No,' Louise said. 'George has something much more important to announce today, but all in good time. For now you must try the fresh oysters and champagne. It appears that George was able to have a consignment of vintage wine shipped from France despite the dangers.'

When Louise was distracted with the arrival of a new guest, Alex took his wife's arm and strolled over to a table almost bending under the weight of the delicacies.

'We get to eat bully beef and biscuits,' Alex said, eyeing the abundance. 'And my brother is able to have French wine. I wonder how much he is skimming off the top of the lucrative army and navy contracts.'

'Your brother is doing his bit to support the war effort,' Giselle said lamely, attempting to defend George. 'Not everyone is able to don a uniform and fight for their country.'

'I have a uniform,' Alex retorted. 'And I am not offered the opportunity to fight for my country.'

Giselle did not reply. She had suffered her husband's despair at being held back from overseas service to train men for the front and somehow felt that she was responsible for his misery at being denied what he felt was his right to prove his worth as a soldier. She had overheard a senior army officer at a similar function months earlier commenting that young Captain Macintosh might be with his father – except that he had married a German national. The officer had glanced up and smiled at Giselle, not recognising her as the German national he referred to. Giselle had not relayed this information to her husband. She was glad that Alex was being held back as she well knew that if he was overseas the chances of him surviving were very poor. He was very much like his father and would feel that he must take terrible risks to prove his worth.

'Do you think that Louise looked different today?' Giselle asked, trying to steer Alex from his brooding. 'She appears to be growing thick in the waist.'

Alex passed a flute of champagne to his wife, before taking one for himself. 'I don't know what you mean,' he said, sipping. 'She looks the same to me.'

Giselle wanted to shake her head at the obtuseness of men. They were so ignorant of the subtle signs that it seemed only women could read. Giselle had noticed a strained expression in her friend's smile when she greeted them. Giselle was determined that she would corner Louise and find out what was behind it. Her opportunity came when her husband was engaged by an old friend, Colonel John Hughes of the British army, who had been on secondment to the newly raised Australian army for many years now. Of all the faces at the garden party, the senior British officer's was the only one Alex wanted to see. Engrossed in military talk as the two soldiers were, neither noticed Giselle slip away to join Louise, who for a moment was alone at the edge of the neatly kept garden.

'The party is wonderful,' Giselle said, approaching Louise from behind. 'You do know how to entertain.'

As Louise turned to face her Giselle could see the pain belying the friendly welcome her friend had extended to all attending. 'You have noticed,' Louise said. 'But then, you are my dearest friend.'

'What has happened?' Giselle asked, gently touching Louise on the hand.

'I am with child,' Louise blurted bitterly, tears forming in the corners of her eyes. 'I have been now for some months.'

'Oh, but that is wonderful!' Giselle exclaimed before stopping herself. Clearly it was not wonderful to Louise. 'But why the tears? Is something wrong?'

'Everything,' Louise replied, wiping her tears with a small, lace handkerchief and attempting to smile for the sake of anyone who may be observing them. 'I want the child, but not under the present circumstances.'

'A child is welcome under any circumstances,' Giselle said, thinking of the birth of her own son, David. 'It is a time to look forward to.'

'It is just that I am not certain that I should be with George,' Louise said, staring across the harbour. 'I know that divorce would be impossible but I would rather be free of him.'

Giselle was stunned; she had thought her sister-in-law's marriage was made in heaven. 'Do you wish to talk to me about this?' she prompted gently.

Louise glanced at Giselle with a rueful smile. 'You were certainly lucky in marrying Alex,' she said. 'He is a man of honour and character.'

Giselle did not reply. She already knew that her husband was the rock of her life.

'I hired a private detective to follow George,' Louise confessed. 'He was hardly at home at nights and rarely went near me in the bedroom. The detective reported that my husband has a place near his office where he entertains prostitutes on a regular basis. It appears that I am not good enough for him.' The tears welled and rolled down her cheeks.

Giselle placed her arms around her. 'I am so sorry, Louise,' she said. 'Have you spoken to anyone about his behaviour?'

'I spoke to my father,' she replied. 'But he only consoled me with the fact that men in George's position often behaved in that fashion, and advised me to ignore my husband's little affairs as long as he was discreet. Would you accept that from Alex?'

'No,' Giselle answered firmly. She knew her husband already had a mistress – the army. 'Oh, my mother has arrived,' she said, grudgingly changing the subject. She broke the embrace and Louise wiped the tears from her face. Together, they regained their poise and strolled back to the guests milling in the garden.

What Louise had failed to tell her best friend was that the private detective had also reported on the many meetings George had conducted with Giselle's mother at George's office. This had been as confusing as it was intriguing. Louise did not think that George was having an affair with

Karolina Schumann. In fact, from what she could ascertain, the relationship between Giselle's mother and her husband was cool. For some reason known only to him George did not seem to like Karolina very much. But this was something Louise thought she should keep to herself.

With a touch of pride, Giselle could see the fine figure her mother presented among the well-dressed matrons. She caught her mother's eye and they exchanged warm smiles, but before Giselle could engage her mother in conversation she noticed that Karolina had attracted the interest of a senior naval officer, who had already placed a flute of champagne in her hand. No matter, Giselle thought, her mother lived with them and she would catch up with her that night. At least she hoped she would be home that night as lately Karolina Schumann was hardly to be seen. It was as if her mother led another life. Confidences were no longer exchanged between them and Giselle resented this rift in their once very close relationship.

'Ladies and gentlemen, distinguished guests,' George said above the chatter. 'I have an important announcement to make.'

The guests fell silent.

'I know that you are curious as to why you have been invited here today,' he continued. 'Louise, my darling, will you please join me?' The guests parted to allow Louise to walk up and stand beside her husband. 'I did not just simply invite you here today to show off my good French wine . . .' A twitter of laughter followed his statement. 'You are here to be the first to know that Louise and I are expecting the next heir to the Macintosh companies.'

Loud clapping and expressions of 'Good show, old chap,' followed the announcement as glasses were raised and a business acquaintance of George proposed a toast.

Alex did not raise his glass. How was it that his son, the first-born grandchild to his father, had not been mentioned? Already a sinister cloud hung over the future.

'To you, sister-in-law,' Alex said, finally raising his glass in toast. 'May the birth of your daughter be a joyous one.'

Laughter and chuckles followed his toast along with a few 'hear, hear' expressions of agreement. Louise smiled sadly as George glared at his brother with an undisguised hatred that was missed by most of the guests now replete with fine champagne and excellent food.

'I hope that you are right,' Colonel John Hughes said softly beside Alex. He detested his good friend Patrick Duffy's oldest son. In fact, from his investigation of George's links with the Germans before the war he suspected that the manager of the Macintosh companies might be guilty of treason. He had not been able to find any direct evidence, however, and well knew that suspicion was one thing, and proof another.

As the sun descended behind the blue hills west of Sydney, the Australian captain and the British colonel continued to discuss military matters. Only Giselle noticed Karolina leave with the distinguished-looking naval officer. She had a feeling that she would not be chatting that night with her mother at home.

East of Sydney, far across the Pacific Ocean, the residents of California were coming awake. Fenella Macintosh felt the silk sheets clinging to her naked body as the sun rose in the clear, blue sky. She groaned softly, realising that the evening before she had consumed more wine than was good for her. As she woke she also realised that she was not alone in the huge bed. Beside her a man snored softly. Fenella focused on him through bleary eyes. It was the handsome Italian actor whose name eluded her for the moment.

'Dominic,' she said, shaking him awake. 'You have to leave.'

The young man awoke and mumbled something in Italian before pulling himself up into a sitting position, rubbing the sleep from his eyes. He too was naked, his clothes discarded on the plushly carpeted bedroom floor. 'Ah, Fiona my love?' he asked with a leering grin. 'You no want to make love now?'

'Enough, lover boy,' Fenella said, slipping from the bed and heading towards the bathroom. 'I have to be at the studio in a couple of hours. And you have to be on your own set by lunchtime.'

'I would like we make love again,' Dominic said, lying back against the bed end with his arms spread to reveal his hairless, olive-skinned chest. 'We make handsome couple.'

Fenella paused by the door to the bathroom and glanced back over her shoulder. She could see the remaining heroin on the bedside table and wondered whether she should partake of some before having her chauffeur drive her to the studio. The drug had returned to her life along with the many lovers, wild parties and alcohol. For just a moment she felt guilty about how her life had evolved, with fame and fortune coming to her from the make-believe world of moving pictures. In a sense she had been able to proudly show her father that, as a woman, she was capable of building her own small empire based on her talent and looks. But she felt uneasy at how readily she had been seduced by the decadence that came with such acquired fame and fortune. Fenella was discreet in her personal life – something that the studio bosses were adamant about when it came to protecting the clean-cut image of their rising stars. On the screen, the public adored the image of a heroine who was pure and chaste. In her private life, however, Fenella had become all that was opposite. She had tasted the forbidden excesses money could buy. There were times she had awoken beside more than one man and occasionally young, aspiring starlets. Drugs and alcohol helped her to forget what she had become but still she had twinges of guilt about the one man she knew loved her more than his own life. The man who had travelled halfway across the world to find her despite his suspicions that she was not faithful to him.

'You are a fool, Randolph,' Fenella whispered to herself, turning to enter the inlaid marble bathroom with its gold-plated taps. But tears welled in her eyes. In her self-loathing she had ceased writing to her father and now it was only a matter of time before she would also lose the only man who loved her as much for her soul as for her body.

Karolina Schumann loathed herself for what she was about to do. The distinguished British naval officer was a man about her own age and had already confessed that his wife had remained in England when he was posted to Sydney to oversee the shipping of troops and supplies to the war in Europe. She stood in his hotel room as he poured champagne.

'Well, Mrs Schumann,' he said passing her a flute. 'Here is to a chance meeting with the most beautiful woman in these damned dreary colonies.'

Karolina raised her glass, accepting his toast, and took a sip. She had convinced the naval officer that she was a Swedish citizen, not so difficult as she was fluent in the Swedish language. The British officer, however, did not seem to care what nationality she was. He was far more interested in what lay beneath her long, expensive dress.

The officer placed his glass on a table and grasped Karolina in an awkward embrace, kissing her passionately on the lips. She did not resist, allowing him to force her back on the bed. In her mind was her husband who had died because the Australians had invaded German territory in the Pacific. He would still be alive had the local tribes living near their plantation not risen up when they heard the rumour that German rule was over. For that alone she would have given her body to destroy her hated enemy. Even her son-in-law was considered to be one of the group that must be defeated by her Fatherland, although this did not extend to her beloved grandson.

In her thoughts Karolina was again on the verandah of their sprawling house on the plantation, standing beside her beloved husband. She hardly felt the enemy officer enter her but before the sun rose the next day he had whispered secrets to her across the pillow, boasting of his importance when she chided him for not being aboard the bridge of a fighting ship. When he asked her to promise to meet him again she had readily agreed. When Karolina left his bed before the sun rose over Sydney, she had in her head not only details of future troop movements to Europe but the names of the ships they would be travelling on. The information would be passed onto Herr Bosch when next she visited the internment camp on the outskirts of Sydney.

Fenella had completed her work on the set of her latest film and had changed to attend a dinner with a group of friends that evening. From there, they planned to go to a nightclub and dance the night away.

When she stepped from the studio onto the street and saw Randolph dressed in the uniform of a Confederate soldier and trailing an old-style musket, she remembered that her studio was making a period production on a lot a few blocks away. He had his back to her but turned to catch her eye. She felt a twinge of guilt and wanted to hurry away to avoid having to confront him. It had been over a fortnight since they had last been together alone and that was simply a meeting on a film set where they chatted, Fenella complaining of the heavy workloads that forced them apart. Somehow, she knew that she had not fooled him and rebuked herself about why she had not already told him that it was all over for them. But another voice nagged her that the man in the Confederate uniform was different to all the others who had come into her life simply on account of her aura of fame.

'Nellie,' Randolph said, walking towards her. 'It has been a long time since we last spoke, let alone shared some time together.'

Fenella hoped that someone would step through the door behind her, providing an excuse not to talk to Randolph. 'Oh, you know how busy I have been,' she said with a forced smile. 'Work, work and more work.' She gave a wave of her hand.

'And at nights?' Randolph replied. 'Is there anything you want to tell me?'

The tension between them was palpable. Fenella was aware that Randolph's eyes were holding her own. 'There is,' she replied. 'But this is not the time or place to discuss the matter.'

'I thought so,' Randolph sighed sadly. 'But I will save you your valuable time,' he continued. 'I leave tomorrow to enlist. I doubt that either of us will have much opportunity to see each other before then.'

'But America is not at war,' Fenella countered. 'Why

would you want to give up the good job you have here to receive a soldier's pay?'

'I didn't say I was enlisting for Uncle Sam,' Randolph answered, a deep sadness in his eyes. 'I am returning to Australia to join up. I figure that I may as well be with your brother and my cobber Matthew in the fight against the Hun. I gave my notice yesterday and my pal Joe has helped me get a berth on a ship steaming for Sydney. As a matter of fact, it is one of your family's ships.'

Fenella paled. From what she had read in American papers about the huge casualties suffered in the European war it was more than possible that she would not again see this man who had loved her with all his heart for so long. She was suddenly confounded by her reaction and impulsively stepped forward, raising her hand to touch Randolph's cheek.

He gently gripped her hand and lowered it.

'Don't pretend to be sorry, Nellie,' he said softly. 'I have known for a long time about your private life – and understood that it does not include me.'

'Randolph, my darling,' Fenella choked, fighting back tears. 'I think that we should take time to talk. I know that my life has been a bit out of control lately but I feel you should not be so hasty in enlisting.'

'Why not?' Randolph frowned. 'You are now a big name in the studios and have the fame and fortune which seem to be so important to you. Why should you be concerned about talking to a man whose only claim to fame is that he can take the falls for fancy actors? At least back in my old life I knew who my enemies were and who would stand by me. I hope that you find everything that will make you happy.'

Fenella realised that tears were running down her cheeks.

She was finding it difficult to accept that Randolph was saying goodbye to her. No man in his right mind could do that, she told herself angrily. She was about to reply when a man stepped out of the doorway behind her.

'Fiona, my love,' he boomed. Randolph turned to see the handsome Italian actor beaming at Fenella. 'I have come to take you to dinner.'

Randolph shook his head with a rueful smile. 'Have a good life,' he said and turned to walk away, even though he had the impulse to smash the smiling Italian's face in. But he knew the beautiful daughter of Colonel Patrick Duffy now belonged to a different, make-believe world and soon enough he would be travelling back to the real world of war.

'Randolph!' He heard her call his name but continued to stride away. 'Randolph, do not walk away from me.' But she did not run to him.

Only George Macintosh remained in the company board-room with its massive teak desk dominating the gloomy space. The pungent aroma of cigar smoke hung in the air. Already George had a portrait of his grandfather Sir Donald Macintosh on the wall at one end of the room to remind the directors who had founded the financial empire in the Antipodes many years earlier. Missing from the wall was a portrait of his own father, Patrick Duffy, in spite of the fact that he was the actual head of the companies. Not that his father could comment on this. He was far away fighting a war, George mused.

The matter of purchasing a substantial share in the Broken Hill Proprietary company had been discussed, and approval given to buying a large package of shares. The mining concern was bringing out lead, silver and zinc from its production, and lead was needed in the manufacture of bullets. George felt that the newly formed company had a grand future and would one day prove to be a good investment.

But he frowned when he realised that he was due to make his routine payment to a member of the New South Wales Police Force. Inspector Jack Firth would be waiting in an out-of-the-way hotel in the city for his envelope containing a generous amount of pounds. It was outright blackmail but keeping the man's silence on certain matters that had occurred before the outbreak of war was essential. George had also curried the crooked policeman's friendship, and he was proving to be unwittingly useful to George's strategic plan to make himself the sole beneficiary of the Macintosh empire. Tonight, he would meet a man whom the corrupt policeman had identified might be employed by George in whatever enterprise he was currently considering.

George counted out two piles of pound notes and slipped them into their respective envelopes before placing both inside folded newspapers. Satisfied, he left the boardroom, wishing the doorman a good evening as he strolled away.

Within minutes he found the hotel Jack Firth had nominated and went inside. It was not far from the docks and was filled with the stench of stale beer, cigarette smoke and unwashed bodies. The patrons were mostly labourers and seamen and George's entry into the bar caused a couple of heads to turn at the sight of the well-dressed man carrying a briefcase. If any of the less than savoury characters thought about robbing the businessman, they changed their minds when they noticed George approaching a table where sat the much feared policeman with his distinctive huge frame. They turned away to continue drinking, allowing the civilian-dressed policeman his privacy.

George took a folded newspaper and pushed it across the table. Firth deftly slid the envelope from inside and slipped it into his trouser pocket. He had no reason to count his payoff; he knew the man on the other side of the table was not about to cheat him. He alone had been able to secure the file containing the notes on the well-known businessman's contacts with suspected German agents. Firth had since discreetly destroyed the paper trail. In a world limited by its ability to reproduce documents, the policeman had been able to track down each and every copy, stopping distribution to all but himself. One hand did not know what the other was doing and Firth liked it that way. George knew that the policeman, now working in a counterintelligence role, had the power to seriously embarrass him.

Firth opened the paper as if reading it. 'The man you want will meet you outside in the lane,' he said softly. 'He expects to see some money up front.'

'Thank you, Inspector,' George replied, glancing around the crowded, smoke-filled bar. 'How do I know that the man I am about to meet is not going to rob me?'

Firth looked up at the businessman with an expression of annoyed surprise. 'Because I told him to look after you,' he replied, presuming that no spivvy crook was about to cross the feared policeman if he knew what was good for him. 'So bugger off and let me take a look at the racing pages in peace.'

George rose from his seat and pushed his way out into the warm Sydney night. He turned down an alley and felt the hair on the back of his neck stand on end as he entered the cobbled, narrow, unlit street that stank of urine.

'You the man I was told to meet?' a voice growled from the shadows behind a pile of empty wooden crates.

'I presume so,' George replied, gripping the briefcase tightly to him. 'If you are able to help me with a small matter.'

The man stepped from the shadows and George could just make out his features. He was thin faced, clean-shaven and around forty years of age. But he moved with the stealth of a cat and George wondered who this man really was.

'I have a job to be done in America,' George said. 'It will pay very generously and I will be able to get you there as a crewman aboard one of my ships.'

'What kind of job?' the man asked, reaching in his pocket, extracting a cigarette and lighting it. When the match flared George noticed that the man had a long scar from the edge of his mouth to his ear. It looked like the result of a very sharp blade. Possibly a razor, George thought. He had read that many in the Sydney underworld carried such in lieu of a gun.

George swallowed nervously and glanced around to ensure that they were truly alone. 'Are you prepared to kill someone? A woman?'

The man looked up at him through the mist of cigarette smoke. 'It don't matter to me,' he grunted. 'Just so long as the money is good.'

'I can promise that,' George said, opening the briefcase and retrieving the second newspaper. He passed it to the man who simply rolled it up and placed it in the pocket of his suit coat without attempting to see what was inside. George was impressed by the way Jack Firth could elicit such trust from a gangster. 'You will find all your instructions with the first payment. Also a ticket. You are to report to the ship in a week's time. If you have any questions I would rather you direct them through Inspector Firth.'

'That bastard,' the man spat. 'I would rather rape that

Jew Big Lenny's sainted mother than work for Firth. But, as he is being generous with your money I will accept the deal.'

Presuming that Big Lenny was an underworld figure, George did not question the relationship the hired assassin had with the crooked policeman. He was not about to correct the thin criminal either on the matter of saints and Jewish religious beliefs.

'If everything you have in your instructions pans out,' the thin man said, 'I will get your job done. I always wanted to see the US of A.' Satisfied that their business was done, he quickly turned on his heel and walked into the darkness of the alley, leaving George alone with his briefcase.

George waited until the man was out of sight before stepping from the dingy lane into the lamplit street. An electrified tram rattled by, throwing sparks from its contacts with the wires. All going well, Fenella would be dead before the year was out. That would only leave Alex, George mused, praying that the army would grant his brother's wish to serve overseas on active service.

5

In the pre-dawn, Captain Matthew Duffy of the Australian Flying Corp vomited. To ensure that he was not seen doing so, he had walked some distance from his tent at the airfield laid out in the arid lands of the Gaza. The bilious attack had not been brought on by any physical ailment but by the fear he was fighting. He knew he was not alone in this when in the company of his fellow aircrew, as death was a constant companion. Just the day before, he had narrowly escaped being shot down by a prowling German fighter plane. It was only because he had been able to outfly his predator and been able to bring the German aviator within range of the airfield's anti-aircraft defences that he had survived the attack.

He had flown without his gunner, Sergeant Bruce Forsyth, who was recuperating from a badly smashed leg, the result of ground fire on a mission in the Romani region.

The squadron commander had suggested that, in place of the forward gunner, Matthew could carry spare fuel drums so as to be able to fly further on his recon missions, then land, refuel and return to base with photographic intelligence of Turkish military formations. The idea had worked and the plan would be repeated with Matthew flying a solo mission towards Palestine.

The Ottoman Turks, along with their German and Austrian allies, were slowly retreating north to Jerusalem and Damascus with the Australian Light Horse relentlessly pursuing them as part of Allenby's forces. This mission was in support of British ground forces and for a short time Matthew would have the protection of his brothers on the ground as he flew north in his fragile aircraft. The desert air still held a bitter chill but with the rising of the sun the day would become unbearably hot. Matthew wiped his mouth with the back of his hand and surrounded by three of the ground crew walked back to his aeroplane. They stood waiting for him to carry out his last-minute ground checks before pulling himself into the rear cockpit. Already the spare drums of fuel had been loaded. Matthew had requisitioned a Lee Enfield with five spare magazines of ammunition to be placed in the forward cockpit, as the twin Lewis guns had been stripped to allow a greater load of fuel. He wanted at least some protection when he was on the ground refuelling.

'She's ready to go, skipper,' a corporal mechanic said. 'Got you a thermos of tea and a packet of sandwiches in your cockpit.'

Matthew thanked his mechanic and climbed into the cockpit. The chief mechanic swung on the wooden propeller until the engine was turned over and spluttered into life. It opened up with a steady roar. The plane vibrated and the chocks were whipped away from the undercarriage. The little biplane bumped its way along the hard earth until Matthew could see the airsock. It lay limply against its post. He glanced over to see his mechanic indicating the little wind for direction and turned the nose into the gentle breeze now rising with the sun.

Matthew opened the throttle and the aircraft picked up speed to eventually drift into the air. Climbing and turning, he pointed the aircraft north, using his compass to indicate the flight path. He was hardly in the air when he began scanning the pale blue sky. He knew the Germans were out there and waiting to finish the job they had started the day before. Matthew had a premonition that this was his last mission, but curiously only wondered what it might feel like to die.

For the first thirty minutes of his flight low over the rugged land of seemingly endless craggy hillocks and jagged ravines he was alone. In his mission orders Matthew was to attempt to locate any rearguard positions laid down by the enemy that might cause problems to General Allenby's advancing army, and photograph and mark such positions on the map squashed on his lap. He passed over one or two nomadic camel trains but did not sustain any ground fire. They were the people of the Bible who had lived their lives oblivious to any Western influence in their lands and would probably do so for another century, Matthew mused, waving down to them.

Around the fortieth minute of his flight Matthew saw the movement. It was a column of around fifty camel-mounted Turkish troops winding their way along the high ground between ravines. He wished that his New Zealand gunner was manning the forward cockpit with his Lewis guns as the Turkish patrol had been caught unawares when Matthew swooped over them, scattering the patrol in different directions. The camels looked so slow and awkward as they were spurred on by their riders but Matthew knew how his Australian mounted infantry cobbers respected these animals for their endurance in this harsh, waterless land.

Leaving them behind, Matthew attempted to lay out his map and mark the position he had observed the camel patrol. He could make a note of what it was and knew it would not be necessary to take a photo. That was usually withheld for fixed fortifications so that those back at base could interpret strong points and wire layouts. So occupied was he in attempting to unfold the map and pencil in the position, he was hardly aware of the extra shudder of his aircraft. But a wire snapping beside him on the wing caught his attention. He was under attack – not from the ground but from the air. Desperately, he swivelled his head. Over his shoulder was the distinctive shape of a German aircraft. Not any aircraft, he realised, but the same one that had attempted to shoot him down the day before. Matthew had instantly recognised the Fokker's colours and it was obvious to him that he was in the German fighter pilot's patrol area. Tiny wisps of smoke had torn away from the barrels of the enemy machine guns and Matthew felt the bullets tear through the canvas and wooden frame of his plane. Turning his head, Matthew realised that he was skimming just above the ground. His only choice was to pull up, although he knew that was what the German pilot expected him to do. Already he could see him raising the nose of his Fokker for the coup de grace.

If he was going to get out of this alive Matthew knew he had only one option. Instead of pulling up he aimed his already badly shot-up aircraft at a stretch of flat ground, praying he could land and get away from the stricken biplane before a bullet exploded the extra tanks of fuel. Fire was the most feared cause of death for pilots, and as the British government had not provided parachutes, pilots couldn't opt to bail out. Many pilots also ensured that they carried a sidearm to end their own lives rather than go down in flames, burning slowly to death. Matthew carried his own revolver for that principal reason.

The ground came up quickly and the flimsy undercarriage hit the earth hard, the aircraft rolling along the ground until a wheel hit a small boulder, toppling the biplane over on its back. Matthew, strapped into his seat, found himself upside down, straining against his harness. He realised that the drums had spilled out and broken on the hard, rocky surface. Already, he could see the vapour fumes fanning out and knew he might be only seconds from being engulfed in flames. Desperately he unleashed himself and fell heavily to the ground. Overhead, he could hear the drone of the German aircraft and knew that it would probably strafe his downed plane to ensure that it was destroyed. But the German had not as yet done so and Matthew was a little puzzled by his adversary's hesitation.

Satisfied that he had no broken bones and that he was still able to use his limbs, Matthew scrambled from beneath the biplane to a good distance away to look up at the German aircraft. It was so low when it swooped over him that Matthew could clearly see the leather helmet and goggles of his adversary looking down at him. The pilot waved and waggled his wings. Matthew now understood why he had not immediately been strafed. His enemy was honouring a rare code of chivalry among pilots, giving him a chance to get free – if he was still alive. Gratefully, Matthew returned the wave and the German aircraft climbed away to the north, leaving Matthew alone beside his now useless aeroplane.

The desert took on its lonely silence, broken only by the steady tick-tick of the cooling metal of the engine. Matthew could see his thermos and rifle lying among the ruptured fuel drums and knew both items may be vital to his survival so far from his own lines in enemy territory. He pushed himself up from the earth to take a step towards recovering them when a sudden whoosh exploded under the aircraft and blew him off his feet. He felt the searing heat from the explosion of the fuel drums as he was blown back to lay crumpled on the hot, hard earth. The explosion was quickly replaced with a loud crackle as the fuselage went up in flames. Black, oily smoke rose into the dry, still air, proclaiming the location of his downed aeroplane for miles around.

Matthew rose once again and brushed himself down. When he took in the terrain around him he could see that he was on a treeless plain of sand and rocks with a rise on the horizon about half a mile away. While he was surveying this rise his feeling he had not cheated death returned. In the shimmering haze of the desert air he could see a line of Turkish camel riders forming up and guessed that they were the patrol he had flown over some ten minutes earlier. Their figures danced in the haze as if they were made of water. Matthew saw a tiny spout of earth erupt about ten feet from where he stood and the crack of the rifle rolled to him a second later. The line of enemy suddenly came down off the rise in a trot as more spouts of hard earth appeared. Matthew was in the open with nowhere to run for cover. And it was obvious that the Turks were not going to take him prisoner.

Matthew drew his revolver from the canvas pouch. So, he had not cheated death on this mission and would be killed in some godforsaken piece of earth where it was unlikely that his body would ever be recovered. As Matthew stood before his burning aircraft, the revolver in his hand, he had a fleeting regret that his beloved mother would not have any grandchildren to carry on her proud heritage. But just as strange, Matthew found that his thoughts were on an old Aboriginal warrior. It was as if Wallarie was actually standing beside him, spear in hand, and facing down the rapidly approaching Turkish mounted soldiers who by now were firing from their saddles in defiance of Wallarie's warrior traditions.

'Wallarie, help me,' Matthew said softly, not expecting an answer but trying to rouse the last vestige of courage to die fighting impossible odds. He raised the pistol to shoulder height and waited until either a bullet took him down or they were foolish enough to get close to him, providing him a target for his shorter-ranged weapon.

Now he could hear the thundering hoof beats of the charging camels and the Turkish war cry of 'Allah akbar!' Matthew was surprised at the eerie calm he experienced as death came closer. He would die in the Biblical lands of Abraham and Moses but with the spirit of the old Aboriginal warrior beside him.

The enemy were now only 300 yards out. Matthew decided to take his first shot into the rank of Turkish soldiers but did not see any camel or enemy soldier fall. He considered keeping the last round in his revolver for his own death, having heard the stories from others of how in the hands of Turkish soldiers torture normally preceded execution.

Matthew fired his second shot. He would only fire five times at the enemy before turning the gun on himself. For a second Matthew stood stunned. Was it Aboriginal magic or had he not just knocked down at least a half-dozen camels and troops with a single shot?

But then he was acutely aware of the chatter of a deadly Maxim gun from his left, beyond the burning aeroplane. The fusillade tore through the line of assaulting enemy, spilling riders from killed or badly wounded camels. The deadly mayhem continued as the machine gun raked the confused Turkish soldiers. Their attack suddenly broke up as they reeled in their mounts to assess the unexpected threat from their flank.

Matthew also scanned the ground. Beyond his wrecked aircraft he could see a crew of three men manning a Maxim gun mounted on a tripod. Its nose poked from just above a tiny rise in the land. From this vantage point for firing down the line of Turkish troops, the heavy machine-gun bullets could not miss their targets. Matthew could see a band of horsemen dressed in the flowing loose garments he had seen the Arabs wear. They were manoeuvring to form a line to assault the now milling survivors of the machine gun. As he watched in awe Matthew saw the line of horse riders charge the broken line of Turkish soldiers. They were firing from the saddle as they came, killing even more enemy. Matthew did not understand the words his saviours yelled as they attacked. It was a language he had not heard before.

Any surviving Turks quickly attempted to whip their camels away from Matthew but the attacking horsemen swept through them, taking out many more until the attacking party of around fifty was reduced to only a half-dozen enemy soldiers on foot with their hands in the air. But it was to no avail as the mounted men poured rifle fire into the survivors, executing them all without any hesitation. A couple of the men dismounted, walked among the bodies lying in pools of blood, firing shots into any that showed any sign of life. Matthew was in part appalled by the callous attitude of his saviours but reserved some sympathy for what they were doing. It was obvious that the wounded would die a slow, painful death in the desert if left without help and he well knew they were a long way from the nearest village or major settlement.

Matthew lowered his pistol as one of the horsemen wheeled away from the mounted men now going through the dead Turkish soldiers' possessions, mostly recovering weapons and ammunition. A horseman trotted to within a few feet of where Matthew stood and brought his mount to a halt. He was dressed differently to the men who had saved him and was in his mid-thirties with a clean shaven, deeply tanned face. He wore a dirty cotton shirt, trousers tucked into riding boots with a bandolier of ammunition across his chest. When Matthew looked closely into the rider's face he could see intelligent eyes behind a grim expression and the demeanour of a leader.

'Shalom,' he said. Matthew knew at least that word was of Jewish origin. 'You know that your bloody escapade almost got all of us killed,' he continued from his height overlooking the downed aviator. 'What are you? British?'

Matthew stared into the face of the angry man who had chided him for his 'escapade', aware how dry his mouth was. But more than the thirst he was suffering was the realisation that Wallarie *had* to be behind his miraculous rescue.

'Saul? Saul Rosenblum?' he croaked in disbelief. 'I thought you were dead.'

The rider peered into Matthew's oil-stained face and his grim expression instantly dissolved. Sliding from his saddle, Saul Rosenblum took a few quick paces to embrace Matthew in a giant bear hug. 'Young Matt Duffy!' he roared, lifting Matthew off his feet. 'You too are alive.'

He released Matthew and stood back to examine him.

'Who under heaven could have told us that we would meet in God's land sixteen years after Elands River?'

Grinning, Matthew shook his head. 'You are listed on the old regiment's roll as missing in action, you know, old chap,' he said. 'So, how is it that you turn up here with what is obviously a band of brigands.'

'Ah, the men from my settlement,' Saul replied, glancing over his shoulder to where he could see his machine-gun crew dismantling the deadly weapon and strapping it on the back of a pack horse. 'We were shadowing the Ottoman patrol when you appeared out of the sky. The Turks are becoming more of a threat to my settlement in their retreat from the Canal. We had planned to ambush them if they appeared to be heading towards the moshava. But the deed has been done and the threat eliminated.'

'Who are you, these days?' Matthew asked. 'And how the hell did you get here from Africa?'

'It's a long story, cobber,' Saul said, slapping Matthew on the back and leading him away from the burning air-craft. 'But we will take you back with us to the settlement, where you will meet my wife and sons. I can arrange to get news that you are safe to your unit and in due time get you back – depending on how secure our lines of communication are back to your army.'

'Sounds like a reasonable idea,' Matthew shrugged. 'I could do with a good drink of anything wet in the meantime. Until you appeared I was about to say my prayers and leave the earth, hopefully on the wings of angels, if I could not use my own.'

'Do you know that I served with the Zion Mule corps as a sergeant at Gallipoli and saw Colonel Duffy?' Saul asked, walking Matthew to a spare horse led by the Jewish fighters now quickly recovered from their ambush on the Turkish patrol. They had incurred no casualties on their own side but were not celebrating their victory. Matthew could see from the way the men were disciplined in their actions that they were seasoned fighting men and their unsmiling faces showed that they did not wallow in the damage they had inflicted on the unfortunate Turkish camel soldiers. 'But then I was under another name and avoided Colonel Duffy – lest he recognise me.'

Matthew did not want to think that his old friend from the South African campaign had deserted all those years earlier but it nagged him. No doubt Saul would tell his story and there would be a good explanation. Saul Rosenblum, former Queensland stockman and mounted infantry trooper, once recommended for the award of the Victoria Cross, was a man of honour. Matthew doubted that the man striding beside him had really changed in character.

When Matthew swung himself astride the horse provided he impulsively glanced back at his still-burning aircraft as if expecting to see the old Aboriginal warrior standing by it. Despite the fact that he did not he casually threw a salute. 'Thank you, Wallarie, old friend,' he said under his breath, and turned to ride with Saul Rosenblum and his band of fighters.

The thin man with the scarred face stood at the rails of the Macintosh cargo ship as it pitched and rolled just beyond the towering sandstone headlands that were the gateway to Sydney Harbour. He sucked on a cigarette and reflected on what lay ahead of him in the next few weeks. Mr George Macintosh had made a substantial down payment for him to carry out a killing on some actress in America. He knew the woman from watching her on the screen in the smoke-filled, darkened theatres in Sydney. She was a bonzer-looking sheila and he wondered why a well-known and respected Sydney businessman would want her dead.

A pod of dolphins followed the wake of the ship that spewed black coal smoke into the air as it prepared for the long voyage across the Pacific Ocean to San Francisco. The thin man flicked his cigarette butt at them as they drew close under the bow. Why Mr Macintosh wanted the woman dead did not really matter to him, he thought, as he unconsciously fingered the closed cutthroat razor in his trouser pocket. He was born into poverty but was an intelligent man and the dreaded Sydney street gangs had provided him with opportunities to make money. He had risen in their ranks because he was smart enough to keep himself out of jail. Even Inspector Jack Firth had grudgingly referred to him as a 'good crim' – that is, one who knew his business rather than one of exemplary morals.

So, he had only a few weeks when he got to Los Angeles to carry out his mission and then reboard the ship he was presently on. Back in Sydney he would collect the balance of his payment. He knew that on American soil he had the advantage of not being known to the local law authorities and so long as he kept to himself he would draw no interest from those around him. He would not live lavishly while he was in the States but simply carry out his observations as to the best place and time to cut her throat. Maybe, if the opportunity presented itself, he would use her for his carnal needs before he killed her. Proof of her death would easily be obtained. It was not every day that a film actress was murdered and it would be in the papers either side of the Pacific.

The thin man cupped his nicotine-stained hands around another cigarette and expertly lit it against the strong breeze blowing off the sea and across the deserted deck. He reflected on how his victim might have been living life to the fullest if only she knew that she had less than two weeks to live. The thin man had killed three times before with his deadly razor – a perfect score as he had only ever been assigned to kill three men. A hundred per cent result spoke for itself.

As if sensing the evil thoughts of the man on the deck above them, the pod of dolphins suddenly veered away from the bow of the ship and disappeared beneath the waves.

On the journey north towards Saul's settlement the former Australian soldier explained that his men dressed as Arab irregulars fighting the Ottomans to disguise the fact that they were actually Jewish settlers. However, he pointed out, two of the men who rode in their ranks were actually Arabs from a nearby village.

'The Moslems have a saying that goes something like this: the enemy of my enemy makes that enemy my friend,' Saul explained. 'Or words to that effect. My old enemy Abdullah from the village near our moshava has allowed his sons to ride with us against the Turks as his people have no love for the foreigners occupying their lands from Constantinople.'

On the evening of the first day they approached a small, squalid township surrounded by sparsely grassed and rocky lands where young boys attended to flocks of goats. Two of Saul's men peeled away from the column to wave their salutes and ride towards the stone hovels.

Saul waved back, shouting something in a language Matthew did not understand but presumed was Arabic. For another hour they continued to ride down into a small valley where Matthew was surprised to see a veritable oasis among the arid hills; vineyards and orchards were laid out in neat patterns and a township of fine stone buildings was located at the centre of the valley. Saul and his men broke into a gallop. Matthew followed them into a cleanly laid out street where healthy, well-dressed men, women and children joyously greeted the return of their fighting men.

Saul slid from his saddle to hug two teenage boys. A pretty young woman wearing a head scarf and in her late twenties stood shyly by holding an infant girl on her hip. She stepped forward and Saul wrapped both wife and daughter in a tight embrace. Tears flowed down the young woman's face.

'My wife, Elsa,' Saul said, turning to Matthew still astride his mount. 'And the princess in her arms is my daughter who rules her two brothers, Joshua and Benjamin, here.'

Matthew dismounted to stand before two young boys he guessed were about twelve and thirteen years old. The eldest, he noted, had a German rifle slung on his shoulder. Both young men looked Matthew in the eyes and appraised him frankly when he shook their hands.

'Pleased to meet you, boys,' Matthew said. 'I am an old friend of your father.'

Both boys nodded.

'I am afraid that their English is not all that good,' Saul said, now holding his daughter on his hip. 'My wife speaks English, but was originally from the Russias, as most of the settlers in our moshava are. We tend to speak Hebrew here rather than Yiddish,' he explained, although Matthew did not have much idea about the difference between the two languages. 'Well, I am sure that you will look forward to a soft bed, a good meal and a bottle of excellent wine tonight, and we can talk about old times.'

Matthew was suddenly reminded of home. Not because of what Saul had just said but because he caught the slightest whiff of eucalyptus on the evening breeze. 'Gum trees?' he asked.

Saul broke into a wide grin. 'My gum trees,' he replied proudly. 'They have helped us reclaim what was useless land and given us the opportunity to turn what our Arab neighbours sold to us into arable soil to plant our grape vines, olive and orange trees. It was one of my first jobs when I came to the settlement after Africa. That, and training the able-bodied to defend themselves against our Moslem neighbours. But that is a long story and I am sure that for the moment you would rather eat, drink and sleep.'

Matthew nodded and Saul guided him away from the horses now being led away to be brushed down, watered and fed by the young men and women of the village. Saul, Elsa and Matthew walked a short distance, all the time being so warmly greeted by the people in the street that Matthew had the impression that Saul was well respected and liked by those of his community.

They reached a neat stone house with a tiled roof. What made the house stand out in the street was a large, dust-covered Packard automobile parked in front. Matthew turned with a questioning look to Saul.

'Oh, that is not mine,' he answered the unspoken question. 'It belongs to a guest, Miss Joanne Barrington of the New Hampshire Barringtons.' Matthew sensed just the slightest hint of sarcasm. 'She's a Yankee archaeologist – or so she says. Her car broke down outside the settlement and we recovered it. The stupid woman is travelling virtually alone in war-torn countryside with nothing else to protect her than the fact she belongs to a neutral country. She feels that being an American abroad is enough to save her neck from bandits and rogue Ottoman troops.'

Before Matthew could ask any further questions about Saul's intriguing American guest a young lady dressed in a white shirt and riding jodhpurs stepped from behind the car. Her freckled face was covered in oil and she held a large spanner in one hand. Her red hair flowed free about her shoulders and she had what Matthew would call a pretty elfish face with large, emerald-coloured eyes. He could also see that she was barely 5 foot 4 inches in height.

'Mr Rosenblum,' she called in a happy voice, 'I am pleased to see that you have come home to us in one piece.'

'My wife likes her,' Saul growled under his breath to Matthew. 'Otherwise, she is a pest around the settlement. Always talking women's rights and them getting the vote. It will never happen.'

Matthew was aware that the pretty young American was looking at him with a curious expression on her face and smiled. She returned his smile, wiping her grease-covered hands on a rag she pulled from the hood of the big American car which surely would have cost a small fortune.

'Miss Barrington, I should introduce another guest,' Saul said. 'Captain Matthew Duffy of the Australian Flying Corps, currently grounded due to the lack of being able to keep his aircraft in the sky.'

'You crashed, Captain Duffy?' Joanne gasped in her concern.

'Shot down,' Matthew replied stiffly as she put out her hand to shake his. Matthew was taken aback at the gesture he normally associated with men. But he had also heard stories that American women were very forward and frank. When he clasped her hand to shake it he was close enough to look directly into her captivating eyes. He had not felt that odd feeling for a long time. Matthew released his grip, realising that he was almost holding his breath. There was so much he had read in those large eyes. Both innocence and courage, but in ways he could not find words to explain.

6

Captain Sean Duffy, MC, had passed his staff college course for company commanders in England. He was to be granted leave before rejoining his battalion in France and was looking forward to meeting with Colonel Patrick Duffy at Patrick's exclusive club in London within a few hours. A knock on the door of his quarters in the officers' mess while he was packing to leave was not unexpected as he had arranged to get a lift up to London with another Australian officer who had also completed the course.

'Captain Duffy, sir,' the officers' mess steward said, poking his head around the corner. 'You are wanted in the orderly room straightaway.'

Sean frowned. He had signed off his mess chits, accounted for his kit and received his course report. Why was he needed so urgently?

Sean left his packing, throwing his kit bag on the bed,

and made his way to the college orderly room where he was greeted by a British corporal slaving away at a pile of forms on his desk. The corporal glanced up. 'I will inform Major O'Shea that you are here, sir,' he said, easing himself away from his desk and disappearing down the long hallway of the old mansion that had been built 300 years earlier but was now a military installation. He returned within a minute.

'Major O'Shea is ready to see you, sir. He is in room 5,' the corporal said, resuming his duties.

Sean walked smartly to the designated office, knocked and heard a muffled voice bid him enter. He opened the door, marched in and came to attention, throwing a salute to the officer seated behind a desk. The first thing Sean noticed was that the British officer had obviously lost his left arm below the shoulder and that, from the badges on his uniform, he had been a member of one of Britain's elite Irish regiments. The major was a man in his late thirties, with thinning, sandy hair and cold blue eyes.

'Captain Duffy, you may take a seat if you wish,' the British officer said, glancing down at a file of papers before him on the highly polished desktop.

Sean took a chair directly in front of the desk.

'Captain Duffy,' the major said. 'I am from the War Office, more specifically the section that investigates reports for recommendations for gallantry. I have a report before me from your former CO, Colonel Patrick Duffy. By chance any relation to you?' he asked, looking Sean directly in the eyes.

'A distant cousin, sir,' Sean answered, mystified as to why this man would want to speak with him so urgently. 'We had not met until I was posted to the colonel's battalion in the Dardanelles.'

'I believe that Colonel Duffy may have mentioned to you in Belgium that he was submitting a report recommending you for a medal for your bravery in silencing a German machine-gun crew at Fromelles,' O'Shea continued, leaning slightly back in his chair.

'He did, sir,' Sean answered, sensing that something was wrong. The demeanour of the man interviewing him was like that of a police investigator clarifying evidence.

'Well, according to your report,' O'Shea said, fingering a thin folder, 'you make no mention of your part in the incident. Why is that?'

Sean frowned. 'Sir, I was hardly aware that I had killed the Germans. Corporal . . . Sergeant Kelly was with me and he informed me that at the time I was suffering concussion from a shell burst.'

'Surely you would remember that singular act of putting the Hun gun out of action?' O'Shea questioned, leaning forward. 'It is an act worthy of recognition by way of the award of the Victoria Cross.'

'Sir, I don't remember,' Sean replied. That terrible day when he had broken down was still a blur in his memory. 'I think that someone else may have put the Huns out of action.'

Sean noticed a change in the almost hostile demeanour of the British officer interviewing him. O'Shea seemed to relax.

'I am glad that you have recognised it may have been someone else, Captain Duffy,' he sighed, leaning back. 'Otherwise, I may have had to recommend from my interview with you that you be court-martialled for conduct unbecoming an officer of his majesty's forces. Claiming another man's courage is a serious breach of an officer's honour.'

'Sir,' Sean said, leaning towards the British officer. 'I have admitted to being confused on the day.'

'I lost my arm at Mons,' the major said, 'But worse, I lost my company to overwhelming Hun artillery.'

Between the two men an unspoken message passed and Sean realised that he had indeed made his point to a colleague who no doubt had also experienced the terror of leadership under fire; an officer must not be seen to lose his grip when so many others looked to him for courage. It was easier to act brave than feel it.

'I am satisfied that you have not deliberately set out to hoodwink the War Office,' O'Shea said. 'You see, we have another report in your file from a company commander in the battalion on your flank in the attack. He says that his men witnessed an NCO killing the gun crew that had them pinned down. As the only NCO at the time was with you, it must have been Corporal Kelly, mentioned in our report. I strongly suspect that he has not reported his role in the act of valour in order to cover you, Captain Duffy. I consider that your CO, Colonel Duffy, may have been just a bit eager in getting gongs shared out in his battalion, and acted somewhat in haste with his report on your part in the attack.'

'Yes, sir,' Sean answered, his face reddening with shame for what he knew he had to be covered for. 'What is going to happen now?'

'I will be passing the report to the appropriate people and recommending that Corporal Kelly be recommended for his act of extreme bravery. I suspect that he will be awarded the Distinguished Conduct Medal. In other circumstances, ones that had not been muddied by contradictory reports, the soldier may have received the VC had you been more in charge of the day. However, I am sure he will be pleased to receive any kind of award, but you will not be returned to your battalion as a company commander, Captain Duffy, Instead, you will fill the position of company 2IC. Let us say that you will do your penance for a time, until you prove you are fully in control of your duty to your men.'

'Yes, sir,' Sean replied glumly. He had so desperately wanted command of his own company and now it had been snatched from him because of what the army had deduced was a temporary lack of leadership under fire. The command of the company would have led rapidly to recognition in the post with the rank of major. Now, he would remain a captain and Sean knew well how the army would have a cloud over his head. Had Sergeant Jack Kelly blurted to everyone of his lapse in the trenches? If so, then his role as a leader was over in the eyes of the men who had trusted him.

'If there is nothing else you want to add to our conversation, Captain Duffy, you are free to take your leave in London,' O'Shea finished.

Sean rose to his feet, snapped off a formal salute and left the room. The trembling he experienced in the trenches had returned. But this time it was not from fear but out of shame for what lay ahead of him in his old battalion.

Whereas Captain Sean Duffy, MC, was sitting in Patrick's exclusive gentleman's club in London while a cold, sleeting rain fell outside, on the other side of the world a policeman wearing a suit sat in a simple wooden office belonging to the commandant of the Holdsworthy internment camp for enemy aliens. Inspector Jack Firth, an officer in the government's counterespionage department, reflected on what a miserable place the camp was: bloody cold in winter and stinking hot in summer. He wished he were back in his office in Sydney where he could duck around to his corner pub for a decent lunch and a cold ale well away from this small town of tents and corrugated iron—roofed huts housing those enemy civilians who had been arrested and put behind the tall wire fences on the outskirts of Sydney.

His duties had forced him to travel to the camp to audit the movements of people visiting those interned. The government suspected that in the camp were German nationals still working for their Fatherland, despite being held as prisoners. It was only natural that they would; patriotism was not the domain of British citizens alone. However, Inspector Jack Firth felt that his visit to the camp was not a complete waste of his time. One name in particular had cropped up in the military logs of visitors. That of Frau Karolina Schumann, who had been meeting with Pastor Karl von Fellmann.

Before the war, Jack had been a detective sergeant investigating serious crime on the streets of Sydney. He had gained a reputation among the toughest and most dangerous street thugs as a man to be feared and respected. Jack had loved his image. He had been a king of the streets but after the war had broken out, even with the promotion, he had found himself stuck away in an office overseeing tedious files on suspected spies. And because most Australians were concerned every person of German heritage was a potential spy, Jack's job of sorting wheat from chaff was far from easy.

Jack knew that Karolina Schumann was the mother-in-law of one Captain Alexander Macintosh. He and his brother George were the brothers of Fenella Macintosh, his chief suspect in an unsolved case two years old that had captured the interest of the public. A well-known Australian film actor, Guy Wilkes, had been shot to death in what the former homicide investigator strongly suspected was a crime of passion. Fenella Macintosh had conveniently fled to America on a ship out of Sydney only hours after the event. He had almost caught up with her in Hawaii via the cable but she again fled the long arm of the law. From what he had come to learn since, the famous American actress of supposed Welsh origins, Fiona Owens, was in fact Fenella Macintosh. Because of his current posting he had been actively discouraged from pursuing his suspect in the Wilkes case. His superiors had explained that Colonel Duffy and the Macintosh family were too important to the war effort for the matter to be followed up in these troubled times. The murder of a drug-using actor of dubious moral standards was not of great concern when thousands of young Australians were being killed and wounded every month on the battlefields.

But Jack Firth was not a man who took well to being told anything. His love was the world of real crime – murder, rape and robbery – not the shadowy world of suspected spies. He would bring someone to justice on the Wilkes murder, despite the war, and now he was seeing interesting coincidences in his work. That Karolina Schumann should be tagged as a person of interest for her many visits to the internment camp was intriguing to the police inspector because of her links to the Macintosh family.

With a deep sigh, he flipped open the pile of reports compiled on the inmates by the prison staff. His first was that of the Lutheran missionary, Pastor Karl von Fellmann. Jack read through the details of the man who had been born in Germany but lived in Queensland for the past sixteen years. He had been married but his wife died on the mission station they had set up to cater to the spiritual and pastoral needs of the Aboriginals of central Queensland. The mission was located on a property called Glen View, belonging to the Macintosh family. According to the commandant's comments the pastor had proved a model prisoner tending to the spiritual needs of the sizeable Lutheran population of the camp. Informants had noted that he did not appear to have any political leanings towards the Fatherland but tended to identify himself as neutral in the conflict, stating that his ministry put him beyond the evil work of men in war. His constant visitor was a former inmate, Frau Karolina Schumann, and some of the informants had suggested that there may be a romantic interest on the pastor's side. Jack Firth was interested to see that the Lutheran missionary was the twin brother of a well-known, high-ranking German officer who had visited Australia just before the outbreak of hostilities.

The policeman continued to read the file, swatting at the clouds of flies attempting to settle on his sweat-stained face. The pastor had a keen interest in playing chess and his main chess companion was one Herr Maynard Bosch . . .

Jack sat up. Maynard Bosch! He and his department had placed the former German consul on the top of their list of principal spymasters. Before the war Bosch had been in contact with Mr George Macintosh and because of that link Jack had been able to blackmail the wealthy captain of industry when he had been transferred from his criminal investigation duties to counterintelligence. At least the transfer had come with a promotion. Coincidence, Firth thought. There was no such thing as a coincidence in the world of crime – only circumstantial evidence. But Jack also knew that all mail coming into the camp and going out was closely scrutinised and so far the people in the intelligence world had not been able to find anything that looked like a code in any of Bosch's letters.

Jack eased his large bulk from behind the table and stood

up to stretch his limbs. He was still stiff and sore from the very rough and tough game of rugby he had played on the previous weekend; his reputation as a policeman made him a target in the forwards to those less than sympathetic to the law. He walked over to a window with a view of the camp grounds. Men, women and children went about their day of limited routine under a hot summer sun. Tiny shops and places of trade had established themselves among the residents of the camp.

Surely Bosch was not stupid enough to send coded letters, Jack mused. He would have a courier and most likely that was the German woman. All he had to do was intercept her after a visit and have her searched. If they were able to find any incriminating documents on her she would face the death penalty. After all, it was good enough for the Huns to execute the British nurse Edith Cavell in Belgium, so why not tit for tat?

'Do you wish to interview any of our inmates?' an army sergeant asked, poking his head around the door.

Jack rubbed his face with a big, meaty hand. 'Not at this stage, sergeant,' he replied. Jack was not about to tip off anyone in the camp about his copper's suspicion that the German spymaster, Maynard Bosch, was still well and truly active and that he had help in the form of Frau Karolina Schumann. As for the Lutheran pastor, he was not so sure. If his suspicions proved to be right then he would be holding high stakes in a dangerous game of blackmail. After all, Karolina Schumann was related to the Macintosh family through the marriage of her daughter to Alexander Macintosh and a scandal of that magnitude could cause the house of Macintosh to come crumbling down. George Macintosh was a man who would be most likely seeking a future knighthood for his services to industry and the Crown would not look kindly on any future recommendation of a man linked to subversive members of the family.

It was time to return to HQ in Sydney away from the dust and flies of the desolate western district of Holdsworthy.

'The enemy is between us and your base,' Saul said, pouring a glass of wine for Matthew and his house guest. 'We have not been able to get word to your army that you are still alive.'

Matthew gazed into his wine. It had the rich red hue of blood. Saul's house was comfortable and would keep out the bitter chill of the winters. None of the rooms were large but the stone building had a solid feel that was comforting. They currently sat in a room that doubled as a kitchen and living room and was lit by a kerosene lantern that cast a yellowish light into the deep shadows.

'They will have listed me as MIA by now,' Matthew replied, guessing that his two weeks' stay in Saul's settlement would warrant such a decision. 'A telegram to that effect will break my mother's heart.'

'I am sorry, my friend,' Saul said. 'But I cannot risk my men attempting to break the Ottoman lines to get you back. The safety of my family and community must be my first priority.'

'I fully understand,' Matthew said, taking a swig from his wine.

It was then that the third party – the guest – spoke. 'I can take Captain Duffy south with me,' Joanne suggested. 'After all, I am an American citizen and therefore a neutral. The Ottomans would not dare interfere with me or my American driver.'

Both men glanced at the young archaeologist. Her plan had merit.

'If we were stopped by a Turkish patrol I would not have papers to say I was a citizen of America,' Matthew reminded her.

'Ah, that can be arranged,' Saul grinned. 'We actually have a former Russian who was a master forger back in St Petersburg before he discovered his Hebrew roots and decided to immigrate to Palestine. Either that, or he was just one step ahead of the Russian police and needed somewhere to run. No matter the reason, he has proved invaluable to us in producing documents. I am sure he could come up with very good papers identifying you as a mad Yankee adventurer – like Miss Barrington here.'

'Your driver?' Matthew asked, looking directly at Joanne.

She glanced down at the table. 'I am, after all, the daughter of William Barrington the second,' she said, looking up and directly into Matthew's face. 'It is only to be expected that my father would supply a driver to look after the automobile.'

'A very impressive automobile at that,' Matthew commented.

'I would presume, Captain Duffy, that as an aviator you would have some knowledge of mechanics,' Joanne said.

'I do,' Matthew replied, taking another swig of his wine. 'Aircraft, automobiles . . . all the same when it comes to a combustion engine. I see that you have had your Packard repaired ready to travel.'

'I did that myself,' Joanne replied proudly. 'I did not need a man to help me.'

'I am impressed, Miss Barrington,' Matthew smiled, admiring the flash of defiance in the young woman's eyes. 'Not bad for a woman,' he added, knowing that he was baiting her.

The American heiress ignored his remark. 'When do you suggest that we leave?' she asked, turning to Saul.

'I will borrow your travel documents and see if our Russian friend can produce what Captain Duffy needs before first light,' he answered. 'If so, I would suggest that you leave at dawn. The weather is starting to turn. It will become very cold and wet soon and your vehicle could easily bog on the tracks south. God knows how you seem to navigate this country as it is,' he added with grudging respect for the American's resilience in the harsh terrain that now was the canvas for a vicious war between invading Christians and defending Moslems with occupying Jews caught in the middle.

'There is just one thing,' Matthew said reflectively. 'I don't like the idea, neutral or not, of travelling south without arms. There are also the bandits. I have my service revolver but that is not enough to protect us if things get a bit ugly.'

'I have my own arms,' Joanne said with a smirk. 'And I daresay that I may be a better shot than you, Captain Duffy, as Miss Annie Oakley herself has taught me to shoot. I carry two rifles and a shotgun in the vehicle to bring down any game that may help in the camp stew pot.'

Matthew shook his head. This tiny woman with the wild red hair had more going for her than most men he knew. And to top it off, she had a pixie-like beauty that caught him in her spell every time she looked his way.

Before the sun rose on a bleak, cold day Matthew felt the gentle shake on his shoulder as he lay tucked under a thick, warm quilt. For a moment the gut-wrenching sickness almost came to him as he imagined that he was being awoken by his batman to fly a combat mission, but as he focused on the room he saw Saul standing over him.

'Time to go, my friend,' Saul said. 'I have the papers you need and it only cost me a good bottle of vodka. I also have a change of clothing for you so that you won't look like a flyer.'

Matthew slowly sat up in bed, rubbing his eyes. A steaming mug of coffee was placed in his hand.

'Miss Barrington is already up and dressed. She is bidding farewell to my wife and children, who have an unexplainable liking for the annoying Yankee. She has a hamper for your trip already stowed aboard.'

Matthew slid from the bed, changed into the shirt and trousers provided and pulled on a heavy woollen coat to ward off the cold. He gulped his coffee down and followed Saul to the front of the house where he saw Saul's family gathered around the Packard. There was hugging and tears.

'Time to leave,' Saul said, placing his hand on Matthew's shoulder. 'I pray that you both make it through the enemy lines without incident.'

Matthew glanced at the pile of papers Saul had thrust into his hands and noticed that they were in his name.

'I thought it best that you keep your name, even if you have changed nationality for the moment. That way you will not be caught out if quizzed.'

Matthew nodded.

'Captain Duffy . . . I mean, Mr Duffy, are you ready to resume your duties as my driver?' Joanne asked with a mischievous grin.

'Yes, ma'am,' Matthew answered, imitating an American accent.

'You do that well,' Joanne commented.

'I spent time in the States before the war . . . even New Hampshire,' Matthew said, climbing into the seat of the open automobile loaded with supplies and spare parts.

Joanne climbed up into the passenger's seat. She was

wearing riding breeches and a heavy woollen coat as well as riding boots that came up to her knees. The floppy man's hat was secured by a piece of cotton cord.

Joanne removed a map and took out a hand-held prismatic compass from a leather case. She examined the map and took a shot with her compass. 'We go that way,' she said, pointing south. 'I believe that will eventually take me to Egypt and, along the way, your airfield.'

'You know where my base is?' Matthew asked, curious.

'Oh, just a guess as to where you might have an airfield,' Joanne answered vaguely. 'You did say that you flew from the south on your mission.'

Matthew nodded as Saul turned over the crank handle at the front of the car to start the engine. It kicked over smoothly and Saul passed up the handle to Joanne. With a wave, they commenced driving out of Saul's settlement and along a track that led between groves of orange trees and lines of grapevines. The cloudy sky and chill wind that whipped around them promised a day of showers. At least Matthew was returning to his squadron and, with any luck, his mother would not receive the dreaded telegram that said he was missing in action.

The track was accommodating enough for a few miles out of the settlement but soon they found themselves manoeuvring through gullies and along craggy hillsides, occasionally passing Bedouin goat herders tending their flocks. But they made significant miles and during a stop Matthew examined the map. At this rate, he deduced, he would reach his airfield within two to three days.

Near dusk they stopped the car and pitched a camp. Joanne carried a tent large enough to accommodate four people. A wind was rising and Matthew pegged it down against the possible tempest. They were camped in a hollow which helped act as a windbreak as on either side were low, bare ridges with just a few scrawny brushes. Matthew was able to find almost fossilised, dry scraps of timber which he made into a reasonable fire. When the sun set, the wind suddenly dropped and the skies cleared leaving a chill in the star-filled night sky.

Joanne had prepared a rich stew from tins of *Fray & Bentos* meats she said she had purchased in London. They were certainly of better quality than the tins of meat supplied to Matthew's squadron mess. The two of them sat by the flickering fire. In the distance they could hear a jackal call in the desert. Matthew had said little during the drive, constantly changing gears to cope with the rough tracks. But now, in the serenity of the night it was as if the world had gone away, leaving just this tiny space of peace in their lives. The place was as far from the war that Matthew could imagine and for a moment he felt that he could have been at home, sitting by the campfire on the vast Queensland plains.

'You did very well today, Mr Duffy,' Joanne said as he stared into the flames reflecting on the peace that he was feeling. 'You must be a good aviator as well.'

Matthew continued to stare at the dancing flames. 'Well, I got myself shot down,' he answered. 'Not a good thing to put in one's flying log.'

'What did you do before the war?' Joanne asked.

'Made my mother miserable with my wandering all over the world,' Matthew answered.

'You must have had some trade or profession, Mr Duffy, or you would not have been made an officer,' Joanne persisted gently. 'From the few facts I have gleaned from Mr Rosenblum you ran away when you were very young to fight against the Dutch in South Africa. And that your family is very wealthy.'

'My father is long dead,' Matthew said, looking away. 'He was an American prospector who came to Australia for the Victorian gold strike of the 1850s. It was my mother who made our fortune on the frontier, hauling supplies to the miners of the Palmer River strike in the 1870s. I suppose I can say that my real profession is flying aeroplanes.'

'Surely that is not a real profession for someone such as you,' Joanne said. 'I might say it is a pastime – a hobby at best.'

Matthew turned to stare into Joanne's face. 'When this bloody war is over, aircraft are going to change the face of our civilisation in ways we can hardly imagine,' he said with conviction. 'Even in your hobby of searching for lost civilisations aircraft will do everything from transporting and supplying to reconnaissance for possible sites of hidden ruins. We don't just go up to ride the wind.'

'My hobby, as you call it, is actually my profession, Mr Duffy,' Joanne replied stiffly. 'I will have you know that I have spent countless hours studying at one of our finest academic institutes to become an archaeologist.'

'From what Saul told me about you I am surprised that your father allowed you to travel halfway around the world to this godforsaken place in the middle of a war just to scrounge around the desert,' Matthew countered, hurt by her opinion that flying was a trivial pursuit.

Joanne poked at the fire with a stick she found at her feet. Tiny red embers flew skyward. 'My father forbade me to pursue my love of ancient things,' she replied softly. 'You see, Mr Duffy, my mother died when I was very young and my father dotes on my older brother. To my father I am his precious princess who has only one role in life – to meet the right man of good breeding stock and marry him to produce babies for my father to bounce on his knee. It is my brother who will one day take the reins of our fortunes while I will simply fade into the background.'

'So that is why you are out here in this place,' Matthew said gently. 'To prove to your father that you are more than simply an item to be married off like a company in a business merger.'

'No,' Joanne said, looking up from the fire and into his eyes. 'I am here to prove to myself that what I do might have an impact on what we know about our past in this part of the world, the crucible of civilisation itself. I am here because I have a desire to experience life beyond the ivy-covered walls of my father's mansion. The only way I was able to finally get my father's grudging support was by threatening to run off with a papist Irishman of not so good breeding from Boston. In my father's world, the Irish and Jews are not acceptable people.'

Matthew broke into a broad smile. 'Would you have run off with an Irishman if your father called your bluff?'

'Am I not with an Irishman now?' Joanne said sweetly.

'Australian of Irish and American descent,' Matthew said, feeling a giddy headiness. He had an overwhelming impulse to reach over and draw her to him, but something warned him she would see this action as boorish. It was a game they both knew they were playing and Matthew wisely held off making a fool of himself. Strangely, he thought, reflecting on the women he had known albeit briefly in his past life, this was one woman he wanted to know more about before he made any move to express his ever-growing desire for her.

'I will lay out my swag under the car,' he said, rising to his feet. 'I am sure you will be comfortable in your tent.' Matthew thought he could see just a hint of disappointment in Joanne's face at the way he had broken the moment between them.

111

'Matthew,' Joanne said as he pulled his pile of blankets from the car. 'I have enjoyed your company today.'

Matthew turned to her. 'I had a good day, too,' he replied, surprised at her small but heartwarming compliment.

'I hope we reach your airfield safely,' she continued, staring into the fire with a distant look on her face.

'Why do you say that?' Matthew asked, frowning at her pessimistic expression.

Joanne looked up at him with a sad smile. 'It is nothing to be concerned about, and you need your rest if we are to tackle the trail tomorrow.'

Matthew shrugged and dropped his blankets on the ground, careful to avoid any scorpions or spiders. But these were not the only nasty things in the chill of the desert night and Joanne knew it.

7

The thin man had a name. In fact, he went by many names depending on who asked – especially the police. Only fingerprinting would reveal that he had been born in one of the tough, inner-city working-class suburbs to alcoholic parents of Irish descent. Written on his birth certificate was the name Michael Patrick O'Rourke but to his criminal acquaintances he was mostly known as Mick.

O'Rourke had not gone to school by choice. He hated any form of discipline but had oddly enough taught himself to read and write. The young thug actually had an IQ to rival the best and because of his natural intelligence had fought his way to the top of most feared killers in Sydney. He was not a man to philosophise on the fact that he felt no empathy for anyone else and perceived that the world owed him. He could be charming when it suited – but only as a means of achieving his own ends.

Disembarking at San Francisco and travelling to Los Angeles, he noticed the difference in the mood of the country he had been sent to on his deadly mission. On the streets he noticed a festive air, whereas Sydney had been draped in sadness for the ever-mounting casualty lists posted in the newspapers. So many young men would never be coming home.

He took lodgings in a hotel that was one level above the mean streets, knowing that if anything went wrong, the local police would turn over the cheap hotels that catered to what the thriving capitalists called the working classes and unemployed. Mick had become fascinated with the writings of Karl Marx and saw himself as a victim of exploitation. His lodgings catered to the middle class: travelling salesmen, those employed in the burgeoning film industry and tourists to the town.

He had been quizzed on his accent the moment he booked into the hotel by a curious desk clerk and told the man that he was English. The clerk had no idea of any accent other than the regional variations of his own country, and accepted Mick's explanation as to his identity. Mick was aided in his deception, producing a British passport supplied to him by an acquaintance in Sydney known – for a price – to help out with documents for the criminal element.

Identifying his target had been easy. She featured in the gossip columns of the local papers which reported on her social life. It had not been hard for Mick to find where she lived and seeing her luxurious house in the better suburbs of the city convinced him that the killing was justified. In his twisted mind, not only was he being paid extremely generously, but he was also striking a blow for the working classes of the world. He only needed to ascertain when she was most likely to be alone and he could complete his assignment.

For nearly two weeks he watched from a distance, blending in with the crowds of people who came to the studios and discreetly following her home. She was rarely alone – except on Sundays. Two Sundays in a row he had seen Fenella from the shadows of an avenue of trees in her street after she'd been driven home in a chauffeured limousine and dropped at her door before bidding her driver a good night. Concealed under the foliage, Mick also observed that on Sunday nights she had no visitors and even gave her cook and housemaid the night off.

Now, all he had to do was fill in a week taking in the sights and sounds of the vibrant City of the Angels which was already celebrating the approaching Christmas. Mick had disciplined himself to stay away from the town's bars and brothels. He knew that his success depended on remaining out of sight of the local police. Even before questions could be asked about her death he would be on a ship returning to Sydney. It was all too easy.

On the other side of the Pacific, George Macintosh strode along the corridor of the hospital bearing an enormous bouquet of flowers for his wife who had presented him with a healthy son. He even smiled at the nurses in their stiffly starched uniforms and distinctive headwear as he passed them on his way to the maternity ward.

Louise had been rushed to the hospital hours earlier and George had waited in his office for the news, before going to her side. His business meeting had priority over waiting at the ward. Certainly he did not see himself as the sort of man who would pace up and down nervously outside the birthing room. He had listened as his accountant read out the financial report. Everything he declared showed that George's shrewd dealings had swelled the family coffers immensely with the war contracts he had been able to obtain through his government contacts. But what pleased George even more was the secret correspondence from Berlin via the Swiss banks that his investments in German chemicals had been protected, as promised, for his assistance to Maynard Bosch. The profits in Germany had swelled even further with the use of poison gases on the battlefronts of Europe. Personally George considered the use of chemicals in warfare a long overdue recognition of the science that had existed for some time. It did not enter his mind for one moment that fellow countrymen were dying agonising deaths or being left with irreparable injuries. After all, war was a temporary state of matters whereas industry was the backbone of civilisation.

A stern matron greeted George with an unsmiling word of congratulations as he entered the private room where Louise lay pale against the clean pillows. The infant lay asleep in a crib by her bed.

'Ah, my dear,' he said, placing the flowers beside her. 'You have done a wonderful job. So, this is my son.'

Louise was still exhausted from the ordeal of giving birth and did not respond. George leaned over to gaze at the wrinkled creature that was to one day inherit the Macintosh financial empire.

'You did not come to the hospital when I was admitted,' Louise said in a weak voice. 'Giselle told me that she had telephoned your office to inform you I was in labour – and that you had got the message.'

George looked away from his son. 'I was tied up in a business meeting and unable to get away,' he replied somewhat unconvincingly. 'But I am here now and that's what matters.'

Louise turned her head away as the tears rolled down her face. 'I know all about your affairs, George,' she said. 'When I am well enough I wish to move somewhere else with my son, and I expect you to pay for it.'

Stunned, George did not reply immediately but stared at the back of his wife's head. 'That will not happen,' he said finally. 'You are my wife and my son belongs to me, not you. You will continue living under my roof and even if you have to pretend, you will be my dutiful wife.'

'Is your son little more than mere property to you?' Louise asked, turning to face him, mustering as much anger as she could in her weakened condition. 'Have I just been a means to breed an heir for you?'

George walked to an open window. He took out a large Cuban cigar he had been keeping for the occasion, lit it and stared into the courtyard below the second storey they were on. The acrid scent of tobacco filled the room, stirred by the slowly moving ceiling fan that clacked monotonously in the still, warm air.

'You must realise that bearing me a son has more importance than you can truly comprehend,' he said with his back to her, puffing on the cigar. 'The Macintosh line has been let down by my weak father, and equally weak siblings. But between you and me, we will make the family name one of the greatest outside England. Your own bloodline is impeccable and that is why I married you. You should be proud that you have borne a son to carry on the Macintosh name when we are gone from the earth.'

'I still wish to move out of the house with my son,' Louise persisted.

George swung around and stared hard at his wife. 'That will happen over my dead body,' he said in a low, menacing voice. 'You do not have the slightest idea what I am capable

117

of when it comes to protecting my interests. No, you will stay by my side. The alternative is not something you would wish to contemplate.'

Horrified, Louise gaped at her husband before answering in a hoarse whisper. 'Are you threatening my life? Me, your wife?'

'Take it any way you want,' George replied with a bitter smile. 'If that is all, I have important business to attend to at the office. I expect that you will be home soon enough and continue as before as my wife.'

Without even a further glance at his newly born son, George left the room, pushing past the matron on her way in with a basin of warm water. The matron glanced at the stricken face of her patient and knew from long experience that this was not a happy marriage.

The sun rose cold and bleak over the Palestinian land. Even wrapped in many blankets and under the protection of the car, Matthew had shivered all night. He awoke to see that Joanne was already up and poking the fire into life. 'I expect a pot of hot coffee when I return,' she said cheerfully.

Joanne picked up her Winchester 30/30 rifle and walked towards the low ridge on one side of the shallow gully they were camped in. Matthew dragged himself out of his make-shift bed and stretched his body that was still stiff with the bitter winter chill of the Holy Land. He scratched his chin and thought about a shave before he made them breakfast. When he glanced in the direction that Joanne had taken she had disappeared on the other side of the ridge.

He decided to pull down the tent and stow it back in the vehicle before attending to a shave and breakfast. He had completed this, packing away the non-essentials, and was bending over the flickering flames when he heard a voice behind him.

'The Australian flyer Captain Duffy, I presume,' the man said with an edge of menace. Realising that his rifle was out of reach, Matthew swung around to see a German officer in the company of two Turkish soldiers who had their rifles levelled on him.

Slowly, Matthew rose to his feet. 'You have the wrong man,' he said, hoping that he sounded convincing. 'I am an American citizen and have papers to prove it.'

The German officer, who Matthew recognised as holding an equivalent rank to himself, took a couple of paces towards him. Matthew deduced that they had quietly come down the ridge opposite to the one Joanne had disappeared behind. He was concerned that the German officer had correctly identified him. Even if the papers appeared genuine they still stated his name as Matthew Duffy. Whoever this army officer was he appeared to know all about him. Curiously, however, the officer still had his pistol in his holster.

'It is no use attempting to lie,' the man said. 'We have informants even in Rosenblum's settlement. Not all his people are loyal to the British and some of his young men have journeyed back to the Fatherland to fight for their country.'

Matthew knew from Saul that when the war had broken out it had split the loyalties of many of the settlers. Those of German blood had cast their lot with the enemy.

'Where is Miss Barrington?' the officer asked almost casually. 'I have not had the pleasure of meeting her since we were both last in Constantinople.'

'You know Miss Barrington?' Matthew asked, surprised.

'Yes, she obtained travel permits from the Ottomans and before leaving was a guest at our embassy some months ago.'

Matthew could see his rifle leaning against the side of a rock but knew he had no chance of retrieving it.

'She is an extremely interesting and attractive woman and . . .'

The German officer did not complete his sentence. The crack of a rifle was followed immediately by the head of one of the Turkish soldiers suddenly jerking back in a mist of red. Before the surviving Turkish soldier could react, a second shot followed and he too crumpled to the cold earth, also shot through the head.

In the confusion, Matthew did not hesitate. He dived towards the rock where his rifle lay, scooped it up and lay on his back, barrel levelled at the German who was now grappling desperately to remove his holstered pistol.

'Don't move!' Matthew barked. The German officer froze.

Matthew could see Joanne, advancing down the ridge, her rifle at her hip. She appeared paler than usual under the smatter of freckles. He nodded his thanks when he caught her eye and when he turned his attention back to the prisoner, he could see that he was badly shaken by the events of the last few seconds.

When Joanne was within a few feet the German spoke. 'Miss Barrington, I . . .' Joanne brought up the tip of the rifle, firing a shot into his head. The German officer slumped to the ground beside the bodies of the two Turkish soldiers.

Slowly Matthew rose to his feet, stunned by this woman's cold-blooded act of shooting a defenceless man. Joanne levered her rifle to eject the spent cartridge and casually reloaded as if she had just been on a turkey shoot. She brought the rifle barrel to rest against the dead officer's head as if to deliver another shot into him.

'He's dead,' Matthew said sharply. 'He was no threat to us and as a prisoner of war might have been valuable to our interrogators.'

Joanne glanced up at him, angling the barrel away. 'I just saved your life,' she said flatly. 'How dare you question my actions.'

Matthew was taken aback by the change in this woman he had come to think of as perhaps a little eccentric but essentially gentle in nature. She seemingly showed no emotion to taking the lives of three men. Then, unexpectedly, she began to tremble uncontrollably and slumped to the ground, sobbing.

Matthew kneeled beside her, holding her in his arms.

'I have never taken a life before,' she confessed, gripping Matthew's shirt. 'I saw that you were in trouble and did what I could.'

'But there was no need to kill the German,' he chided gently. 'We could have taken him as a prisoner.'

'How do I, as a neutral American, explain that I am holding a German officer as a prisoner of war if we are stopped by Turkish patrols?' Joanne asked.

Matthew had to agree with her reasoning but the fact that the officer already knew Joanne troubled him. He had a momentary deep suspicion as to the answer but immediately dismissed it. Perhaps he was becoming paranoid. But war did that to a man, he thought.

'We have to hurry and get away from here,' Joanne said, wiping the tears from her face with the back of her hand. 'I suspect that Hauptmann Klaus may have others with him if he has continued to track me from Jerusalem.'

'You know his name?' Matthew asked incredulously. 'And what do you mean, track you?'

Joanne rose to her feet, scanning the low ridges around

121

them for signs of further Turkish troops. 'It is a long story, but since I arrived in Constantinople the Ottomans have suspected me of spying. It is not true,' she sniffed, bringing her emotions under control. 'I am nothing more than an archaeologist, as you know.'

Matthew watched her walk unsteadily towards the Packard. He shook his head as he followed her. He knew so little about this extraordinary woman who could kill so easily one minute and then break down with remorse the next.

Fenella stepped from her limousine and bid her chauffeur a good night. It had been a long day attending a luncheon organised to raise funds for the Red Cross but she felt the effort worth it given her beloved father was fighting on the Western Front. Sunday evenings had become a tradition for some time alone, away from the constant swirl of people around her during the working week and her frenetic social life of night clubs, parties and dinners. She opened the door and stepped inside her luxurious house with the idea of a long soak in the tub, flute of champagne in hand and a good dose of bath salts to soothe her weary body.

The cook had left a selection of cold meats and salad vegetables in the refrigerator and Fenella opened it to retrieve the chilled bottle and nibble on a slice of cold beef. Closing the door, she walked towards her bedroom to disrobe, magnum and glass in hand. She paused in the doorway of her bedroom. One of the windows was wide open. The silly housemaid must have overlooked it before she left, Fenella thought, annoyed at the oversight. But then a chilling thought crept into her mind. She stared at the open window. There were distinctive smudges of garden dirt on the sill. Immediately, Fenella stepped back into the hallway.

But she was too late. An arm wrapped around her throat, a razor blade against her chin.

'Don't struggle or I'll cut ya,' a voice hissed in her ear.

Fenella instinctively swung her arm up, bringing the large bottle of champagne over her head and slamming it on her assailant's skull. The thick glass did not break but the man let go with a noisy grunt.

Fenella twisted around to face her attacker, a thin man, bleeding profusely, blood running down his face. She hefted the magnum to swing again at him but despite his initial shock, he reacted quickly, slashing at Fenella's raised arm. Fenella felt a searing heat burn her wrist and reeled back, dropping the bottle. Blood spurted from the severed artery, spraying the walls and her attacker, who was cursing her as he advanced with the cutthroat razor.

'You bitch,' he screamed at her. 'Why'd ya do that?'

Fenella backed into the bedroom, attempting to stem the blood pumping from her almost severed wrist. But her fear was not helping slow her heart and the blood continued to pour stickily between her fingers. She hardly recognised her own voice as she screamed at the top of her lungs for help.

Her assailant was shaking his head, dabbing at the laceration to his skull. 'I'm gonna cut you from limb to limb, you bitch, for what you done to me,' he muttered as he advanced on Fenella.

Fenella suddenly felt tired. She wanted to just lay down and go to sleep. The blood was pumping furiously from her wrist as she slumped down on the edge of her bed. The advancing man was becoming a blur to her. The last word Mick O'Rourke heard from his victim was a man's name. 'Help me, Randolph.'

O'Rourke dropped his blade on the bed beside Fenella

and went to find a towel to swab his head. The bleeding was severe and he knew that he must seek medical attention. His intention to rape her first had been thwarted by her resistance, and he was angry. His consolation was that he could now return home and collect the balance owed to him. All he had to do was get out of the house, find a hospital where he could have his head wound stitched, and be at the docks before midday on the morrow to embark for Sydney. Considering everything, Mick O'Rourke was satisfied that he had done his homework well and there were no witnesses.

His head throbbing, the killer made only two mistakes. Instead of leaving the house the way he came in where the shrubs concealed him, he took the quickest route and went out the front door. He also left his razor on the bed beside his victim. He would be well away from the scene of the crime before he remembered it and by then it was too late to retrieve it.

An elderly lady who lived across the street had thought she heard a woman scream. When she went to her front window she saw nothing unusual but remained by the window watching the street. She was rewarded by seeing a man leave the house, holding a bloody towel to his head which he tossed into the garden by the front path. The witness had a good view of the man as he stood for a moment under a street light looking up and down the roadway. She could even see the scar on his face and from the blood on his clothing she knew all was not right. As the man strolled away, disappearing into the darkness at the end of the street, the elderly lady telephoned the local police sergeant who responded quickly. When he and one of his uniformed men found Fenella's body slumped over her bed shortly afterwards, the sergeant immediately called a number which he knew would get him through to a studio head. This was Hollywood where the power of the men who ran the main industry was able to reach into the portals of the justice system. He would give them a half hour to discuss their strategy before calling his own detectives to investigate.

It did not take long for the news concerning the death of the famous actress in her mansion to reach the media. Before dawn the house was surrounded by a bustling crowd of reporters trampling Fenella's once immaculate lawns and gardens. Within days, the news would spread around the world and be reported in Australian newspapers. The media would reveal that it was rumoured that the actress Fiona Owens was, in fact, Fenella Macintosh, a person of interest in the death two years earlier of the Australian actor Guy Wilkes.

When George Macintosh read the headlines days later at breakfast he felt no grief for his murdered sister. Her death had been an economic necessity, as far as he was concerned, if the family business was to flourish under his sole management. Now only his younger brother remained and George cursed the army for not releasing him for active service. He reached for his cup of tea and continued to read the scandal that was unravelling about the beautiful young actress's sordid life before her tragic death.

'Typical,' George muttered, placing his cup on its saucer. She even brought shame to the family name in death, he mused. With a sigh, George rose from the table and folded the paper. He must relay the news of Fenella's death to his father overseas, he thought, smiling, as his driver pulled into the driveway.

8

Winter was coming to the Northern Hemisphere and Captain Sean Duffy knew that the men on the Western Front would feel its impact in the trenches. As he sat behind his desk in a tiny room warmed by a coal burner he cursed the army and all its bureaucrats. At the end of his staff college course for company commanders, he had expected to be posted back to his old battalion, if not as a company commander at the least company second-in-command. But this had not happened and for the last two months he had found himself posted to London to the War Office in a role that any clerk could fill.

Sean suspected that the matter of the incorrect report nominating him for a gallantry award had somehow brought about what he saw as a punishment posting. It had not been his report that had brought him to this office safe from the bullets and bombs his comrades suffered every day. He felt like a coward. Even the fact that he had been able to occupy Colonel Patrick Duffy's comfortable flat a short walk from his office had not negated his feelings of shame and hopelessness. He should be back on the front with his men, not skulking in an office job.

The clerical corporal knocked on Sean's door and entered to drop a pile of papers on his desk. 'Never seems to end, sir,' he said, stepping back. 'Oh, there is a message that a Colonel Duffy will be returning tonight from France and requests your company at his club this evening at 6pm.'

'Thank you, Corp,' Sean answered as the English NCO departed the room.

It had been months since he had seen his distant cousin and Sean was pleased to hear that he had returned safe and well from his posting with divisional headquarters. If anyone could get to the bottom of why he had been posted to the War Office for liaison duties it would be Patrick.

When his working day had ended, Sean took his greatcoat from the stand, slipped on a pair of leather gloves and made his way along the London street to Patrick's club. He passed civilians and soldiers alike. The civilians hardly gave him a glance but British soldiers were wary enough to salute the officer. Sean wondered at the seeming complacency of the city's residents towards the war, although Patrick's upper-class civilian friends constantly complained how it was interrupting their social lives and causing shortages in goods. Not that they went short on anything, he'd noticed when he was an occasional guest at their country houses, usually to make up numbers for the many single women and even unescorted married women who attended.

Sean had found himself in one or two young women's beds after such parties but felt nothing for his sexual partners.

It was as if something had died in him and although the young ladies found him dashing and glamorous with his award of the Military Cross for action at Gallipoli, sex was not the answer. Sean would gaze down at each partner knowing that he could not say the words they wanted to hear. Self-loathing for being safe or simply that none of the women attracted him for more than the relief of the moment, he wondered. More often than not he did not even know when he left in the mornings.

Except for the rare zeppelin raid over England the war was contained to the Continent, and only the streams of badly mangled bodies being off-loaded at railway stations and the men with trembling hands and nightmares returning on leave reminded civilian observers of the horrors experienced in the trenches.

When Sean reached the club he was shown in by an elderly former soldier who relieved him of his bulky greatcoat. He found Patrick lounging in a large leather chair that no doubt had also warmed the backsides of generals who had served anywhere from Tibet, India and Africa to China and even the Australian colonies many years earlier. Patrick rose as Sean crossed the floor of the elegant room filled with pipe and cigar smoke. Only the clink of ice in the tumblers of gin and whisky seemed to disturb the quiet ambience.

'Sean, it is good to see you well and hale,' Patrick said with a warm smile, stretching out his hand. 'What can I order for you . . . a gin, whisky?'

'Whisky would be fine, thank you, sir,' Sean answered, glancing around at a few frowning faces who obviously disapproved of a young colonial officer in their midst. At least the colourful purple and white riband on his jacket deflected some of the looks of disapproval.

'Make yourself comfortable,' Patrick said, gesturing to a chair similar to his own and at the same time signalling to a white-jacketed waiter hovering nearby. 'A whisky, neat,' he said to the waiter. 'On my chit, James.'

The waiter nodded and moved away to fill the order.

'I am sorry for your loss, sir,' Sean said, taking his seat. 'The news of Nellie's death reached me in the papers over here.'

'It was not just a death – but murder,' Patrick replied, taking his seat.

For a brief moment Sean thought the tough, professional soldier might burst into tears. 'The American press seemed to have exposed Nellie's true identity,' Sean said, hoping to steer the colonel away from his grief. 'They should be damned to hell for the lies they have printed in the press over there about Nellie's private life.'

'I know that you were very fond of my daughter,' Patrick said. 'I expect that you are missing her too.'

'I never really had the honour of pursuing my feelings for Nellie,' Sean answered, lowering his voice as the waiter returned.

Patrick signed the paper handed to him. 'I cannot dwell on Nellie's death at the moment. So many are dying over in France, as a result of outdated tactics that should have been left on the veldt of Africa.'

Sean could see that Patrick was forcing himself not to dwell on the reports of his daughter's murder, and admired him for his strength to focus on what he could change.

'It's not going well, is it, sir?' Sean said, swishing his whisky around the ice cubes before taking a sip.

Patrick sighed. 'We need to review our tactics,' he said. 'Just hopping the bags and attempting frontal attacks does not work. The Huns are too well entrenched, better than we are, and the little ground we win is lost in counter-attacks. We need to look at using small groups of men, well armed, attacking weak points in the lines to push through to strike at the Hun rear echelon while we push forward our arms to finish off any pockets of resistance left behind.'

Sean listened dutifully as the divisional officer outlined his idea of forming units of a new kind of soldier trained to carry out shock attacks on the enemy.

'But the bloody politics I come across at divvie level does not have the brains or imagination to see my ideas.'

'Maybe the Hun will one day beat us to the punch and form units of what you call shock troops,' Sean suggested by way of acknowledging that he had been listening to Patrick's tirade against the military establishment. 'At least we do attempt to learn from the enemy.'

'Probably,' Patrick replied gloomily. He took a long swig from his drink, before turning to gesture to the waiter to refill it. 'But the troubles of a staff officer are not those of a captain about to be posted back to the battalion in France.' Sean almost dropped his tumbler at Patrick's unexpected announcement. 'You will receive your movement orders tomorrow,' he continued casually. 'I hope that you will be ready to move within twenty-four hours.

'Sir, you have obviously pulled some strings,' Sean said, leaning forward and almost hugging his cousin. 'I am still damning to hell that bloody Irish major who had me trans-ferred to the War Office.'

'It was not he who had you seconded,' Patrick said. 'You were posted to the War Office on my request.' Stunned, Sean slumped back in his chair to stare at Patrick. 'You see, I felt that you were not ready to return to the battalion straight after your staff college. I thought that a spell away from France might help you get your thoughts straight.'

'I was ready, sir,' Sean protested indignantly. 'I realise that there was some confusion in what I did at Fromelles that day but I was ready to lead again.'

'Sean, you are one of the best officers I have had the honour to command,' Patrick said. 'I saw you lead at Gallipoli and was proud to see you recognised with the award of the MC, but I have been a soldier for a long time and know that we are sometimes asked to go beyond what I would call the breaking point. The doctors are naming this nervous sickness shell shock and I feel that you were on the edge of losing your reason. The medical people believe that rest and time away from the front goes towards curing a soldier. I am not sure if they are right but the army needs good men such as you to lead others – to their deaths, if necessary.'

'Did Sergeant Kelly say something about my behaviour that day?' Sean asked.

'When I questioned him for the report he was nothing but supportive of your actions,' Patrick answered gently. 'From reports I have seen of him in the last couple of months he is a bloody good soldier and I would hope that one day he takes a commission. But despite the fact that he would say nothing against you I was able to read between the lines. You should have been sent home to Sydney after Gallipoli for a rest before returning to France.'

'Sir, I think I lost it that day and do not know why,' Sean choked. 'Sergeant Kelly should have got the VC for what he did that day clearing the trench.'

'Sadly, because of my eagerness to see you rewarded again, the British are punishing me,' Patrick replied. 'And the British government has downgraded Kelly's nomination from VC to a DCM. However, it is certainly a higher award than the Military Medal. He should be pleased.'

'I am sure he will be,' Sean agreed, without sounding very convincing. His actions that day had cost the gallant soldier the high award he deserved. It should have been him submitting the report, not Colonel Duffy. No, Sean well knew that he had let down Sergeant Kelly.

'The battalion is currently resting up behind the lines so you will have the opportunity of squaring away when you join them,' Patrick said. 'I will be returning to France within the week and may come across you from time to time.'

'I hope so, sir,' Sean answered. 'I would appear churlish if I did not thank you for all that you have done.'

'No thanks required,' Patrick replied, waving off the young officer's gratitude. 'I just pray that my old friend John Hughes continues to be successful in detaining Alexander in Australia for the duration of the war,' Patrick confessed. 'I know that my son would not appreciate my efforts to keep him away from the front but he does not realise just how important it is that he remain alive to one day take the reins of the family companies.'

Sean was not surprised to hear the colonel confess to his secret manoeuvring to ensure Alex remained away from the war. If he had a son he would have done the same. Deep down he knew it would only be a matter of time before the bullet with his name on it took away his life. The former solicitor had resigned himself to death and just prayed that when the time came it would not be painful. Worse still was the thought of being mutilated like some of the pitiful creatures he had seen survive their wounds only to be terribly disfigured or lose their limbs. There were some things far worse than dying.

*

For hours after Matthew and Joanne fled the scene of the killing they had said little to each other. A cold, bleak wind that cut through them like icy bullets reminded them that winter was hovering, about to descend on the ancient lands.

Before leaving the gully, Matthew had scouted a short distance to see if there had been more than the three men but only found their hobbled horses. Perhaps only three had come out in search of them because of the shortage of horses in the Turkish army. Hopefully, if a Turkish patrol found the three dead in the gully they would assume that they had been killed by Arab irregulars under the British officer, Lawrence. Bearing that in mind, Matthew had stripped the bodies and taken the uniforms and weapons to dump them in the desert somewhere along their route. Stripping bodies was the trademark of Arab irregulars and hopefully the scattered items would not be found too soon by the Turkish patrols.

Near midday the big American vehicle bogged down in soft sand and Matthew dismounted to place the metal strips carried for such circumstances under the wheels. Grunting and heaving, he pushed while Joanne drove. Eventually they were able to free themselves from the shifting sand.

'I think we should have a hot drink,' Joanne said, standing beside the heavily packed vehicle. 'This cold could cause us some concern.'

Brushing down his clothes, Matthew nodded. While Joanne set about brewing a pot of coffee on a fire of petrol in a sand-filled tin, Matthew took the opportunity to scan all the horizons with her binoculars and check their bearings on the map. All he could see was a relatively flat surface of rippled sand and tiny pockets of tough, tussock grass. He calculated that they were at the edge of the Sinai, which meant they were not far from his airfield.

Joanne passed him a mug of steaming, black coffee and he sat down with his back against the front wheel. She sat next to him, sipping at her drink.

'Who are you, really?' Matthew asked, unable to reconcile his earlier impression of her with what he had seen in the gully that morning.

'I am what I seem to be,' she answered, staring at the flat horizon to the east. 'An American archaeologist touring the Holy Land in search of undiscovered ruins. The war between the European powers does not concern me.'

Matthew gave a short laugh. 'So, executing that German officer was not of great concern to you?'

As Joanne turned to him he regretted his taunt. There was great pain in her eyes and he thought that she might be on the verge of tears.

'I have never killed anyone in my life and the death of those three unfortunate men will haunt me forever. But I knew if I did not do what I did you might have lost your life. The German officer I killed has . . . had a reputation for extreme cruelty towards prisoners. I know that as a neutral in this war I have now compromised myself but it was either that or you being taken prisoner and possibly killed.'

'I am sorry,' Matthew said in a humble voice. 'I don't mean to sound ungrateful. It's just that you did it so efficiently and, well, I had a stupid idea that you might be working for someone in intelligence. You cannot deny that you admitted to knowing the Hun you killed.'

'My father is a good friend of our president, Mr Wilson, and I could not risk compromising my country in your affairs, Captain Duffy,' Joanne said. 'To do so could possibly cause an international incident.'

'Call me Matthew,' the Australian said. 'If I may call you Joanne?'

'I would like that, Matthew,' Joanne said, softening. 'You have a fine name.'

'For an Irish papist,' Matthew said and saw the glint of humour in her eyes at his joke.

'You must know, Matthew, that I find you an attractive man,' Joanne said impulsively. 'But I must also say that there is no future in anything other than a lasting friendship.'

'I did not suspect that there was anything else,' Matthew lied. 'I am flattered that you think I hold some attraction to you, as I have thought since we met at the settlement that you are nothing other than a lady to be respected. However, I have to say that since saving my life you have somewhat endeared yourself to me.'

'Nothing else?' Joanne queried.

Matthew could hear the disappointment in her question but it gave him some satisfaction not to reveal his true feelings. It was obvious that she was a strong-willed woman who was used to getting her way with men. Had she not persuaded her father to fund her expedition into a war zone?

'Nothing else,' Matthew shrugged, rising to his feet.

'Then, that is good,' Joanne said, tossing the remnants of her coffee to the wind.

They continued the journey south and near sundown saw a faint cloud of dust rising before them. Matthew stopped the car and reached for the binoculars.

'Is it a sand storm?' Joanne asked anxiously.

'No,' Matthew replied, focusing. 'It's a column of mounted troops and they have changed course. They are coming this way.'

'If we turn about we may be able to outrun them,' Joanne said.

'Not necessary,' Matthew answered, rubbing his eyes. 'They are my countrymen. From their uniforms they appear

135

to be mounted troopers. It seems that we may receive an escort to my base.'

Matthew had been correct about the slouch hats the men wore. Within minutes a patrol of ten troopers rode cautiously towards them, their rifle butts resting against their hips.

'G'day,' the leader of the patrol, a tough-looking sergeant said when he had his mount alongside the car. 'Who in hell are you?'

'Captain Matthew Duffy of the Australian Flying Corps and the lady with me is Miss Joanne Barrington, an American citizen,' Matthew answered. 'We would like an escort to the nearest airfield.'

The sergeant scratched his chin. 'You have any proof of who you are?'

'I am afraid I have only forged documents to get me through the enemy lines – thanks to the help of Miss Barrington,' Matthew responded. 'However, proof of my identity can be made by my squadron commander as soon as you get us to the airfield. I was shot down some weeks ago and, no doubt, am currently listed as MIA.'

'Okay,' the trooper sergeant replied, wheeling his horse around and signalling to his men who were now staring with great curiosity at both the American automobile and the two passengers. It was not a sight they expected to encounter on their patrols pursuing the retreating enemy.

Matthew put the car into gear and slowly followed the lead men of the patrol while a section fell in behind them. They reached the airfield just after sunset and Matthew was welcomed with pleasure by his commanding officer who thanked the troopers for their assistance.

Matthew had found his kit already stowed away as few had given him much chance in the desert when he did not return.

It took him some time to unpack it and find another uniform, and after a debriefing with the unit intelligence officer joined the merriment of the men of the squadron at rest.

Joanne was given a tent to stay in for the night and invited to the officers' mess that evening for drinks before dinner was served. The mess was an open-sided tent during summer but with the bitter cold creeping in the sides were down and a coal brazier provided some heat. Such a pretty guest attracted every male to offer their guest a drink and Matthew quickly became jealous at seeing his brother officers turn on the charm. He had sidled unobtrusively up to Joanne, surprised to see her wearing a rather elegant dress for the occasion. Despite the wear and tear of the harsh desert lands she shone like a precious stone, he reflected.

A British major who Matthew knew held some aristocratic title in England joined the ring of men surrounding Joanne. 'Joanne, my dear, what a very pleasant surprise finding you all the way out here in this godforsaken place. When we last met it was at a party in Kensington around '14,' he said with a broad smile. 'How the devil did you get to be in here? I should add my condolences for the death of poor Freddy,' he continued. 'He was a damned good chap. We heard of him going down over France.'

The merriment in Joanne's face momentarily faded.

'Thank you, Harry,' she replied. 'But it has been some time now and I have chosen to get on with pursuing my work as an archaeologist. I know Freddy would not want me to just sit around and grieve for him, but make something of my life.'

'Annabelle will be tickled pink when I write to let her know that we met out here,' the major continued. 'You and Freddy made a grand couple. I say, we heard that you rescued Captain Duffy, what.'

'I would not say that I rescued Captain Duffy, but simply gave him a ride,' Joanne replied. 'I am sure that Captain Duffy is resourceful enough to have made his own way back without my assistance.'

'But we heard that you shot three men,' the major persisted. 'Devilishly brave of you to do so, if I must say so, and a tad dangerous, as a neutral.'

Matthew felt a twinge of embarrassment. No doubt his debriefing, where he had accounted for all that had occurred since his aircraft had been shot down, was no longer a secret. Very little was kept private among this tight-knit band of flyers.

'Oh, I see Captain Duffy wishes to speak to me,' Joanne said, turning to Matthew who was standing a few feet away pretending to be engrossed in his drink. She excused herself and pushed her way to him.

'Matthew, I hope that I have not embarrassed you,' she said gently, touching his arm. 'But I said nothing of what has happened on our journey together.'

He looked up from his glass and into Joanne's eyes. 'It was I who informed of all that had occurred, when I gave my debriefing. I had to give a full account but did not say how you killed the German officer. I said that he was killed from a distance by you protecting my life.'

'Thank you,' Joanne said, taking her hand from his arm. 'There would be people who might get the wrong impression of me.'

'Who was Freddy?' Matthew asked quietly.

The pain returned to Joanne's expression.

'Freddy was Lord Frederick Norman-Smith, and he was a flyer like you with a unit he commanded in France. He was shot down and killed early last year over France. We were engaged to be married,' she answered softly.

'I am sorry,' Matthew replied. 'I guess that flyers are at the top of your list as not the kind of men to become involved with.'

Although Joanne did not reply Matthew knew he was right.

'Thank you for your company on our trip,' Joanne said, stepping away. 'I must retire after dinner to get an early night as I am continuing my journey to Cairo tomorrow with one of the Arab servants your commanding officer has been able to obtain for me. He says that he is trustworthy and reliable.'

'I am sure that if he is not you will know how to take care of him,' Matthew said without thinking. He noticed a cloud come over Joanne's face. 'Sorry,' he hastened to apologise. 'You know what I mean. You are not only beautiful but one of the most remarkable women I have ever met, Miss Barrington. Please be careful.'

'Duffy, old chap,' one of Matthew's pilot friends called to him across the throng in the mess. 'It's your shout. You have a few days to catch up.'

'I should leave you to your friends,' Joanne said. 'But I hope that we meet again under better circumstances.'

Before Matthew could think of anything to say she was gone, leaving him with a multitude of swirling thoughts. A glass was thrust in his hand and Matthew let the company of his fellow officers lead him in a night of hard drinking.

When he finally rose the next morning for breakfast Joanne and her Packard were gone. Matthew gazed south across the arid landscape but saw no sign of her. All he knew for the moment was that he had to survive the war and find her again.

9

In early December Randolph Gates stepped onto Australian soil at Circular Quay in Sydney. Hefting his swag, he strode away from the ship that had brought him from San Francisco and set about finding a cheap hotel. He said little to those who attempted to engage him in idle chatter, but brooded on what he must do next. He had returned to enlist in the Australian armed forces but Fenella's death only days before he was booked to return to Sydney had changed his plans. The papers had run accounts of the killing and even provided a good description of the man suspected of the murder. The American newspapers also published that the weapon had been left behind – and that it was a cutthroat razor with the letters MOR scratched into the bone handle. The newspaper reports also pointed out that the particular brand of blade was only made in Australia, suggesting that her murder may have links to the death of an Australian actor two years back.

Randolph, however, did not accept that Fenella's murder had anything to do with the death of Guy Wilkes. In his gut he felt it did have a link to Australia but it was difficult to accept what his instincts told him – that George Macintosh was behind his own sister's murder. How could it be possible that a man could have his sister murdered so brutally? It had to be the work of some deranged Australian with a morbid fascination for the actress he knew as Fiona Owens. Still, the nagging doubt persisted.

Randolph only had Alexander Macintosh to turn to as he knew from the occasional letters that reached him from Matthew Duffy that Alex was still in Australia. After cleaning up, Randolph telephoned Alex's home and a delighted Giselle answered. He was immediately invited to have supper with them that day and Randolph dressed in his finest suit of clothes for the visit.

That evening he knocked on the door and was met by the valet, Angus MacDonald, who greeted him with a broad grin and crushing handshake. The tough, solidly built Scot in his mid-fifties was a very fit former British NCO who had served with Patrick Duffy in Africa.

'The colonel's gonna get me over with him as soon as he is settled,' Angus said hopefully. 'I heard that you will be joining up,' he continued.

'That's right, Angus,' Randolph replied just as the Scot led him into a spacious sitting room where Giselle stood, holding her son in her arms. She passed the baby to their nanny so that she could greet Randolph.

'Mr Gates, it is good to see you after such a long time away,' Giselle said with a sweet smile. 'I have the pleasure of introducing you to Master David Macintosh.' She pulled back the blanket wrapped around the infant, who screwed up his eyes and balled his fists at being disturbed from his sleep.

'He is beautiful,' Randolph dutifully observed, poking gently at the little boy's tummy with his finger.

'You may take him away, Lizzie,' Giselle said to the nanny. 'Alex should be home very soon and I know that you will have much to talk about,' she continued. 'Angus, could you be a dear and serve up a drink for our guest?'

'What will it be, Mr Gates?' Angus asked.

'Whisky will be fine,' Randolph replied just as Alex entered the room in his army uniform. He kissed Giselle on the cheek and thrust out his hand to Randolph.

'Welcome back, old chap,' Alex said with a broad smile. 'It has been a long time since we stood on the wharf together when you left us to find Nellie.'

At the mention of Fenella's name Randolph paled. He had trouble coming to grips with her death. 'A lot has happened to us both since then,' he replied. 'But it is good to be back in Australia.'

Angus quickly had a glass of Scotch in both men's hands and discreetly left the room, as did Giselle with an excuse to oversee their dinner for the night. When they were alone Alex raised his glass in a toast.

'To friends and family who cannot be with us at this moment,' he said and Randolph also raised his glass in silent salute.

'Your brother had her murdered,' Randolph said without any polite chitchat. 'Don't ask me how I know. It is just a strong hunch. I have no evidence at all.'

Alex frowned. 'That is a very serious accusation,' he replied. 'My brother is a man with little expression of feeling but conspiring to murder Nellie . . .'

'I know that you are his brother and must defend him but I feel in my soul that, somehow, George was behind Nellie's death. Call it a gut feeling but he has a lot to gain from you and Nellie not being around to share the family fortune if anything should happen to the colonel, your father.'

Alex took a long swig on his drink and stared for a moment at a portrait of his long-dead great-grandfather Sir Donald Macintosh, speared to death in central Queensland on the family property of Glen View. The eyes had been faithfully painted to show the tough, determined soul of the Scot who had ordered the killing of the peaceful Aboriginal tribe on his land so many years earlier. In those eyes he could see a family disposition to ruthlessness. But for his brother, George, to order the murder of his own sister . . . Was it possible?

'If what you suspect is true,' Alex said in a considered way, 'I would need evidence.'

'You must also know that you stand in your brother's way as well,' Randolph said. 'Who is to say that he is not already plotting your demise?'

'A bit hard to get rid of me when even the army will not send me on active service,' Alex answered with a short, bitter laugh. 'He would be doing me a favour if he could wrangle a posting to France.'

'Don't put anything past him,' Randolph cautioned. 'Even getting you posted to the front.'

'If I may ask,' Alex said, 'what makes you suspect my brother of being behind Nellie's murder?'

It was Randolph's turn to frown. 'I can't put my finger on it,' he replied, 'but something deep down in my belly tells me he has been able to reach even across the Pacific.'

'My father has good friends in the American community

143

here,' Alex said, finishing his glass of Scotch. 'I will prevail upon his contacts to have everything the American police have on the murder sent to me. It may help you one way or the other.'

'I was hoping that I might be able to depend on you,' Randolph said, also finishing his drink.

'I heard that you came back to enlist in our army,' Alex queried.

'I will,' Randolph said. 'As soon as I get to the bottom of who was behind Nellie's death. To that means I was hoping that you would authorise my expenses – as your father did to originally find her.'

'You know that will be done,' Alex answered. 'Anything to see justice is done, one way or the other.'

'Dinner is ready,' Giselle said, poking her head into the sitting room. Both men exchanged looks that said their conversation remained in the room.

Randolph wasted no time in initiating his own discreet inquiries. As he sat on the edge of his bed, he reflected on how George Macintosh might have organised the murder of his sister, and concluded that George would most probably recruit his killer in Sydney. If so, it would have to be from the side of the city where the criminal gangs roamed. At least he had somewhere to start his search.

Randolph stood up and wiped the sweat from his brow with a clean handkerchief. He had formulated a plan of action and knew that he would have to call on the considerable resources of Alex Macintosh. A telephone call to Alex with a special request was completed earlier in the day and now it was only a matter of waiting for his order to be filled. Because of its sensitive contents he could not afford to have it delivered to the hotel so Alex informed him he could pick it up from his residence.

Outside in the corridor he could hear a woman's raucous laughter and the muffled sounds of a man speaking soft words to her. The hotel's bar downstairs was packed with soldiers and sailors in uniform, standing shoulder to shoulder, drinking as much as they could as quickly as they could. Most were on a short leave before steaming for England and then onto the battlefields of Europe. Randolph had endured a few snide remarks passing through the bar to the stairs that led to his stuffy room in the living quarters; that he was in civilian clothes and not a uniform had brought scorn on him from the armed forces men.

The woman's laughter stopped and Randolph heard a door open just down from his room. Alcohol was not the only thing on a soldier or sailor's mind before he steamed away to war.

The thumping of the bed down the passageway and the intensity of the woman's cries told him that the act was not going to be very long.

Randolph decided to indulge himself with a cold beer in the hotel's bar. The barmaid was a busty young woman with red hair and a loud voice. But she softened to Randolph's accent and asked him what it was.

'Canadian,' Randolph answered.

'What's your name, love?' she asked, wiping down the top of the bar with a rag. 'I see that you are one of our residents.'

'Joshua Smith,' he answered, using the name he had signed in under. It paid to leave no tracks when you were targeting one of Sydney's most powerful men.

'What you doin' here?' she continued.

'Come to get away from the war,' he replied.

'I thought you Canadians were fighting with us,' she said with a frosty edge.

'So I heard,' Randolph answered, raising his glass to swallow the refreshing cold ale, as the barmaid tossed her head and moved away to serve a customer in a khaki uniform.

The following morning, Randolph caught a taxi to Alex's house and was once again met by Angus.

'Mrs Macintosh and the captain are not here,' Angus said. 'But you came at the right time because there is a package that Captain Macintosh told me to give to you delivered a few minutes ago.'

Randolph accepted the thick envelope from Angus, thanked him and left.

Back in his room, Randolph opened the envelope. Sheets of paper and a revolver spilled onto the springy bed. The papers were lists of names of Macintosh crew members covering the last three months of employment. For the next few hours he pored through the names, sifting out those he was able to cross-reference against permanent positions, and those who had only been employed for one trip with the Macintosh ships.

Randolph then went further to see if any of the names on the crew lists had made a journey back to Australia about the same time that he had. He found only one name. That of a Michael O'Rourke whose home address was listed in Surry Hills, Sydney. Randolph sat up . . . MOR . . . the initials on the murder weapon . . . Michael O'Rourke! He read a description of the man in a column down one side of the sheet . . . thin build with a scar to the face. It had to be him!

*

No-one took much notice of the tall civilian who quietly slipped out of the hotel and commenced walking towards the infamous suburb. The first hotel he came across was filled with rowdy patrons. But this time there were very few uniformed men to be seen holding up the bar. Instead, the hotel was filled with sweat-stained working men. A few men who knew little of hard manual labour had propped themselves against a wall opposite the bar, and were smoking cigarettes with the air of those who feared very little from others around them.

Randolph was closely watched as he entered and he suspected that the hotel was the place that a local gang used as their own meeting place. He hoped so. Buying a drink, he made his way unobtrusively to the back wall to stand by one of the flashily dressed men, who was chewing on a toothpick and holding a beer.

'I'm looking for a buddy I met when he was in the States a few weeks back,' Randolph said. 'His name is Michael O'Rourke. I owe him a drink.'

The man turned towards Randolph, slipping his hand into the pocket of his trousers. Randolph tensed.

'You mean Mick,' the man said, looking Randolph up and down while twirling the toothpick around between his lips. He was young and had the hard look of a man used to violence. 'I 'eard Mick had done a trip to America. 'Ow do you know him?'

The question had a chilling edge to it and Randolph could see the man's eyes narrow. But he had hit pay dirt. 'I met him in LA,' Randolph parried. 'In a bar.'

'I can see that you are a Yank,' the man said, looking Randolph up and down. ''Eard the same accent before aroun' the docks when we was down that way doin' jobs.' He turned to the man next to him who Randolph could see was cut from the same cloth. 'You 'ear if Mick is aroun'?'

The man shook his head.

'Maybe if you buy me Mick's beer I might be able to tell you where you might find 'im,' the toothpick-chewing tough said, leaning slightly towards Randolph.

'Yeah, I could do that,' Randolph agreed and made his way through the crowd to purchase a large beer.

'Mick usually drinks up the road with his cobbers,' the man said, grasping the fresh glass of beer. 'You might find 'im there.'

Randolph knocked back his beer, nodded to the tough and left the bar to step onto the dimly lit street. He was walking deeper into the dangerous suburb but did so with the certainty he would find the killer of the only woman he had truly loved.

Randolph found the second pub and was not surprised to see that it was very similar to the one he had just left. It was the same kind of working-class hotel catering to shady, relatively well-dressed young men avoiding military service to their country. Randolph did not even have to ask if Mick O'Rourke was there that night. Entering the public bar his eyes fell on a thin man with a long scar down his face, sitting at a table drinking with men much like himself. Randolph felt his blood chill and instinctively felt in his pocket for both the small calibre revolver and bowie knife he had armed himself with. He heard the man called by his name by one of the men he was drinking with.

Randolph forced himself to tear his gaze away. He ordered a beer and stood alone at the end of the bar, keeping a small crowd of patrons between himself and the group Mick O'Rourke was drinking with. Randolph noticed that the Surry Hills thug had a lot of money and was generously waving around notes to buy drinks for his cronies.

Randolph took his time finishing his beer before

leaving the hotel. When he stepped out onto the dark street he immediately scanned the area for locations to ambush O'Rourke. He was fortunate in that there was a narrow alley beside the pub, used to bring in crates of beer and spirits. It had no lighting and appeared to only have an exit into the backyard of the hotel.

Randolph glanced around. The street was deserted. There were lights on in a few of the windows in the surrounding tenement houses and Randolph was not surprised to see that the street was deserted; this was not a place any sane person would want to go wandering late at night. Randolph waited patiently for over an hour and at last was rewarded to see O'Rourke step out onto the street in the company of three drunken cronies, all singing raucously as they stumbled away from the dark alley.

Randolph followed at a discreet distance and was pleased to see that one by one O'Rourke's companions peeled away, leaving him alone in front of one of the narrow terrace houses.

O'Rourke stepped inside and minutes later Randolph saw a light in a window facing the street. He looked up and down the street, reassuring himself that he was not seen. He approached the front door cautiously, staying in the shadows until he was able to glance inside. O'Rourke was sitting at the kitchen table, attempting to slop down a plate of stew and dumplings he had retrieved from the oven of the wood combustion stove. Beside the plate stood a bottle of beer which O'Rourke swigged from between mouthfuls. The front door was not locked and Randolph pushed it gently open. It creaked but he was inside before O'Rourke could react.

Startled, O'Rourke looked up from his meal and immediately reached into his pocket for the razor. He flipped it open and started to rise from the table, scattering his plate of stew in the process. But he froze when he saw the pistol in the intruder's hand.

'What are you?' he snarled. 'A copper?'

'Your death – if you do not answer some questions I have,' Randolph said quietly, stepping forward into the yellow, flickering light of the candle on the table. 'So just sit down and shut up, unless I want you to answer a question.'

O'Rourke slumped back into his chair, the razor on the table within reach of his hand. 'If yer not a copper, then you are a dead man,' he said with as much menace as he could muster. 'You don't come into Mick O'Rourke's territory unless yer invited, and I don't ever remember invitin' you. If yer out to robbin' me you can have any money I have but I can also promise you that you won't keep it.'

'You have just returned from America,' Randolph said, keeping the pistol levelled on the thug. 'To be specific, from Los Angeles.'

'No secret 'bout that,' O'Rourke replied, shaking his head. 'So what's it to you?'

'Who paid your way?' Randolph asked.

'None of yer business, cobber, and from yer voice you have to be a bloody Yank,' O'Rourke answered in a surly, arrogant tone. 'I don' 'member meeting you over there.'

'You met a dear friend of mine,' Randolph said slowly. 'And you killed her.'

O'Rourke paled. 'I didn't kill that actress sheila. Yer got it wrong.'

'Funny that you should allude to Miss Owens when I didn't say who it was. All you have to do is tell me the truth about killing Miss Owens – including who paid you to do the job – and I will let you live.'

Sweat dripped down O'Rourke's forehead. 'You swear

on yer word of honour that if I tell you who paid me to kill that Yankee sheila you will let me go?'

'You have my word,' Randolph answered. 'I want the man who hired you more than you.'

O'Rourke seemed to relax but in a split second he had upended the rickety wooden table, slamming it against Randolph. The candle was snuffed out in the process and the room was now pitch black. Clearly, a man's word of honour meant little in O'Rourke's world.

Even worse, Randolph realised that he had dropped his pistol when the table hit him and he was now unarmed, apart from the bowie knife he also carried. With great haste, he slid it from his pocket and crouched in the classic stance of the experienced knife fighter. Randolph could hear his opponent moving in the dark and wondered if he had armed himself. Neither man spoke, fearful of giving away their position to the other.

Suddenly, Randolph was aware of a quiet, swishing sound in front of him. He stepped back, but the finely honed steel caught him across the chest, slicing open his shirt and upper layer of skin. Randolph thrust forward with his blade only to meet air.

'Gotcha, yer Yankee bastard!' came the triumphant shout in the dark. 'How's it feel to die like yer sheila friend?'

Enraged at the taunt, Randolph had no doubt that O'Rourke would pay for killing Nellie. All thoughts of keeping the Sydney criminal alive to question him were gone. Just a red, killing haze filled the American's thoughts. If it was the last thing he ever did on earth it would be to kill O'Rourke. So intent were they on hunting each other in the dark, neither man was aware of the sound of footsteps crashing down the stairs off the kitchen. Suddenly the room was lit by a kerosene lantern held high by a young woman.

The unexpected illumination gave Randolph the opportunity to see his target in the split second he needed. He flung himself across the small space to plunge his knife into O'Rourke's chest with all the strength he had. The knife went in deep and the thin man screamed as he fell back, with Randolph still holding the knife, twisting it to cause more damage. O'Rourke's scream did not last long. The blade had ruptured his heart and he lay coughing up blood, his eyes glassing over as he stared at the greasy, smoke-stained ceiling of the kitchen. Meanwhile, the young woman was no longer screaming but backing away from the kitchen door with the lantern in her hand.

Randolph yanked the knife from O'Rourke's chest. 'I'm not here to harm you,' he said to her reassuringly, looking up from the body of the man he had killed. 'So please don't scream again and I will leave you in peace.'

In the flickering light Randolph could see that the young woman's face was a mass of recent bruises and guessed that the man on the floor may have inflicted them. She must be his wife or mistress – the American did not know – but she at least nodded her head, eyes wide with fear and mouth agape with shock.

Randolph stood slowly. 'He killed someone I loved more than my own life,' he said sadly, looking down at the dead man at his feet. 'I am sorry for your loss.'

The young woman still did not speak and Randolph brushed past her on his way to the street.

'This belong to you, mister?' the woman called to him when he was at the front door.

Randolph paused, turned around to see his pistol being held by the woman and pointed at him. She stepped forward and pushed it towards the American. Randolph took the weapon from her and stepped out into the street. Her screaming had not appeared to attract interest. Perhaps it was something the residents of the area were used to and besides, it probably did not pay to become involved in Mick O'Rourke's regular beatings of his girlfriend.

As Randolph walked away he remembered seeing a look almost of gratitude in the battered woman's eyes as she passed the revolver to him. He knew that as a witness he should not have left her alive but she was an innocent and seemingly another victim of the man he had just killed.

Before midnight, Randolph had reached his hotel and bandaged the long but shallow wound across his chest. Maybe he should have it stitched but he'd had worse before when travelling with Matthew Duffy in the years prior to the outbreak of war.

Randolph reached for a bottle of rum he had stored in his kit and drank straight from the bottle. The shot helped ease both his physical and emotional pain. In the morning he would contact Alexander Macintosh and tell him that the police reports from the USA would not be needed. Maybe Alex would understand what that meant without becoming an accessory to the killing. Sadly, Nellie's killer had not admitted to being hired by George Macintosh but Randolph had no doubt he was behind the assignment. Randolph did not believe in coincidences. That the man he had killed had been employed by the Macintosh company and sent to the USA had to have the hand of George Macintosh on it. Confronting George was not an option for the moment as the killing of the Sydney criminal would surely attract police attention. No, that could wait for another day when things cooled down in Sydney, Randolph mused, adjusting the bandage strapped across his chest. For the moment he would need to get out of town. One day, he would return and finish his mission to avenge the woman he had loved despite her rejection of him for the glamour of the world of film.

Detective Jack Firth always read the daily police reports typed out at headquarters. One item attracted his attention this morning. It was about the stabbing murder of a well-known criminal from Surry Hills. Not that his death was of a great priority to police resources for the moment, and besides homicide was no longer the counterintelligence officer's concern. It was the name of the dead criminal that struck Jack – the man he had put in contact with Mr George Macintosh. Jack had a good idea from what he had read that O'Rourke had been involved in the murder of the Hollywood actress. But as he had also been complicit – and the murder had occurred outside Australian police jurisdiction – he preferred to let the matter slide on the off-chance it might in some way lead back to him.

At the change of the shift in the busy office Jack ambled over to the uniformed constable who had compiled the report on the death of Michael O'Rourke. The constable was a man in his early thirties who had served in the South African campaign, where he had been wounded and so was unable to pass the rigorous physicals for volunteer service in this war.

'Constable,' Jack said, holding the clipboard with the report. 'You questioned Molly Canning, Mick's lady friend, about his death. You think she did him in for all the beatings he gave her?'

The constable looked up from the paper-strewn table where he was writing up the last of his patrol reports before going off duty after a hectic night. 'No sir,' he replied wearily. 'I don't think she did him, but we do have a description of the man she claims she saw kill Mick. She says he was tall, about in his thirties and spoke with a funny accent she had not heard before. Thinks he might have been from Queensland from the way he spoke. She reported that Mick was killed in the early hours when she got hold of me on foot patrol down near Surry Hills. When I got hold of Sergeant Prowse we went with her and found Mick dead on the kitchen floor in a pool of blood. It looked to me like he had been dead for a few hours but she claimed he had been killed just a few minutes before she fetched us. I think she is lying and possibly knew the person who killed Mick.'

'Interesting,' Jack mused. 'Give all you know to the investigators – especially since you suspect she may have been in some way protecting Mick's killer.'

'I will,' the constable replied, returning to signing off his patrol report.

Jack Firth strode away, heading for his office down the hall where he would continue his duties in the world of finding spies. There was no such thing as a coincidence, he brooded. What if the funny accent that Molly, a simple girl who had never been out of Surry Hills, had heard was that of an American? If he remembered correctly from his Wilkes case before the war there had been an American who was keen on the Macintosh girl. What if the Yank had somehow learned that Mick O'Rourke was her killer? Was he capable of murder? If so, would the Yank also suspect George Macintosh's involvement in hiring Mick? A lot of questions – and the detective inspector knew the best way to get answers was to get the suspect. How hard would it be to track down a Yankee in a former British colony?

10

The leaves on the trees in Sydney's Hyde Park lay limp under the sweltering summer day. Great thunderheads boiled up in the afternoon sky and as he sat on a bench in the park under the shade of a large European tree, George Macintosh knew that one of the city's cooling storms was imminent.

He was not alone in discarding his coat and loosening his tie as he waited for the meeting. Others in the park moved listlessly along the avenues of trees and George had time to reflect on the state of affairs in his life. He now had an heir for his dynasty and although matters were very strained between himself and Louise she still dutifully carried out her social obligations. People who attended their soirees remarked on what a fine couple they made but that all changed when they were alone. Louise had made it plain that she wanted nothing else to do with her husband and slept alone in another room next to that of their infant's nanny. Not that George really cared. He had access to other women to slake his perverse desires and the fact that he alone virtually controlled the Macintosh companies was enough to fill his life. All was going well – except for the matter of his brother still being alive.

'Bloody hot day,' the large framed man who slumped down on the bench beside George grunted, wiping his brow with the sleeve of his shirt. George did not turn to greet Detective Inspector Jack Firth as this was their way of concealing their meetings. Instead, he slid an envelope containing the monthly payment along the seat to the policeman who deftly pocketed it.

'Thought you might like to know that I think your life might be at risk,' Jack Firth said without turning to George. 'The man you hired to go to America was found stabbed to death a couple of days ago.'

'Wouldn't that be an expected means for his demise, considering the world he lived in?' George asked.

'The detectives investigating the stabbing leaned on the only witness to O'Rourke's killing,' Jack continued. 'It seems that she finally gave up that a tall man with a funny accent said something about getting even for the death of someone he held dear. You know what he might have meant?'

George paled. He was not aware that Randolph Gates had returned to Sydney but somehow the information seemed to fit. If it was him, was he aware that George had contracted the killer to dispose of Fenella? 'It is not of any concern to me,' George lied. 'But I would venture that a Yankee by the name of Randolph Gates might fit the picture of the man you should be looking for.'

'That's what I thought,' the policeman answered. 'It's not my case but I will pass his name onto the investigators looking after the stabbing. I just wonder if he might not have killed that actor, Guy Wilkes, before the war. Maybe your sister was not the only person we should have been looking at.'

George did not reply. He already knew who had killed Fenella's former fiancé. He had witnessed the accidental shooting by his father and knew full well that it had not been murder. But this information was his ultimate ace in any future dealings with his father and not a card he needed to play now.

'Oh, there is one other thing,' Jack said as he rose from the bench. 'Macintosh correspondence being mailed to Sweden is being read by our people in the GPO. I just thought I should warn you as I would hate you to be accused of aiding the enemy.'

The second bit of information also worried George. Although the seemingly routine business correspondence was cleverly coded he was not sure how smart the intelligence people intercepting mail were. The war was a nuisance in his dealings, but also a God-sent opportunity to make money off misfortune. If the Germans won, then his secret support would be recognised by them, George considered optimistically. After all, when it came down to winners, it was really in the interest of the family's fortune that Germany won the war, and there was a good chance yet that it might.

As George watched the policeman walk away into the heat of the afternoon, he was jerked out of his reflections on the dangers posed to him when lightning tore the sky, followed by a loud crack of thunder. It was time to get out of the park and seek the sanctuary of his office.

★

Whereas those in the Southern Hemisphere sweltered under a summer sun, the men on the Western Front of Europe froze under bitter winter skies. Sean Duffy was finally returning to his unit but with some trepidation. How would he be received when he reached battalion HQ in the trenches behind the front lines?

He was vaguely aware that it was a mere few days before Christmas. Time had lost meaning in a world of sudden death – or worse, lifelong mutilation. At Gallipoli he had always thought that death was meant for the next man but life on the Western Front had changed that view. Now, all he knew was that death or mutilation was waiting for him from a bullet, bomb or artillery shell. It was surely only a matter of time before he too would join the lists of dead and wounded.

The resupply party he was going up to the front with pointed him in the direction of a narrow, communications trench. Sean made his way along, his boots clogging with mud that had not frozen, past soldiers huddling and shivering in small alcoves that had been dug out of the side to afford even the slightest protection against artillery rounds and the weather, but which were shared with rats and lice. The men he passed smoked pipes or cigarettes, their rifles always clutched in one hand ready for use. Hardly a man gave Sean a second glance as he trudged to the entrance of a bunker dug under the trench to provide the battalion with a relatively safe forward HQ. Here he reported to the duty officer, who greeted him with a brief handshake and a mumbled welcome and duly directed him to his company commander located further along the trench.

Sean found the company HQ, a similar style bunker to battalion HQ and went inside. He noticed a map attached to a board on the wall reinforced with corrugated iron sheets and a tiny table strewn with pencils and notepads. Behind the desk sat a tall, lean man wearing the rank of major.

'You must be Captain Duffy,' the major said. 'Rather ironic,' he continued, scribbling a message on a notepad and hardly looking at Sean who was still standing to attention in the cramped earthen bunker lit by a kerosene lantern. 'One of the reinforcements being sent up to the company today is a Private Duffy. You wouldn't have seen the man by any chance?'

'No, sir,' Sean replied.

The major finally looked at him from behind his tiny wooden desk. 'I suppose you are one of those damned Irishmen who supported your Papist bishop Mannix in the referendum to conscript men for the war,' the major said belligerently, making Sean feel uncomfortable.

The Labor prime minister of Australia, Billy Hughes, had called for Australian males to be forced into military service to help out England in her war against the Germans and their allies. But the issue had been defeated and the blame for the government defeat had fallen on Australians of Irish descent perceived as being anti–British because of the occupation of the old country by the British army. It had also been a significant result in that most troops fighting overseas had also said no to conscription, based on the philosophy that they did not want the men beside them in the trenches being reluctant soldiers as each and every man fighting on the war fronts was a volunteer. As for Sean, he did not consider himself Irish and had little interest in the politics of his ancestor's homeland, but he had voted against conscription for the same reasons most fighting soldiers had.

'How one casts their vote is meant to be private,' Sean replied. 'It is that idea of democracy I fight for, sir.'

The major looked sharply at Sean, glaring in a way that

said: do not disagree with me. 'I am Major Hartford,' he said. 'Before the war I was the principal of one of Victoria's best boys' colleges. As such I understand that men – like children – need firm discipline. I also disagree with our weak politicians that we do not have the ability to shoot our men for cowardice as our British cousins do. And I resent being sent a second-in-command of Irish blood. It is well known that the Irish cannot be trusted. They are men of little intellect, and less courage.'

Sean stared at his commander with disbelief. The man was a blithering idiot, he thought.

'Sir, if I may ask?' Sean said, attempting to keep his temper under control and feeling his hands begin to tremble. 'How long have you been out here?'

Major Hartford stared at him. 'I have been here for over two weeks, Captain Duffy. Why would you want to know that?'

'I think that you will find men with Irish blood in our ranks die just as easily as those with Anglo-Saxon blood, sir,' Sean said in the most diplomatic way he could.

'You are verging on insubordination, Captain Duffy,' Major Hartford said, his face reddening with anger. 'I think it is time you learned how arduous our work is here compared to the time you spent swanning around the War Office in England. No, Captain Duffy, you are in a real war now.'

'Is that all, sir?' Sean asked.

'That is all,' Major Hartford said, looking down at his pile of papers. 'You will report to the acting CSM who will brief you on our current layout of defences.'

Sean turned and pushed his way through the narrow entrance to glance up and down the trench. His eyes rested on a familiar face among so many new ones.

'Captain Duffy, sir, welcome home,' Sergeant Jack Kelly said with a broad smile, extending his hand. 'It's been a while.'

Sean gratefully accepted the gesture and when he looked into the acting company sergeant major's face he could see no guile. The welcome was genuine.

'I gather you have met our esteemed company commander.'

'I have, sergeant,' Sean replied. 'I see that you have come a bit of a way up the ranks with your current posting.'

'I am just filling in until Major Hartford can find someone with a real English name to replace me,' Jack grinned. 'Been a bit hard lately, with the casualties we have had here.'

'In my opinion, Sarn't Major,' Sean said, 'you should be at officer training and be commissioned.'

'Sir, my parents are wed, so that is not possible,' Jack replied with a straight face, causing Sean to laugh. He sensed that it was the South Australian prospector's way of telling him that he held no animosity over the Fromelles incident. 'I have been briefed by Major Hartford to give you a tour, so you can familiarise yourself with our little piece of paradise,' Jack continued. 'It will give you a chance to catch up with the few remaining mob from the time you were with us.'

Sean thanked Jack and, as they made their way along the trench, occasionally Sean recognised a face from his days with the company. It seemed a lifetime ago rather than six months – but then half a year was a lifetime on the front. The men who he knew greeted him warmly enough and Sean wondered at how, perversely, he felt so at home among these dirty, lice-infested, disease-ridden men with hollow eyes when only mere years before he'd sat in an expensive legal office in Sydney and would have considered any of the men strung along the trench as beneath his social position.

Even in hell there was a comradeship he knew that could never be repeated in his life – if he lived to see the war out.

'Our two new members, who joined us today,' Jack said, indicating the pair wearing relatively clean uniforms now standing on a parapet beside a corporal holding a crude periscope propped above the sandbags. The corporal was briefing them on the German trenches to their front.

'Privates Duffy and Frogan, this is the company 2IC, Captain Duffy,' Jack said, causing the two men to glance at their CSM. 'You any relation of Captain Duffy, Private Duffy?' Jack asked.

'I don't think so, sir,' Tom answered. 'Not unless Captain Duffy comes from Queensland.'

'I have distant relatives in Queensland, Private Duffy,' Sean said, looking up at the tall, handsome young soldier who obviously had non-European blood. 'A Mrs Kate Tracy, and her son, Matthew.' Sean was startled to see a fleeting expression of surprise on the young soldier's face.

'Aunt Kate is a relative of mine,' Tom replied. 'She helped me to get in on this show although I was supposed to be with the Light Horse. Some backroom bastard had me assigned to the bloody infantry instead.'

Sean now stared at the soldier who he knew must be related. The only confusing part of the relationship was how a Duffy could have Aboriginal blood! 'We might get the opportunity to catch up and discuss family matters some time,' Sean replied, his thoughts still awash with the coincidence of sharing a piece of the front line with a distant relative.

As he continued his tour of the trench, Sean was aware that Jack was shaking his head and chuckling. Sean dared not ask him why but his unasked question was answered anyway when Jack Kelly finally blurted, 'A blackfella in the family,' he said without being derogatory. 'Even in the best of families you will find a black sheep.'

It was only on the second day of Sean's time with the company that he realised just how badly the company was being commanded. He had been called to HQ to be informed by Major Hartford that he would not be able to attend the battalion CO's daily order group, and that instead Sean would attend and give his apologies, telling the CO that his company OC was indisposed with a touch of dysentery. From what Sean could gather this was a lie and left to make his way back behind the lines to the rear HQ.

He was greeted warmly by the newly appointed commanding officer in what had once been the living room of a French country house. Pictures of the former residents' family still hung on the walls and the living room had been converted to an operations centre with maps, field telephones connected to brigade headquarters and soldiers going about their tasks of taking reports and dispatching signals.

The new CO had been a company commander when Sean was acting company commander and Lieutenant Colonel Millington had also once been a school teacher, knowing Major Hartford when they had been civilians. Sean congratulated his former comrade on his well-deserved promotion. The colonel took Sean aside out of earshot of his staff. 'You know a touch of the runs is no excuse to miss my O group,' he growled softly. 'Hartford up to his old tricks, eh?'

'I am sorry, sir, but I have just joined the company and cannot comment on my commanding officer's behaviour,' Sean replied diplomatically.

Colonel Millington shook his head. 'He always was a lazy bastard, and he has a Napoleon complex,' he muttered. 'No matter, welcome to our little piece of real estate. We are hoping that in the future we might buy out some of the Hun's prime land from him. The word is that you did a stint at the War Office and met our General Monash?'

'Yes, sir,' Sean answered. 'A good soldier, who knows what he's about.'

'I have also heard that,' Millington said reflectively. 'I even heard that he is a favourite of Churchill to command the armies here – except that he has four strikes against him, being of German heritage, a Jew, colonial and a former militia officer.'

Sean nodded. The former Victorian militia officer who had been trained as a civil engineer seemed to apply a bit of science to warfare but his aptitude was dismissed by those above him. Sean had first met Monash when they were on the Gallipoli peninsula and had the opportunity to meet him again when the Australian general had been recalled to England for conferences.

The adjutant called the company officers to gather for the daily briefing and Sean, representing his company, took notes. He was pleased to see that the new CO had not ordered any offensive operations in the days before Christmas as he had been informed by Sergeant Kelly that they and the Germans opposing them across no-man's-land had a tacit agreement to let Christmas 1916 pass by in peace. War could re-commence after the day held sacred by both sides.

After the briefing Sean took tea and caught up with some of his old companions. Most had been promoted because of the terrible casualties among the officer staff but there were some fresh faces from Australia via England. When he had completed his tasks at battalion HQ, including those as the company 2IC, he made his way cautiously back to the front lines, keeping his head down to avoid snipers.

As soon as he reported to his commanding officer's

bunker he found him asleep. He woke him and delivered the contents of the briefing.

Hartford sat on his tiny bunk, rubbing his eyes, and from the irritable expression on his face Sean could see that he had not liked being disturbed by such trivial matters as the CO's orders for the day. He skimmed through Sean's notes and without looking up said, 'Thought I might inform you, Captain Duffy, that I have given the CSM orders to organise a patrol for tonight, to go out and snatch a couple of Hun prisoners for our intelligence chaps.'

'But the CO said in his briefing we were to stand down for Christmas,' Sean protested quietly. 'It's Christmas Eve and the men deserve just a little peace for the day.'

'Are you questioning my command, Captain Duffy?' Hartford said, rising from his bunk.

'No, sir, but we could put off the raid until after Christmas,' Sean answered.

'The last thing the Huns will expect is a raid on their trenches on Christmas Eve,' Hartford said with a satisfied smirk. 'It has a brilliance that only a good commander can recognise. I have informed Sergeant Kelly that he is to select the new men from the replacements to go over the bags at midnight. It will give them the experience they have yet to know of war.'

'Then, may I suggest that I go with them, sir,' Sean volunteered stiffly.

'I have given the task to Lieutenant Grant,' Hartford said, rifling through his belongings for a mug. 'He has just joined us and I feel that the patrol will stiffen his backbone for his future duties as one of my platoon commanders.'

Sean had briefly met the young officer mentioned and from his experience knew that he was not ready to go on such a patrol. It would surely mean his death.

'I still think that I should go,' Sean persisted.

'Captain Duffy, you are my second-in-command whether I like it or not, but it is not the job of captains to lead raiding parties,' Hartford answered, finding his mug. 'If you attempt to go out with Mr Grant I will personally ensure that you are court-martialled. Do we understand each other?'

'Yes, sir,' Sean answered dutifully and wondered if he would also get six cuts of the cane for what he was already planning. 'If that is all?'

'You are dismissed,' Hartford said, waving his mug in Sean's direction as he called for a pot of hot tea to help ward off the bitter cold of the snow lightly falling outside his bunker.

Sean left the bunker and in the dark of the trench felt his way along, requesting the location of the acting CSM. He finally found Jack Kelly squatting in a section big enough to hold a party of ten men. In the dark Sean could make out three other men squatting in a semi-circle fronting the CSM. He knew them as the platoon commander, Lieutenant Grant, and privates Duffy and Frogan.

'Come to join us, sir,' Jack said as Sean joined the group, squatting beside the CSM.

'I have just been informed by Major Hartford that he is sending out a prisoner snatch patrol,' Sean said.

'Yes, sir, we hop the bags in an hour's time,' Jack replied.

'Are you going?' Sean asked, knowing that Hartford would not have sanctioned his acting CSM to join the patrol.

'I can't let them go alone,' Jack replied in a pained voice. 'They wouldn't last three seconds out there.'

'Then I am coming with you,' Sean said.

Jack placed his hand on Sean's shoulder. 'You don't have to prove anything to anyone, boss,' he said out of hearing of the raiding party. 'What happened at Fromelles can happen to anyone of us, and I know that you didn't put yourself in for a gong. It was just a typical stuff-up by the army. I know the men who served with you at Gallipoli said you were one of the best bloody officers in the army and you saved my life from that big Hun that day. Besides, if anything goes wrong, the men are going to need you to stand up to that pompous bastard, Hartford.'

'I'm coming with you, Jack,' Sean insisted. 'And that is that. Mr Grant, have you been issued the appropriate weapons and kit for the raid?' he asked, turning his attention to the three men who had been waiting nervously in the dark.

'Yes, sir, bombs, clubs and pistols,' the young officer answered in a strained voice.

Sean could hear his fear. He was not ready, Sean thought. God help him. 'Good,' Sean said. 'The CSM and I will accompany you on the raid. Are there any questions?'

None were asked and Sean knew that they were probably as numb with fear as he was. The snow was falling and the strip of land between the trenches was covered in white, bringing a deceptive sense of peace to the front. Sean armed himself with extra grenades stuffed into the pockets of his heavy greatcoat and checked his pistol. The five men waited in silence, each coping with the mounting fear in his own way.

'Happy Christmas, sir,' Private Frogan said quietly. 'I am glad you will be with us.'

'Thanks, Private Frogan,' Sean replied. 'When we get back I will ensure that you all get an extra ration of rum – to go with the roast turkey and plum pudding.'

A ripple of soft laughter followed. They knew the best they would get in the forward trenches would be bully beef and rock hard biscuits to be washed down by a mug of tea.

'I'll settle for a good kip behind the lines,' Tom said and

all nodded in agreement; that would be the best Christmas present they could get – a place away from the stench of the garbage heap called the front line.

Sean pulled out his fob watch, battered by the extreme conditions of soldiering. It was a good watch and kept accurate time. He peered closely at the glowing face.

'Okay, boys, time to go,' he said, replacing the watch and drawing his pistol. One by one the five men slithered over the top of the sandbags past their sentries to enter the badly cratered land that lay as a buffer between two enemies. They would use the craters to conceal their movement as they made their way towards an outpost in the German lines identified by intelligence reports as the most likely weak spot in front of their own lines.

They had around 400 yards to cover before reaching the identified position described as an assembly area for the change of shifts on a nearby machine gun. With any luck an enemy officer would be present when the shifts were changed. They froze whenever a parachute flare popped in the sky above them to illuminate the battlefield before drifting with the wind to eventually extinguish itself in the snow. When the flares were floating above them they were acutely aware of how vulnerable they were to observation from any alert sentry in the German lines. But it appeared their luck held. The Germans must have considered their foe would respect the temporary truce and leave Christmas Day as a time of peace and goodwill to all men.

Sean could feel the biting cold of the ground beneath him and was aware that he had crawled across a couple of bodies whose decomposition had slowed in the cold. Needless to say, the sticky mess that clung to his arms was something he did not want to think about as a whiff of rotting flesh assailed him. He had taken the lead and his group moved within a short distance of him. Every five minutes he would pause to ensure they were all still together. Getting there was working out to being a bit better than Sean had pessimistically considered. The Germans were off guard.

Sean called a halt when he could actually smell cigar smoke drifting on the air. The snow had stopped falling and the muffled voices of their enemy could easily be heard.

'You speak German, Jack,' Sean whispered in the CSM's ear. 'What are they on about?'

'Not much,' Jack replied, straining to differentiate the voices. 'I can hear one of them talking about his kids . . . I think he is showing his cobbers photos of them. Mostly stuff our own mates are talking about right now.'

'A bastard of a night to be doing this,' Sean muttered angrily and Jack knew what he meant. Would the man talking with love about his family die in the next few hours at their hands? The company commander should be out here with them to see what his orders came down to on this sacred day. Then the German voices broke into a song whose tune Sean recognised – 'Silent Night'. Their singing was accompanied by a harmonica and each man on the deadly patrol felt a lump in his throat.

Sean signalled to his patrol to close up and gave final orders of what they were to do in the next few minutes. Absolute surprise was on their side and the shock of their assault should carry the day. Each man armed himself with a grenade and when they had carefully cut their way through the barbed wire, ensuring that they did not rattle any of the empty tin cans strung out to warn of an approach, Sean rose up and tossed his primed grenade into the trench before them. It was followed immediately by four others and before the first bombs had hit the floor of the trench they were followed by five more.

Confused and frightened voices greeted the arrival of the egg-shaped explosives, but they were cut short, turning into screams of panic and pain as the bombs exploded in the confined space. The raiding party followed Sean by leaping into the trench that was now a mass of writhing, wounded German soldiers. The acrid smell of smoke caught them as they fell on the men. Sean's landing was buffered when he landed on a dead soldier who lay face down amid a heap of scattered photos of a young woman surrounded by three children. Sean could feel his heart pounding as if ready to burst out of his chest.

A wounded soldier attempted to sit up and reach for his rifle but Tom Duffy swung his metal-studded, home-made club to smash in his skull, spraying blood and brain tissue into his own face. Sean searched around desperately for a prisoner and saw a German NCO clasping his head, hands over his ears. He was stunned and appeared to have been deafened by the proximity of the grenades exploding.

'That one!' Sean screamed at Jack, who understood, grabbing the still stunned soldier and wrapping rope around his wrists.

From around the corner of the trench, Sean could hear the sounds of the Germans rapidly organising to launch a counterassault against them. Already four armed men appeared from below a well dug bunker, firing wildly down the trench. In an instant Sean saw Lieutenant Grant crumple and it was obvious he had been caught in the rifle fire. He lay on his back and in the flickering light of the overturned brazier flames, Sean could see that his face had been smashed by a bullet and another had hit him square in the chest. He was choking on his own blood and desperately attempting to cough to clear his lungs. Sean knew that the young officer was as good as dead and impossible to rescue as the German infantry spilled from their deep bunkers and down the trench towards them.

Both Tom Duffy and Dan Frogan fought well, priming grenades and tossing them at the bend in the trench either side of their flanks, deterring any enemy from rushing them down the length of the trench they now occupied.

Sean plucked to his lips the whistle that he had secured by a lanyard around his neck and gave the long blast of the prearranged signal to get out of the trench and return to their own lines as best as they could with their prisoner.

The raiding party, now reduced to four men, hauled themselves over the top of the sandbags to find the gap they had cut in the wire. They had hardly gone 10 yards when the night sky was suddenly filled with parachute flares, their magnesium white lights dangling, reflecting off the field of snow, but also lighting up the silhouettes of the fleeing Australians. A machine gun opened fire from their flank, churning up wisps of snow around them. Jack was yelling at his reluctant prisoner in German, urging him to do what he was told.

Sean glanced around to see Private Frogan following, running in a crouch, stumbling as bullets tore over his head, then scrambling back on his feet to continue running. Machine guns had opened up from their own lines in a futile attempt to provide cover fire but the machine gun firing at them was too well entrenched.

At first Sean could not see Tom Duffy but then spotted him as a flare settled in the snow in front of the German lines. He was running back to the German lines towards the machine gun, a grenade in each hand.

Sean shouted to him to leave the gun and run, but Tom knew what he must do if they were to live. He was on the gun before the crew could traverse the barrel to kill him when he threw his grenades. They exploded on target and the gun fell silent.

'Bloody marvellous!' Sean shouted, impressed by the raw courage of the new recruit.

He turned to run when the world exploded. He was not even aware that he had been blown off his feet by a German trench mortar bomb, brought into action to counter the raid on their lines.

Sean lay in the snow beside the small scorch mark where the mortar had exploded. Winter was the worst time for the spread of shrapnel, he thought, as he lay on his back, staring up at a sky filled with tiny swinging lights like those he remembered on Christmas trees at home. When the ground was frozen, the artillery rounds and mortar bombs exploded on impact, scattering the deadly shards of hot metal to shred men's flesh, whereas mud absorbed the rounds before they exploded and muffled the effects of shrapnel. It was so peaceful, as he could not hear anything. It was as if the war was over, and he was back home in the Redfern hotel that had always been a part of his family heritage. There was the aroma of a lamb roast and the clink of bottles of cold beer to wash down the Christmas lunch.

The face of Jack Kelly loomed over him and he felt Jack's strong hands under his arms, dragging him into a shell crater. He was shouting something but Sean could not hear him and was annoyed that the CSM was disturbing his Christmas Day. Then the darkness crept over Captain Sean Duffy, MC; he was truly at peace for the first time in the past two years of his life.

PART TWO

1917

PART TWO

1917

II

Captain Sean Duffy lay between clean, starched sheets in the English manor house converted to a hospital for wounded officers. Outside it was cold and Sean was vaguely aware that the men of his battalion were many miles away across the English Channel, shivering and dying in the trenches he had left behind. He had jumbled memories of being dragged through no-man's-land by Jack Kelly while every inch of the journey caused screaming agony. After that, a maze of recollections of being transported back to the field hospital behind the lines and the operating table tended by a grey-faced army surgeon before being subjected to a gas that took away his pain and any recollection of what occurred next: the train trip with others mangled by the science of modern weapons to the coast, before being shipped to England to be loaded on a lorry and transported to the fine old home with its ivy-covered walls.

When the operation was over, Sean knew what had happened to him, and he tried not to weep for what he had lost. But in the darkness of the long hospital ward, his tears flowed freely among the screams and shouts of his fellow wounded, reliving in their troubled sleep the awful shell fire and machine-gun chatter that had brought them to this place. The ward echoed with shouted commands to long dead platoons and companies of soldiers that had followed these now shattered men who had been their leaders.

For almost a month Sean had not received any visitors; his world had been reduced to extreme pain and the cheerful encouragement from the doctors and nurses who tended to the shattered men under their care. He had befriended the wounded officer occupying the bed beside his own, a Canadian major in his early forties, married and now minus his arms from the elbows down. From the little that the Canadian shared, it appeared his wife had left him when she heard that her husband had been severely wounded. She had in fact written to him apologising for meeting another man, a civilian working in the civil service, and thought that he had the right to know she would ask for his cooperation in seeking a divorce.

Major Herbert Lancaster was tough, but at night Sean could hear him sobbing from the pain of betrayal. Sean had joked that between them the doctors should be able to put together a whole man: Sean's legs amputated below the knees and the major's arms, on one body. Whenever the weather allowed and both men were not being subjected to their recuperation procedures for the fitting of artificial arms and legs respectively, they would spend time on a bench in the garden, Sean lighting and placing a cigarette in the Canadian's mouth. Major Lancaster sucked on the smoke and sighed. 'As soon as I get my new arms,' he said, 'I'm going to wipe my own arse, then light my own cigarette and finally punch the bastard who has taken my wife from me. Just a few of life's little luxuries one takes for granted when one has arms.'

The late winter chill carried the smoke from their cigarettes skyward while Sean gazed at the water dripping from the trees as the country emerged from the winter.

'At least we don't have to go back,' he said softly, hunching against the day and staring down at the grass struggling to break through the last ice of winter. There was no response from the Canadian sitting beside him; both were beyond feeling any guilt about leaving their units on the battle front. Both were numbed by constant pain and the effects war had on their futures. When Sean had learned that his comrade had also been a solicitor with a firm in Ontario, they had warmed to each other, often revealing private thoughts on everything from how the war was being prosecuted to the way they went about their legal work in civvy street.

'Well, old chap,' Herbert Lancaster said one day, gazing at the stately building that was their temporary home. 'It appears that you may finally have a visitor – as he is not wearing the uniform of one of ours.'

Sean looked up to see Patrick Duffy strolling towards him in the uniform of a divisional staff officer. Sean's instinct was to rise to greet his senior officer but he quickly remembered that was something he was not about to do given his current condition.

Patrick reached the two men.

'Sorry that I cannot salute you, sir,' Herbert said with a touch of lazy sarcasm. 'Captain Duffy does all the saluting for both of us.'

Patrick shook his head, brushing off the apology.

'May I introduce Major Lancaster, sir,' Sean said. 'He's

one of those mad Canadians we have had the misfortune of serving alongside of from time to time.'

'Can't shake hands either at the moment,' Herbert replied, the cigarette dangling from his lips.

'Herbert, this is my cousin, Colonel Duffy,' Sean continued with a weak smile.

'I have heard that there are a lot of you former convicts in Australia,' Herbert said with a wide grin. 'But I did not think it was that bad that captains could be related to colonels.'

'It is a pleasure to meet you, Major Lancaster,' Patrick said and, beyond military protocol, raised his hand in a lazy salute, a gesture not lost on the Canadian.

'I suspect that you two have a bit to talk about,' Herbert said, rising from the bench. 'So, I shall see if there is a brew on in the ward. A pleasure to meet you, sir,' he said before ambling away towards the old manor.

Patrick took a seat on the bench beside Sean. 'I was saddened to hear you copped it,' he said. 'I only learned about you being evacuated a couple of weeks ago and, as fortune has it, I was sent back here to complete a staff college course. How are you, old chap?'

'I'm supposed to be alive,' Sean replied bitterly. 'But it does not feel like it.'

Patrick nodded his head, understanding the handsome young man's meaning. 'You know that your wounds will have you on a ship back to Sydney soon,' he said. 'I presume that you will return to the practice.'

'I suppose so,' Sean answered, hardly thinking much about the future.

'Do you still have the pain?' Patrick asked.

'It's not so bad now,' Sean answered as a raven took flight from a tree denuded of leaves. 'They are helping me with a set of artificial legs. I was fortunate that I kept some of my legs below the knees. It helps in my mobility.'

'I know that what I am about to tell you is no consolation to losing your legs but it has come through divisional orders that you have been gazetted to major. You proved to be a good student on your staff college course and I was able to slot you into a vacancy. You would have had your own company,' Patrick said. 'I wanted to be the first to congratulate you, Major Duffy.'

Sean blinked at the news. He had finally received the rank to go with the position he most desired but it was all for nothing now. He would be recuperated back to Sydney and discharged from the army to return to civilian life.

'Thank you, sir. I appreciate the gesture.'

'I know that you are going through the bitterness of losing a part of your life but you will be of great value to myself and the family when you return to Sydney,' Patrick said awkwardly, his face twisted in a grimace. 'I need you to act on my behalf for the family interests when you return. You are, after all, linked by blood to me.'

Sean glanced at Patrick and could see a pained expression in his face. 'What I can do to help, I will,' he said. 'I suppose as a solicitor I might be able to do something.'

'You know that I have two sons,' Patrick continued, staring into the shrubs and rockeries. 'My youngest, Alexander, is currently posted to a training battalion as a company commander. And my eldest is running the family business. Alexander is a soldier through and through. Perhaps that is my fault for allowing him to follow me in as many ways as he could. Sadly, Alex does not have a head for business, whereas George does.'

'Then your family matters appear to be well and truly under control,' Sean responded.

'I know this will sound shocking coming from a father who is not supposed to differentiate between his children, but I do not trust George any further than I could kick him,' Patrick said, tapping his swagger stick unconsciously against the side of his boot. 'So I have drawn up papers giving you full authority to make any decisions that you might think I would make, if I were back home. With that authority is, I hope, a generous salary to oversee my interests. You see, we have shared much in the last two years and I trust you as if you were my third son. I think you will have Alex's support in your endeavours. He has his military career, but as my proxy you have the requisite legal background to keep an eye on the company affairs.'

Sean was stunned by what his cousin was telling him. It was a huge responsibility and a show of great trust in him. For a moment he was speechless.

'I beg you to take up my offer,' Patrick continued. 'I would trust you with my life.'

'Sir, you know that I will,' Sean answered.

Patrick extended his gloved hand, taking Sean's mitten-covered hand in his own.

'Then, it is done.' Patrick rose from the bench. 'You do not know how much it means to me to have you home looking after the family interests in the competent way that I know you are capable of even when the chips are down.'

'Sir, you must know I disobeyed orders when I got my wound,' Sean said in an attempt to test his cousin's resolve to grant him with the power of attorney.

'I know all about the trench raid,' Patrick said, standing over Sean. 'There was a formal charge submitted by that blithering idiot of a company commander of yours to have you and Kelly court-martialled. But your CO overrode his report and even recommended you both for a decoration.

I am afraid the army brass would not come at that, but they did quash the request for a court martial.'

'Is Hartford still the commander?'

'I am afraid so. But learning what I have about Kelly, I suspect he will do a good job protecting the men of the company. In fact, Jack Kelly has been recommended for officer training.'

'That is good to hear,' Sean answered, nodding his head. 'Jack is a highly intelligent and brave man with outstanding leadership qualities.'

'That's what I deduced,' Patrick said. 'I had the pleasure of interviewing him at Div HQ last week. He said that if the army recognised him for anything good, it was because he had the honour of serving under you – as brief as it was.'

Sean felt his face flush. After all that happened, Jack Kelly still had a good opinion of him. Although Sean knew his military career had come to an end his heart was still with his old battalion with which he served from the first weeks at Gallipoli up until his wounds in weeks past. 'I know that Jack will make the grade,' he said. 'His men will be ably led.'

'Is there anything I can do for you?' Patrick asked.

'No, I will be okay,' Sean replied. 'Just a matter of getting the hang of my new legs and then getting settled back into the practice at home.'

'Well, time I made it back to London, old chap,' Patrick said, placing his gloved hand on Sean's shoulder. 'Chin up and we will meet home in Sydney as soon as this damned show is over.'

'Yes, sir. See you when I see you.'

Patrick walked away, leaving Sean alone in the sprawling garden. He gazed at the back of his distant cousin and sighed. He would be going home but some part of him besides his legs would always remain in the filth and mud of the front. His soul would linger over the battlefield forever. He was glad that there was no woman waiting for his return. After all, he was no longer a full man in either body or soul.

Tears rolled down Sean's cheeks until he found himself sobbing quietly. He cried not for just himself but for the friends he had left behind in the hell of war. Those young men he knew he would never share a drink with in a pub back home.

George Macintosh waited at his table with its starched white tablecloth spread with expensive silver. The hotel dining room was in Sydney's finest establishment catering to the needs of the well-dressed and wealthy patrons who used the facilities to carry out much of the government of the country as well as businessmen clinching deals. George had extended his invitation to his guest for such a meeting over some excellent food and wine. The purpose of the meeting had been played out in previous casual meetings at dinners and tea parties he had hosted to curry the favour of the right people. He rose as his guest approached the table, a grey-haired, middle-aged man wearing a fashionable suit. George knew the man was a government public servant occupying the position of department head. He also held a knighthood for services rendered to the Empire but was nondescript in every other way.

'Sir Hubert, I am glad you could break your busy schedule,' George said, extending his hand. 'I hope you do not mind but I have ordered for us both, knowing how busy we both are.'

'Not at all, George,' Sir Hubert said, taking George's

hand. 'I am sure that you have chosen well, knowing your reputation for enterprise and taste in food.'

The two men sat facing each other as a waiter poured an excellent claret. They waited until he withdrew before getting down to business. Sir Hubert opened first. 'You know that another round of honours is pending,' he said, sipping from his goblet. 'Despite your youth, your services to the government have been noticed.'

George experienced a wave of euphoria at the veiled hint of being honoured by the King. 'Oh, one does what one can for his country in these difficult times.'

'Come, old chap, your donations to the party have been invaluable in keeping our policies in the public's eye,' Sir Hubert replied. 'Not that a little more would not be appreciated – if you understand what I mean.'

George knew exactly what he meant. Despite being a senior civil servant, Sir Hubert secretly supported a political party against the ethics of his employment. George had covertly funnelled financial contributions to the party he suspected would eventually take government owing him favours. 'Would this be enough?' George said, scribbling a figure on a page from a notebook and sliding it across the table.

'In time, enough to buy you a knighthood,' he said, raising his eyebrows. 'However, first things first. A rather splendid decoration for services rendered to the country will be announced in the next honours list which I hope will be to your satisfaction and the envy of your father. After all, it is about time the Macintosh family received another knighthood.'

George smiled to himself. The thought of receiving an honour from the King would certainly be a shock to his father who considered such matters the domain of men serving their country in the armed forces. The eventual knighthood would cement his legitimacy to the Macintosh empire.

The meal arrived and as they ate the two men chatted about popular issues of the time. When the meal was over and the claret consumed they rose to leave.

'Just one other matter,' George said, extending his hand to the older man. 'Would it be possible for your colleague controlling the army to have my brother transferred to the Western Front?'

Sir Hubert looked at George with an expression of surprise. 'One would have thought that you would do anything to keep your brother on safe shores.'

'It's just that my brother has his heart set on seeing active service,' George replied.

'From what I have heard,' Sir Hubert said, dropping his voice, 'your brother is married to a German woman and that makes him somewhat doubtful – if you know what I mean.'

'My brother is a lot of things, but he is a true patriot to his country,' George said. 'It would mean everything to both of us if you could use your influence to have him released for active service in Europe.'

'I will do all I can,' Sir Hubert shrugged, taking a large cigar from a bulky silver case as they entered the spacious foyer. 'I am sure that we can get him his posting. Maybe even to your father's unit.'

'That would be wonderful, Sir Hubert,' George said with a broad smile of appreciation.

In a matter of minutes they had parted leaving George with a pending honour in the civil list as well as the prospect of a future knighthood. But, more importantly, an opportunity had been created to have red tape cut to release his foolish brother for service in the front lines. George was sure that Alex would get himself killed. He was the kind of stupid man who was likely to put his own life second to others'. People like his brother tended to win medals – but posthumously. In all, it had been worth the cost of the best bottle of claret in the hotel.

Detective Inspector Jack Firth sat in his cramped, untidy office of paper-filled crates and overflowing timber filing cabinets. In his role as the coordinator of police counter-intelligence services he received a daily mountain of reports on enemy alien activities. The vast majority of the reports were nothing more than false claims against innocent men and women who had the unfortunate circumstance of having German or Austrian blood in their family.

It was early autumn in the Southern Hemisphere and the day outside was mild. Jack preferred winter – a time the burly policeman welcomed as a chance to get back on the rugby field and mix it with other tough men. He glanced at the big clock on the wall opposite his desk and could see that it was almost midday, which meant he would have to prepare his notes for a combined police military intelligence meeting at Victoria Barracks in a few hours. Jack groaned. He hated sitting through the meetings. If he had his way he would be back doing real police work. He missed mixing with the colourful elements of the city's dark side where he was treated as a king by both those he worked with and the criminals he hunted. Counterintelligence work was mainly boring but he had no choice in his posting.

Jack leaned back in his chair that was hardly strong enough to bear his weight, placed his booted feet on the table and stared up at the fly-specked, soot-stained ceiling. His mind was not on the forthcoming meeting but on the report he had read down in the criminal section of the office complex months earlier. It had occupied his thoughts because of the investigation he had led into the death of a famous Australian actor, Guy Wilkes, just before the outbreak of war. At the time his prime suspect was the man's lover, Fenella Macintosh, but in retrospect he blamed himself for not looking at others associated with her. Especially the Yank Randolph Gates, who he had since come to learn was also a lover of the now murdered actress.

As Jack had persuaded Mick O'Rourke to work for Mr George Macintosh, he knew in his gut that Macintosh had used the infamous Sydney criminal to murder his sister, although Macintosh would not admit it to him. That O'Rourke himself had been killed by a man described as being identical to Gates was no coincidence. It was most likely the Sydney criminal had been killed as an act of revenge.

Jack placed his feet on the floor, leaned forward, retrieved his new pipe, filled it with a plug of tobacco and lit it. The thick smoke filled his office as the policeman contemplated a variety of leads. Was it possible that the American had actually killed Wilkes? Randolph Gates' alibi had been supplied by a drunken old night porter at the pub Gates had been staying in. But Gates had motive – the elimination of a rival in the affections of the beautiful young actress. Had Fenella Macintosh helped her American lover kill Wilkes?

Only one person could answer his questions now and according to Jack's enquiries he had disappeared. If only he had been able to put someone in the dock for the murder of the well-known actor, he would have taken front page on every newspaper in Australia, Jack thought wistfully. He wanted to be remembered as the copper who had the reputation for solving the high-profile murders. Working in the shadowy world of counterintelligence had little appeal for a man who loved the adulation of the press.

Jack puffed on his pipe and sighed. If only he could track

down the Yank he would have the case solved. It was interesting, he mused, how the whole Macintosh family seemed to be riddled with dark secrets which extended to all they came in contact with – including himself.

'Sir?' a female voice questioned from the door to his office. Jack looked up to see a uniformed policewoman holding a ribbon-tied folder in her hand. 'I have the collated report on Mrs Karolina Schumann.'

'Just drop it my desk, love,' he grunted. What would be next in the police force? Dogs? The recruitment of females to the male world of policing was the last straw.

His colleague stepped forward, unafraid of the famous detective's reputation for savaging junior police and placed the folder on his desk, where it was immediately buried among the other unopened folders. She turned on her heel and left his office without another word.

Karolina Schumann – another in the Macintosh web, Jack thought, pushing the folder with the stem of his pipe. He would look at it later. Now it was time to grab his hat and head down to the local for a beer and pie before catching the tram to Victoria Barracks for the meeting.

As Jack stood to retrieve his hat from the stand, a thought occurred to him. Maybe the best way for a man to disappear after a killing would be to join the armed forces. After all, one or two of the crims he had chased in the past had done the patriotic thing and enlisted to fight rather than face him on the street.

A wide grin split the tough policeman's face. He remembered that there was a Pommy colonel who attended the meetings in his capacity as a liaison officer for British intelligence. He was also known to be a close friend of the Macintosh family – or rather a close friend of Patrick Duffy. Colonel John Hughes, Jack remembered. If the Yank had enlisted for service surely Hughes would be able to track him down and supply his whereabouts. After all, as a commissioned officer of His Majesty he was bound by his office to be truthful.

The young police officers working in the HQ noticed that their superior had a strange smile on his face when he departed the building. It could only mean that he was close to arresting some well-known crim.

The meeting at Victoria Barracks was over in a couple of hours and to cement police–military relationships, tea and scones were served, courtesy of the army, in the spacious conference room.

Jack was quick to sidle across to the tall, grey-haired British colonel wearing his uniform adorned with campaign ribands. 'Colonel Hughes, isn't it?'

John Hughes turned to the man whose height brought them eye to eye and saw a cold steeliness behind the gaze. 'I am, Inspector Firth,' John Hughes replied.

'I was hoping that you would be at today's meeting,' Jack continued. 'There is a matter that you may be able to help me with.'

John Hughes frowned. 'Do you mean outside the items we covered at the meeting?'

'Well, yes,' Jack replied. 'It's a matter of confirming that police and army have a good working relationship.'

'If you feel that I can be of some assistance to ensure that, Inspector Firth,' John said, taking a sip of his tea, 'please feel free to discuss the subject.'

'It's about one Randolph Gates, an American citizen whom I have an urgent need to contact,' Jack said, staring the British colonel directly in the eyes.

'Why would you ask me?' John questioned, without blinking.

'Because I suspect that he has enlisted – most probably

in the army – considering his past skills. And I also know that you have met him in the past in reference to the Macintosh family.'

'I do know the man,' John replied. 'But I do not know of him enlisting in the army.'

'You realise that if you are not telling the truth I could have you,' Jack said bluntly, dropping any semblance of politeness.

'I don't take threats kindly, Inspector,' John said in a low, menacing voice, easily overheard by those around them. 'On my honour as an officer of His Majesty's army, I do not know of any Randolph Gates enlisting in the army.'

'Please excuse my manner, Colonel,' Jack relented. 'I've been too used to dealing with society's dregs, and old habits die hard.'

'Your apology is accepted,' John said stiffly, placing his cup of tea on the end of the conference table. 'If there is nothing else I must excuse myself but promise to inform you if I learn that Gates has enlisted.'

Jack watched the British colonel stride away, his swagger stick under his arm. He sensed that the man had lied to him but also knew he could not bully a soldier of John Hughes' stature. Being a member of the bloody toffs' class meant he had privileges beyond those of the criminals he was used to standing over.

Jack swilled down the last of his sweet tea and exited the conference room. If he could not get information from the damned Pommy he had one other he could approach. As far as he knew, George Macintosh was not aware of where the Yank was but his brother, Alexander, most probably knew. They'd been linked as friends when Jack first became involved in investigating the Wilkes murder.

12

Major Alexander Macintosh had his request for a transfer to an active service battalion overseas approved and when he returned to his house to announce the news he was met by his wife. Standing behind her was Colonel John Hughes, a grim expression on his face.

'Oh, how could it happen?' Giselle sobbed, throwing herself into her husband's arms.

'It is what I have trained for all my life,' Alex said softly, holding his wife as if he would never let go. Only now were the full ramifications of his leaving dawning on him. The chance that he may never return had always been something he dared not confront. Looking over his wife's shoulder, he could see John Hughes still standing in the hallway.

'Sir, your presence is rather a surprise,' he said, disengaging from his embrace of Giselle and straightening his uniform.

'I know my visit is a waste of time, but as soon as I saw your transfer order for England cross my desk I knew I had to see you and explain a few things you are not aware of. I would prefer do so in private.'

'I have already spoken with John,' Giselle said, excusing herself from their conversation. 'When you two are finished, I will have tea brought to the living room.'

Alex watched as his wife disappeared with Angus into the kitchen, leaving him and the colonel alone in the hallway.

'We should go to the library,' Alex said, leading the way and closing the door behind them. He walked over to a liquor cabinet and selected a whisky he knew the colonel liked.

John stood at a window overlooking the driveway and stared out, his hands clasped tightly behind his back. 'You know that your brother is behind you being posted overseas, despite all my efforts to ensure you remain at home.'

'The best thing he has ever done for me,' Alex said, raising his glass in a salute. 'You don't know how hard it has been training men, watching them steam away and hearing of their deaths when I am safely tucked up at home. I have always felt like a coward skulking behind the safety of a home posting, when men like my father and cousin are posted to the front. But I am dismayed to hear that you have been using your influence to keep me here.'

'I am sure that George wants you dead,' John said, sipping his whisky. 'Your father made me swear an oath that I would do all within my power to keep you here.'

'Father!' Alex gasped. 'I have always thought that he wanted me to follow in his footsteps.'

'He does,' John said gently. 'But alive. I was able to use Giselle as an excuse not to let you go by reminding the transfer board that you had a German wife. But some damned politician has stuck his beak in and over-ridden my protests. Your father knows the terrible risk you take by going on active service,' John continued. 'You know that I suspect your brother of traitorous acts but I cannot prove anything without evidence. But I have suspected him of treachery since the mission you undertook to Rabaul a couple of years ago. I have brought the subject up with your father, but he prefers not to accept that his eldest son is a traitor – not only to his country but also to his family. If anything ever happened to you I am afraid that George would control everything. You have lost dear Nellie and that only leaves two of you to control your brother's lust for sole power over the family companies. You may be a commissioned officer of the King, but you are also a man with a family and all the responsibilities that entails.'

Chastened, Alex slumped into a big leather armchair. 'Many men with families have volunteered and given their lives,' he sighed. 'I am no different.'

'You are,' John said forcefully. 'If anything happens to Patrick then it must be you who takes control of the family enterprises, not George.'

'He is in a better position to manage the companies,' Alex conceded.

'But not completely control them,' John retorted. 'Dear God, your family companies are among some of the most powerful in our former colonies and we rely on the products you deliver to help us win the war. George has no sense of loyalty to the Empire – although I hear at cocktail time he is in for a gong from the King for his so-called assistance to the Empire's war effort.'

'I have to go. I understand that my father has been well meaning but he also has to accept I am a soldier who must do his duty for country and King.'

John shook his head sadly. 'When you get over there, all noble thoughts of fighting for King and country will be shot away with your first time on the front, believe me. All you will be fighting for is the men around you and the hope that you will come home in one piece. It has always been that way for soldiers from the dawn of time, ever since men began fighting each other for some stupid political reason or other.'

'Maybe so. But I must find out for myself. I know it will be a strain on Giselle but I have to do my duty as a soldier.'

John stepped forward and offered his hand. 'Well, old chap, I tried. The jolly best of luck to you.'

Alex accepted his firm grip. 'Thank you, sir. Are you able to stay for dinner?'

'I'm afraid not. Gladys has her friends coming over this evening for bridge – although I must say, your cook is much better than the one we employ.'

Both men laughed, allowing some relief from the tension. Alex would see the colonel out and then deal with the dreaded task of facing Giselle.

A week later, a troop ship docked in Sydney Harbour to offload stretchers of wounded men from the front. Sean Duffy refused to be carried down the gangway. On the voyage back to Australia he had fought the agonising pain of his recently healed stumps and forced himself to use the wooden legs he had been fitted with. At first, attempting to walk the decks of the troop transport, once a luxury liner, he had used two walking sticks. But on account of his stubborn character he had eventually been able to hobble using a walking cane. The onboard medical staff had praised him for his dogged insistence and learning to walk again in such a short time. He had refused morphine for his pain whenever he could. The memories of how it had ruined the life of the woman he loved were still painfully fresh.

When the ship docked in Sydney there were no crowds of people waiting on the wharf to welcome home these war heroes – just a few relatives and military staff with ambulances to convey most of the passengers to hospitals. Sean limped his way down the gangway, guided by a nurse wearing a starched uniform with the distinctive emblem of a red cross.

'Thank you, sister,' Sean said when he eventually reached the wharf, bathed in a lather of sweat. He had shared his ward with men with no faces, or with weeping wounds that would eventually turn septic in an age that did not as yet have effective antibiotics. There were others whose minds had been lost along with their body parts. In comparison, Sean felt grateful and did not feel any self-pity for the extent of his own wounds.

'You will continue to have nightmares,' the sister explained gently. She was an attractive woman in her mid-thirties, whose eyes reflected what she had experienced nursing the wounded of this terrible war. Many nights she had sat in the semi-dark of the ward, holding the hands of dying men as they called out for their mothers or cursed God for not doing anything to help them. In Sean's case she had admired the major who only allowed his troubled soul to escape in his sleep when he tossed and turned, screaming orders to phantom soldiers.

'Your care has gone a long way towards healing me,' Sean said gallantly, allowing her to release her grip on his elbow. 'From here on, it's up to me.'

'Take care, Major Duffy,' she said, turning to walk up the gangplank to fetch the next patient. 'I know that you will learn to live with your disability.'

Then she was gone, leaving Sean alone, leaning on his walking stick. With difficulty, he made his way along the wharf, sweat streaming although it was a mild autumn day. He would take a taxi to his old office in the city and catch up with his staff. Later, he would pursue all the matters the army had for his discharge.

The loneliness of the returning soldier assailed him. 'Major Duffy, sir,' a voice deep with a Scottish brogue called to him.

Surprised, Sean turned to see a solidly built man in his mid-fifties wearing a good suit striding towards him in the manner that marked him as a former British soldier.

'I am he,' Sean replied.

The stranger thrust out his hand. 'My name's Angus MacDonald, sir,' he said with a broad smile. 'You dinna think the colonel would not have someone here to meet you when you returned. I work for the colonel.'

Angus MacDonald. Sean had a vague recollection that this was the former Scottish soldier who had campaigned with Patrick Duffy in Africa during the colonial wars, although he had never met him in person.

'Major Macintosh was unable to meet you in person as he is preparing to go over there himself. And Mrs Macintosh is ill from a bad cold so she organised for her friend, Mrs Louise Macintosh, wife of the colonel's eldest son, to come with me to fetch you back to Major Macintosh's house.'

As he spoke, Sean was aware of a woman walking up to join them. Sean was simultaneously struck by her beauty and puzzled by the sadness behind her expressive eyes.

She held out a gloved hand. 'You must be Major Duffy,' she said with a wan smile that had Sean wondering if it was in response to his disability. 'I offer Major and Mrs Macintosh's apologies for not being able to be here in person

197

to welcome you home. However, it is my pleasure to meet the man about whom Colonel Duffy has written so many glowing letters.'

'I must say, this is all so unexpected,' Sean said, reluctantly releasing Louise's hand from his own. 'I was planning to nip down to my office and then to the old local for a counter meal and beer.'

'Well, I am sure that Giselle will be up and about to organise a feast fit for a returning hero,' Louise said, attempting to sound gay.

'A car is just outside the terminal, sir,' Angus said. 'I have already organised to have your kit picked up.'

'Thank you, Sarn't Major,' Sean said, causing the tough Scot to look at him with an expression of surprise. 'Oh, the colonel told me all about you when we were at Gallipoli. You know that he holds you in the highest esteem.'

Just a little off balance, Angus mumbled a thanks. 'Do you need a hand, sir?' he asked to cover his temporary embarrassment.

'No thanks.' Sean leaned on his stick and forced himself to take steps towards the end of the wharf. 'Got to get as much practice as I can.' But he did allow Louise to slip her arm under his for balance.

'In my own time I visit the hospitals for our wounded men,' she said quietly. 'I am used to assisting soldiers who are usually too proud to ask.'

Sean was touched by the gesture. So, this was the wife of George Macintosh. Bloody shame such a gentle soul – and physical beauty – should be mixed up with him.

'No explanation needed,' he said through gritted teeth, pleased to see the exit a few feet away. The occasional soldier threw him a salute but he was unable to return the courtesy other than to nod. After the longest 200 yards he had traversed in a long time they reached the vehicle, a shiny luxury import. Angus helped Sean into the back seat and Louise sat down beside him as Angus closed the door to take his place behind the wheel.

'I believe that you have a law practice in the city,' Louise said, breaking the silence between them as Angus steered onto a street where automobiles vied for a place among the horse-drawn wagons and rattling electric trams.

'I am a junior partner in my family's practice,' Sean replied.

'I have been told that you were of wonderful assistance to Fenella before the war. It is interesting that we did not meet then.'

I wish we had, Sean thought. 'The Duffys and the Macintoshes come from a different social strata,' he said. 'We did not have much chance to mix socially.'

'Well, Major Duffy, I know that you are held in high esteem by the Macintosh family,' Louise said kindly. 'I hope that we will have more opportunities to meet again.'

'Does that high esteem also extend to your husband, Mrs Macintosh?' Sean asked.

Louise turned to face him. 'I am sure that it does,' she answered – somewhat defensively, Sean thought. 'However, as far as I know you have not met George.'

'No, I haven't,' Sean replied, regretting his pointed question. The wife did not bear the sins of the husband. 'But I am sure that we will meet before much longer, as I have been appointed by Colonel Duffy to oversee his legal matters.'

Louise registered some surprise at Sean's words but turned away, hiding any further expression.

'Do you experience much pain with your legs, Major Duffy?' she asked, changing the subject.

'Please call me Sean. My military past is behind me now, and hearing my name less formally delivered would assist in my recovery.'

Louise smiled. She sensed that this man beside her had a cheeky sense of humour. One could not help but like him. 'I don't know what to say to you about your . . . wounds,' she said carefully. 'I doubt that you are a man to allow your . . . disability to stop you forging a successful life.'

'I am fortunate that my life is working as a solicitor,' Sean said, turning to gaze out the window at his first real sights of home. How strange it was, he thought. Men were killing and dying even as he sat here, and to see the way people went about their routines on the busy streets of Sydney one would not even know there was a war on. 'I was lucky compared to many that I met in the English hospitals.'

'I am sorry, Sean, it is just that I don't know what to say. I am afraid that, other than visiting soldiers recuperating from their wounds, I have no comprehension of what you must have been through. Please forgive me my awkwardness.'

'There is nothing to forgive,' Sean said. 'What we experienced can really only be shared with those who were with us. But so much for that subject. You have not told me anything about yourself.'

Louise was surprised but pleased at Sean's interest. Falteringly at first, she began to speak about her life, her son, Donald, and her friends. But as Sean was quick to notice, she did not once mention her husband.

Captain Matthew Duffy had mixed feelings about his new aircraft. It was a Martinsyde single-seat biplane designed for scouting and bombing missions. Although it had a longer range than previous aircraft he had flown, it was less manoeuvrable, hence its nickname 'elephant'. But in the desert skies over Palestine it rode the wind at a speed of 55 mph although it could reach 96 mph if pushed. On this lone mission to scout ahead in support of the ever-advancing forces under General Allenby, Matthew was aware he was flying into territory still under air superiority of the Turks with their German air support and, as usual, the AFC aircraft were no match for the nimble, fast-flying fighter aircraft of the enemy.

Matthew's armament consisted on this mission of a swivel .303 Lewis gun mounted above his head on the top wing and a Lewis machine gun fixed aft to deter enemy on his tail. He was also carrying 260 pounds of bombs in case he located a target of opportunity. His route took him back into the area he had been shot down in almost six months earlier and he knew that nearby was the Jewish settlement he had been taken to. Flying low over the ancient, rugged landscape, he startled some Arab boys tending flocks of goats and the occasional wandering caravan of camel traders. He missed having the second set of eyes that his former New Zealand gunner, Sergeant Bruce Forsyth, had provided in a forward cockpit and was acutely aware that he was alone in the sky with little hope of help should he bump into one of the prowling German fighters.

All Matthew prayed for now was that he survive the war – something that had become even more important since meeting the American girl who had helped save his life. Joanne was always in his dreams; he would fantasise that they were on a Queensland tropical island surrounded by lush, green forest with babbling streams of cool, clear water to swim in. But his reality now was the roar of the engine, oil spattering his face and goggles, and the rush of a hot wind by his plane.

He was two hours into his mission and had seen nothing worth reporting and was making a last check of the map strapped to his leg to mark his route. He was grateful that the mission had been uneventful because with any luck he would be back at the officers' mess tent before sunset, sharing a drink with his fellow flyers.

Pulling on the stick he slowly swung the nose of his Martinsyde around and began to level off for the return flight. He craned his neck to observe the ground below and blinked in shock. Dipping to one side for a better view he sought out what had caught his eye and prepared to turn back on his original path. As he had been flying at around 500 feet everything had rushed past his vision but this time he had a clear view of the ground below. There it was! He could not mistake the lines of the Packard Tourer that he had driven months earlier and the face looking up at him was Joanne's. She waved and Matthew waved back, waggling his wings before beginning to search for ground suitable to land on. Fortunately, a clearing that was a wide part of the track loomed up.

With expert ease, Matthew settled his aeroplane and rolled to a stop. He did not even consider that he had landed in enemy territory and his only protection was the revolver in his canvas side holster, but scrambled out of the cockpit, even as the Beardmore 6 cylinder engine growled to an idle.

The Packard came to a stop a few yards from where he stood and he could see Joanne standing in the open cabin gaping at the airman blocking her way.

'Matthew!' she screamed, leaping from the car to run towards him with her arms wide. Despite her slightness, she almost knocked him over. Suddenly he was aware that she was kissing him passionately on the lips. He returned the kiss and they stood embracing on the dusty track. Matthew wanted the moment to last forever. Finally, they broke apart slightly.

'Matthew Duffy,' Joanne said, half-laughing, half-crying. 'I missed you so much after I went to Cairo. I could not get you out of my thoughts.'

'That was mutual, I can assure you,' Matthew responded. 'I truly think that we were destined to meet in this place at this time . . . Anyway, what the hell are you doing in the middle of nowhere once again? And don't give me that archaeology story.'

Joanne gently pushed herself away from Matthew and her expression became more serious. 'Matthew, my big brave airman, you should not ask too many questions but, as you have, I am on my way to meet someone – a mutual friend.'

As if on cue, a troop of heavily armed horsemen appeared on the crest of a low ridge a hundred yards away. When he scanned the faces Matthew saw his old friend Saul Rosenblum waving his rifle over his head in his direction by way of greeting.

When the troop reached the aircraft Saul dismounted, walked over to Matthew and hugged him. He then turned to Joanne and held out his hand to her. She accepted the gesture, even as Matthew's arm was protectively about her waist.

'So, an old cobber and Mr Churchill's lady are together in the land of Joshua,' Saul said with a broad smile.

His statement puzzled Matthew. 'I just happened to be flying by when I thought I saw a lady in distress,' Matthew said, grinning. 'Who would think that a lady such as Miss Barrington would have much more to do with bandits like your lot.'

'Miss Barrington is much more than meets the eye – and very pleasantly so,' Saul said, staring at Matthew's aircraft, now softly purring on idle. 'And I think God has sent you to us. Are you able to fly to my settlement?'

Matthew frowned at the request. 'From what I remember

of the distance, I daresay that I can but I am not authorised to do so.'

'Ahh, just a bureaucratic matter of little consequence,' Saul responded, waving off Matthew's concern. 'I am sure that Miss Barrington's friends in London can settle that little situation for us. Is that not so, Miss Barrington?'

Joanne nodded. There was a lot more to this American woman than he could ever guess at – especially the reference to her being Churchill's lady.

'Matthew, be assured that whatever it is that Mr Rosenblum is proposing will be cleared by the War Office,' she said. 'I am sure that we will be able to get the news to your superiors that you have been temporarily put under the direct control of the British government.'

Matthew shrugged. 'Well, about time I went up and landed at your settlement, cobber,' he said.

'You will find a suitable area on the western side of the village where you can put down,' Saul said. 'We will all meet there tonight and I will ensure a feast to announce the arrival of both of you. We will escort Miss Barrington from here so she does not have anything to worry about.'

Still mystified, Matthew walked over to his aircraft and clambered aboard as the horsemen trotted up to the rise to give him clearance on the track. Matthew opened the throttle and let his plane bump and grind over the rough, dry surface until the nose rose into the blue sky. He circled overhead, scanning the skies for enemy aircraft and then set a compass bearing to where he remembered the settlement was. As he flew away, leaving Joanne and Saul behind, his thoughts were troubled. In effect, he was disobeying orders. He could only hope that whatever Saul was implying would indeed be sanctioned by the British War Office.

13

Matthew found the cleared ground on the outskirts of the settlement. He had sufficient fuel to make a low pass and ascertained that the surface was as good as anything outside a constructed airfield. When he returned to make his landing he noticed a large crowd of men, women and children gathering below. Clearly, an aeroplane attempting to land out here was something of a novelty.

The light was fading and Matthew braced himself for the touchdown. It went smoothly and he was able to bring his aircraft to an idle not far from the end of the improvised strip. With the help of a few eager men, one or two of whose faces he recognised as being of those who had rescued him from the Turkish patrol months earlier, he clambered from the cockpit and stretched his legs. Matthew was quick to note that all the able-bodied men – and a few young women – were armed with rifles and pistols;

a few sported Mills bombs in their bulging pockets.

'You come back to us, Captain Duffy,' one of the men helping him from the cockpit said in a heavily accented Russian voice. He was in his mid-forties but had a tough look in his eyes that did not invite contradiction. 'My name Igor. We look after your aeroplane and hide it.'

Matthew accepted the assistance, noticing that men and women were already throwing a great, dun-coloured mesh cloth over his aircraft. To any observer from the air it would appear to be a mound of earth.

'Is a, what you say . . . precaution,' the Russian said. 'German aircraft fly over our village. We find camouflage net at deserted German airfield. Think it might be good to use one day.'

Matthew was escorted to the settlement where he was met by a party of long-bearded men who greeted him solemnly in a language he did not understand.

'They say you are sent from God,' the Russian man said. 'We do not know why you land here but Saul will tell us when he returns.'

Matthew guessed the older men with the long beards were probably rabbis and if he was God's answer he wondered what the problem was.

Matthew was escorted to Saul's house where he was welcomed warmly by Saul's wife and youngest son. He was given a good meal and, just after sunset, Saul arrived with Joanne.

'Good to see that you landed safely,' Saul said by way of greeting, brushing the dust from his clothes and being chided by his wife for littering her clean floors with half the Sinai desert at the same time. But her eyes were full of relief and love at his return.

Matthew glanced at Joanne, who returned his look with

a warm expression. 'Saul is not the only one who is pleased to see that you did not crash this time,' she said.

'I was shot down,' Matthew growled, falling for her mischief. 'Maybe later on you might be truthful with me and tell me who the hell you really are.'

'I am an archaeologist. That is the truth – well, most of it.'

Matthew nodded. 'And who are you really working for – us, or your government.'

'Possibly both,' Joanne answered with a mysterious smile. 'You can be assured that your diversion from your mission with your Flying Corps will be fully sanctioned in London – as soon as I am able to make contact with the War Office.'

This did not make Matthew feel any easier at not returning to his base.

'Elsa has fed you,' Saul said, noting the bread still on the table. 'Miss Barrington and I will eat now while we discuss why God has sent you to us.'

Matthew sat down as Elsa served up a chicken stew.

'Elsa is also a crack shot with a rifle,' Saul said, devouring a piece of bread dipped in the juices of the delicious, herb-flavoured stew. 'She should be. I trained her when I first came here and she has killed many Arabs.'

Matthew thanked Elsa when she poured a glass of rich red wine for himself and the others. The fact that Elsa was a very attractive woman, with a flair for cooking and killing, had not informed Matthew why he was needed.

'To luck!' Saul said, raising his glass. 'Here is to you and I fighting together again – like we did back in Africa.'

Matthew glanced at Joanne who had also raised her glass silently. 'So, what are you two up to?' he finally asked.

'The Ottoman army is retreating towards Jerusalem,' Saul said, wiping gravy from his chin with the back of his hand. 'The Arab village nearest us has, over the years, alternated between friendship and hostility, depending on who they listen to from outside. Intelligence from Lawrence's men has informed us that they have been able to obtain a German field gun with a plentiful supply of shells, as well as a number of Maxim machine guns. They intend to use it against us and wipe us out – every man, woman and child. We need you to deliver that big bomb you carry on your aeroplane down the barrel of their artillery piece.'

Matthew shook his head in disbelief. 'You cannot tell me that London would sanction me getting involved in a tribal fight between you and the Arabs,' he said. 'My squadron has probably already listed me as MIA again, to say nothing of the ramifications of going off on a mad mission to help you – as much as I would like to.'

'It is not only Saul and his people who you would be working for,' Joanne cut in quietly. 'We also have good information that the Arab village is currently harbouring a religious fanatic who has returned from Berlin to convince the Arabs to turn on the British and Lawrence's nationalist army. We would rather see him taken out of the picture.'

'We?' Matthew asked, frowning at Joanne. 'The British government? But you are an American citizen. How much do you trust this Lawrence chap?'

'I met Mr Lawrence in Cairo and we share a love of Biblical archaeology. I got to know him through our conversations concerning sites that we had worked before the war. He may be a somewhat odd man but he is devoted to the Arab nationalist cause. I trust his intelligence, as does London. Very soon, my country will be in this war on the side of Britain and her allies,' Joanne continued. 'I suppose you could describe me as a liaison officer between the British and my country. In my position as an archaeologist specialising in the Biblical lands, I was very well placed to move between settlements, as was Mr Lawrence before the war. I have had access to the highest Ottoman circles in Constantinople because I was neutral – and because of my father's financial influence in this part of the world. But, with our entry into the war looming, I am restricted in my movement. Saul has been assigned to provide me with a base and help me in my mission.'

'Are you working for the bloody Poms too?' Matthew exclaimed, looking at his old army comrade.

Saul grinned sadly. 'I had little choice,' he sighed. 'You could say my unauthorised leave of absence from our post at Elands River eventually caught up with me. But the Poms were very accommodating when it came to finding a solution. So, there it is.'

'It is very important that the man we wish to silence is killed rather than captured,' Joanne said. 'I have the authority to make that decision.'

'From whom?' Matthew growled. 'King George?'

'No, Winston Churchill,' Joanne retorted defiantly. 'Lord Balfour has compiled a report to create a Zionist state when the war is over. Winnie has a deep interest in this part of the world and the matter of an Arab agitator attempting to turn the local people against the Allied cause is not in Britain's interests. My mandate was to collect information and, if possible, act on that intelligence. To do so will help both Saul and the war effort.'

'You do realise that I am putting both my career as a pilot with the AFC and my very life in your hands,' Matthew said to Joanne. 'I must truly love you to do that.'

Joanne leaned across the table and took both his hands in her own. 'When this is all over I want you to meet my father,' she said. 'He despises Papists.'

Matthew broke into a chuckle. Here was the strong-willed

daughter who was out to defy her father just to prove that she could do so. Hopefully he and Joanne would never have a daughter together. She might just turn out to be like her mother. 'Well,' Matthew relented. 'I am on board. What is the plan?'

Saul looked relieved, stood up and retrieved a map sketched by his scouts. He placed it on the table before launching into a briefing outlining Matthew's role as well as explaining how he and his men would launch an assault on the Arab village. As Matthew listened, occasionally asking questions on logistics, he experienced a sense of dread. Why did he feel something was bound to go wrong?

That night Matthew did not sleep well. From what Saul had told him, the Arab village was heavily defended. The war between the two settlements had waged for as long as Saul had lived in Palestine, and with the rise of Arab nationalism the small Jewish population was in danger of being eliminated – every man, woman and child.

Despite assuring Joanne he trusted that she would sort out his new mission with his superiors in the AFC, Matthew could not help but harbour a small doubt. Just exactly who she was continued to puzzle him. He now knew that she worked as a spy and he certainly admired her courage working virtually alone in these dangerous lands. But still she had not really explained her motivation to risk her life when she was the heiress to a fortune and would inherit all the trappings that went with that.

Matthew listened to the silence of the settlement at sleep. When the door to his room creaked, instinctively, he grasped his pistol.

'I can't sleep,' he heard Joanne say in a whisper. 'I would like to lie beside you.'

Surprised, Matthew moved over in the narrow, single

bed to allow her to settle beside him. She was wearing little else than a silk slip and Matthew was aware of her flesh underneath when he placed his arms around her.

'I am armed, so don't get any ideas, Captain Duffy,' she said softly with a hint of teasing in her voice, her back to him.

'I am an officer and a gentleman,' Matthew said lightly. 'But you have to be careful of your choice of words when you make a request like wanting to lie with me,' he continued. 'If I remember my few forays into the Bible, over here that means a lot more.'

Joanne laughed, attempting to stifle her mirth. 'I couldn't sleep thinking about what is ahead in the morning,' she said. 'I wonder if I should not have stopped you from volunteering your services in this mission when it has so little to do with you. It has only been in the last few hours that it has dawned on me that you could be killed.'

'That fear has been with me ever since we got into this war,' Matthew said, reassuring her. 'So, do not feel any guilt if anything goes wrong.'

'Saul has told me that when you were only a boy you lied about your age and went off to fight in South Africa,' Joanne said. 'He said that you and he were separated at some place called Elands River.'

'Like a lot of my life, I would rather not talk about it,' Matthew sighed. 'It seems like a lifetime ago. What I would rather know is why you are risking your life in this damned cruel land when you could be at home going to parties and balls.'

'Oh, I could not explain fully in one night,' Joanne said quietly. 'But I guess it is just part of who I am. I seek the adventure normally denied to my sex unless we are independent enough to grasp it ourselves.'

'This is not adventure,' Matthew reminded her. 'This is

a deadly game where you can forfeit your life in a thousand horrific ways.'

'I know,' Joanne answered in a soft whisper. 'It just seems that I have been caught up in a situation that has got out of hand.'

'You are free to quit and go home any time,' Matthew suggested.

'That may have been true until this year,' Joanne replied. 'But my country is gearing up for war against the Germans and now, as a patriot, I have little choice.'

Matthew knew that for the moment he had asked enough questions. Joanne wriggled around to face him. 'Life under these circumstances can be desperately short,' she said, her mouth so close he could feel her moist breath on his face. 'Love me, Matthew,' she said with a passion that could not be mistaken for anything else than the invitation he had dreamed about since first meeting this remarkable woman.

Their night of lovemaking took Matthew to a world he had never experienced before. He had known many women over the years of his travels but they had only been a means of satisfying his lust. Now he was in a world where love and lust came together. It was not until the early hours of the morning that he and Joanne finally fell asleep in each other's arms. Before he drifted off, Matthew vowed that he would make this woman his wife. To do that he still had to survive this war. Joanne had already lost one flyer in her life and he did not want to be the second.

On the other side of the world, Inspector Jack Firth could also be in trouble if the commissioner learned one of his best men was neglecting the task of counterintelligence in order to pursue an old murder inquiry. Jack had chased down everything he could on the American Randolph Gates, and was sure that he had enlisted in the Australian army. Although the British officer had not been forthcoming with any knowledge of Gates, Jack felt his best bet would be to corner Major Alexander Macintosh, as he knew he and Gates had been friends before the war.

Firth's investigation brought him to the door of the infantry officer's headquarters in Sydney to confront the man himself. Alex had just about tidied up all his admin matters in preparation for departing overseas when he was informed by the orderly room clerk that a policeman was asking for him. He asked the clerk to usher the man through, and within moments Jack Firth strode into the room.

'Major Macintosh, you may remember me from a matter I was investigating before the war,' Jack said, not bothering to remove his hat. 'The murder of Guy Wilkes.'

'Ah, yes, Inspector.' Alex rose from behind his desk so that he did not have the intimidating policeman standing over him. 'How can I be of assistance?'

'I was informed that you have access to all persons enlisting in the army,' Jack said bluntly. 'I would like to have a copy.'

'Inspector, I doubt that is within your jurisdiction,' Alex answered firmly. 'I am afraid you would have to produce written authority for me to provide you with that.'

'Like this?' Jack asked, retrieving some papers from his pocket and throwing them on Alex's desk. 'You can examine them, if you like, but you will see that the authorisation comes from your own HQ command.'

Alex picked up the two sheets of paper and could see the signature of a high-ranking staff officer he knew.

'You could save us both a lot of time and heartache by telling me where the Yank is,' Jack said. 'You know that you have a duty to the law of this state.'

'I am aware of that,' Alex snapped. 'But I also have the responsibility of training the men out there to go to war. I assume you're referring to Randolph Gates, but I can swear on my commission as an officer that no American by that name has enlisted.'

'I am not a fool, Major,' Jack replied. 'As Gates is wanted for questioning not only concerning the death of a Mr Michael O'Rourke but also in regard to the matter of Mr Guy Wilkes, I expect that he would have signed up under an assumed name – perhaps even as a Canadian citizen to hide his accent. So, the list of all men who have been through your battalion in the last six months, if you please.'

Alex had not expected this. He had told the truth when he said no man by the name of Gates had enlisted. Randolph had put down his citizenship as that of a Canadian. He glared at the policeman on the other side of the desk.

'Corporal Hardy,' he called loudly. 'Fetch me the carbon copy of the battalion roll covering the last six months.' Alex was satisfied that it would not reveal Randolph's true identity in the training battalion. Forewarned by John Hughes, Alex had discreetly altered Randolph's enlistment nationality to Scot.

'Yes, sir,' came the reply from the orderly room and within moments the clerk entered the room holding a thick wad of papers in a bound folder. He placed it on the desk.

'Thank you, Corp,' Alex said, dismissing his clerk. 'That will be all.'

The corporal departed, a puzzled expression on his face.

'I must insist that you sign for the battalion roll, Inspector,' Alex said, dipping a pen in an ink pot and passing it to the policeman.

'The copy of the roll will be returned within twenty-four hours,' Jack said, hefting the book from the table. 'I expect that your cooperation will continue for the sake of good relations between the police and army.'

Alex did not answer but watched as the detective inspector left his office. When he was sure he was gone Alex bawled down to his clerk to have Private Maurice Green report to him immediately. The clerk hurried off and within a few minutes Randolph reported to the company HQ building where he was ushered into Alex's office. He saluted smartly.

'You wish to see me, sir?' he asked as Alex closed the door.

'Stand easy, Randolph. We are pretty safe from being overheard here. Take a seat.'

Randolph removed his hat and sat down. 'You look worried, Alex,' he said, glancing at the door.

'We have to cut short your training and get you out of the country,' Alex said. 'That copper Inspector Firth is looking for you in relation to the death of some man called Michael O'Rourke, and also wants to talk to you about the death of Wilkes.'

'You know that I did not kill Wilkes and, as for the other matter, it is best you do not know. But he was the man who killed Nellie.'

'It should have been me to settle that matter,' Alex said, turning from the window. 'But you shouldered the responsibility and now it's my turn to protect you. I am going to draw up orders to put you on a ship leaving tonight with a complement of men going to Egypt. From what I can gather they will be most probably disembarking for deployment to Palestine. I am sorry that you will not be able to serve with the cobbers you have made in training.'

A broad smile crossed Randolph's face. 'You could not have done me a greater favour. Matt is somewhere in

Palestine and there's a good chance I will be able to track him down – maybe even get a transfer to his unit.'

'I had not considered that. Let us hope that you get to catch up with my wild Irish cousin and, when you do, please give him my compliments.'

'What happens next?' Randolph asked.

Alex laid out his movement details for embarkation on the troop ship. When all was in order, Alex reminded Randolph to pick up his documents authorising his travel from the orderly room. Randolph rose and Alex extended his hand. 'Well, old boy, let us hope that we get the opportunity to meet after this war and share a cold beer.'

'You take care, and if you see Colonel Duffy give him my regards,' he said, gripping Alex's hand firmly.

'I will tell him all that you have done for the family,' Alex said, stepping back. 'Just keep your bloody Yank head down.'

'I will,' Randolph said, grinning. 'See you when I see you.'

The American stepped back, replaced his slouch hat and saluted his superior officer with genuine respect. Once Randolph was gone Alex sat down at his desk. Soon, it would be his turn to steam across the Indian Ocean. Would there be a reunion after the war? He was acutely aware of the ever-mounting death-roll of soldiers from all theatres of the war.

The coded papers secured under her corset, Karolina Schumann walked towards the main gate of the internment camp. She was greeted by the corporal of the guard who had become used to her frequent visits. But as Karolina approached him she noticed that this day his greeting was strained. Suddenly she felt a sick feeling in her stomach. To add to her growing concern, the corporal unslung his rifle from his shoulder.

'Mrs Schumann, I have orders to take you to the commandant,' he said in an awkward voice.

'Why is that?' Karolina responded indignantly.

'I dunno,' he replied with a shrug of his shoulders. 'I just have orders to escort you to the office.'

Karolina felt the cold grip of fear. This had never happened before, but she allowed herself to be taken to the main building housing the camp administration. The office was not the commandant's, but when a male voice bid them enter, Karolina was ushered inside. The room was virtually empty, with just two old chairs and a burly looking civilian standing in the middle.

'My name is Detective Inspector Firth,' he said. 'And I have reason to believe that you are in possession of papers deemed to be subversive.'

Even though she always thought she might be able to bluff her way out of any such situation, the shock registered on Karolina's face. 'I do not know what you are saying,' she replied, her face pale with fear.

Jack took a threatening step towards her, towering over Karolina. 'Don't make it hard for yourself, Mrs Schumann,' he said in a low, menacing voice. 'We have had a file on you for some time. I have the power to have you stripped and searched by a woman authorised to do so. The choice is yours.'

Karolina glanced around the room. There was an open window but it was foolish to think of fleeing. She knew she would not get far. Jack waited a moment while Karolina stood in silence. 'Corporal, fetch Mrs Jenkins for the search,' he said in a tired voice.

'Wait,' Karolina said, raising her hand. 'That will not be necessary. I will give you the documents you demand.'

Jack nodded to the corporal who remained in the room while Karolina turned away from the men. Lifting the front of her long skirt, she took out the papers and passed them to Jack.

'You do realise, Mrs Schumann, that if these prove to be subversive documents you will be charged with espionage, a crime that carries a death sentence in this country? But, if you cooperate now I may be able to mitigate your sentence.'

Karolina's hands were trembling. She felt faint. Observing her distress, the policeman pushed a chair towards her.

'Please, have a seat,' he said in a gruff tone. 'We are not in the habit of bullying women, regardless of their nationality.'

Karolina gratefully sat down and stared at the dusty floor. She knew that the Australians would soon discern that the papers she carried were in code – and if they broke that code she would be found guilty of spying. The death threat was not an idle one. In her two years of active work for her country she had not really considered the consequences. Now the reality hit her. A death sentence would mean never seeing her grandson grow up to be a man.

'What do you want to know?' she asked in a beaten voice.

'Who is coding the documents?' Firth asked, glancing at the unintelligible words. 'Is it the pastor, von Fellmann, or the former consulate assistant, Herr Bosch?'

Karolina realised that the authorities knew more about her contacts than she gave them credit for. 'I am afraid that I cannot tell you,' she said. 'To do so would be handing them a death sentence.'

'Fair enough,' Jack said. 'I admire your courage and would probably give the same answer if I were in your shoes. But for now you are under arrest and will be taken back to Sydney to be formally charged and put in prison until your trial. Just remember that if at any time you wish to speak to me, it might help in sentencing. I know that your daughter has married into a prominent Sydney family and that your son-in-law is currently on his way overseas. That will be hard on her. You will have to think about your family. Your death would not help either your daughter or your grandson.'

Karolina knew the policeman spoke sense but she also realised that she had a duty to fight for her country and thus must share the dangers faced by her countrymen on the battlefields of Europe.

Jack did not handcuff her as he escorted her to the waiting car. Did they shoot spies? Karolina wondered. Or would she have to resign herself to death on the gallows?

14

Karolina sat in the front seat beside the police inspector, who drove in silence until they were some distance from the camp. He suddenly pulled off the dirt road to park a short distance away among a stand of gum trees. Karolina now experienced real terror. Was she about to be executed on the side of the road?

Jack leaned towards her. 'I want you to listen very carefully, and if you have any sense you will do everything I say,' he said. 'Right now I am the only one who has your file and if you want to stay alive you will listen to what I am going to tell you.'

Karolina had shrunk back from him, fearing that he was about to rape her before killing her. 'I am listening.'

'Good,' Jack said. 'As I said, I am the one who has been assigned to follow up your file and we both know that the papers you were caught with would probably get you executed if they were passed onto the intelligence people. But it is a queer world and you just happen to be related to a well-known and respected Sydney family. I am sure if you were arrested for spying it would bring shame on the Macintosh name so I am going to return you to your daughter's house, but you will not step out of the place unless I say so.'

Karolina was stunned by her reversal of fortune. 'Why do you do this?' she asked.

'Let's just say that it is in both our interests,' Jack said, removing his pipe from his pocket and tapping it on the steering wheel. 'If you do not agree with me, believe me, I will make sure you swing on a rope.'

'I will do as you say,' Karolina said meekly. 'But I will not tell you what you want to know about my friends.'

'Bugger that,' Jack snorted. 'I have other plans. So, we are clear on what I have told you?'

Karolina nodded, still trying to fathom how she had escaped certain death. Jack then swung the car back on the road and drove to Alex Macintosh's residence, where Giselle was surprised to see her mother escorted to the front door by a burly policeman.

On his way back to his office Jack Firth made another stop. In Kent Street he parked in front of the Macintosh building and told the receptionist he wanted to speak with Mr George Macintosh immediately. The receptionist attempted to protest but was silenced by George, who had come out of his office when he heard the raised voices.

'Come in, Jack,' he said. 'It must be bloody urgent for you to meet me here.' He closed the door behind them.

'I have just arrested your brother's mother-in-law for espionage,' Jack said without any preliminaries. 'I had no choice. It seems that a separate file on her exists with the army intelligence people but I was able to convince them to leave the arrest in my hands. I will be needing your influence to make the arrest go away.'

George slumped into the big leather chair behind his desk. His immediate reaction was the impact such a matter might have on his being awarded an honour by the King. 'Is Karolina currently in a prison?' he asked.

'Not exactly,' Jack said, walking to the window overlooking the harbour. 'I have placed her under unofficial house arrest at your brother's house until something can be worked out.'

'Why would you do that?' George asked, feigning innocence but knowing full well the shrewd police inspector was most probably jockeying for a bribe.

'To prevent you and your family suffering the public disgrace of having a traitor in the family,' Jack said with just the slightest of satisfied smiles. 'Right now, I am the only one with Frau Schumann's file. I ensured all other copies were destroyed – except the army one, which I need you to make go away. Now, I know you fully appreciate what her arrest might mean so you must also appreciate that I need compensation for risking my pension.'

'How much?' George cut across the policeman's explanation.

Jack pushed a scrap of paper across the desk. George glanced at the figure, raising his eyebrows at the large sum.

'You realise that I will need something more in return for paying you the figure you ask,' George said, already scheming to recover the amount. 'I would need the file you have. I am sure it could be easily lost in your busy department.'

'When I get the money you get the file,' Jack said, pleased to see that the wealthy businessman had not queried what he had asked for. 'But I will have to take steps over the next week or so to have Frau Schumann returned to internment at Holdsworthy – just to cover my arse. That way I can be sure she will not continue her spying and cause us any future embarrassment. There would be a good chance that your sister-in-law's mother might meet with an unfortunate accident in the camp if it was circulated that she had betrayed her fellow agents to our intelligence people. In the meantime, you have to ensure that the file the army keeps on Schumann is lost.'

'That sounds like a very good arrangement,' George concurred, knowing it probably meant he would not have to pass on the coded papers she brought him. 'I will arrange to drop off the money to you at our usual meeting spot,' he continued. 'I just need a day to arrange withdrawals. As for the other file, I am sure that a well-placed friend of mine in government can take care of that for me in return for a party contribution.'

'Keep to the plan and all will work out for us both,' Jack said. 'If there is nothing else, I will bid you a good day, Mr Macintosh.'

When Jack had left the office, George leaned back in his chair. His success in business was largely the result of having the mind to recognise an opportunity. And right now he was about to be played a hand that would help him realise yet another dream. He would be able to rid himself at last of the woman who had been the only link he had with the German agent in the internment camp. Finally he had an excuse to cease acting as the courier for the coded letters.

George rose from his desk, walked over to the window and gazed out at the view. His kingdom. One day, the Macintosh family would be the most influential in Australia, he mused. He returned to his desk and lifted the telephone receiver. His public service contact, Sir Hubert, would make the army file disappear. As for Karolina Schumann, he trusted the corrupt policeman to make her also vanish.

Matthew did not require anyone to wake him for his mission. Years of early rises had equipped his internal clock to bring him out of his sleep. The first thing he noticed as he heard the settlement stirring was that Joanne was no longer beside him.

He dressed in his flying kit and left the house under the last veil of night to go to the improvised airfield. Here he met the Russian who had first greeted him.

'I have checked guns and bomb,' the Russian said in the dawn's half-light, shaking Matthew's hand with his own grease-plastered one. 'We paint out your identification.'

Matthew turned his head. All AFC roundels had been painted out. His aircraft was now one that seemingly did not belong to any nation, which made the Australian flyer apprehensive. He was helped into the cockpit by the Russian, who made his way around the nose to spin the propeller into action. With a choking roar, the engine spluttered alive. Matthew checked his instruments – especially his compass – and waved to the small crowd of curious men and women who had gathered to see him take off. The operation was well sketched in his mind and he pulled out his fob watch to check the time. According to Saul's plan he should have just about put his raiding party in place for the surprise attack.

The Russian stood back, throwing a salute which Matthew returned with a wave of his hand. He could barely make out the end of the strip and prayed nothing had changed since the evening before. When he was satisfied his revs were up he let the heavy bomber lurch forward, picking up speed until he was confident there was enough wind on his wings to lift her skyward. With a final bump she was in the air and Matthew was pleased to see the dawning day was proving to be clear of clouds.

He pulled on the stick to get altitude before swinging around and checking his compass for the bearing he had calculated the night before. Soon, he had levelled off and was flying in the direction of the unsuspecting Arab village. He would have the sun at his back when he made his approach, thus blinding any observer on the ground as he swept in.

It did not take long to reach the sleeping village below and, as he passed over a ridge, Matthew could make out Saul's force of around fifty men dismounted and waiting on the reverse slope. They waved to him as he continued his flight towards the village.

With the sun rising behind him, he levelled off at almost roof level to make his approach on the cluster of square mud and stone buildings. According to the map Saul had shown him, his target was a large mud building at the edge of town, bordered by a low, stone wall. He had been assured that if the bomb dropped cleanly there was little chance of killing the women and children of the village. But that was a great trust in his own ability to deliver the deadly iron canister accurately.

As he approached Matthew could see his target and also noticed men spilling from the stone building. The sound of his engine had obviously alerted them and he could see dark faces staring at him as rifles were raised to challenge his approach. When Matthew was satisfied that his height, speed and angle of delivery were right he pulled the stick to release the bomb. It fell away cleanly and the release of weight caused his aircraft to lurch upwards. He was over the village before the bomb hit the building and exploded.

But it was the second explosion that almost blew his flimsy aircraft from the sky. He could feel the heat rise up to grasp at him and realised that his bomb must have set off a store of high explosives. Buffeted by the secondary explosions, Matthew fought to keep control of the Martinsyde. He put on more speed and, as he did, pulled up and around to fly back over the target. From his cockpit he could see dust rising on the plain below from Saul's assault force charging the stunned survivors of the blast. Matthew could not hear the rattle of gunfire as both attackers and attacked engaged in a savage skirmish. The roar of his engine and the air whistling past his ears drowned all sound from below.

He swooped again over the area, now covered in black, boiling smoke, and saw the remains of men mutilated by his bomb. A few more fortunate survivors wandered aimlessly around the area scorched by the explosion, clearly with ear drums blown out and suffering concussion. They were no longer interested in firing on him and ignored his fly over.

From his vantage point, Matthew could see Saul's men already firing in the narrow, twisting alleys of the village, fighting any armed men who came out to engage them. There was little else he could do but return to the settlement and land to await the final outcome.

'We could hear the explosion from here,' the Russian said when Matthew had brought his aircraft to a halt and cut the engine. 'You do good.'

Matthew climbed out of the cockpit and jumped to the earth, taking off his goggles and leather head cap as he did. The Russian passed him a bottle of vodka.

'We drink,' he said. Matthew took a long swig of the fiery liquid and passed the bottle back.

'How long before Saul returns?'

'Maybe before noon,' the Russian replied. 'If all go well.'

The Australian airman walked over to a stand of olive trees and wearily sat down in the shade. He soon fell asleep but just before midday was awoken by the loud wailing of women coming from the settlement. Blinking away the snatched sleep, he stood up and walked quickly to the township. When he entered the main square he was shocked to see Saul holding his eldest son, Benjamin, in his arms. He was covered in blood. Elsa sobbed, clutching frantically at her son. Matthew spotted Joanne, alarmed to see that she, too, was covered in blood. He rushed to her.

'It did not go well,' she said in a tired voice. 'I was left on the ridge to observe until the signal was given for me to identify the body of the man we were supposed to kill. When I went in I saw that Benjamin had been severely wounded. Saul allowed his men to run amok and they killed every male they found, sparing only the very elderly, women and children. Saul forced them out of the village and set it alight. We only had one casualty – Saul's son.'

'Have you been wounded?' Matthew asked, ignoring for the moment the brutal tactics of his old army friend.

'No, this is Benjamin's blood. I tried to bandage his wound after we ensured the Arab agitator was among the dead. Benjamin appears to have been hit in the upper chest with a dum dum bullet and if he does not get first class medical treatment he will surely die. There's a medical clinic here but it is not equipped for major surgery.'

'Thank God you have not been injured,' Matthew said. 'I don't know what I would have done.'

'Well, we are both alive,' she said softly, touching his cheek with the tips of her fingers.

'What do we do now?' Matthew asked as the men who had accompanied Saul on his raid mixed with wives and children joyous to have their men back safely.

'I have to help save Benjamin's life,' Joanne said. 'I know a Syrian surgeon from Damascus who has a practice in Jerusalem. He is reputed to be one of the best in the Holy Land.'

'Jerusalem is still held by the Turks,' Matthew cautioned. 'It would be too dangerous.'

'We don't have much choice,' Joanne answered. 'I have the Packard and will be able to transport him. As a US citizen I am still classified as a neutral, and the Ottomans respect that. I will not be harmed.'

'It is still risky,' Matthew frowned. 'The last I heard, your country is on the verge of declaring war.'

'I have survived this long. Just trust me.'

Matthew agonised. How could he stop her? When it came to looking after herself in these harsh and dangerous lands she had more than proved to be the better of most men he knew. 'Promise that you will contact me as soon as you can,' he said.

'I will,' Joanne answered. 'We will leave within the hour and should be in Jerusalem before nightfall. All I can hope is that Benjamin is strong enough to make the trip.'

Matthew joined Saul and between the people of the settlement they were able to make up a litter to fit in the big American touring car. Elsa insisted on tending to her son for the journey and against Saul's protests won her argument. With a sigh and shrug he watched as his wife cradled her son's head in her lap, crooning soothing words of encouragement. Both Saul and Matthew stood shoulder to shoulder as Joanne set out to drive north to the ancient city with her cargo which was precious to both men.

'They will be safe,' Saul said when the automobile was out of sight. 'May God look over them.'

Although Matthew was not particularly religious he

found himself thinking about Wallarie, and silently asked his protection for the woman he loved.

'I suppose that I should return to my base,' Matthew said as both men walked away. 'I will need your Russian to make sure I am displaying AFC markings and top up my tanks from the fuel supply I see you have in the village.'

'That will be done,' Saul answered. They had seized the drums from a hastily deserted German airfield in one of their raids. 'We thought it might be best if your aircraft was not identifiable to the Arabs.'

'Joanne said that you pretty well slaughtered all the men of the village.'

Saul stopped walking and stared across the fields covered in vineyards and orchards. 'Ever since I have lived here the Arabs from the village have periodically attempted to wipe us out,' he said. 'Had you not helped us they would have used the German gun to shell our settlement and the Ottomans have no real desire to protect us. Today, I solved the problem of any future threat from our Arab neighbours. We spared the women and children and I know that they can settle further up the valley with their relatives. This country has been at war forever,' he continued. 'Even Moses sanctioned the complete destruction and death of his enemies in the past. He ordered that every man, woman and child be put to the sword when his people entered the lands promised by God.'

'That was then,' Matthew argued. 'This is now, and what you have done is going to come back on you in the future.'

'This is my land now,' Saul said. 'I have given the blood of my eldest son in the defence of freedom from persecution. We are merely returning to the land the Romans forced us out of – not attempting to take someone else's land.'

Matthew desisted from continuing the argument with

his old friend. He could see that Saul had grown to be a pioneer in his adopted country. After all, had not his own relatives on the Macintosh side slaughtered the Aboriginal people of the lands they took for themselves? Who was he, as an Australian, to judge another's ideas on the occupation of land?

With his crowd of curious wellwishers waving goodbye, Matthew took off to make his way south to his airbase. He was dreading the homecoming as he'd have to account for being so long overdue. He knew that he would have to answer a lot of awkward questions and only hoped Joanne had been able to get a message through to London to explain his unplanned mission.

His return flight was without incident and he landed just before sunset to be met by his ground crew who beamed broad smiles of relief for his return. Forced landings due to mechanical problems were not uncommon, and Matthew guessed that his squadron comrades would have presumed his overdue return had been put down to such an event. His name would be removed from the MIA list.

When his aircraft came to a stop and he cut the engine he was met by the sergeant in charge of the ground crew.

'Heard the news, sir?' he asked, helping Matthew from the cockpit.

'Sorry, Sarge,' Matthew said, adjusting his hearing to the silence of the desert airfield. 'What news?'

'The Yanks are in the war,' he replied. 'The show should be over soon enough, when they arrive to give us a hand.'

Matthew paled. If that was so, Joanne would now be considered an enemy alien by the Turks. She would surely be taken prisoner and, knowing the Turks, possibly tortured. After all, from what he had learned about her, she was already a suspected spy.

He turned away from the sergeant and vomited in his gut-gripping fear.

Sean Duffy had hardly settled back into his life as a solicitor when he had his first matter to deal with concerning the Macintosh estates. With utter disbelief he had read the contract delivered by George Macintosh's legal representatives, and when he had telephoned Giselle to confirm the papers before him she had instructed him that her signature on the contract was indeed genuine. When he asked her why she should be a party to such a ludicrous contract, Giselle had made it clear that she had her reasons and that her husband's power of attorney had given her absolute authority to make such a decision.

Sean pleaded with her to reconsider but she remained firm in her resolve to be a party to the contract as it stood.

With a sigh of frustration, Sean had replaced the handset. He flicked through the formal papers that gave George full ownership of his brother's house and land on the harbour in the event of his death. Why in hell would Giselle sign such a ridiculous agreement? What did George have over his sister-in-law? Whatever it was, Sean knew it was legally binding in a court of law.

'You had better come home alive, Major Macintosh,' he said quietly to an empty room. 'Or your wife and son are going to be homeless.'

It was now that Sean could see why Colonel Patrick Duffy had appointed him to take care of his legal matters in his absence. He eased himself away from his desk to stretch his legs. Reaching for the walking stick he pushed himself to his feet and, with unsteady steps, walked towards his office window to gaze out at the busy street below. It was as if his three-year absence from legal practice had never occurred. The staff and his fellow lawyers treated him with the amount of respect due to a decorated war veteran but, other than that, every time he took a step he was reminded of what he had given for his country. Sweat broke out on Sean's brow. He turned and tottered back to his desk where he opened a drawer to retrieve a bottle of Scotch. He took off the top and gulped down a large mouthful – followed by another. The soothing liquor soon began to flow through him. His reliance on alcohol had been noted by the senior partner of the firm but he had been given some leeway considering this was to be expected of someone who had lost his legs for his country and King.

But this time he was drinking because he felt impotent to stop Giselle Macintosh's stupid decision. How could he protect the colonel's interests if his own daughter-in-law was signing away rights to a bastard like George Macintosh? A knock on the door and Sean slipped the bottle back in the drawer.

'Yes,' he answered.

'Major Duffy, a Mrs Macintosh would like to see you,' a young articled clerk of seventeen said. 'She does not have an appointment but said it was urgent.'

'That's okay, Harry,' Sean replied. He was annoyed that the young man persisted in using his old military title, but had been informed by his receptionist that the young trainee solicitor idolised him as a war hero. 'Please show her in.'

Sean wondered at the unexpected appearance of the wife of the man who had virtually robbed his own family. He was curious as to what brought her to see him. When Louise entered the room, he remembered just how beautiful she was.

'Louise, please take a seat,' he said without rising, as would be his normal custom.

'Thank you, Sean,' she replied. 'I know my visit is unexpected, but I have learned of my husband's despicable act.'

'I presume you mean getting Giselle to sign over the deeds on the house in the event of Alex going west?' Sean said.

'Yes,' Louise answered, folding her hands in her lap. 'My husband was boasting last night how he was gradually taking his rightful place at the head of the family, and there was no place for fools like his brother to share it. It was then that he told me what he had done.'

Sean shook his head in disgust. It was obvious that the man who had remained behind to manage the family fortune was some kind of mad megalomaniac. 'I am surprised that you have come here,' Sean said. 'Is that not being a disloyal wife?'

'Wife!' Louise snorted. 'A wife according to the law. I have attempted to gain a divorce, but George has threatened to take my son from me, and I know that he is powerful enough to do so. I have no feelings for my husband other than hate and loathing.' Sean was taken by surprise at her candid confession and left at a loss for words. 'I am here to explain that my dear friend and sister-in-law signed over the deeds because she had no real choice. You may not know, but she confided in me that her mother, Karolina Schumann, has been threatened with being arrested as a spy and possibly executed. George claims he has evidence that he would release if Giselle did not sign the papers.'

'God almighty!' Sean swore. 'I hate to say it but your husband is more of a bastard than I gave him credit for. His father and brother are overseas risking their lives, and he skulks back here sitting on his shiny arse, robbing his own family.'

'Is there anything we can do?' Louise asked. 'I could not

bear to imagine my dear friend thrown out on the street penniless should anything happen to Alex.'

'It helps that you sympathise with Giselle's situation,' Sean said. 'I will need time to make a case to break the agreement and at the same time protect the interests of Frau Schumann. It will be like a war fought on two fronts. But for now, all I can say is thank you for your generous help protecting your sister-in-law. Be careful though. George is still your husband and I presume if he found out that you were helping me he might do something rash.'

'He cannot hurt me anymore,' Louise replied defiantly. 'But I fear for my son. I am afraid that he will find a way to take him from me. With that in mind, I have secretly employed the services of a legal firm.'

'Well, you also have my assistance if you need it,' Sean offered.

Louise nodded her thanks and rose to her feet. 'I must excuse myself. I have an appointment to attend the theatre tonight. I have been told it is very good show.'

'I understand,' Sean said, this time rising awkwardly behind his desk.

Louise was about to say that he should not bother considering his recent wounds but stopped herself. She could see the gritty determination behind the grey eyes and took Sean's hand lightly in her own. 'I hope that we have the chance to meet again in the future, under more pleasant circumstances,' she said with a warm smile, releasing Sean's hand.

'So do I,' Sean replied. When Louise had gone Sean called for the articled clerk.

'Yes, Major?' he asked.

'I want you to get me a ticket to the theatre for tonight's performance,' he said, taking some pound notes from his pocket and passing them to the boy. 'Bribe the ticket sellers if you have to.'

Sean opened the drawer of his desk to remove the bottle of whisky. He stared at it for a moment and then replaced it unopened back into his drawer, closing it. If nothing else he was getting his confidence back, and the company of a beautiful woman would be a welcome change from the monastic life he was living in his city apartment. That she was the wife of the powerful George Macintosh made the chase even sweeter, he thought, brooding on what lay ahead in both his social and legal worlds. Morality was also a casualty of war and Sean Duffy cared little for the judgments of others. After all, he had lost his legs so why not his moral scruples about courting a married woman?

15

Over the week Karolina had been placed under informal house arrest, the tension between mother and
daughter was inevitable. Karolina had reluctantly admitted
the circumstances of her arrest after the policeman had con-
veyed her to the house with instructions that she was not
to leave without his permission. For a week mother and
daughter avoided the situation until Giselle could no longer
control her exasperation.

'How could you do it?' she finally asked in her anguish.

Karolina continued with her sewing as they sat in the
drawing room of the Macintosh mansion. 'I was doing
my duty to my countrymen and the Kaiser,' she answered
simply.

Giselle stood up and paced the room. 'Your son-in-law
is an officer in his country's army, and all the time you have
been sending information to Germany that could endanger

his life. We are fortunate that your activities have been concealed by George or the revelation may have cost you your life – and shame on my husband's family name.'

Karolina glanced up from her sewing. 'Because of the actions of the Australians at the outbreak of the war by invading the Fatherland's territory in the Pacific your own father is dead. Have you even considered that?' she snapped. 'Or is your father's memory nothing to you?'

Giselle slumped into her chair. 'You know I loved Papa. But his death at native hands is not the fault of the Australians.'

'You can convince yourself but I was just doing my duty,' Karolina said, returning to her sewing. 'As it is, I am a virtual prisoner here and it seems that you and I will just have to learn to get on.'

Giselle stared at her mother sitting so serenely amid the storm of her own doing. How had it come to this? That her beloved mother should become so estranged from her? At least David was still too young to know of his grandmother's treachery, and Giselle prayed that Alex would never find out. The contract that she had signed depended on her husband returning from the war – otherwise she and her son could find themselves homeless. For a moment she had a fleeting image of Sean Duffy. The poor man bravely struggling to walk with the aid of a cane and the obvious pain in his eyes, not only because of the loss of his legs, but the terrible things he had witnessed. At least Giselle and her mother shared a common love of David. Karolina could not be a more doting grandmother. She would sit by her grandson's cradle at night and sing to him German lullabies until he drifted off to sleep.

'You do know that George Macintosh has corrupt policemen working for him,' Karolina said. Giselle strongly suspected that Alex's brother was a cold, ruthless man – but corrupt was something else. 'The policeman who came to arrest me must be working for George, considering the deal you made over the deeds to the house.'

Giselle pondered her mother's statement and had no reason to think that she might not be right. She had always felt something evil lurked in her brother-in-law's soul. How could two brothers be so different? But all she could do now was pray that her mother remained safe, and that her beloved husband returned to his family.

'Mrs Macintosh,' Angus said quietly from the open door to the drawing room. 'There are some policemen at the door demanding entry. They say that they have a warrant for the arrest of Mrs Schumann.'

Karolina stopped sewing, looking with fear towards the Scot.

Giselle rose. 'You must let them in, Mr MacDonald,' she said, ashen-faced, reaching out to grip her mother's outstretched hand.

Escorted by Angus, two uniformed policemen entered the room. Although they looked awkward in such palatial surroundings, without any preamble the first of the policemen, a sergeant, looked directly at Karolina. 'Are you Mrs Karolina Schumann?' he asked.

'I am,' Karolina answered.

'I have a warrant for your arrest under the enemy aliens act and have been instructed to take you from here to the internment camp at Holdsworthy.' He then turned to Giselle. 'Who are you?' he asked bluntly.

'I am Mrs Macintosh, and my husband is Major Alexander Macintosh, currently on active service,' she answered stiffly. 'You are arresting my mother and I protest at your intrusion.'

'You can arrange to have your mother's personal possessions delivered to the camp out at Liverpool,' he said. 'I apologise for intruding on your privacy but the warrant was issued this afternoon and all I am doing is my duty, Mrs.'

The police sergeant nodded to Karolina who rose from her chair. Giselle hugged her mother to her before she left and whispered in her ear, 'I will fight to have you returned home.'

Karolina pushed her away gently. 'My home is with my people,' she said sadly. 'It was inevitable.'

The sergeant took his prisoner by the elbow and gently escorted her from the room. Angus stood by, bristling at the invasion of his house. When Giselle glanced his way she could see that the tough Scot was ready to resist the police. She shook her head, warning him not to put himself in a position where he could be arrested for obstructing the police.

Sitting in an automobile a short distance away in the dark, Detective Inspector Jack Firth watched his men escort Karolina from the house. Satisfied the arrest had occurred, he only had to telephone Mr George Macintosh to confirm that Karolina Schumann was on her way to the internment camp outside Sydney. When the vehicle conveying her pulled out of the gravel driveway, he put his own car into gear and drove back to his office in the city, where he immediately put through a call to George at his home.

George Macintosh was alone in his library when the call was transferred to him. Satisfied that his plan had worked, he put down the receiver and slumped back in his big leather chair. Had Karolina Schumann fallen into the hands of the intelligence people, she might have spilled the fact that she passed on her smuggled papers to him for transmission to Sweden and it would not take the counterintelligence

239

officers much time to link him to a German spy. George shuddered. He had been named in the honours list for an imperial award and the scandal would have destroyed his scheme to rise to the top of his industry. He smirked. How easy it was to control one's destiny when one had the brains and instinct for survival. It helped that he had absolutely no conscience or moral scruples.

From down the hallway he could hear his infant son, Donald, crying to be fed and the reassuring footsteps of the nanny going to his nursery. George glanced at the big clock in his office. It was near midnight but there was no sign of his wife. For the past two weeks she had not returned home until the early hours of the morning and then had gone directly to her room. He was sure that she was seeing someone, and had considered that she was attempting to provoke him into a divorce, which he would never give her. She would remain as his dutiful wife to accompany him to the functions he must attend to retain his high profile among those who counted in politics and business. It had occurred to him that he might, one day, throw his hat in the ring for a position in federal politics; he knew he had what it took to run the country.

The baby had stopped crying and George pondered his son's future. He would ensure that Donald had every advantage so he would naturally take the reins from him one day. But there was also the matter of his brother's brat and under the terms of his father's will he had an equal claim to the family enterprises. That his damned brother should go and marry a Jewess and breed, he thundered to himself.

George rose from his leather chair and made his way to the door of the library. David and his mother were a problem he would deal with at some other time.

★

Processed in the early hours of the morning, Karolina found herself behind the barbed wire of the internment camp. When she was released to her quarters she was met by the Pastor von Fellmann.

'Oh, Karolina, it is so tragic to see that they have returned you to us,' he said. 'I did not think this day would happen again.'

'It is good to see you again, Karl,' Karolina said with a tearful face, thinking of the separation from her grandson. 'But I am satisfied being among our people.'

'Come,' Karl said, taking her by the elbow. 'I have made a pot of coffee and I am sure that after your ordeal you will welcome a strong brew.'

Gratefully, Karolina allowed herself to be guided to Karl's tent where he had made himself comfortable with a few items of home-made furniture. He sat her down in a rickety chair and poured her a mug of coffee, sweetened with sugar.

'The commandant is a good fellow and told me that you were to be expected this day,' Karl said, sitting opposite Karolina, nursing his battered tin mug in his hands. 'Herr Bosch has asked me to inform him of your return to us.'

'Herr Bosch,' Karolina said with a note of unease. 'When did he ask?'

'About an hour before I was able to welcome you,' Karl replied, sipping his coffee. 'It would be expected that your friends here would be glad to see you.'

Karolina blew gently on her coffee. She was exhausted from the ordeal of being transferred and processed into the camp but she was also aware that her internment might be construed as her failing in her mission to assist the espionage efforts of her government. Why she felt uneasy about meeting with Bosch was a mystery to her but a tiny seed of doubt was growing; she was now a person suspected of betraying their activities. She tried to shake off the rising paranoia, explaining to herself that she was wrought with fatigue.

She was aware that Karl had taken her hands in his. 'I am being selfish when I say that it is good to have you here,' he said softly. 'I found the camp empty whenever your short visits were over and you left to return to your daughter's home.'

Karolina looked down at his hands wrapped around her own. Tears welled in her eyes and she withdrew her hands to fumble for a handkerchief. Dabbing her eyes and bowing her head, she said softly, 'Oh, Karl, if you only knew what I had to do . . .' She trailed away, realising that by confiding in her friend of her espionage activities she would be drawing him into being a conspirator.

'Do you mean what you have done for the Fatherland?' Karl asked.

Karolina looked up sharply. 'You knew!' she gasped.

'I would have had to be the biggest fool not to know what transpired between you and Herr Bosch,' he said. 'I have always feared for your safety.'

'I revealed nothing to the Australians,' Karolina said. 'They asked – but I refused to name anyone.'

'I believe that you are the kind of woman Germany can be proud of,' Karl responded. 'But, if it meant your life I would prefer that you told all to the Australians.'

'It did not come to that,' Karolina said, shaking her head. 'They did not threaten me. For some reason I was allowed to remain with my daughter and grandson for a short time until last night when the police came for me. I do not understand what is happening. The policeman who initially arrested me let me go. I suspect that he is working for a Mr George Macintosh – brother-in-law to my daughter – and an evil man.'

Karl stood and walked to the flap in his tent to gaze out at the recently established little town within the wire going about its daily business. Some instinct told him that Karolina's life may be in jeopardy; there would be those in the camp who might consider her a traitor who would inform on them. He turned to gaze at her.

'I would like it if I visited you often,' he said. 'Just until you settle in.'

Karolina could see the concern in his tanned face. 'Thank you, Karl,' she said. 'That would be good.'

Suddenly Karl noticed Bosch standing with two men at the end of the street. They were staring intently in his direction, and the Lutheran pastor did not like the expressions he saw on their faces.

Second Lieutenant Jack Kelly, newly commissioned and returned from officer training in England, huddled against the cold. The field was bathed in the glow of German parachute flares drifting through the night sky to light up the snow in red and green shadows. It was April but the northern winter had not given up its white cloak.

'Bloody freeze the balls off a brass monkey,' his batman muttered beside him, eager to finish the recon mission and return to the relative safety of their lines. 'What's that village over there?' the private soldier asked, gazing westward to the dim silhouette of a church spire against the night sky.

'Bullecourt, I think,' Jack replied.

There had been so many alien names in the advance on the Hindenburg Line through France. Jack only remembered the little village's name because, as a platoon commander, he had ensured he was able to identify landmarks in the area of his platoon's operations. What he saw now worried him – a gradual rise leading into a re-entrant and a lot of open ground. From a tactical point of view it was a nightmare for infantry to cross; they would be exposed to artillery and small arms fire in the open.

He had also seen the name of the village on a big map at Brigade HQ when he had been summoned by the brigade commander. Mere second lieutenants did not usually find themselves in the company of brigadiers but this time Jack had been pleasantly surprised to recognise the face of Patrick Duffy in his newly appointed position.

Jack had waited outside the farm house, seconded by the army to use as its headquarters until he was ushered in to meet the brigade commander. Patrick stood in front of a large map with its crayon squiggles in blue and red marking positions and units – both friendly and enemy. Jack saluted and Patrick returned with a wave of his hand in the lazy manner of officers.

'Mr Kelly, I just wanted to personally congratulate you on your promotion and award of the DCM,' he said. Jack thanked his brigade commander although wondered why he would be summoned when it was normally the battalion CO who delivered the congratulations.

'I know that you are probably wondering why I have had you report to me,' Patrick said quietly, not wanting to be overheard by the soldiers and officers manning the HQ. 'You have truly earned your commission and I expect to see you acquit yourself well with your command,' he continued. 'But mostly I wanted to personally tell you that at Fromelles your actions warranted the award of the VC. It was my fault that you were not suitably recognised and I apologise for that.'

'Sir, I was only doing what I was trained for,' Jack countered quickly. It was unheard of for a brigadier to apologise to a lowly officer or soldier, but Jack admired this man for his honesty and the ability to recognise a mistake. Jack had not expected anything for silencing the German machine gun.

'You also were loyal to your superior officer at the time,' Patrick continued. 'I hope that your own men give you the same loyalty.'

'Yes, sir,' Jack responded. 'I was fortunate in getting a few old hands I soldiered with before the promotion.'

Patrick nodded. 'Well, Mr Kelly, good luck to you and your men.' He thrust out his hand to take Jack's. 'I think that the two best commands a soldier can have are a platoon and a battalion. Brigades are okay, but one becomes somewhat isolated from the camaraderie of the men around you. I will see you when I see you.'

As Jack stepped back a few curious looks were cast in his direction from more senior officers in the brigade HQ.

That had been two days ago, and now Jack crouched in the snow behind a stand of low brush, scanning the fields before him. Other than the German flares being a reminder they were within rifle shot of the enemy, the night was relatively peaceful; it was as if the war no longer existed. Jack instinctively touched the top pocket where he carried a fading photograph of his wife and son living back in Adelaide. His son had been born while he was overseas and now all he wanted to do was just survive to be able to hold his son in his arms. He would be two years old now, Jack thought, his mind wandering from his mission for a moment. The crack of a bullet passing overhead soon snapped him back to reality.

'Think it's time we went home,' Jack said to his batman, who was already on his belly wriggling rearward.

Two days later Jack led his platoon as part of the brigade attack on the German trenches. They were supposed to have the newly invented English tanks supporting them to crush the vicious barbed wire entanglements piled up in front of the German lines, but the tanks proved to be ineffective, either breaking down or being knocked out by artillery fire.

Jack found himself on his side hacking at the wire with his bayonet, attempting to cut through the resilient material. Along the stretch of wire frontage he could see that his men were using their bayonets or wire cutters to make a gap to rush through. All the time he could hear men screaming or grunting as machine-gun bullets ripped into their bodies as they were tangled in the barbed wire and exposed to the merciless fire from the enemy trenches. In the early hours after sunrise blood quickly turned the white snow red across the battlefield swept by snow flurries and a bitter cold. Even as an officer responsible for approximately thirty men of his command, Jack had little concern for the grand strategies and tactics of those in headquarters, plotting their battle far behind the trenches and out of immediate danger. The war that he and his men fought was on the ground they could see and against the enemy occupying that piece of the world. To survive meant defeating the enemy on that little patch of earth and, at the same time, staying alive. That the names of the places he fought would likely become the talking points of military historians in the years ahead was of no concern to him. He desperately wanted to finish this operation and go home to his family, and the same hope was shared by his men.

To one side he could see Lance Corporal Tom Duffy urging his section on. Jack guessed that the section commander, a corporal, was out of the fight and Tom had taken over. He was directing his Lewis gunner to put down suppressing fire on a group of Germans foolish enough to momentarily expose themselves about twenty yards away on the other side of the wire. Jack's batman, a private soldier slotted for a section commander's promotion, cursed and swore – then began to pray. Jack could feel the barbed wire tear at the back of his hands, cutting them in deep scratches. He joined his batman in the cursing – but not the prayers. Blood splashed Jack's face and he blinked. The batman had ceased praying and when Jack turned he could see that a bullet had hit him in the face. The dying man had not been able to scream; he stared at Jack with imploring eyes. Jack felt a surge of nausea at the sight of the hideously maimed soldier and struggled in his pack for a battlefield bandage for the horrific wound, but his batman jerked as another bullet took him through the tin helmet, closing his eyes forever.

As Jack looked away he had a sneaking suspicion that a marksman had targeted his section of the wire. Although Jack was an officer he preferred to arm himself with a rifle instead of relying on the pistol issued to officers. Not only did it make him less conspicuous but it was a better weapon in hand-to-hand combat.

In the overwhelming din of the battle, Jack could see Tom Duffy on the other side of the wire. His section had been able to cut through and Tom rose into a crouching position to rush forward with his bayoneted rifle extended, all the time screaming unintelligible words. Jack watched him safely sprint through a hail of bullets as if protected by some god of war. His dash had taken the German defenders on Jack's small front by surprise, and now Jack took advantage of the success.

'C'mon boys!' he yelled at the top of his voice, rising from the snow. 'Up and into 'em!'

What was left of his platoon followed him through the small gap Tom had opened and they tumbled into the trench where Jack could see the lance corporal fighting for his life against the German troops massed to resist the attack. It was vicious fighting where no quarter was asked, and none given by either side. Fighting with sharpened entrenching shovels used like medieval axes, knives, bayonets, knuckledusters and their hands, soldiers of either side screamed, yelled or died with a grunt of surprise. The Australians were masters of bayonet fighting and soon forced back the German defenders, clearing their stretch of trench. In retaliation the Germans retreated to shower them with the distinctive stick grenades. Men went down but Jack could see that along his section of the assault they were slowly winning, so long as their breach was reinforced by others in the company. In a very brief respite, the bodies of friend and foe were piled to provide a barricade in the narrow, deep trench. Jack knew the enemy would inevitably mount a counterattack and also knew that his platoon would not be able to hold the ground they had captured without company support.

'Private Gould,' he said, snatching one of his soldiers by the shirt. 'Get back to the OC and tell him we have broken through. Tell him that the platoon needs support.'

The soldier stared at his commander and Jack could see that he was in shock. He shook him and repeated the message. The soldier nodded, then scrambled over the parapet and the edge of the trench to make the dangerous journey to the position in the assault he knew was company HQ. Under intense fire he was able to find the company commander surrounded by a group of soldiers pinned down by small arms fire. They were at the edge of the barbed wire and had not broken through.

'Sir, Mr Kelly sent me to tell you that we have breached

the wire about fifty yards to the right. He says he needs the company to bring up more ammo and men to stop the Huns.'

The company commander was visibly shaking and seemed to ignore everything around him so the runner repeated his message.

'What?' the company commander snapped. 'We are going to fall back,' he yelled. 'Not possible to get through.'

'Mr Kelly is in the Hun trenches,' the soldier reiterated. 'If we get reinforcements we can move onto the next objective.' The soldier from Jack's platoon could clearly see that his company commander had lost it but this did not surprise him. He was hated by one and all in the company for his officious manner and incompetence.

'Tell Mr Kelly that he is to withdraw his platoon and provide covering fire for the company's withdrawal.'

'But . . .'

'But nothing, Private,' Major Hartford yelled hysterically. 'Just tell Mr Kelly to obey my orders.'

The runner turned and in a crouching sprint was able to cover the fifty yard distance to the break in the wire. He dropped to the wooden duckboard floor of the trench.

'Major Hartford says we are to pull back,' he gasped, attempting to suck air into his lungs. 'He says that we are to provide covering fire for the company's withdrawal.'

'You told him that we had made the breakthrough?' Jack questioned with a frown.

'I told him, boss,' the runner answered.

'Damn the bastard to hell!' Jack exploded. He was about to declare the company commander a yellow gutless dingo when he remembered he was now an officer and such things could not be said in front of the men who were now looking to him for leadership.

Snow whipped his face and blood was rapidly clotting

on the wounded. Jack looked wearily up and down the stretch of trench they had captured. He could stay and fight or relinquish what had cost him so many of his men's lives to win. His platoon objective was the next line of German trenches but without the company in support they would all be slaughtered. Prisoners had been taken and he had his own wounded to consider. He could see the expressions on his men's faces. They looked as if their souls had long left their bodies and they had gone to hell. The whole bloody show had been a fiasco, he thought. Just another waste of good lives to achieve nothing.

'Pass the word that we are pulling back,' Jack said wearily. 'We are to move by sections.'

'Hardly enough of us to make up a section, boss,' Lance Corporal Duffy said. 'What do we do with the Huns?'

Jack stared at the five Germans sitting in the trench in their heavy, grey greatcoats. 'It is your lucky day,' he said to them in fluent German, surprising the prisoners. 'I am going to let you live, but if you attempt to recover arms and fire on us as we are leaving, I will personally come back and cut your testicles out.'

A senior NCO among the German prisoners grinned weakly at Jack. 'I have not yet fathered children, Lieutenant,' he said. 'We will respect your orders.'

'What did he say?' Tom asked Jack.

'He said he wants to bear your children,' Jack replied, leaving Tom puzzled at the joke.

Within minutes, those wounded able to walk made ready and the couple of soldiers unable to move without help were provided with mates to carry them. The withdrawal went off well back to company HQ, where Jack saw Major Hartford arguing with a soldier Jack guessed was a runner from battalion HQ.

'What is it, sir?' Jack asked his commander.

'The bloody fool has sent a message up from the CO that we are to advance to the second line of Hun trenches, but you can see that it is impossible. It seems we are now down to around one third strength.'

Jack knew absolute fear when he saw it, and he could see it in his commander's eyes as he stumbled over his words, crouching low in an almost foetal position.

'Maybe you should hold here with a couple of men to act as a link with BHQ,' Jack said, barely able to restrain his contempt for the man who was supposed to provide leadership. 'I can push on with the rest of the company and send back a runner to keep you up to date with our progress.'

For a moment Major Hartford stared with unseeing eyes at his platoon commander, but slowly comprehended the suggestion.

'A good idea, Mr Kelly,' he finally replied. 'You take the men forward.'

Jack rallied the survivors fit enough to continue the assault. He chose to return to the trench he had abandoned and wondered at the reception he would receive from the German soldiers they had left behind. Warily, the men went over the top but found the trench deserted, only the dead and dying having been left behind.

'Lance Corporal Duffy,' he called.

'Yes, boss,' Tom replied.

'You are now my acting CSM,' Jack said with a grin. 'But don't expect to draw a sar'nt major's pay.'

'Yes, boss,' Tom replied with a serious expression. 'I will do my best.'

Jack issued brief orders to his men, redistributed grenades and ammunition from the dead and wounded, and they clambered over the rear of the German trench to advance into hell. It was around 7am and Jack wondered why he was not seeing supporting artillery falling on the German lines, but he was not privy to the decisions being made in a confused situation well back from the edge of the battle. German fire continued to pour into the Australian ranks and, in his concern for the few men he had left, Jack had long forgotten his fear of dying. When the bullet or shard of shrapnel found him his worries would be over, Jack accepted with the soldier's sense of fatalism. To the men that he led it seemed that their commander had ice in his veins. They were supposed to think that, despite the fact Jack Kelly, former gold prospector born in South Australia and who worked in the tropical jungles and mountains of exotic Papua and New Guinea, was barely in control of his fear.

'Boss!' Tom called. 'They're coming!'

Jack's attention was drawn to a grey line of German infantry slowly, and some what reluctantly, advancing across the snow towards his outnumbered company.

'Back into the trenches!' he yelled.

He took his men in a sprint back to the trench they had vacated, dropping down on the bodies of those they killed earlier. He knew that the Germans would counterattack and also knew that he was short on men and ammunition. Jack scrambled to a makeshift parapet to observe the advancing force of grim-faced soldiers wearing the distinctive coal scuttle tin helmets. His job now was to coordinate his thinly stretched defence. His men were firing into the advancing ranks with rifles and Lewis guns, attempting to keep the Germans out of grenade range. Jack moved along the line with encouraging words and, when he was standing behind Tom Duffy calmly firing his Lee Enfield, Jack noticed that with each shot, Tom dropped an advancing enemy soldier.

Jack admired the young man's deadly accuracy. Jack's two Lewis guns were firing a lethal enfilading cone of death into the German ranks and a couple of enterprising soldiers had heaved a German Maxim gun into position to rake the advancing troops. It was a murderous fire and he could see the advancing ranks falter under its effects. If they were close enough he would order the use of hand grenades, and if those failed it would come down to fixed bayonets and hand-to-hand fighting. Instinctively, Jack touched the photograph of his son and wife in his top pocket.

The German line ceased its advance and turned to withdraw. No-one cheered. The men simply stared into nothing, trying to light cigarettes with hands that trembled so badly the task was impossible. Even Jack dared not attempt to plug his pipe lest he betray his fear with his own shaking hands. He knew from experience this was just the beginning of a battle that before it was over would take the lives of so many good, young Australians.

16

It was cold at the edge of the Sinai desert. Captain Matthew Duffy stood at the entrance to his tent, holding a mug of hot tea. He stared at the activity on the airfield with the frustration of being grounded. When he had attempted to explain his mission over the Arab village to his CO he had received a hostile reception.

'I am afraid that I would like to believe you,' his CO had replied. 'But until I receive evidence confirming that your mission was authorised by London, as you say, then I have no choice but to ground you. I must also caution you that you are to remain within the lines. You are free to join in the mess but say nothing of why you were late returning to the squadron. That's all, Captain Duffy.'

Two weeks later the words still echoed as he watched his comrades take off and land on the dirt strip while all he could do was write letters, take his time as duty officer, and drink mugs of tea and coffee. Matthew's ground crew were a little more sympathetic. They had a close bond with their flyer and knew that it was not just the grounding that had caused him to look so depressed; it had to be something more.

They were right. Matthew could hardly sleep, wondering about Joanne's fate in Jerusalem and frustrated that he seemed impotent to do anything to ascertain her whereabouts. Asking for leave was out of the question, as was setting off across the desert to make his way to the ancient city now occupied by the Turkish army. He was about to return to his tent to complete a letter to his mother when his eye caught a tall figure wearing the distinctive dress of a light horseman striding towards his tent. Matthew blinked, wondering if he was suffering some kind of hallucination.

'God almighty!' he roared, dropping his enamel mug and rushing forward. 'Bloody hell!' he said, coming to a stop in front of Trooper Randolph Gates, whose slow grin spread from ear to ear. Grasping each other's hand, they stood staring for a moment.

'Good to see you are still alive,' Randolph said. 'How have you been?'

'What in hell are you doing impersonating an Australian soldier?' Matthew asked, punching Randolph in the shoulder.

'It's a long story. I don't suppose you flyer types have a stock of half-drinkable coffee for a Yank masquerading as a Canadian by any chance? If you do, I will tell you everything.'

Matthew led the American back to his tent where he dug into his private supply of precious food items including the jar of coffee sent by his mother and some biscuits made of treacle and oatmeal. He pulled up his one and only folding chair for Randolph, and sat on his camp stretcher while Randolph cradled the jar of coffee he had just been given as a gift and drank the tea Matthew had one of his passing ground crew fetch from the mess. Over the mug of tea, Randolph filled Matthew in on his life from the USA to his present posting as a member of the Australian Light Horse. He explained how he had to leave Australia one step ahead of the law and had wrangled a position with the Light Horse in Egypt when he was able to prove his ability to ride, shoot and handle horses.

'I asked around and found someone who thought you might be here. My squadron commander is a pretty good bloke and gave me leave to visit as we are only a couple of miles away.' Randolph said. 'I also heard that you were in a bit of trouble.'

Matthew stood and stretched his legs in the small confines of his tent. A cold, bitter wind howled outside, flapping the canvas with the crack of a gunshot. He pondered telling his oldest friend the truth and decided that they had shared sensitive secrets before. Matthew related the events that had taken place at Saul's settlement and his love of the American woman.

'So, the gay bachelor has finally met his match,' Randolph said with a smile.

'How about you?' Matthew countered, and saw the smile disappear.

'Not since Nellie,' Randolph replied in a pained voice, and Matthew knew not to ask any further. 'My philosophy is that it is best to avoid any permanent relationships until this god–damned war is over. What are you going to do about finding Miss Barrington?'

Matthew gazed out through a slit in the entrance to his tent. 'We are so bloody close to Jerusalem,' he said. 'If only I could fly there and search for her.'

'I heard some scuttlebutt that we might be the first into the city,' Randolph said. 'The Turks are on the ropes and falling back.'

'I hope that you are right,' Matthew said, still staring out through the small space of the flap. They had been deep in conversation for a long time. The sun was already making its way to the western horizon. Randolph also could see that it was time to return to his unit and shook hands with Matthew, promising to return if his squadron was still in the area. The light horseman was hardly gone when a corporal from the orderly room poked his head through the flap.

'Sir, the CO would like to see you at HQ immediately.'

Matthew thanked the clerk and tidied himself for the meeting. It had to be important to be summoned, and it was with some trepidation that he made his way in the gloom of the coming night to the kerosene-lit tent of the CO, who gestured for him to step inside. The tent was large enough to accommodate the tables and chairs for the administration of the flight, and its sides were covered in maps and clipboards with signals and operational orders.

'You wished to see me, sir,' Matthew said, giving his CO one of his best salutes.

The Commanding Officer rose from his chair and returned the salute.

'Well, Captain Duffy, it appears your story was true,' he said in a friendly voice. Matthew felt a huge weight fall from his shoulders. He had feared a court martial and then being sent home in disgrace. 'I have just had a signal delivered from Cairo stating that you had been temporarily detached to carry out a top secret mission authorised by the War Office in London. Needless to say it says little else but it has been signed by Mr Winston Churchill. I only wish the bloody English government had the courtesy to inform me that they would be using your services – just damned good manners to do so.'

'In defence of the War Office, sir, it was a bit of an impromptu show and if I may ask, sir, how did the War Office know of the mission?'

The aristocratic-looking Australian pilot commander stared at his subordinate officer. 'How the devil would I know, Captain Duffy?' he replied sarcastically. 'I am just a mere colonel.'

'Sorry, sir,' Matthew answered dutifully. But he experienced a surge of hope. Joanne had not cleared the mission with London before he had been involved, and for London to know of it being carried out they would have had to have heard from their agent after she had left for Jerusalem with Saul's son. It was not much, but at least it was a small hope that she was alive.

'As you can deduce, Captain Duffy, you are returned to flying duties, active as from now and no longer confined to the lines,' the CO said. 'I don't know all that occurred on your mission as you have rightly kept mum, but I suspect the bloody British will probably give you a gong from the way they praised your cooperation. In the meantime, I would like to say that I am pleased to have one of my best and most experienced pilots back on full duty.'

'Thank you, sir,' Matthew answered with real feeling of gratitude.

'There is nothing else for now so join your brother officers in the mess and ensure that you are fit to fly tomorrow,' the CO said, resuming his chair behind his wooden table piled with paperwork. 'We are going to be busy supporting the Light Horse in their advance so pass the word on that all my pilots are to be at an O group oh four hundred sharp.'

'I will, sir,' Matthew said, snapping a salute and turning on his heel.

He marched out of the HQ tent into the night of sleeting, cold rain that had crossed the airfield. At least now the chains had been taken off he felt that he was in a position to being one step closer to Joanne – wherever she was. He remembered an expression Saul used. It was almost two thousand years old: *next year, Jerusalem.* Matthew prayed that he would soon reach the city of three faiths.

Major Alexander Macintosh had stared out the window of his carriage at the bleak, snow-covered fields on his railway journey to a small French village behind the Allied lines. From there he was taken by a motor truck to divisional headquarters to meet his father. It had been well over two years since he had last shaken Patrick's hand, when he embarked for Egypt, and then onto the shores of Gallipoli. At the time Alex had bridled at not being posted with his father on active service, but now all that was in the past.

The truck delivered him to an old chateau that had seen better days. Uniformed soldiers in clean dress stood guard and passes were carefully checked before entry was allowed into the building where tactics were being planned for troops miles away in the snowy fields of France and Flanders. He knew the soldiers hated the bitter cold for more than itself; artillery shells were designed to explode upon impact with the frozen earth. In the mud many were buried before exploding, mitigating the effectiveness of shrapnel to spread and tear men apart. But in winter the soldiers cowering in trenches experienced the full effects of a shell releasing its lethal shrapnel balls or fragmented casing.

At a clearing station nearby rows of wounded men were

lying outside the makeshift surgery. Alex noticed a medical orderly dumping severed arms and legs into a pile awaiting burial. He shuddered. It was his first sight of what lay ahead in a war where technology had developed to make the most of killing or maiming.

'You can wait here, sir,' an immaculately dressed NCO told Alex. Soldiers and officers moved smartly about inside the once grand house as well as outside in the gardens now going to ruin from lack of attention. 'Brigadier Duffy is currently in a meeting with the divvie commander.'

Alex took a seat in the foyer but was forced to stand many times, saluting the high-ranking officers passing him by with important expressions on their cleanly shaved faces, although they hardly gave the Australian major a second glance. After a half-hour wait Alex was overjoyed to see his father stroll into the foyer, alongside a colonel whose some-what less-than-looked-after uniform denoted him as a field commander. Alex stood up, saluted and waited. His father's expression bespoke his love and pride.

'Colonel, if you will excuse me for a moment,' Patrick said, not taking his eyes from Alex. 'My son has just arrived.'

The colonel nodded and walked away. Patrick so badly wanted to crush his son to him but he was well aware that military protocol did not condone such behaviour between a brigadier and major. Instead, he extended his hand and gripped Alex's with as much force as he could.

'It is good to see you,' he said, barely able to keep the tears from his eyes. 'How is Giselle and my grandson?'

'They are well, Father,' Alex answered quietly. 'It is good to see you.'

'We do not have much time as I have to return to the brigade,' Patrick said, reluctantly releasing his grip on his son's hand. 'I have organised a posting for you to one of the companies in the best battalion I have. It seems that a vacancy has arisen with one of the company commanders being sent home, a Major Hartford. Apparently a victim of shell shock, I have been informed.'

Alex was startled by the news that he was stepping into the boots of a man who had commanded nearly a hundred men but had succumbed to breakdown under fire. He thought only soldiers suffered shell shock – an officer had a duty to set an example – and realised that he had a lot to learn about combat. 'Thank you, Father,' he replied. 'You do not know how much the posting means to me.'

'Be careful what you wish for, Alex,' Patrick cautioned as they walked towards the main entrance. 'I know that you are a fine officer but you have to experience what those poor, bloody men are suffering out there before you know just how much you can take before you lose your mind.'

It was a sobering sermon and Alex knew his father was concerned for him. 'I am sure that the brigade commander is a damned good soldier and will see to it that we stay safe,' Alex replied with a mischievous smile.

'Your old man will be looking forward to hanging the sword over the mantelpiece after we go home,' Patrick sighed. 'This is definitely my last campaign.'

'Well, you have me and, in time, little David to carry on the family tradition,' Alex said when they stepped outside where a car and driver awaited Patrick.

'I pray that this war will be the last we ever have,' Patrick said, taking the salute from the driver holding the door open on the former French taxi. 'You can ride with me back to Brigade HQ before continuing to your new home in the battalion.'

Alex stepped into the back seat beside his father. It was strange. All his father talked about was the grandson he had yet to hold in his arms. He did not mention George or his other grandson at all; it was as if they did not exist. Never before had Alex felt as close to his father, even when they lapsed into silence. They drove along a road clogged with horse-drawn wagons, artillery pieces and files of men with rifles shouldered, trudging in lines towards what Alex ascertained was not thunder but the sound of the big guns booming out across battlefields. So this was it, he thought. Real war.

'We have arrived,' Patrick said, breaking the silence.

Alex alighted from the car to a strange odour on the chill evening air. It was a mix of cordite and blood.

The man kept to the shadows as he trailed his target. It was a busy Saturday night in the city and the war was a long way from the bright lights of the swank hotels catering to the needs of wealthy patrons. Louise Macintosh was easy to keep in sight as she was unaware that she was being tracked.

George had first attempted to dismiss the idea that his wife was having an affair. He had his women whenever he desired and now she had provided him with his heir. But his male ego began to speak to him and it was time to discover who she was meeting.

The private investigator made his way across the street busy with automobiles and horse-drawn wagons until he reached the footpath where Louise stood as if waiting to meet someone. The investigator leaned against the front of a sandstone building with his hands in his pockets, appearing to be just another larrikin on a night out. Before long a man using a walking stick and striding stiffly made his way to Louise. The investigator could not help but let out a soft whistle. He did not need to attempt to identify the mystery man as he already knew him from appearing to give evidence in the courts of law. He was the solicitor Sean Duffy, and the last the private investigator knew of him was that he had been wounded overseas and decorated for his courage.

The private investigator made his way back to his office to write his report on what had to be one of the easiest cases he had ever taken on. As he sauntered away he glanced over his shoulder to see the pair disappear into the hotel. No doubt the food was good there, he thought, and so were the beds.

The following day he delivered his report to George at his office.

'Do you want me to follow up with pictures of them together in what one might term a delicate situation, Mr Macintosh?' He could see that his client had paled at the mention of Sean Duffy's name.

'No . . . no need, at this time,' George replied. 'Just the identification of my wife's lover is all I require.'

'Well, if that is all I will only bill you for two days' work.'

George Macintosh appeared to be in a state of shock, the investigator thought. But it was an expression he had long come to recognise from cuckolded husbands when they were told the identity of their wife's lover. He left the office wondering what the esteemed businessman would do. From what he had heard on the streets from the shady people he mixed with, it appeared you did not cross Mr Macintosh, who had friends in many places – including the police. But that was not his concern. For now he had no reason to doubt that George Macintosh would pay the bill when it was tendered for his services.

★

The first battle of Bullecourt had been a terrible blunder and everyone knew it. The tanks had failed in supporting the infantry, the artillery did not provide the covering fire so badly needed, and the infantry were bled dry on the bleak battlefield. When he returned to his lines Lieutenant Jack Kelly realised that he was one of the few officers not to be killed or wounded. He was met by a replacement for Major Hartford who had been rumoured to have fled back to safety, shaking and rambling incoherently about God punishing him for his transgressions with choir boys. At the time Jack had been leading the remainder of the company to occupy and eventually withdraw from the trenches they had captured. In the meantime the battalion CO quickly bundled Hartford off and had already accepted his replacement from the reinforcements arriving from England.

Major Alexander Macintosh would now command the company and he made a point of gathering all surviving officers together at a copse of trees behind the lines. Jack sat back on the cold, wet fir needles.

'Gentlemen,' Alex started, standing, as his three acting platoon commanders remained sitting in a rough semicircle. 'I appreciate that we have taken a terrible toll over the last few days and I suspect that things aren't going to get any better. I am new to the battalion but have a policy of allowing my commanders to organise their platoons as they see fit. Mr Kelly,' Alex said, turning to Jack, 'I am appointing you company 2IC and you will nominate your replacement until we are able to get reinforcements to fill out our complement of officers and NCOs.'

Jack nodded; he had a man in mind who could take command until a replacement arrived.

'If there are no questions you are dismissed to return

to your platoons. We will meet back here for a briefing at nineteen hundred hours.'

The three platoon commanders rose to their feet, none saluting lest there be a German sniper in the area. Jack returned to the remnants of his platoon resting amid another copse of trees where they had erected improvised shelters from ground sheets. Tom Duffy sat alone, cross-legged, cleaning his rifle with great care while his comrades sipped tea or simply rested with their heads on their tin helmets.

'Duffy,' Jack said, causing Tom to glance up. 'How would you like to be a marksman?'

Tom slipped the well-oiled bolt back into the rifle. 'You mean work alone?' he replied. 'I don't mind.'

'Good,' Jack said. 'I am being pushed up to company HQ as 2IC so I will make sure you are looked after.'

'Thanks, boss,' Tom said and returned to cleaning his rifle.

Jack gazed around at the survivors and wondered if they could take another battle. They were all volunteers and might not have been so keen to fight for King and country if they had known when they enlisted what they did now on the front.

Tom lay out in no-man's-land among the dead of both sides. He had been given his orders and passed through the sentry point in the deep of the night to slither forward until he could find a spread of dead soldiers. He would lie very still whenever a star shell burst in the night sky, temporarily illuminating the ground between the lines. Settling himself among the stiff corpses, he set himself up with a fully charged clip and waited for the dawn. At this time of day men were at their least aware, shaking off the little sleep they got. Tom knew instinctively that camouflaging himself was the trick to surviving, rather than simply being the crack shot that he had proved himself to be. He was aware that there was a marksman on the Western Front by the name of Billy Sing who was already celebrated in the English press as 'the assassin'. But to the enemy, the Australian sniper was known as the murderer. Tom accepted that he would never match Billy Sing's incredible record of hundreds of men shot dead since Gallipoli, but in his new assignment with his company he would make it very uncomfortable for the enemy.

The sun rose over a bleak, flat land of snow-covered mounds that were once living men. The snow had also settled on Tom's back, making his night miserable. He gently squeezed his cold-stiffened hands to regain circulation. Satisfied that he was prepared, he quietly slipped the safety catch and scanned the line of German trenches a hundred yards away. Very slowly, he set his rear sight to 100 yards and then patiently watched the trench line. For an hour he saw nothing. Then a head appeared. The man was holding binoculars, staring out at no-man's-land. He had to be an officer, Tom thought, when he noticed he was wearing a cap rather than a tin helmet. Tom's target was cautious, keeping as low as possible while carrying out his observation. Tom dared not breathe as the man's gaze passed over the pile of bodies he lay among.

Satisfied that the German officer had been fooled by his camouflage, Tom very slowly levelled the foresight on the man's head and took a deep breath, exhaling naturally and increasing pressure on the trigger at the same time. The rifle cracked and Tom saw the man's head jerk back violently as he disappeared behind the earthen works. Tom did not feel any emotion at his first kill as the company marksman.

When the sound of the shot rolled away, Tom resumed his pose as a corpse among corpses, praying that he had not been detected. His ruse worked as he heard a machine gun open up, spraying a slight rise to his left. It had been too obvious a place for a sniper to make his post, as Tom knew.

Now the German machine-gun post had revealed itself Tom knew his next target. The Maxim had to have a slit to fire through. The former stockman from Queensland cautiously let his eyes slide along the trench line until he found the tiny opening in a section of sandbags. He knew that the machine gun must be manned at all times and very slowly moved the barrel of his rifle until it was pointed at the slit. Then he waited, not taking his eyes from the tiny aperture until he could just focus the merest portion of flesh. Part of a man's face. Tom fired again and the white disappeared. It took a few minutes for the machine gun to open fire again, spraying the area with bullets, some passing very close to Tom and thudding into the already dead men around him. It was obvious that the gunners were extremely wary of manning their weapon from the way they fired, intent on killing the marksman who was taking their comrades with deadly stealth.

Tom fired again and was rewarded with the gun falling into silence as the dead gunner's fingers fell away from the trigger. Three men in three hours. Before the sun went down on no-man's-land, Tom Duffy had accounted for nine men. With the dark it was time to slither back to his lines where a hot cocoa awaited him.

'How many?' Jack Kelly asked as he stood by Tom in the deep trench.

'Nine,' Tom answered. 'Including a Hun officer.'

'You can't take up the same position tomorrow,' Jack said. 'The Hun will be smart enough to see that one of the dead has miraculously got up and left the battlefield.'

'I know,' Tom replied, cradling his mug in his gloved hands to warm them. 'But I couldn't see any other possie out there.'

'I think I have a position for you,' Jack said. 'I had a good look today. We will move you down the line, away from this part of the front. Hopefully your reputation there is not known among the Hun.'

Reputation, Tom thought. He had already established himself as an unseen killer on this section of the front. He had not thought of himself developing a reputation as a hunter and killer of men. Nor did he think of the men he had shot as people but rather as targets. He knew he would never allow himself to consider the full reality of what he was doing. That was the way of war.

That night, Lance Corporal Tom Duffy curled up in a corner of the trench and slept soundly. At least his duties as the company marksman got him out of sentry duty. He knew that he was bloody good at what he did but still he did experience an unusual dream that night as he lay curled in the alcove carved out of the side of the trench, wrapped in a pile of mud-stiffened blankets. He was a young Aboriginal warrior, crouching in the scrub near a creek. There were women and children screaming, as a troop of blue-uniformed Aboriginal men rode down the helpless community of Darambal people. He had a spear gripped in his hands and knew what he must do to defend his clan. *It is time to take back the land*, a voice said.

The dream forced Tom awake. Not so much a dream but a nightmare, he thought, as he lay in the shadow of a star shell fired into the sky. Lying on his back, Tom tried to make sense of what he had dreamed. He could have sworn that he had gone back in time and seen something terrible, but recalled the stories his father had told him and knew it must have only been a bad dream.

'Wallarie,' Tom whispered. 'You were the warrior by the creek.'

But what did the dream mean? How could he take back the lands that Wallarie had once hunted in the days when his people lived in harmony with the brigalow scrub of the semi-arid plains? He was on the other side of the world and did not expect to survive. But while his white blood inferred that he was only having a nightmare, something in his black blood told him that what the Aboriginal warrior had said in the cave before he enlisted was coming to fruition on the snow-covered fields of France and Belgium.

17

Karolina Schumann sensed the hostility towards her as she went about the monotonous routine of life behind barbed wire. Only Pastor Karl von Fellmann offered a warm smile when he greeted her. Herr Bosch was cool in his greetings and Karolina had heard the rumours that she had betrayed the patriots in the camp to the Australian authorities, and that she was now collaborating with them as a spy for the Allied cause. She had, however, remained friends with the cobbler whose tiny store was piled with shoes to be mended. He was a Jewish man in his late eighties, stooped from the years of his work bending over his awl. Karolina would sit with him as he worked, sharing the precious supply of coffee brought in by her daughter.

'You should be careful, Mrs Schumann,' the little cobbler said, tapping in a row of tiny tacks to the edge of a well-worn shoe. 'There are people I hear say that you are a traitor.'

'I know,' Karolina sighed, staring out across the dusty road between the ramshackle shops that had cropped up within the camp. 'It is not true.'

The cobbler took another tack from between his lips and tapped it into the leather. He had the ability to carry on a conversation with a row of tacks between his teeth. 'It does not matter to them,' he said. 'Just be careful.'

'I have the friendship of the Christian pastor,' Karolina replied. 'He is a good man who ensures that I am left alone.'

'I think that the pastor is in love with you,' the cobbler chuckled, using the last of his supply of tacks to mend the shoe.

Karolina looked at the little man who now sat up straight on his stool, his hunched back prominent. That Karl had any romantic feelings towards her had not occurred to her.

'Do you think so?' she asked, looking over the rim of her chipped enamel mug. 'He is a Christian minister, and I am a Jew.'

'I have been on this earth for many years and I have found that love can be a stronger emotion than religious conviction,' the cobbler said, stretching his weary limbs.

Karolina wondered at his perceptiveness. She had in fact found Karl attractive in his own way. He was respected by the people in the camp, as well as by the enemy guarding them. He had a moral strength she admired and was rather handsome, although he appeared to be a man who would turn the other cheek rather than stand up to any act of violence. She had not thought about Karl as a lover – until now. Finishing her coffee, she bid the cobbler goodbye.

Karolina unfurled a battered parasol to walk along the street towards her quarters. She passed Bosch, who was sitting at a chessboard playing a game with a stocky, scarred man. She knew the man to be a sailor taken from a captured

German merchant ship and imprisoned in the camp. It was rumoured that he was violent and Karolina shuddered as she passed them as the brutish, former seaman appeared to be friendly with Bosch. He glanced up at her and in his eyes she could see something that made her afraid. Karolina hurried on, and decided to visit Karl – if for nothing else the assurance that she had a protector in the camp.

She found him poring over a pile of paperwork in his tent. So engrossed was he in his work, he did not seem to be aware of her standing in the entrance. He had his coat off and wore only a shirt and tattered trousers with braces. Karolina noticed that his trousers had a long tear down the leg.

'I could repair your trousers,' she said by way of greeting. He looked up at her smiling face. 'I am a good seamstress. It is something that I was able to master, while living on our plantation in New Guinea.'

'I would be very grateful,' Karl replied. 'I have little time for such things and I am afraid I must look rather shabby to my congregation.'

Karolina stepped inside and found herself noticing the broadness of the pastor's shoulders, his slimness of waist and fine features. He was very Germanic with his blonde hair and blue eyes and the cobbler's comment had sparked mixed thoughts about the man standing before her.

'Please, have a seat,' Karl said, pulling out a chair he had made from scrap timber. It was sturdy and had the touch of elegance one would associate with a qualified cabinet maker.

Karolina sat down, furling her parasol. A sheen of perspiration glistened on the smooth skin of her cheeks. Age had been good to Karolina, despite the fact that she had lived most of her life in the tropics.

'I presume that you crafted this chair,' Karolina said, causing Karl to look slightly alarmed.

'Is something wrong with it?' he asked.

'Oh, no!' Karolina exclaimed reassuringly. 'I was actually admiring your versatility. You excel at many things.'

Karl resumed his chair and stared through the entrance to his tent. 'When I was ministering to my flock at Glen View station I was forced to learn how to survive in this land that can be so harsh,' he sighed. 'One learned to be everything from doctor for the poor Aboriginal people, to negotiator with the Europeans who owned their lands. Carpentry was an essential skill for a missionary.'

'Did your wife like the missionary way of life?' Karolina asked boldly.

For a moment, Karl did not reply, as if considering his dead wife's feelings. 'She was a good wife, but I think that she yearned to return to the life we once knew in Prussia. She did not complain, however, and her passing is still something of great sadness to me. I feel that I let her down by remaining among my people and not heeding her feelings.'

'Your wife must have loved you to remain with you.'

'I suppose she did,' Karl answered softly, remembering the beautiful sunsets and sunrises in central Queensland. 'But God has taken her to his bosom for her selfless work among our people.'

Karolina could see the pain in his eyes as he remembered the past. 'You knew that I spied for the Fatherland,' she said softly.

Karl turned his attention to her. 'Yes, I knew,' he said. 'But I am a man of God and do not concern myself with the issues of whose side God is on in this terrible war. He is taking so many good men from both sides. But I do know that I have always loved you.'

Surprised, Karolina rose from her chair and moved towards him. She could see tears in his eyes and was not certain if they were for his declaration of love to her or the memory of his dead wife. 'Karl, I have feelings for you but I do not know what the future has planned for me. I cannot bring myself to tell you of what I have had to do for the sake of the Fatherland.'

'I think I know, and I do not care,' Karl said, reaching up to take her hand. 'What you did was motivated by your need to serve your country, but this country is where I will die. People may not be able to choose where they are born but they can choose where they eventually die. For me, I have fallen in love with the vastness of this country's far places, where one can reach up and touch the face of God when the night sky reveals the beauty of the universe. I would not expect any woman to ever share that loneliness again.'

'Karl, I . . .'

The pastor cut her short with his finger to her lips. 'You do not have to tell me,' he said sadly. 'I am a fool to think that a woman of your great beauty and position would even consider a life with a poor missionary.'

'We both share this life behind the barbed wire,' Karolina replied with a bitter smile. 'There is no social line drawn in the sand here.'

'When this war is over I will return to my outpost at the Glen View station to be with my old friend, Wallarie,' Karl said. 'I will always hold you in my heart to the day I become part of the night sky as Wallarie has promised is my fate. There, he tells me, we will wander with friends hunting the kangaroo which will be in abundance, and we'll never know starvation or pain again.'

Karolina felt her tears running down her face and

wondered if they were for herself or this man sitting before her. She pulled away gently. 'I should be going now,' she said, wiping the tears from her face with a small handkerchief. 'People have enough to gossip about and any rumours that you have feelings for a Jew might ruin your reputation.'

'I don't particularly care what people think,' Karl said. 'My love for you is true, and times have changed because of our situation.'

'I must go,' Karolina said, turning and unfurling her parasol to step into the heat of the day.

She walked quickly, head down and past the men playing chess. She did not give them a glance but Bosch noticed her pass. He turned to his chess opponent who, it was rumoured, was a murderer who had escaped Germany by signing on as a merchant seaman. He preferred to be addressed only as Sailor and was a good chess player.

'She is the one,' Bosch said, returning his attention back to the game and moving his bishop. 'And tonight you will act.'

The sailor nodded, ruminating on his next move. Bosch had supplied him with the knife to carry out his killing of the perceived traitor. Not that he cared for politics, but Bosch was able to pay him in a large amount of British currency, which he could use while in internment to purchase a few luxury items.

'You must be very careful. The Australians will consider the killing of any one of us as murder under their law, and hanging is the penalty for that crime in this country. Needless to say, you will not mention my name – if you happen to be unlucky enough to be caught.'

'I will not be caught,' Sailor replied irritably. 'I know what I am doing.' He moved a pawn, knowing it would be lost but putting his opponent in a compromised position.

'Good,' Bosch said, not falling for his opponent's move. 'Frau Schumann will be alone tonight and there will be no moon.'

Karolina lay on her rickety bed and stared at the canvas ceiling. Her emotions were in turmoil. The sun beat down, and she reflected on Karl's expression of his feelings towards her. The heat of the day had made her weary and before long she fell into a deep sleep, awaking late in the evening when a noise alerted her to the fact that someone was in her darkened living space, looming over her bed. Struggling from her sleep-induced stupor, Karolina attempted to scream but felt a callused hand clamp over her mouth. She could smell the sweat of an unwashed body and knew that death was a mere few seconds away as the cold steel brushed her cheek. Instinctively she knew Bosch had sent his assassin to kill her.

The snow had gone from Bullecourt and now mud splatters would rise with the terrible earth-shaking explosions of the heavy artillery raining down on the Australians facing the German lines. Frontal assaults had been mounted to capture the village and allow the men to pass through to the enemy trenches beyond, but the attack had cost many lives of young men, blasted by explosives into meaty fragments, cut down by the high-velocity bullets of rifles and machine guns, and shredded by the shrapnel of hand grenades. At times it had been death by the bayonet in close combat where a man could see into the eyes of the soldier he had killed and watch the life fading from them.

Over the weeks he had been in command, Major Alexander Macintosh had proved his ability as a company commander, and earned the respect of his officers and men. He was no longer seen as just the son of the brigade commander but as a bloody good officer on account of his concern for his men and his sound planning in the missions they had as a rifle company. On this day they had fought a vicious battle as part of a brigade operation on the outskirts of the village. They had been given the mission, as the reserve company, to mop up any enemy resistance from German soldiers who had not reached their second set of entrenchments north of the shattered town.

Lance Corporal Tom Duffy had been tasked to move forward of the company in the role of a scout and marksman to clear his opponents whose deadly skill could bring a disproportionate number of advancing men to a halt. Prior to his mission he had blackened his foresight with the smoke from an oily rag, ensuring that the metal blade lost its shine and was clearly highlighted. Now he was in the village, moving stealthily forward of the company, seeking out opposition marksmen. The shelling from both sides continued but had moved further north as the sun slowly made its way to the shattered skyline beyond the little French village.

Tom's nerves were on a razor edge. He was fully aware that an unseen marksman might even now have him in his sights as he lay among a pile of smashed masonry in a narrow roadway. Most of the still-standing buildings faced the street, their windows empty. Like a man with blind eyes, Tom reflected. He had his rifle levelled on a German soldier scurrying across a cleared space between the rubble. But he did not fire, preferring to see where the soldier disappeared. In his grey uniform, he entered a largely intact building sporting jagged shrapnel scars from a shelling by heavy artillery. From his position buried in a pile of rubble, Tom had a good view of both the narrow street and the surrounding high places.

Barely moving a muscle, he noticed a civilian accompanied by two high-ranking officers. They had arrived on foot, the road being too shell-cratered for an automobile to get through, and had entered the building where he had seen the soldier disappear. He held his fire, considering he would be able to kill one of the enemy but the civilian and the other officer might gain protection before he could fire again. He had also been tasked to gain intelligence on enemy movements and could later report on the presence of the two senior officers in the village. Tom's attention was drawn to what was left of the sign painted on the building and drawing on his little knowledge of French made it out to be a former bank. From what he had seen of one of the German officers, he had been able to identify his rank as being equivalent to a British general. Immediately, Tom's mind queried the presence of such a high ranking officer so far forward in the lines. The officer accompanying him was the equivalent of a colonel, and this only heightened the mystery. Tom knew that he should report back, but curiosity overcame him. If he could actually take the high-ranking officers prisoner then they might be extremely valuable to the intelligence men of the division. What could be gleaned from them in interrogation might save many of Tom's mates' lives. It was worth the risk.

Very slowly, Tom rose from the rubble and made his way between piles of bricks and mortar brought down by explosive shells to within twenty feet of the open door of the bank. So far he had done so without being seen but a bullet cracked so close to his feet he felt stone chips hit his shins. Tom leaped forward straight towards the door, knowing his only means of getting out of the unseen marksman's sights was to get inside the building where he had seen the enemy enter. But it would be a case of out of the frying pan and into the fire.

Tom burst through the door to see a soldier levelling a rifle at him. His reflexes were honed by many weeks of living out in no-man's-land, however, and his own shot took the soldier square in the chest. The dead man slumped to the floor and in the semi-dark Tom was aware of the grey uniforms around him. He had already reloaded a round into the chamber and fired quickly at the nearest soldier who was bringing a pistol to bear on him. As the man went down, Tom realised that he had killed the German general whose presence had caused him to risk his life in the first instance. Because the room was so small, the second man he had identified as a colonel was now on him, struggling to bring his pistol into a position to fire point-blank at Tom who had no time to reload. He brought up the heavy, brass-plated butt of his rifle to smash into the German officer's face, crushing his nose in a shower of finely misted blood. The plan to take a prisoner was long gone as the Australian merely fought to stay alive. The officer went down. Tom smashed the butt of his rifle into the moaning man's head, splitting it open. His desperate strength had come from his instinct to survive and when Tom ripped back the bolt to chamber another round he realised that only he and the civilian remained standing amid the carnage.

Tom was covered with blood and when he swung on the civilian he could see that the man was terrified. He half-stood, half-crouched with his hands in the air. Tom could see that he was well-dressed, wore expensive spectacles and was in his middle age.

'Monsieur, please do not shoot,' the man pleaded in a cracked voice. 'I am not Boche. You are English, no?' he asked.

Quickly, Tom scanned the room for any sign of enemy activity before returning his attention to the French civilian he had captured.

'Australian,' Tom corrected the terrified man. 'What the hell were you doing with these two Hun officers?'

The French civilian realised that the man who had killed the three men with such ferocity was not about to kill him. He lowered his hands. 'I am a banker,' he answered. 'These men were here to . . .' The Frenchman checked himself.

'You were here to do what?' Tom asked, bringing up his rifle in a threatening way. 'From what I can see you are a bloody collaborator, and that means before I leave this room, you join your Hun mates on the floor with a bullet between your eyes. I'm sure your Froggie mates would give me a medal for doing your country a service.'

The banker paled. 'If you spare my life I can make you a rich man beyond all your wildest dreams,' he said. 'I was here to turn over a large consignment of stones to the German government.'

'Stones?' Tom queried. What did the Frenchman mean?

His puzzled expression caused the Frenchman to explain. 'Diamonds from Antwerp,' he clarified. 'They have been here since the beginning of the war, and we were using them to bribe the Boche to leave alone certain French interests in Germany.'

Tom was not interested in any French interests but the thought of the diamonds did interest him. A vague memory returned. What had the old Darambal warrior said, something about fiery stars?

'God almighty!' Tom gasped.

The French banker took his stunned reaction to be one of pure greed for what he offered in return for his life. 'I can give you the diamonds and you will let me live.'

'A deal,' Tom replied. 'So, where are they?'

'I have them,' the Frenchman answered, turning to a

desk where Tom noticed four, black velvet bags lying in full view. 'They are yours for the taking.'

Tom edged across the room, stepping over the body of one of the Germans he had killed. He picked up a bag and pulled the cord, releasing the contents. The room was lit with the sparkle of beautifully cut gems as they spilled onto the table. But so entranced by the fiery beauty of the diamonds was Tom, he failed to notice the banker sidle to the body of a German officer to retrieve the pistol still gripped in his hand. Some survival instinct warned Tom that he was in dire peril and he turned to look directly at the pistol levelled at him. Before he could swing his rifle around, the banker pulled the trigger. A bullet ripped through the flesh between Tom's neck and shoulder. Tom fired from the waist and his high velocity .303 round tore through the forehead of the banker, ripping out the back of his head and splashing fragments of bone and brains on the wall behind him. The man stood for a second before toppling backwards, waving the pistol before him.

The pain came very quickly but it was not enough for Tom to forget the four velvet satchels containing the fortune in precious stones. He scooped the diamonds back on the table into the bag, his blood splashing them in the process. With the diamonds secure in his gas mask bag, Tom found a battlefield bandage in his kit and wrapped it in place over the wound. He was bleeding profusely and was having trouble remaining alert as the pain swept in agonising waves. It was time to get out of the bank and report back to Major Macintosh.

He had hardly exited the bank when the unseen marksman opened fire on him again, but this time the bullet from his rifle tore through his side. Tom was flung sideways by the biting impact and fell into the street, exposed to a clear shot. He lay in the dust and masonry fragments, knowing that the marksman would probably leave him alive to attract those who might attempt to rescue him. Tom remained very still, wondering if whoever had fired might decide to finish him off instead of using him as bait. From his own experience Tom knew it depended on how professional the enemy marksman was. If it had been Tom in the other man's place he would have left him alive to claim the rescuers attempting to recover him.

'Tom, are you okay?' a voice came to him from about forty feet away.

He recognised it as that of Jack Kelly. The company had caught up with him in the sweep of the village.

'Yeah, boss,' Tom responded. 'But I don't know where the bastard is who is trying to kill me.'

'Okay, just stay there and we will locate him,' Jack answered.

The pain in Tom's side and neck continued to sweep over him and he fought not to slip into unconsciousness. Groaning, he stared at where he knew Jack and the company were concealed. Tom was reassured, as at least Jack Kelly knew what he was doing; he had not attempted to send anyone to retrieve him. All Tom could do was wait patiently, and pray that his cobbers would find the enemy marksman.

Jack Kelly lay on his stomach on a pile of broken bricks and earth, scanning the road and high buildings still left standing. His best bet was that the man he was hunting was most probably a soldier left behind to harass the advancing Australians. Had he been an expert marksman, he would have brought Tom down with his shot and not simply wounded him. At least the Hun had been smart enough to leave his wounded target as bait.

'See anything?' Alex Macintosh asked, crawling up beside his 2IC.

'Not yet,' Jack replied. 'We have to get the bastard before we clear this road.'

Alex retrieved a short pencil stub and a small notebook from his pocket to write a brief report for the company runner to take back to battalion HQ as regards their location and situation.

'There!' Jack hissed, causing Alex to pause in writing his report. Alex looked up, following the direction of Jack's finger. 'The Hun is in the middle level of that three-storeyed house . . . third window from the left.'

Alex squinted against the failing light. 'Sorry, old chap, I can't see him.'

Jack turned to his company commander. 'He's good,' he said. 'He has placed himself back in the room so as not to expose the barrel of his rifle. But that also means his vision is restricted and I reckon I can get into the house and take him out.'

'If you brief a couple of the men they can clear it,' Alex said.

'Sorry, boss, but Tom Duffy is kind of special to me,' Jack answered. 'I'm not going to ask any of my men to risk their lives in what I should be doing for Tom Duffy.'

Alex understood. His 2IC had the task of providing their marksman with his deadly tasks. Each time Jack sent Tom into no-man's-land or on these recon missions he was virtually taking years off the young man's life. It was a special relationship between officer and enlisted man that only they could understand but a partnership that would probably lead to Tom's death.

'Okay, Jack, I understand. But be bloody careful. Good 2ICs are hard to come by,' Alex said, placing his hand on Jack's shoulder.

Jack slid rearwards from his position and quickly briefed

the leading platoon as to what he was about to do. He directed them to pour as much fire as they could through the window he pointed out to them, expecting that the German would have enough cover inside his hide to protect himself from their small-arms fire. At least it would keep his head down to avoid the stray rounds, and there was less chance of the enemy finishing Tom off if he was preoccupied with staying alive himself.

Jack armed himself with two primed grenades and a captured German Luger he carried besides his rifle and, when the covering fire commenced from his men, he made his way along behind the protection of the rubble to a narrow alleyway behind the building where the sniper was located, wary of any German stragglers or other enemy marksmen. At the rear of the house he found an open door, previously blown off its hinges by the explosive force of a shell. Inside the building it was dark, with just the last light of the day filtering through the cracks of the broken structure. Jack made his way up the stairs, his pistol in a holster at his hip and the two primed grenades – minus their safety pins – in his hands ready to be thrown into the room he identified as the one where the German was hiding. Jack was very careful on the rickety steps as he moved towards the second floor.

Halfway up, Jack froze. The enemy marksman had vacated the room for another hide where he could continue sniping at the advancing Australians. Jack was acutely aware that the hand grenades he held in each hand were now useless – if not dangerous to him – as the German soldier came down the stairs towards him. It was obvious that he had not seen Jack in the dim light until they were only mere paces away from each other. Both men stared, frozen in fear at what would happen next.

Jack could see that his enemy was a man in his late thirties with the look of an experienced soldier.

'Don't move and put your rifle down!' he shouted in German, temporarily confusing the soldier standing three steps above him.

But the German quickly recovered, bringing his rifle barrel up to fire. In desperation, Jack dropped the live grenades, which rattled down the steps behind him. At the same instant he attempted to throw himself at the enemy but fell short instead. Jack's sudden lurch forward had distracted the man, however, and the shot went high, missing him. Virtually unarmed, Jack heard the rifle bolt chamber another round as he lay on his face on the steps, knowing the second shot would not miss.

Then the blast of the grenades at the bottom of the stairs tore at Jack and the man standing over him. Jack knew he had taken shrapnel but in the confined narrowness of the stairs the man standing over him had taken the full brunt. Jack felt him tumble over to slide down the steps. He twisted around, his ears ringing from the twin explosions, to see the German soldier attempting to rise to his feet. Jack grappled for his Luger, removed it and fired into the dying man, each bullet plucking at the grey, bloodied uniform. Satisfied that the soldier was dead, Jack attempted to stand, but screamed in pain. Some of the shards of iron had ripped through his feet and up his legs. He collapsed and fell on the body of the dead German.

Jack did not have to wait long for rescue. Men from the company had advanced and brought up stretcher bearers to litter him out and back to a medical aid station. Jack knew that he would live. Maybe it was a blighty – a wound that got a man sent back to the comforts and safety of a hospital in England – but somehow Jack also knew he might be treated in a French hospital, to rejoin his battalion when his wounds healed.

The stretcher bearers carried Jack out past Tom Duffy, now sitting in the street and apparently arguing with the company commander. Jack requested the stretcher bearers to stop beside Alex and Tom. Tom turned to Jack with a pleading expression.

'Boss, please ask Major Macintosh to allow me to remain with the company, and not go back to an aid station. I am all right and the wounds are just bad cuts. The bleeding will stop soon enough.'

Jack was stunned that the wounded marksman would want to stay at the front when he had the opportunity to be taken out of the firing line. 'Don't be a fool, Corporal Duffy,' Jack said. 'You could die from your wounds.'

'You have to get treatment, Corporal,' Alex said. 'That's an order.'

'Sir,' Tom pleaded, returning his attention to his company commander. 'I beg you in the name of an old man who lives in a cave on a hill to let me stay. I cannot tell you why I must stay but to do so might change the course of a lot of lives back home.'

'What old man?' Alex asked scornfully.

'His name is Wallarie, and he is a blackfella,' Tom answered. 'He is kin to me.'

Alex paled, visibly shaken by the name he had heard his cousin Matthew Duffy mention so often when they served together before the war. 'Wallarie is kin to you,' he whispered with a tone of almost reverential deference. 'I know of the man. He lives on my family's property at Glen View.'

Now it was Tom's turn to look surprised and both men's eyes met in an instant of understanding, leaving Jack

Kelly sensing that something outside his understanding was occurring. He felt as if he was intruding.

'You do what Major Macintosh tells you to do, Tom,' Jack said, asking the stretcher bearers to continue with him back to the regimental aid post at the battalion. 'And good luck, old chap.'

With a smile on his dirt-covered face, Alex stared at the wounded marksman sitting in the dust of the street. 'If you say that Wallarie has a hand in you wanting to remain with the company instead of going back to division for hospitalisation, then who am I to argue?'

'You know about Wallarie?' Tom asked.

'Let us just say that he is one of the most important people in my family's history,' Alex said, waving off the stretcher bearers. 'You stay, but if I see even the slightest twinge from you because of your wounds I am sending you back. We clear on that, Corporal Duffy?'

'Yes, sir,' Tom said, raising himself unsteadily to his feet and gripping his side. 'I will get the RMO to look at my wound and inform him you have given me permission to remain with the company.'

'I am sure the RMO will consider you a shell shock case for wanting to stay and send you back for psychiatric treatment anyway,' Alex said, grinning.

Tom retrieved his rifle from the road and made his way painfully rearwards towards battalion HQ to have the battalion's doctor look at his wound. He was sure the bullet from the German marksman had passed cleanly through his side and now infection was the greatest concern. But of the most importance to Tom was that the four bags of diamonds would remain undetected. Had he been evacuated as a wounded soldier they would have certainly been found by the medical staff treating him and forfeited to the

British government – or simply stolen by a rear echelon soldier. Tom had to remain with the company until he had the opportunity to dispose of the precious stones in a way that ensured they were transported to Australia unseen – or converted into hard cash in France.

There was only one man Tom trusted to help him, but he was now being carried back to the regimental aid post. Jack Kelly had once been a gold prospector and must know something about the disposal of precious stones. In the meantime, it was his duty to protect the small fortune in any way he could.

18

The flat of the blade slid across Karolina's cheek and she could feel the weight of her assailant press her down. She could even smell his foul breath and forced herself not to vomit.

'It's been a long time since I had a woman,' the man hissed. 'It would be a waste to kill you without a sample of what's under your dress.'

Karolina wanted to scream but knew he would surely kill her if she did so. She was going to die and so had nothing to lose but her scream was strangled by the hand clamped over her mouth. Unsuccessfully she attempted to bite him as he crushed her lips with the pressure of his arm. Even as she prepared for death she was thinking about her beloved grandson whom she would not have the opportunity to see grow to be a man.

The attacker had massive strength. Karolina could feel

his free hand groping under her long dress and calculated that he had put down the knife. She used all her strength to resist him but to no avail. He was too strong and Karolina continued to pray for her death to be quick when her desperate struggles failed.

Suddenly, the man on top of her went limp. She thought she had heard a loud crack a split second before her attacker lost his strength. In the dark she sensed the presence of another and for a moment thought it was an angel sent to save her.

'Are you hurt, my love?' a voice asked gently as the body of her attacker was pulled off her to thump to the ground next to the bed.

'Karl!' Karolina gasped. 'Is it you?' She felt a hand stroking the loose hair away from her face and strong hands lifting her into a sitting position.

'I am sorry that I was not able to be here for you earlier,' Karl apologised. 'But a loyal member of my congregation just informed me that Sailor was on his way here.'

Karolina flung her arms around Karl's neck and began to sob. 'Oh, Karl, I love you,' she said with passion. 'I think I may have loved you from the first time we met but had always denied that feeling. Please, never let me go.'

Despite her pleas, Karl gently untangled himself from Karolina's embrace. 'I have something to do – if you are to remain safe,' he said softly. He reached out for a kerosene lantern which he lit, illuminating the would-be rapist and killer who now lay sprawled on his face beside the single bed. The back of the man's head was caked in blood and Karolina then noticed the heavy, wooden club Karl had obviously crafted. When he noticed her gaze fixed on the makeshift weapon, he explained almost apologetically, 'I made it for the rats that plague our living quarters.'

'I am glad you did,' Karolina answered with a short, bitter laugh. 'Not all rats have four legs.'

Karl noticed the assailant twitch and groan. 'He lives, but will have a bad headache when he comes round. He is a very tough man.'

'What should we do?' she asked, the gravity of the situation replacing her initial terror and then relief at her rescue by a man whom until now she had secretly considered too gentle for such a violent act.

'You will leave it to me,' he replied, straightening up and looking around at Karolina's few possessions until his eyes fell on a small patch of linen. He picked up the cloth and tore it into strips, using them to tie Sailor's hands and feet. Satisfied that the bindings would hold, he reassured Karolina that her attacker would not be long in her tent, and disappeared with his club into the darkness.

When Karl located Herr Bosch's tent he was not surprised to see he was still awake and playing cards with one of his cronies. Without invitation Karl stepped inside the tent and swung his club down on the tiny wooden table between the two men, smashing it into fragments and sending the cards flying. Both Bosch and his companion leaped to their feet, seeing before them the terrible spectre of an avenging angel, not a meek Lutheran pastor.

'The blood on this club belongs to the sailor,' Karl snarled. 'If anything happens to Frau Schumann it will also be coated with yours, Herr Bosch. Now, go and retrieve your man from her tent. He is barely alive and will require medical attention.'

Bosch recovered quickly from Karl's sudden fury. 'I don't know what you are inferring, pastor,' he said.

'I don't care, Herr Bosch,' Karl snapped. 'If anything bad should happen to Frau Schumann I will hunt you down and kill you regardless of the consequences. That is all I have to say.'

Bosch glanced at his card partner, and could see real fear in his eyes. The other man nodded politely. Karl turned to him. 'You can spread the word among all those you speak to that Frau Schumann is a loyal and dedicated German for the Fatherland, and is under my personal protection.'

Satisfied that he had made his point, Karl stepped out and strode back to join Karolina, who met him outside her tent. 'He is conscious,' she said, her arms folded over her breasts.

'Then you should stay with me tonight,' Karl said. 'Until Herr Bosch has someone remove him from your tent.'

Karolina did not baulk at the pastor's suggestion, slipping her arm through his as they made their way down the narrow street. 'What will your congregation say about you having a single woman stay with you tonight?' she asked, half in jest and half out of concern.

'That I am a sinful man not worthy of my office. But, I do not care. My real congregation is much further north of here.'

Karolina shook her head, puzzled. Karl was a complex man with so many sides to his character. One, which she had witnessed this night, she hoped she would never have to see again.

For Lance Corporal Tom Duffy the possession of a fortune in diamonds was becoming more of a concern than even death itself. He had grasped the chance to sit back in the relative protection of the trenches and clean his rifle. It had been two weeks since he was shot and the wounds had commenced healing under the care of the RMO who kept a careful eye out for infection, and rubbed garlic on the bullet's entry and exit points. 'Wog stuff,' the RMO had muttered. 'But it seems to work.'

With his wounds healing, Tom volunteered to continue as the company and battalion marksman, but now under the supervision of the battalion intelligence officer, a young second lieutenant who proved to be competent in his job. Tom's comrades respected and admired him for his cold-blooded courage. To creep out into no-man's-land and kill with a single shot took a very special breed of man and Tom was becoming something of a celebrity among those who knew of his deadly reputation along this stretch of the front. Some even said that he might eventually rival the legendary Billy Sing himself, who had killed his first two hundred men before leaving Gallipoli. Tom had refused to keep tally of the number of enemy who had fallen victim to his marksmanship, although his comrades did. Unbeknown to Tom they kept a book on how many enemy he would kill in a day, and the nearest to the number would take the pot on the final tally.

Tom knew that keeping the diamonds concealed was difficult and so secreted them in his meagre kit whenever he went out to take up a hide for the day's sniping. He had made the young intelligence officer promise him that his kit would not be disturbed if he appeared overdue from a mission in no-man's-land. The IO promised that his wish for privacy would be kept. He wondered why his marksman should be so obsessed with his kit, but kept his word.

Eventually the battalion was pulled back for a badly needed rest behind the lines and Tom was able to obtain leave from the company commander to visit Captain Jack Kelly in a nearby French hospital. Jack's wounds had been ascertained not serious enough for him to be evacuated back to England and he had already been notified that when he recovered he would be posted to another battalion where a company commander was desperately needed.

When Tom found Jack Kelly, he was in a bed between a wounded South African officer who had taken shrapnel in his stomach and a New Zealander blinded by mustard gas. The Canadians, New Zealanders and South Africans were very much like their Australian counterparts, enjoying a reputation as being among the best soldiers on the front.

Jack was sitting up in bed with a copy of CJ Dennis's latest release on the exploits of Ginger Mick and his mates. He greeted Tom with a broad smile. 'Well, Tom, I thought you would have been sampling the wares of a pretty mad-emoiselle, rather than visiting the man who tried to get you killed every day.'

Tom held out his hand and grinned at his friend and superior officer. 'The battalion has someone else doing that now,' he said. 'Figures he can do a better job of getting me sent west.'

'From the look on your face I get the feeling your visit is more than social,' Jack said, losing his smile as Tom pulled up a chair beside him. The ward was clean and bright and the French nurses in their stiffly starched uniforms moved among the wounded men with gentleness and competence.

'I wanted to see if you were okay,' Tom said, glancing around at the beds on either side of Jack. Satisfied that the Canadian and South African were asleep he leaned over to speak quietly to the wounded Australian captain. 'You remember when we both copped it back at that Froggie village?' Jack nodded. 'Well, something happened while you blokes were still coming up.'

'I heard you killed a couple of very high-ranking German officers,' Jack said. 'Pity that you couldn't have taken them alive.'

'There was a Froggie there I was forced to kill when he pulled a pistol on me,' Tom said quietly. 'He was carrying a lot of diamonds.'

Jack glanced around to see if his fellow patients were in a position to overhear their conversation.

'What do you mean by lot of diamonds?' he asked with the professional interest of a former gold prospector.

Very carefully, Tom withdrew the four black velvet bags from his trouser pockets and placed them on Jack's lap. Jack undid the string on one and looked inside. He was barely able to restrain himself, whistling at what he saw before indicating that Tom should conceal them again. 'You have enough stones there to pay an army's wages for a year,' he said in a whisper. 'How in hell did you come across them?'

'The Froggie told me that they were meant to pay the Fritzes for what he said were French interests in Germany,' Tom explained, securing the bags. 'If I had not been there they would probably be in some Berlin bank by now.'

'You know you should hand them over to the army,' Jack said.

'Would you?' Tom countered.

'No, I would be working out how to dispose of them, so that I did not have to worry about some rear echelon scab stealing them. If I were . . .' Jack's face broke into a grin. 'So, that is why you refused to be stretchered out of the lines when you were hit.' Tom returned the grin, acknowledging Jack's perceptiveness. 'How did you get Major Macintosh to let you stay on?'

'That's just it, boss,' Tom answered with a frown. 'I mentioned the name of an old blackfella I know, and Major Macintosh looked like he had seen a ghost. It appears that my kinsman lives on a Macintosh property I visited a while back. He agreed to let me stay so long as the RMO agreed – which he did – but thought I was a fool, when I could have been back here in a ward with clean blankets and good food.'

Jack chuckled. 'Not when you are the richest lance corporal on the Western Front,' he said. 'Now, it is time for an old friend of mine in Paris to take care of your problem and turn the stones into hard, cold cash. I once met a prospector in New Guinea who was born an Alsatian. He had problems with identifying which side he should be on in this war as his mother is German, like my own mother was, and his father French. I heard that Henri is now in the business of trading gold and precious stones. As we spent a few months together up in the old German territory, I got to know him, indeed saved him once from a native arrow. He owes me one – and I can vouch for his honesty. But you will have to trust me.' Tom looked at Jack with a blank expression. 'The doctors here tell me I will be released tomorrow and going on wound leave to Paris. I had intended on catching up with Henri anyway as he also deals in excellent wines and spirits. Are you able to return tomorrow when I am to be discharged?'

'I have a forty-eight hour leave pass and the battalion is only three hours away. I can make it,' Tom answered.

'When I am let out I will take the parcel from you and get the stones to Henri who will convert them into cash and place it in an account you nominate with a Swiss bank.' Tom had no real understanding of high finance, but was reluctant to admit so. 'Henri will take a commission but of no more than ten per cent, I promise you,' Jack continued quietly. 'And I don't want a cut. You earned it fair and square for all the risks we . . . I have asked you to undertake.'

'I don't have any idea of how to set up an account,' Tom finally admitted. 'Can you do that for me?'

'I can,' Jack replied, realising the total trust the young soldier placed in him. 'If in the event something happens and you go west,' Jack continued, 'who do you nominate as your next of kin?'

For a moment Tom thought on the matter. 'Mrs Kate Tracy.'

'A lady friend?' Jack asked, raising his eyebrow.

'My aunt,' Tom replied. 'She lives in Townsville and will know what I want done with the money if I don't make it home.'

Both men knew that the way the war was dragging on it was probably only a matter of weeks – if lucky, months – before they would be killed, as such was the lot of the infantryman on the front.

'There is one thing,' Jack said as Tom rose from his chair to return to the house where he'd been billeted with a friendly French farmer and his family. 'I have no knowledge of what you have confessed to me.'

Tom nodded and the next day, as Captain Jack Kelly prepared to go on leave in Paris, he had a visit from Lance Corporal Tom Duffy who passed him a brown paper parcel. All Tom could hope for was that he had made the right decision in trusting the former prospector.

Within a week, Tom received a letter from Jack Kelly saying that his Swiss bank passbook had been posted to Kate Tracy in Townsville. He was also given the number of his account and a statement that the bank book had been sealed with instructions that it was only to be opened upon notification of Lance Corporal Tom Duffy's death.

In time, Kate Tracy received the thick envelope addressed to her and opened it. She did not recognise the handwriting but the instructions on the outside of a second, sealed envelope were clear enough. She placed the mysterious packet in her sideboard and when a week later a letter arrived from Tom she read of his further instructions on what she should do with the contents of the account should he be killed in action.

Kate sat back on her verandah, a cup of tea at hand, and frowned. Tom's instructions would be near to impossible to satisfy, she mused, considering her past efforts in the same field of endeavour. The amount of money required to do as Tom wished was unimaginable. It was not likely that a soldier would be able to save even a fraction of the amount.

Kate sipped her tea and sighed. Tom had been consistent in sending her letters, unlike her only son, Matthew, who she only knew was somewhere in Palestine flying missions over the Holy Land. He had always been a poor correspondent in his travels before the war so Kate was delighted to open the second letter that she had received that day. It was from her old leading hand, Randolph Gates, to say that he was in contact with Matthew and that he was well. Kate's eyes dimmed as she read that they were advancing towards Jerusalem with Matthew's squadron in support. That Randolph was riding with the Australian Light Horse brigade did not surprise Kate, who knew he was both a superb horseman and a crack shot.

'Mrs, you want a fresh pot of tea?' Angela, her young Aboriginal housemaid, asked from the door.

'No thank you, Angela.' Kate carefully folded the letter and replaced it in the envelope marked with sweat and gun grease.

The damned war just seemed to drag on and from the news in the daily papers there was no end in sight, despite the appearance of fresh American troops on the European battlefields. Kate placed her reading spectacles on a small table and leaned back in her chair to rest, soon falling into a deep sleep in the balmy afternoon sun.

A voice was calling to her gently and Kate opened her eyes. The sun was softening the day on the horizon and her attention was suddenly drawn to her sweeping lawn below. 'Wallarie,' she gasped in her shock. He was standing, staring up at her, but he was very young and carried his array of spears and war clubs. Their eyes met and he gave the slightest of nods to acknowledge that he had seen her. She heard no words, except in her head, and Wallarie's face broke into a wide smile, as he relayed his message to her.

'Mrs, Mrs,' the voice called to her from somewhere close.

She could feel a gentle nudge at her shoulder. Kate came out of her trancelike state, rubbing her eyes with the back of her hand. Angela was shaking her. Kate glanced back to the lawn to see that Wallarie was gone.

'Did you see him?' Kate asked, still scanning the lawn.

'Who, Mrs Tracy?' Angela asked, clearing away the long-cold pot of tea from the table.

'Wallarie. He was just here speaking to me.'

Angela paused, looked out to the lawn with its long shadows. Wallarie was the name of the *debil debil* man whose name was invoked to keep children out of the dark when she was much younger. It was said that he could not be killed because he turned into a great eagle and flew from his enemies.

Angela shuddered. 'I not see the old blackfella,' she replied but felt a superstitious awe. She had come to learn that her kindly mistress had spiritual powers and could see beyond the world of the living. If she was sure that the old man had been here she must be right.

'What did he say?' Angela asked, noticing the radiant look on Kate's face.

'He told me that I was about to become a grandmother,' she replied, still puzzled by the message, as her son had not mentioned any woman in his life. As far as she knew, Matthew was constantly at the front flying his missions and would have had little chance to meet a woman. But if Wallarie had brought the message then it must be so. She would write to Randolph and try to ascertain if he knew of any romantic interests in Matthew's life.

Kate rose stiffly from her chair and followed Angela inside. She paused for a moment at the door of her sprawling house and looked back to the lawn.

'Thank you, old friend,' she whispered, closing the screen door behind her.

Captain Matthew Duffy lined up the hard-packed earthen runway and prayed that his aircraft would take the landing. He had been so badly shot up on his mission to track the retreating Turks that he wondered if his undercarriage would sustain the impact of setting down. He waved to the ground crew observing his return with binoculars and guessed they had anxious expressions on their faces since seeing the damage he had taken from ground fire. But Matthew brought his aircraft down safely and to a halt in front of the operations tent to the cheers of his fellow pilots.

When the engine spluttered to a stop he was aware that the ever-present drone was gone, leaving the ringing in his ears he had come to live with. His ground crew were on his aircraft immediately and one of his fellow pilots strolled over with a mug of tea for him.

'Bad one, old chap?' he asked, examining the myriad of bullet holes that had punctured the flimsy fabric of the fuselage. He passed the mug up to Matthew, who had trouble holding it, his hands shook so badly.

'I got caught between two ridges,' Matthew said,

attempting to sip the hot tea before realising that it was coffee with a strong lashing of rum.

'Thought you wouldn't mind,' the pilot said. 'We raided your supply while you were gone. The mess seems to have run out.'

Matthew swallowed the contents of his mug before easing himself out of the cockpit and jumping to the ground. His ground crew were already working out the repairs required to keep his aircraft in the air as Matthew walked away with his fellow aviator, a young chemist from Queensland who was around the same age.

'Any word on Allenby's advance?' Matthew asked.

'Not much to report,' the pilot answered. 'I have heard a rumour that you may have a lady waiting for you in Jerusalem.'

Matthew glanced at his companion as they approached the gaggle of pilots lounging about and enjoying the last of the day's sun. 'I hope so,' Matthew replied, falling into a silence that his comrade sensed meant no more references were to be made to Matthew's hopes of finding Joanne. Many of the men still remembered the visit of the pretty, American archaeologist months earlier and envied Matthew.

The sun was long down as Matthew returned to his tent after supper. He was in no mood to share the evening drinking with the other pilots in the mess and sat down on his cot to write a letter home. The months had passed without word of Joanne's fate and the year was drawing closer to Christmas. The light from his lamp flickered and, startled, Matthew glanced up to see the familiar face of Saul Rosenblum outfitted like a desert bandit. The Jewish settler had contacts with the intelligence section of the squadron and thus as a trusted ally was able to move freely among them.

'Saul!' Matthew exclaimed, jumping to his feet to greet his old friend. 'How the devil are you?'

Saul stepped inside the small tent and embraced Matthew with a great bear hug. 'It is good to see you, Matt. But I bring both good and bad news. Do you have any whisky or rum?'

Matthew had a half bottle of whisky among his few personal supplies and retrieved it. He poured some into an enamel mug and kept the bottle for himself. Saul took a long swig, draining the shot while Matthew took a short sip from the bottle.

'Miss Barrington is safe,' Saul said at last. 'But she has been sent to Berlin. The Germans are civilised, however, and will treat her with respect given her father's position in the USA.'

'Your son?'

'Benjamin is well,' Saul replied. 'The Syrian doctor was able to treat him and have him smuggled back to us. Our spies in Jerusalem passed on the news of Miss Barrington.'

'Why would the Turks send Joanne to Berlin?' Matthew frowned.

'I don't know,' Saul shrugged. 'But, at least she is alive.'

'What are you doing here?' Matthew asked.

'We are working with your Light Horse, assisting them in intelligence gathering, but we do not advertise the fact in case the Ottomans find out and take reprisals against my settlement,' Saul explained. 'Besides, I have enough German supporters in the moshava to make me nervous.'

Matthew poured another half mug of whisky for the Jewish guerrilla who again swallowed the contents, before wiping his mouth and passing the empty mug back to Matthew.

'Well, old cobber,' Saul said. 'Time to go and find the

Light Horse HQ and report in. They need the information we have on Ottoman dispositions forward of your base.'

Matthew was always surprised at how Saul Rosenblum could sound so Jewish, and yet in Matthew's presence use Australianisms so readily. 'Yes, well, take it easy, and next year – Jerusalem.'

Saul's face broke into a wide grin. 'Ah, you know of our prayer. But I think the way you and the British are going, it will be this year.'

With a handshake, Saul disappeared into the night. Matthew sat down on his cot and picked up his pencil and pad. But he was no longer in the mood to write to his mother. He downed what was left in the bottle before collapsing on his cot and falling into a troubled sleep, haunted by the image of Joanne being raped by German soldiers.

19

George Macintosh waited like a hunter in his hide as he sat behind his great wooden desk listening to the monotonous ticking of the grandfather clock in the hallway. When it chimed the first stroke for the morning he heard his wife's car pull into the driveway outside his window. He knew the sound well. She was met by a very sleepy manservant who took over driving it to the stables converted to a garage.

George let the curtain fall back and left his office to greet his wife in the foyer. When door opened, Louise was startled to see her husband standing before her, wearing his smoking jacket.

'Have you been with him?' he demanded.

Louise stepped inside, wearing the chic dress she normally wore to the theatre. 'With whom, George?' she asked, confronting her husband.

'That cripple.'

'If you mean Major Sean Duffy, yes, I have.'

'How could you shame me?' George spat. 'Every one of our friends must know of your infidelity and you don't give a damn.'

'I give a damn when I know that you visit my son's nanny in her room even as I am lying a bedroom away,' Louise flared. 'But that does not seem to cause any problem with your conscience. I care that you have the power to separate me from my son and I care that you are a craven coward.' Louise paled when she saw the riding crop dangling from her husband's hand. He took a step towards her with the crop raised. Louise cowered, her hands above her head as it came down with a vicious thwack on her arms.

'Whore!' George screamed. 'You have no idea of the risks I take to maintain the family companies and provide for this family.'

He raised the riding crop again and slashed down on Louise's face, drawing a thin stream of blood and raising a welt. Louise was initially stunned by the attack but she was also the daughter of a tough father who had risen in business to establish an empire in his own right. She fought back, striking at her husband's face with her fingernails. But he was now in a blind rage, thrashing his wife until she was forced to her knees, curled into a foetal position to protect her body. The attack seemed to go on forever until George found himself physically spent but sexually aroused by the punishment he had meted out to his wife.

He stepped back, sweat rolling from his face, and stared down at the woman he thrashed before turning to walk away, leaving her huddled on the floor and moaning in pain and frustration.

'I will call the police and show them my injuries,' she

cried after him as he began the ascent up the stairs to the nanny's room.

'Call the police,' George retorted. 'See what they will do about interfering in a husband's right to chastise a disloyal wife. If you like, I will give you the name of a friend I have in the force who might listen to you.'

Louise forced herself to her feet and clung to the foyer wall. She could feel her face swelling from the strike to the cheek and painful throbbing throughout her body. She felt shame and fury at the same time. 'I swear I will kill you if you ever do that again,' she screamed at the back of her husband.

George paused at the top of the stairs and looked down on his wife with a smirk of satisfaction. 'Who? You and that cripple?' he jeered. 'A man with half a body?'

Louise glared up at him. 'Sean Duffy is a real hero who has killed many times, so I would not be so complacent if I were you,' she answered bitterly, sneering at George's taunt. But he simply turned his back and disappeared from sight.

Louise thought about her son in his nursery. She could go to him and take him from the house, but knew that George would prevent that. She also knew that he kept the room locked when she was out at night to stop her from going to her son.

Wiping the streak of blood from her cheek with the back of her hand, Louise was already contemplating revenge. She would not remain under the roof where her husband kept her son from her, and lay with the nanny in her room.

Louise stepped back into the night where she saw the manservant hovering in the darkness, no doubt afraid to enter the house when he heard the violent attack inside.

'Herbert, I wish to be driven to Master George's brother's house,' she said with as much dignity as she could muster.

Herbert, still in his dressing gown, did not question her

order. At least with her out of the house he would not be a witness to any further violence.

It was the tough Scot valet, Angus MacDonald, who answered the door in the early hours of the morning. 'Mrs Macintosh,' he said, blinking away the sleep. 'Is something wrong?'

As Louise stepped into the light Angus blanched at the sight of her badly bruised and cut face. He helped her inside, nodding to her driver to leave. Very gently he led her to the kitchen, sitting her down at an old table used to prepare food. Louise was grateful for the kind attention and smiled weakly at the burly man fussing about in search of medical supplies. He retrieved a half bottle of Scotch he secretly shared with the cook.

'Here, have a wee tot of this, Mrs Macintosh,' he said, offering her a full shot of the fiery liquid. 'It will cure anything that ails you.'

Louise gratefully accepted the drink and swallowed half of it before coughing at the cheap liquor burning her throat. 'I doubt that it will cure what ails my life, Mr MacDonald,' she gasped, getting her breath back. 'I did not mean to disturb you this late at night, but this was the closest place I could think of to find sanctuary.'

'I will fetch Mrs Macintosh,' Angus said. He already had a good idea how her injuries had been sustained.

'Please don't disturb her,' Louise said, waving her hand.

'I am sure that Mrs Macintosh would be angry if I did not,' Angus countered. 'She has a good knowledge of medicine. I believe that she used to treat the natives on her father's plantation.'

Louise wanted to laugh when she remembered how Giselle had always dreamed of becoming a doctor before the war, but motherhood had curtailed that dream for the moment and now with Alex away at the front she felt responsible to remain at the hearth to await his return before pursuing her dream of a career in medicine. Louise envied her sister-in-law for the love she knew existed between her and Alex.

In a short time, Louise was joined by Giselle who immediately went to her sister-in-law and examined the ugly cut and welt on her cheek. She did not ask what had happened as she had also guessed.

'I will apply some antiseptic oil to the cut,' Giselle said, bending over, the worried expression still on her face. 'It will sting, but will help with the healing.'

'I did not want to disturb you, but I could not think of anyone else to go to tonight,' Louise said as Giselle located a small bottle of antiseptic oil from a medical cabinet she kept in the kitchen.

'I am glad that you came,' Giselle said, applying the oil with a small, clean gauze. Louise winced at the stinging oil but was grateful for Giselle's medical skills. 'Was it George?' Giselle finally asked.

Louise nodded. 'He knows about my affair with Sean,' she replied, knowing that Giselle frowned on her behaviour of having an affair while still married.

'You are welcome to stay here with us,' Giselle said, replacing the phial back in the cabinet. 'I can arrange to have your things brought over. I am sure that George will not mind you visiting for a while.'

'And my son?' Louise said bitterly. 'Can you arrange to have him join me?' Giselle looked away and Louise realised that she was taking her anger out on the wrong person. 'Oh, I am sorry,' she hurried to say. 'I did not mean it that way.'

'I understand,' Giselle said, placing a kettle on the stove and turning on the gas. 'These terrible times make us tense.'

'You have reason to be tense, with Alex on the front,'

Louise said gently, going to Giselle to assist her prepare the tea. 'Sean sweats and screams in the night,' she continued. 'It is as if he is still back fighting in the trenches. I wake him but it takes a long time for him to recognise that I am beside him. The war changes men forever.'

'I cannot imagine my Alex changing,' Giselle said, staring at the wall. 'He is a gentle, brave and intelligent man, and a wonderful and warm human being, whose love for me and David cannot be questioned.'

Louise put her arms around her sister-in-law. 'He will return to you as that same gentle and loving man,' she said gently as she hugged Giselle, not really sure she was telling the truth. She could only pray that she was right. But even as she held her friend in the embrace, she was seething with rage. How could she see her husband humiliated – or even dead? The thought frightened Louise because she had truly considered the possibility. If her husband was dead then she would have her son back and could be with Sean. The idea of seeing her husband gone permanently from her life was becoming an obsession.

Thousands of wives, mothers, sisters, daughters and lovers dreaded the arrival of the telegram boy on his red GPO bicycle. Kate Tracy was no exception as she sat with her sewing in her lap on the wide, shaded verandah of her house in the tropics. Each day the mail man was welcomed as he rode up the long driveway to her house and delivered the precious letters from friends and relatives and, most importantly, those rare letters from overseas stained with the dust and mud of the battlefields. But the boy on the red push bike was not welcome.

It was a warm day and the world seemed at peace. Kate

tied off the cotton thread on a shirt she was stitching for one of the gardeners when she glanced up to see the uniformed young boy riding towards her on his distinctive bicycle.

'Oh, dear God,' she heard herself groaning. 'Let it be a mistake.'

She dropped the sewing at her feet and staggered to the railing as the young boy dismounted, propping his bike against a gum tree before walking towards her with an envelope in his hand. Kate knew the boy as she had sat with his mother only weeks earlier when the news arrived that her husband had been killed on the Western Front.

'Mrs Tracy,' the boy said apologetically as he walked up the steps to her. 'I am sorry, I have to give you this.'

Kate did not say a word but accepted the telegram as the boy ducked his head and hurried away. Too often those he delivered the telegrams to fainted, and he did not like being around women who fainted or screamed out in their grief. It was unnerving. Besides, all he wanted to do was be old enough so that he could also sign up and fight the Huns.

Kate half-staggered back to her chair and slumped into it. She could barely bring herself to slip open the unsealed envelope and spread the single page.

It is with regret . . . killed in action.

From the drawing room where she was dusting the sideboards Angela heard the long, anguished groan and hurried to the verandah to see her mistress ashen-faced. 'He's dead,' Kate said, holding out the single typewritten page to her. 'Killed in Palestine.' Then Kate broke down, tears streaming down her face as she sobbed for the loss of one more soldier in this terrible war.

★

Behind any such telegram is always a story of a moment in time, when a man faces death in his own way. Under the competent British General Allenby, the men of the Australian forces were on the road north to Damascus and Jerusalem. The advance had been spectacular, with thousands of Turkish and German soldiers taken prisoner as Allenby's combined forces of French, British, Indian, Australian and New Zealand infantry and horsemen flowed forward, swamping the enemy. It had become a fluid war, unlike the bogged-down battlefields of Europe, a war designed for horsemen with the wide, sweeping plains to manoeuvre across.

In the air, Matthew, flying a new Bristol fighter, carried out recon and interdiction missions with his gunner, Sergeant Bruce Forsyth, now occupying the rear cockpit with his Lewis gun for rearward protection against enemy fighter planes. Matthew liked the new aircraft, as it was, despite being a two-seater, very agile and capable of engaging any of the German fighter planes they might come across on their missions.

On the ground, Trooper Randolph Gates rode with the advancing troops but a bout of malaria was dogging him. It was not only the enemy and the scorpions and snakes of the desert taking the lives of men, but also mosquitoes carrying the deadly disease. Randolph slumped in his saddle, shivering from the effects of the fever as they trekked ever northwards. They were advancing through low, craggy hills, and Randolph could see aircraft from Matthew's squadron diving like angry bees into the gorge. The airmen had come across a Turkish transport column which had unwittingly made itself the perfect target for the aircraft circling above. The lead vehicles were immediately attacked with bombs and machine-gun fire; then the airmen went to work on the strung out column of troops, flying a few hundred feet over their targets, dropping bombs and strafing the desperate soldiers as they attempted to take shelter.

Matthew aimed the nose of his aircraft at a cluster of men he could see spilling from the back of a truck. Satisfied that he had a good sight on the soldiers, he fired the forward, fixed machine gun and saw the dust spouting up in tiny bursts as men caught in the bullets fell, riddled with high velocity .303 rounds. Horses were also hit and reared in agony before collapsing on the ground. Some of the braver troops on the ground were answering their persecutors with rifle fire, but to little effect as those aircraft with bombs remaining under their wings dropped them into the packed convoy, exploding ammunition and petrol. Behind him Matthew could hear the chatter of Sergeant Forsyth's Lewis gun picking off targets of opportunity. The scene below was that of a slaughter but Matthew felt no emotion about the carnage he was helping to create. From his height, the men he killed hardly had features, certainly none he could discern, and were simply targets to be tallied at some later time.

From a safe distance, Randolph's unit watched the slaughter, hoping that the Turks might surrender. But the Turkish troops were as brave as any on earth and fought back despite their losses. In the time that Randolph had been with the Light Horse he had not seen the scale of death he was now witnessing.

'Poor bastards,' a trooper mumbled beside Randolph.

Out of ammunition and bombs, the aircraft flew away to re-arm, leaving a shattered column drowning in their own blood. The order was given to Randolph's troop to find a way down to engage the survivors. They drew their rifles from the buckets and charged a group of Turkish soldiers attempting to set up a machine gun to cover the rear of the column.

Randolph let out a rebel yell he had heard as a kid in Texas from his uncle, who had fought the Yankees in the war between the states. He felt a thump in his chest that flung him from his galloping horse. Winded, and his lungs filling with blood, Randolph lay staring at the sky, knowing that he was dying. He could hear the shouting of his comrades as the crack of bullets in the air around him faded into another world, one that no longer concerned him.

Hardly able to breathe, Randolph lay still, clutching his rifle. 'Nellie,' he whispered hoarsely, although he was alone and no-one would hear him. 'I loved you.'

When his comrades returned they found him dead. According to records in the regimental HQ, his death was to be notified to a Mrs Kate Tracy in Townsville. Randolph Gates, former cowboy, stockman, adventurer, one-time film actor on two continents and now a mounted infantry man would be buried in the earth where so many armies had fought and died before him.

Winter was returning to the Northern Hemisphere and Major Alex Macintosh was still alive, although he had long given up on any hope of surviving the war and returning to his wife and child. Since his arrival in France he had taken command of a company of approximately a hundred men, but in the months that passed he had written so many letters to next-of-kin that the names of the dead blurred.

Other than a mild case of trench foot, Alex had remained unscratched. He and his men had pushed on as a tiny part of a juggernaut always attempting to break through to the green fields beyond. Though they were hard to pronounce for non-Gallic speakers, Alex clearly remembered the names of the places he had led his company in the slog of taking a few miles of land. Names like Messines, Ypres and Bullecourt were forever burned into his memory, and now they were advancing along the Menin Road to a place called Passchendaele.

The rain was constant, with a biting cold creeping into the air heralding the snow ahead. In the next few months, Alex led his company, with the slatted wooden duckboards providing the only firm footing in a sea of churned, sticky mud. They struggled along, careful not to slip lest they drown in the liquid earth. Shoulders slumped against the rain, they groped through a stark landscape, the complete desolation brought on by the constant pounding from artillery guns of both sides. At least they were under the command of General Monash, Alex consoled himself. He admired the former civil engineer for the careful planning he brought to the art of war, but this time Alex wondered about the Australian general's intelligence when he saw before him a sea of mud.

Eventually they trudged past a group of demoralised English soldiers huddling in an old concrete pill box, scarred by shrapnel and bullets.

'Good on yer, Aussie,' one of the young English soldiers cheered weakly. Alex glanced in the English soldier's direction and caught the expression of a man who had come to the end of his nerves, experiencing too much of hell to function anymore as a soldier. Alex felt pity and respect for the soldier whom he guessed was barely seventeen years of age and should have been home with his mother.

The sun was gone by the time they fumbled their way into what had once been trenches and Alex was called to battalion HQ for the nightly briefing for company

314

commanders. He moved from man to man in the dark until he eventually found a soldier who knew where the CO was located. Alex's hands were covered in mud that stank of decomposing flesh by the time he reached a section of the trenches that had collapsed from the effects of the constant torrential rain.

A star shell popped in the sky, illuminating the sea of stinking mud, and Alex cursed the glutinous earth that held him fast as he stepped into a collapsed section of the trench and became aware that he was clearly exposed. Frantically he fought the clinging mud to reach the intact trench ahead, but the artillery shell exploded only a matter of yards away. Alex felt the short, sharp wave of heat and a burning, stinging sensation to his face and body. He was knocked sideways and immediately knew that he had taken the brunt of the shell's force. The pain caused him to scream.

'Stretcher bearers!' a soldier yelled.

Major Alexander Macintosh lay in the mud, raising his hand weakly to feel his face. He knew that much of it was missing. Then mercifully the darkness came to the Australian officer before the stretcher bearers were able to reach him. But Alex was not alone as a casualty that night; the German gunners poured in a barrage to welcome the Australians to Passchendaele.

For a brief moment Alex found himself conscious. In the dark he heard a voice speak.

'Poor bastard. He ain't a pretty sight.'

Alex guessed it was one of the stretcher bearers. What would his beautiful wife think of her husband returning home without a face?

20

Louise was afraid to tell Sean about her husband's behaviour, lest he take steps to confront George and leave himself open to charges that would end his career as a solicitor. She knew that George had many powerful contacts – including the police. She remained as Giselle's house guest, having had a few personal possessions brought over from her home with the help of Angus MacDonald. But as each day passed she felt the separation from her child and her waking hours were filled with thoughts of getting him back. George had not objected to her moving out and told friends that she was staying with her sister-in-law for a short time while his brother was serving overseas. For the time being, the explanation covered the fact that all was not well in his household.

Sean Duffy continued with his work as a solicitor and at Louise's gentle insistence had cut back on his drinking.

He had long disregarded the tenets of his strict religious Irish heritage concerning morality and lost any belief in God after his experiences on the battlefields of Europe. In the case of another man's wife he had a bitter satisfaction that he was sleeping with the wife of a man whom he considered a slacker – one who had avoided military service while others made the ultimate sacrifice. But he had also grown to love this beautiful and intelligent woman who had preferred to keep their affair private, even from her circle of friends.

Sean was preparing to take his briefcase full of notes to the Court of Petty Sessions on the Monday morning to defend his list of clients when the articled clerk delivered a note to him.

'Who gave you this?' he asked the clerk whose expression reflected some concern.

'That copper, Inspector Firth,' the boy replied, knowing the policeman from the photographs that appeared from time to time in the daily papers.

Sean glanced at the note and frowned. It was a threat that he should not associate with Mrs Louise Macintosh or he may find himself in dire trouble. The note was not signed. The boy glanced at him with an unspoken question. 'Don't tell anyone that you got this note,' Sean said, pocketing the single sheet of paper.

'I promise,' the boy said. Major Duffy was his hero and he would have died for him if he had asked.

Sean painfully walked the couple of blocks to the court house where the flotsam of Sydney's criminal underworld waited inside for the decisions that would be made against them. Sean's first client was a former soldier who had lost his eye at Ypres and been returned home to be discharged onto a pension. His name was Harry Griffiths and he had

317

been arrested in a bar room brawl and charged with drunk and disorderly behaviour and causing damage to the property of the public house.

Harry had been granted bail by a sympathetic magistrate whose own son was serving on the Western Front. He stood at the steps to the magnificent sandstone building waiting for his legal representative. 'Hello, Harry,' Sean said, shaking his client's hand. 'Are you ready to face the beak?'

Harry Griffiths was a man in his mid-thirties. He wore a black leather eye patch and was tall and broad shouldered, denoting his physical strength. Sean knew that his appearance alone might prejudice the magistrate into believing the publican who would appear as a witness for the prosecution.

'As right as I will ever be, Major Duffy,' Harry replied, letting go of his bone-crushing grip on Sean's hand. 'I see that you are getting around pretty good on your cane now.'

Sean had forced himself to learn to walk again on his artificial legs and now was able to cope with the nagging pain. 'I will be presenting the story that you did not cause all the damage and that you had been provoked to defend yourself,' Sean said, walking with great care up the broad stone steps to the entrance of the court. 'But I doubt you will be able to get off scot-free even in the best-case scenario.'

'I know that, Major,' Harry said and suddenly paused halfway up the steps. Sean glanced in the direction that had caught his client's attention to see Detective Inspector Jack Firth speaking with another man at the top of the stairs.

'That bastard!' Harry spat. 'He's still around.'

'You know Inspector Firth?'

'Before I went away to the front, I was a copper in Sydney,' Harry answered. 'Firth was a sergeant at my station and we had a falling out that helped me decide on joining up.'

'What happened?' Sean asked.

'Firth was on the take and one day, while I was on my beat, he turned up drunk to get me to help him do over a shopkeeper who had not paid his dues,' Harry explained. 'I refused and then he had it in for me. I got hauled up before the divisional boss who chewed me out for not being worthy of my uniform. Firth had told lies about me and I was on the fast road to be dismissed anyway.'

Sean shook his head in sympathy.

'How much is having you represent me going to cost?' Harry continued. 'The pension don't pay a lot.'

'My services are free to ex-servicemen. But I might have a job for you that pays a bit on the side.'

Harry turned to Sean with an expression of interest. He had been unemployed since his discharge and had trouble finding work, attempting to support himself, his wife and three children – all under ten years of age – on his meagre pension. 'I will do anything, Major,' Harry said.

'Don't worry, it's legal,' Sean hurried to add in case this former police officer and soldier thought he might have to break the law. 'Our firm is looking for a man,' he said. 'Kind of private investigator, you could say.'

'Sounds bonzer to me,' Harry replied. 'The Mrs is getting a bit sick of me hanging around, and I wouldn't be in trouble now if I were working instead of getting drunk at the pub.'

'Good, now let's see if we can get you off for good behaviour,' Sean said, glancing over his shoulder as they entered the doorway. He could see Jack Firth staring at him with a smirk on his face. Sean would work towards wiping off that smirk.

Sean knew that the magistrate had a son at the front and argued his defence along sympathetic lines. He also knew that the presiding magistrate was an Irishman and

Sean cunningly introduced that the publican who had laid the complaint was a firm supporter of the Australian prime minister, Billy Hughes, who had crusaded to have eligible Australian males conscripted for service in the British war against Germany and her allies. Two referendums had been fought and the second clearly supported the first in defeating the bill to introduce conscription, and so all the Australian troops fighting were still volunteers. Sean even added that the publican was known to provide hospitality to shirkers. His case was blatantly aimed at the magistrate's sympathies with the men who had fought, giving a major part of their life to the country.

The magistrate leaned back in his chair and made his decision. The defendant was found guilty of being drunk and disorderly, but not of inflicting the damage to the licensee's property. The now outraged man sitting behind the police prosecutor had not produced any witnesses to prove his case. Besides, as the magistrate looked down from his bench, he saw two wounded war heroes appearing before him.

Sean and Harry left the courthouse with Harry beaming his satisfaction.

'Thank you, Major,' Harry said, vigorously shaking Sean's hand. 'I thought I was for it.'

'We were lucky,' Sean answered and reached into his pocket for a handful of notes which he passed to Harry. 'Call this an advance on your retainer,' he said, pressing the notes into the startled former soldier's hand. 'It comes with the condition that you remain away from licensed premises unless you are on an investigation for me.'

'I can promise that,' Harry said, remembering the hunger in his wife and children's tiny faces and the shame was enough to satisfy the promise. 'Thank you, Major.'

'I want you to learn as much as you can about Inspector Firth's activities that might be deemed unlawful,' Sean continued. 'Especially any links that he might have to a Mr George Macintosh.'

Harry nodded. 'I still have cobbers in the force and I know one or two good crims who have had dealings with Firth.'

'Good,' Sean replied. 'As soon as you get something worthwhile you are to report to me and I will pay a bonus if I feel it can be used. In the meantime, you will be paid your retainer each Friday at my office.'

'You are a good man, Major, and from what I have heard, a bloody good soldier in your time.'

Sean did not respond to the compliment as he still carried the guilt of losing his nerve at Fromelles. It was a private guilt he would carry to the grave. But from the threat Firth had delivered earlier, Sean knew that the corrupt policeman must be on George Macintosh's payroll and Sean would use the law as his weapon in his fight against Macintosh.

Major Alex Macintosh hardly remembered being stretchered out of the lines. He was not alone, as the Germans had delivered a barrage of artillery shells on the Australian troops, killing and wounding many. He wavered between life and death as he lay in a row of stretchers outside a former farm house, now being used as a medical clearing station. A doctor had bent over him in the rainy night and under the pale light of a hurricane lantern examined him briefly. Alex's face was swathed in bandages and he heard the medical officer grunt that he was to be left with the last of the wounded for treatment. In his pain now slowly dulled by the morphine, Alex knew that he had probably been exiled to those that had been deemed in triage as hopelessly wounded and likely to die. He could taste blood in his mouth and found it hard to breathe. Beside him a dying soldier whimpered for his mother. Alex wanted to comfort him but could not see the soldier in the wet, dark night. Alex found his own comfort as his thoughts drifted to Giselle and his young son. His last thoughts were about his family before the blood filled his lungs and drowned him, shrapnel having also ripped through his chest.

When the sun rose in a sky swept with low, scudding clouds delivering drizzle, the medics came to sort the still living from the dead. One bent over to prise a blood-spattered photograph from the dead Australian major's fingers and glanced at it. It showed a very pretty young woman holding a smiling baby. He rifled through the dead officer's clothing for any personal effects to be sent home to his next of kin, and removed one of his identity disks, leaving the other on the body for future identification.

Then the medical assistant moved onto the dead body beside the Australian major. He was a young German soldier, whose bleary eyes stared up at the sky. The medic knew that he must work quickly, because the stretchers would be desperately needed for the coming battle for Passchendaele.

Giselle received her telegram before the public release of Alex's name in the newspapers. Her grief was so great that she fainted. She was revived by Angus MacDonald, who called Louise to the room to assist him. Louise picked up the crumpled telegram from the floor of the foyer and read it quickly. She only needed to see Alex's name and the three dreaded words, killed in action, to know why Giselle was in such a state. Now more than ever Louise would have to call on all her own strength to nurse her best friend through her dreadful grief.

As she helped carry Giselle to a couch, an awful thought crossed Louise's mind. If Alex was dead then George would take possession of the house, leaving Giselle and her son homeless. Louise despised her husband but now she felt raw hate for him. How could a man do such a thing to his brother's family? If Alex's father was ever needed to stop his eldest son from carrying out such a dastardly act it was now. The secret had been kept from Alex and no-one other than Giselle and George seemed to understand such an outrageous arrangement. Whatever the gamble had been, Giselle had lost her husband and her home.

They lay Giselle on the couch and she curled into a foetal position, whimpering like a child. Upstairs, her young son, David, began to cry and was soothed by the nanny. Louise looked across to the old sergeant major and realised that he also would be without a home when George took possession. Maybe all was not lost. Patrick would ensure that his daughter-in-law and grandson would not find themselves destitute on the streets. Ironically, by George seizing the house he was also taking his father's home from him, as Patrick had signed over the title to Alex at the outbreak of war, much to George's fury who thought that he was entitled to half the house. But Patrick had quietly explained that George already had the former residence of the White family given to him by the Macintosh companies as part of his package of benefits for managing the family enterprises. It had nothing to do with his feelings for his eldest son but was merely a matter of providing for them both in appropriate ways.

Louise knew that Sean was fighting to have the contract made null and void but was having little success in the courts. If anyone could help Giselle it had to be Sean.

Meanwhile, Sean's decision to hire Harry Griffiths was already paying off. The former Sydney policeman had used his skills, influence and good rapport with the Sydney underworld to garner information. Harry had been known as tough but fair in his time on the beat. He would ensure that the families of the men he put behind bars were looked after by charitable services, and this brought respect. His nemesis, Jack Firth, also garnered respect, but that was through fear.

Harry, like Jack, was a man whose life shifted between the two worlds of the good and the bad. When he reported to Sean at his office his appearance did not cause any curiosity. The firm was used to seeing such characters pass through its doors in search of legal advice. Sean sat the big man down and offered him tea, which he politely declined.

'Picked up some interesting things about our Jack from some of a dead crim's mates,' Harry said. He'd had conversations with both serving police who had been friends when he had served his community in the blue uniform as well as a few criminals he had known walking the beat. 'A bloke known as Mick O'Rourke had a big mouth, and it appears Firth is definitely on the take big time. From what I learned he is also on the payroll of George Macintosh.' Sean was not surprised to hear this bit of news. 'There is also a rumour that Firth did a job for George Macintosh and paid Mick O'Rourke to travel to America to kill this Macintosh's sister.'

Harry was confirming Sean's suspicions, albeit ones that were based on simply hearsay. If anyone in New South Wales deserved to swing on the gallows it was George Macintosh, he thought bitterly. He was a man born without morals or scruples. 'Harry, I want you to dig as deep as you can into the connections between George Macintosh and Jack Firth,'

Sean said, retrieving an envelope from his desk drawer. 'See if you can find anything to do with a German woman, Mrs Karolina Schumann, and Firth.' Sean was working on a hunch. The fact that Giselle's mother had been mysteriously released from the internment camp and then returned just as mysteriously played on Sean's mind. He felt there was some connection between Karolina's fate and Giselle signing the contract without telling her husband.

'I know a cobber who works in Firth's office,' Harry said, pocketing the envelope Sean had passed to him across the desk. 'Jack is now working for the secret service – or something like that. My cobber can get to see his files but I will have to make it worth his while to put Jack in harm's way.'

Sean opened his desk drawer again, located a five pound note and passed it to Harry.

'I think that should do the job,' Harry said, raising his eyebrows. 'But don't expect him to sign a receipt for the money,' he added with a grin.

'I trust you, Harry,' Sean said, noticing the expression on Harry's face. It was an open and honest look that Sean rarely saw in his business but understood when he saw it. 'Believe me, if all goes well we will nail Detective Inspector Jack Firth.'

'Other than getting my eye back, seeing Firth go down will be the next best thing happening in my life to date,' Harry said, rising from his chair. 'I will get back to you as soon as I have something.'

Sean watched the man leave his office. When the telephone rang, he lifted the handset. It was Louise.

'Darling, have your heard?' she asked.

The smile faded from Sean's face at the tone in his lover's voice. 'Heard what?' Sean replied.

'Giselle has just received a telegram informing her that Alex has been killed in action.'

Sean felt his heart miss a beat. He did not know the man well but had sworn to Patrick Duffy to protect the interests of Alex and his family, and felt a twinge of guilt for not being able to be of much good to date in voiding the disastrous contract Giselle had signed. 'Oh, God!' he groaned, 'How is Giselle taking the news?'

'Very badly,' Louise answered. 'I am with her now and she has just been administered a stiff dose of laudanum. You know what George will do when he learns of Alex's death?'

'I know.'

'Is there anything you can do legally to stop him?'

'Not at this stage,' Sean sighed.

'Then possibly I might be able to do something,' Louise said, alarming Sean.

'I hope that you do not have plans to kill your husband,' Sean countered, considering the worst. 'Not that he does not deserve to be put down like some rabid dog.'

'No. That would give Giselle a home but for the moment please don't ask me what my idea is.'

There was pain in Louise's voice but Sean respected her wishes. In good time she would reveal how she planned to ensure that her sister-in-law was not made homeless and destitute. It was all so bloody messy, Sean thought as he hung up and stared at the bookcases opposite his desk. He had survived one war but his involvement with Louise and the Macintosh family had dragged him into another, where his opponent was capable of cold-blooded murder. Sean could only rely on the former soldier Harry Griffith to get all the information he could to bring both Jack Firth and George Macintosh before the courts. But this would not be easy. Both men were held in high regard by the conservative higher classes in Sydney, and the corrupt policeman also wielded power on the streets of the city.

Brigadier Patrick Duffy was not the only senior officer to have a son killed in this bloody war. When he received the news at his HQ behind the Passchendaele lines, he put on the stoic demeanour of acceptance expected of a senior commander. After all, his own battle plans inevitably resulted in the deaths of soldiers who had fathers trusting in him to keep their sons alive. Patrick could not make an exception with his son but, when he was able to secure time alone in his quarters, he sat on his bed and wept with overwhelming grief at the loss of the son he loved most.

Outside the door to Patrick's quarters, his batman heard his pain and quietly kept all away until the respected brigadier was ready to come out and resume his duties. The batman, an old soldier of many colonial campaigns, had seen this terrible situation before when soldier fathers lost soldier sons. It was not right that fathers outlive their children, he thought, as he waved off a young officer attempting to deliver a signal to Brigade HQ.

'The boss will be out in a sec,' the batman said to the young, fresh-faced second lieutenant. 'He just needs a little time to himself.'

Despite the fact that the batman only wore the two chevrons of a corporal, the more senior commissioned officer knew well he spoke on behalf of the brigadier and quickly removed himself. Within fifteen minutes, Patrick emerged, dry eyed, and returned to his operations room in the former chateau. It was time to get back to this grinding, never-ending war that minced the bodies of young men into the mud, snow and dust of the battlefields without any glimmer of hope for an end. In a couple of weeks he was scheduled to return to England to attend high-level meetings with the British prime minister's office. Normally, he would have welcomed a respite to Blighty but now, with the death of his son, Patrick preferred to remain in France either until he was killed or they won the war.

21

Louise sat behind Angus in the back seat of her sister-in-law's car in a dark mood. She expected to find her husband home. He was usually a stickler for routine, and after six in the evening could be found in his library poring over documents and files pertaining to the management of the family enterprises.

Angus stopped at the front door of the Macintosh house, turned off the engine and got out to open Louise's door. He remained standing beside the car, hoping his physical presence would be a warning to George Macintosh.

'You are certain you do not wish me to accompany you inside?' he asked as Louise stepped out.

'No thank you, Angus,' Louise replied with a weak smile. 'I am sure my husband will prove to be a reasonable man.'

Angus was not so sure. He had watched George grow

329

into the despicable person he had become and was well aware of his violent character.

Louise took a breath, walked to the front door and knocked. She was greeted by a young girl of around fifteen years of age whom she did not recognise. The girl looked Louise up and down suspiciously as she stood with the door ajar.

'Is Mr Macintosh in?' Louise asked, returning the young girl's surly stare with an imperious one of her own.

'Who are you, Mrs?' the girl asked insolently.

'I am Mr Macintosh's wife, and I would mind your manners if I were you,' Louise said, pushing past the girl to enter the foyer and call out, 'George, I wish to speak to you.'

The girl stepped back and in the light Louise could see that she was very pretty. Louise stood for a moment before her husband appeared at the top of the stairs.

'What do you want?' he asked with his hands on his hips. 'I thought that you had decided to leave.'

His rebuke caused Louise to feel a flush of fury but she forced herself to remain calm. 'I would rather speak with you alone,' she replied, glancing at the girl with an expression of distaste for her appearance. 'Has our nanny gone away, George?' she asked, climbing the stairs to confront her estranged husband.

She did not receive a reply. No doubt her husband had made the young nanny pregnant and quickly shipped her off to some country town until the girl had given birth. Louise knew that Macintosh money was being funnelled into the expenses, and she felt just a short flash of pity for the girl whom her husband had probably promised the world to.

'You can leave us, Jenny,' George said to the girl wavering in the foyer. 'I wish to speak with Mrs Macintosh in private.'

The girl nodded and disappeared from the foyer to the kitchen.

'I also notice that Herbert is no longer to be seen,' Louise said. It had been Herbert's job as the valet to answer the door to visitors.

'He was old and useless,' George answered. 'I had to discharge him.'

'Or was he seeing more than he should under this roof?' Louise countered.

She did not get a reply from her husband who turned his back and led her to his library. Louise followed, closing the door behind her.

'My time is valuable,' George snapped, fiddling with a pile of papers on his desk. 'Why are you here?'

'I came to see my son, among other things,' Louise said, preferring to stand in the dark room that smelled of old timber and cigar smoke.

'You gave up the right to see my son when you left this house,' George snarled.

'I have simply been staying with my sister-in-law on a family visit,' Louise answered mildly. 'And now I am back.'

'My son is in good hands with his new nanny,' George replied.

'You don't mean that young girl who met me at the door?' Louise scoffed.

'No, Jenny is the sister of the new nanny, a very capable young woman who came with good references,' George said, pushing the sheets of papers aside and glaring at his estranged wife. 'I know that you must be here to discuss the eviction of my sister-in-law from the house.'

Louise took a step towards his desk. 'How could you do it?' she asked, still desperately attempting to keep her calm, despite seeing her husband through a red haze of hate. 'Your own brother is killed fighting the King's enemies, and you sit back here in your comfortable world of dinners and parties with shirker friends as equally as despicable as you, and decide to make the wife of a hero homeless and destitute.'

'I hear in your words an echo of your crippled lover,' he said, smirking, feeling that he had the upper hand in what was about to unfold. After all, the real issue in the world was money and how it could be used to obtain power. War was simply an irritating digression in the world of international finance, and those who went off to fight like his father and brother merely idealistic fools.

'Major Duffy is not a cripple in bed,' Louise countered. Her words had a stinging effect which registered on her husband's face as he shifted uncomfortably in his leather chair. But she knew that she must not provoke him in this meeting. Far too much was at stake. 'But that is not why I am here,' she continued, attempting to defuse the anger she could see in her husband's eyes. 'I have come here to ask you to reconsider evicting Giselle.'

George shook his head. 'I am sorry, but that is not negotiable. She has a week to get herself, her brat and any of her staff out of the house, or I will have the law do the job for me and that could prove embarrassing for her. I would not be the only landlord in these times to evict the wives and families of dead servicemen from their residences, because they are no longer able to meet the rent.'

'If I return as your wife would you consider allowing Giselle and her son to remain in their home?' Louise asked in a quiet voice.

'No,' George answered with the trace of a smile. 'But I would provide Giselle somewhere to live and a small stipend.' Louise frowned at his answer as George leaned forward to continue. 'The family has a cattle station in central

Queensland called Glen View, currently under the management of a man appointed by my father. He is in need of a housekeeper and I am sure my sister-in law could learn to do what is required if she wishes to have enough money to raise her son. But to return home you would also have to give up your crippled lover – only then will I allow you unlimited access to my son.'

Louise took in all her husband had proposed. If she was living under the same roof as her hated husband she could at least monitor matters concerning Giselle and her son's welfare. But giving up Sean was something else. 'That offer of financial security is to also extend to Mr Angus MacDonald,' she responded. 'He is to be given employment at Glen View as well.'

For a moment George mused on the possibility of the valet living in the semi-arid lands of central Queensland and remembered the stories he had heard of his father and the old Scot soldiering together in the deserts of the North Africa and the Sudan. Maybe it would be like going home for him to be surrounded by miles of empty land. 'If he wishes, he may travel with Giselle and I will ensure that he has a home on Glen View. You see, I am not as hard as you may think. But there is nothing to negotiate about that lawyer lover of yours. You return home and desist in ever seeing him again. If you attempt to meet with him I will know, and promise that I will take steps to prevent you ever seeing my son again. You know that I have enough influence to do that.'

Louise knew that her husband was not bluffing and realised, as she stood in the library staring at the collection of Aboriginal spears on the wall behind him, how much she would dearly love to remove one and thrust it through his body. Her gaze returned to him as he sat smugly watching her, waiting for an answer.

'I will do as you wish,' she said in a flat voice. 'You are to provide travel for Giselle, David and Angus to Glen View and ensure that they receive a fair – and even generous – allowance from the Macintosh company funds. In return, I will promise not to see Major Duffy and you will allow me unlimited access to my son.'

George rose from behind his desk. 'There,' he said, reaching out to touch her face. Louise recoiled from his touch and he dropped his hand. 'You see how easy it is to get what you want when you are prepared to discuss things in a civilised manner. I will have one of the company employees go over to the old family home and fetch your things tomorrow morning.'

'And Jenny?' Louise spat. 'What of her?'

'Do you expect me to put the poor girl out on the streets? Where could she go?'

'You can put the widow of your brother on the street,' Louise retorted, knowing full well that the girl would remain as her husband's plaything.

George turned his back and strode to the large French window to gaze down at Angus standing in the driveway with his brawny arms folded across his broad chest. He had always hated the man and was pleased to be able to exile him to the wilderness. When he had received news that his brother had been killed in action, George had trouble pretending to grieve for his loss and had awkwardly accepted condolences, uttering words such as that Alex had such a promising future. Now, only his father stood in the way. George had already taken steps to cut Patrick out of any interests in the family enterprises by suggesting that he was not demonstrating any real management interest, and therefore that he should be retired if the financial future was to be assured. Very few of the directors of the family's numerous companies disagreed with his arguments, and steps were already in place to remove Patrick on a generous annual allowance. How much kinder could he be?

'Well, if there is nothing else, you should be on your way back to discuss the matter we have settled,' George said to his wife. 'I feel that much has been achieved between us this evening.'

'How do you think your father will react when he hears what you have done?' Louise asked, hoping that the veiled threat might unsettle her husband from his smugness.

'Oh, I suspect that he will be outraged,' George said casually. 'But his opinions no longer carry any weight in the running of the family companies. I have already seen to that.'

Louise turned to walk away. Short of murder, nothing could stop this evil man. She had once been smitten by his debonair demeanour. Now all she could see was a creature as loathsome as any that had been spawned by the devil. As she left the library she heard her husband's parting words. 'When I conclude a contract it is final.'

Louise knew exactly what he meant. At least now she could be with her son and have some time to scheme for a future free of George's influences. How she would do that was still a mystery to her but it would not include Sean Duffy. She had agreed to parting with Sean for she knew that as long as she was linked to the former soldier, his life would be in peril.

Nursing David on her lap as they sat in the drawing room, Giselle listened as Louise explained the deal she had made.

'I have little choice,' Giselle finally replied. 'I suppose it will be a little like living on our plantation when I was growing up.'

'Angus has agreed – if you accepted the offer – to go with you to Glen View,' Louise added. 'I will make sure George keeps his word to pay you an allowance to help in the education and raising of David.'

'You have always been a wonderful friend, more like a sister,' Giselle said, stroking her son's curly locks in a distracted way. 'I don't know what we could have done without your help. I was expecting to be on the streets and living in one of those slums.'

'That will never happen so long as I draw breath,' Louise said forcefully and, leaning forward, resting her gloved hand on Giselle's knee. 'You are my sister for life.'

Giselle broke into tears, confusing her son who slipped from her lap to stare at his mother who was now being hugged by Aunt Louise. But among the tears there was laughter for the small victory Louise had won, and the boy heard the laughter knowing all was well with his world, his father but a dim memory.

Stunned, Sean Duffy read the letter delivered to his office. In her fine handwriting Louise explained that she had decided to return to her husband for the sake of her son – and other reasons she did not wish to elaborate on. Sean felt ill as he placed the two pages on his desk. There had not been a hint about the sudden break-up and the last time they had lain together she had spoken softly against his chest, saying that she would love him forever.

Anger replaced his shock and Sean sensed the breath of George Macintosh in the words. Somehow he had been able to manipulate his estranged wife into returning to him, he thought, reaching for the walking cane. He hobbled to the window of his office. He was expecting Harry Griffith to report to him and the knock on his door announced his appointment was on time.

'Major,' Harry said when he entered. Sean turned to him and Harry could see the concern in his face. 'Everything okay, Boss?' he asked.

'Nothing that can't wait,' Sean replied, making his way back to his desk. 'Do you have anything for me?'

Harry beamed at the question. 'My cobber at Jack's office gave me some good information on that Mrs Karolina Schumann,' he said. 'He was able to have a look at the files old Jack keeps locked away – except that my cobber knows where he hides the key. He read through them and it seems that the sheila you mentioned is on the list of German spies who was supposed to be arrested, and although Jack makes no notes, it seems she is still in the Holdsworthy camp out Liverpool way.'

'She was temporarily allowed to live with her daughter,' Sean said.

'That has to be crook if she is a Hun spy,' Harry said, frowning. 'Inspector Firth is in serious dereliction of his duty if he did not arrest her as he was instructed.'

'But how could he cover it up? Surely his superiors would know about Frau Schumann's status as a confirmed spy and be questioning why she is still at Holdsworthy and not in a prison cell?'

'In these times the left hand don't know what the right hand is doing,' Harry surmised. 'He has the file under lock and key and I wouldn't put it past old Jack to do away with her, solving the problem of not bringing her before a court.'

Sean did not question his investigator's conclusion that the corrupt policeman was capable of killing anyone. Sean also was aware from the threatening note that on behalf of George he was under the policeman's scrutiny. And despite displaying confidence that he could not hurt him in any way, privately Sean was not so sure. Accidents did happen – and he might just end up as another one on the city streets.

'I think that I should travel to the camp and speak with Mrs Schumann,' he said. 'It is possible that she may be able to throw some light on matters I am now dealing with concerning her daughter.'

Sean's mind was racing as he attempted to put the pieces together. He looked up at the big man standing over him and, with a mumbled thanks, reached into his desk, passing the brown envelope to Harry who thanked him and bid him a good afternoon.

When Harry stepped onto the street he was startled to see Detective Inspector Jack Firth walking straight towards him.

'Hello, old son,' Jack said, without offering his hand. 'I've heard talk around the traps that you have been asking a lot of questions about me.'

Harry stood nose to nose with his former police superior but, strangely, did not feel intimidated. 'Good to see that you made inspector,' he replied. 'Lucky for you there is a war on, and the department is scraping the bottom of the barrel.'

The insult caused Jack Firth's smile to turn into grimace. Harry instinctively balanced on his feet as if ready to receive a bayonet attack from a German soldier and the policeman sensed his defensive stance. He could see that war had changed the former policeman.

'I heard that you are working for that slimy cripple, Duffy,' Jack responded, taking a step back. The street was crowded with workers and shoppers and neither man could afford a brawl. It was a standoff where words were the weapons. 'Just a word of advice. If you don't want to end up on the wrong side of the dock, keep away from Duffy.'

'Don't know what you mean, Jack.' Harry smiled. 'Major Duffy is my legal representative.'

Jack Firth was frustrated that he could not intimidate his former junior police officer and glowered at him. 'You think the army made something of you,' he snarled. 'Think again, boyo. You are back in my world now – and so is your family.'

A cold fury swept over Harry and he braced himself to launch an attack on the smirking police detective.

'Inspector Firth, is there anything I can do for you?'

Both men turned their attention to Sean Duffy, who stood leaning on his walking stick a few paces away.

'Nothing I know of,' Jack replied before turning to walk away.

'I just happened to be looking out my window and I noticed you and Inspector Firth getting reacquainted,' Sean said mildly to Harry, who was still bristling with fury. 'I would hate to have to defend you again for an assault on one of the city's most well-known policemen.'

Harry felt the adrenaline easing, realising that the police inspector had been baiting him. He was suddenly grateful for Sean's timely intervention.

'So help me,' he said softly, 'I am going to kill that bastard one day. I killed men in the trenches whom I didn't even know, and I can bet they were blokes who I could have sat down and had a cold beer with as cobbers. The government gave me a medal for killing those men, who were not much different to me – but Firth is a born bastard, deserving of being killed.'

'Needless to say I did not hear that,' Sean said, slapping his investigator on the shoulder. 'But I promise you that one day Firth is going to answer for all his corruption and evil.'

Harry stared at the solicitor with a slight expression of

amusement. The trouble with gentlemen is that they had a belief in justice, he reflected. Harry had long come to realise that there was justice and the law – and neither existed together. One day he would find his kind of justice with Firth, the kind that the law did not condone.

It was very still and hot. A heat haze shimmered across the brigalow, but a bank of black and white clouds boiled up over the sea of stunted scrub, promising a drenching that would bring alive the very earth itself.

Wallarie gazed across the plains at the growing cloud bank to the west, hoping that the rain would come to cool his body and run in rivulets down his sacred hill to splash into cooling rockpools he would be able to drink from. He would return to the sacred cave and sit listening to the life around him as the ancestor spirits watched down upon the earth where they once walked. If he was lucky on his journey home he would find a spiny anteater for the cooking fires. He could make the flour cakes and wash them down with heavily sugared black tea.

Lightning flashed and seconds later the thunder reverberated around the hill. From under his overhang the old Aboriginal felt a twinge of fear. He relished his reputation for being a magic man who could turn into an eagle or appear to those who first met him as a young warrior. But he also feared the forces greater than himself and, right now, he was looking directly into the face of the lightning spirit, who had the power to turn the scrub into a raging inferno.

A strong breeze pushing ahead of the summer storm washed over his scarred body. A voice was speaking to him in the old language that only he and the pastor knew. Pastor Karl said he was writing it down so the world would not forget that the Darambal people once lived in these lands. Wallarie had not understood why the Lutheran pastor should spend all his time recording the words when only he and Wallarie spoke the language anymore.

With a sudden roaring the wall of water swept towards Wallarie, flattening the scrub and swamping the hill. It was not just the deluge of heavy rain but a release of some savage spirit, bringing a terrible fear to the man who could soar on the wings of an eagle. In the roar of the wind and rain he could hear the old men who were now his ancestors talking to him softly.

Wallarie retreated to the dark cave and the voices became louder. They told him that a rent would appear in the fabric of Glen View, and warned him that he must leave this place and wander in the wilderness for many days and nights before returning.

The old warrior trembled at the message he had received, and through the mist of time he saw people coming to Glen View from the south. They were strangers he had never met and yet he knew them from his dreams. Wallarie began singing to appease the spirits but his tired voice was drowned by the sound of the storm rising over the plains.

22

Sean Duffy made the journey to the internment camp where he was granted an interview with the acting commandant. A major in his sixties, he had served in the Boer War and had a fatherly demeanour. After chatting about Sean's experiences on the Western Front and his own on the veldt of Africa, the two had established that they shared the common bond of battle.

'You telephoned ahead and left a message that you wish to interview Frau Schumann, as her legal representative, Major Duffy,' the commandant said, fingering the message sheet that had been written out at the switchboard.

'Yes,' Sean answered, hoping that Karolina had not mentioned that he was not in fact her legal representative. 'It is in relation to a property dispute on which she may be able to shed some light.'

The commandant leaned back in his chair, hoping the

space between his expanding stomach and the desk would let some air flow past. The summer heat had already hit Sydney and the ever-present smell of bushfires surrounding the city drifted on the little breeze there was in the room. 'I suppose there can be no harm in that,' the commandant answered. 'I will get one of my men to escort you to Frau Schumann's quarters.'

Permission granted, Sean was taken by a soldier to a large building made of timber and corrugated iron. When Sean stepped inside he could clearly see that the building was a hall, and judging from the religious icons on the walls most probably doubled as a chapel.

'Mrs Schumann usually spends her days in the company of the Lutheran pastor,' the soldier explained.

Sean saw a tall, gaunt man approach. He was wearing a shabby black suit that was much patched.

'I am Pastor von Fellmann,' he said without offering his hand. 'How can I assist you?'

Sean introduced himself and stated that he had come to interview Karolina about a property matter, while the escorting soldier hovered to one side, obviously bored with his job of monitoring the lawyer.

'Karolina, you have a visitor,' Karl said.

Karolina stepped out from a small alcove, immediately recognising Sean from his visits to her daughter's house.

'Major Duffy, I hope that you have not come here to bring bad news,' she said, extending her hand.

'Yes – and no,' Sean replied. 'I do not know if you have been told of your son-in-law's death at the front.'

'I am sorry,' Karolina responded with genuine concern despite having always considered Alex her enemy. 'I was not informed. He was a good husband and father.'

'Well, to cut a long story short, that also means that your

daughter is now without her home as a result of the contract she signed with Alex's brother. George has, however, found her employment and a place to live on a cattle station in central Queensland. I am here to ask if you know why your daughter would have signed such a foolish contract in the first place.'

'My daughter did not tell you?' Karolina asked, appearing genuinely surprised at the news.

'No, but I suspect that she may have confided in you as her mother.'

'I will find you chairs to sit on,' Karl said, walking away.

'Giselle was forced to agree to the contract in exchange for my life,' Karolina replied wearily. 'I think that the policeman who came to arrest me on spying charges is a friend of George Macintosh, and something was arranged to trade my life for the deal made with my daughter.'

'Was that policeman Inspector Jack Firth?' Sean asked.

'Yes,' Karolina replied. 'Since I have been returned to the camp only the protection of Pastor von Fellmann has kept me from being killed by certain people in here,' she continued. 'What he has learned from loyal members of his congregation is that a rumour was circulated that I had informed on those loyal to the Fatherland. That could only be started by the policeman who arrested me.'

Sean had already taken that leap in his reasoning; Firth would be rid of the woman's embarrassing existence if she were dead.

The pastor returned with two chairs and placed them in the centre of the hall. Sean could see from the looks that passed between the Jewish woman and Christian missionary that their relationship was close.

'I can assure you, Mrs Schumann, that I am looking after your daughter and grandson's wellbeing, and I also extend

344

that to you if you wish to avail yourself of my legal services,' Sean said.

'Thank you, Mr Duffy,' Karolina said. 'I have not yet expressed my sympathies for your injuries.'

'Just the bloody luck of the draw,' Sean replied, waving off her kind thoughts. 'I know that you are a loyal citizen of your country and I hope the damned war ends soon so that no more legs and arms go west on either side.'

'Yes,' Karolina nodded. 'The war seems to have no end and soon there will be no young men to return home from either side.'

Sean chatted with Karolina for a short time before excusing himself and going back to the commandant's office to sign out. He was met by the commandant, who said he hoped that Sean's visit had been fruitful.

'Is there any chance of any of your internees being released?' Sean asked, leaning over the big book with its columns of names of visitors and times.

'Yes,' the commandant replied. 'Some of the internees have been proved to be loyal citizens and are being released back to their homes. I have men and women in here with German or Austrian names, who were born in this country and hardly speak German. A damned shambles, if you ask me. At the beginning of the war neighbours often used the hysteria to settle old scores. I believe you met Pastor von Fellmann. He is a good example of a man who should be back on his mission station and not locked up here at the government's pleasure. I have a feeling he may be released within the next couple of months if the paperwork goes through without any hitches.'

'What about Mrs Karolina Schumann?' Sean asked, placing the fountain pen back on its cradle.

'Mrs Schumann is an odd one,' the commandant

frowned. 'She does not attempt to hide the fact that she is loyal to her Fatherland – but what damage can a lone woman do, I ask you?'

Sean could have answered but he now saw himself in the role as her legal representative and kept quiet on the matter. 'Is there any chance of having her released?'

'I doubt it,' the commandant replied. 'She is under a bit of a cloud. One moment she is free and then she is returned to us without any explanation.'

'What circumstances might get her freed?' Sean persisted.

The commandant scratched his balding skull. 'Maybe exceptional family circumstances,' he finally replied.

As he drove back to his office along a dusty, rutted road Sean reflected on what he now knew about George Macintosh and Jack Firth. The link was beyond doubt, and it appeared that Macintosh pulled the strings. The two made a dangerous pair and Sean felt even more unease for his safety, despite the fact that Louise had made it plain she wanted nothing else to do with him. He had attempted to telephone her, but she refused to take his calls. Not satisfied that she had suddenly fallen out of love with him, he also realised that he would have to find some resolution to the problem of her husband's ever-growing power in the Macintosh family.

Sean found himself thinking about France and Patrick Duffy. It would be winter on the battlefields and the icy ground would be ideal to spread shrapnel. He shuddered at the memories. He honked his horn at a horse-drawn dray occupying the centre of the narrow road and pulled past it with some difficulty. The bloody government had to do something about the roads around the city, he thought angrily. The advent of automobiles meant they needed better roads to ensure safety. But Sean was pleased that he had something else to think about other than the men he had left behind to continue living with frostbite, bitter cold and barbed wire.

The fighting along the Passchendaele front had exhausted the Australians and New Zealanders, and those in high command recognised that the weary, battle-worn men would have to be pulled out of the Ypres salient. As usual, for all the tactical victories achieved with sheer courage and blood, the Germans had not been dislodged from the Belgian coast, thus denying the Allies the ports badly needed for resupply. Under orders, Patrick had gladly withdrawn with his brigade to a quieter section of the front. He hoped that they would remain out of the fighting until his battalions could be reinforced, and his men given rest from standing and sleeping in the mud of their trenches. Looking back, he remembered how his men had bled in the lowlands of Flanders the previous year and throughout the year now drawing to a close.

Patrick had established his brigade headquarters behind his lines in a green field shivering under the grey skies of the coming winter. He appreciated that his HQ must be located out of enemy artillery range, but close enough to coordinate the movement of his battalions. It was always a juggling act to find the right distance. The days would pass as he oversaw his staff officers, planned the logistics for his brigade, and prepared orders for the day-to-day defences of the battalions. Signals flowed, were logged and intelligence summaries updated. Brigade HQ was the brain of the body, and Patrick's HQ had a reputation of competency due to his quiet but firm leadership.

He stood over a large photographic map beside his operations officer, a major who had once been a grazier from Victoria, pondering on the movement of long-range German artillery batteries photographed by a recon aeroplane.

'Still no threat,' the major commented, tracing the distance between their location and that of the enemy artillery units with a ruler.

'The information is two days old,' Patrick reminded him. 'I would like to have the Poms do another fly over and confirm the current position of their big guns,' he said. 'Arrange to have a signal sent to our English flyers for a mission on that sector.'

'Yes, sir,' the major replied, straightening his back while scribbling down the coordinates of the German artillery's location.

Patrick was aware that a young signals corps captain hovered like an excited terrier behind him, clasping a sheet of paper. Patrick turned to him. 'Yes, Mr Grant?' he asked.

'Sir, I think this might be of interest to you,' he said, passing the sheet to Patrick who quickly read the abbreviated contents, raising his eyebrows and returning his attention back to the captain.

'Send a signal to say that I request the company of our esteemed prisoner. He is to be escorted here by eighteen hundred hours to dine with the officers of our mess.'

'Yes, sir,' the captain replied and hurried off to telephone divisional HQ.

'Well, I will be damned,' Patrick muttered.

His ops officer had not seen his boss smile since the death of his son.

'Some good news, sir?' he asked politely.

'Not good news for the Hun, Major,' Patrick said. 'They had one of their regimental commanders captured just a bit too far forward from his HQ by one of our forward patrols. It also happens that he is a distant relative of mine, General Major Kurt von Fellmann, and is now a prisoner of war. He will be dining with us tonight in the mess and I think you will like the fellow. He speaks fluent English and is a likeable sort of chap.'

It was kind of funny, the major thought, that the capture of a high-ranking enemy general could bring some happiness to the brigadier.

That evening, Kurt von Fellmann arrived at Patrick's HQ under guard by two red-capped British military police. Patrick met him outside his HQ in the driveway and both men saluted each other before exchanging firm handshakes, as a small but curious crowd of Australian staff officers lingered briefly at the entrance to the HQ, looking on.

Kurt was dressed in his grey field uniform and Patrick could see that he had lost a lot of weight since he had last seen him in Sydney before the outbreak of the war.

'I must congratulate you, Patrick,' Kurt said, accepting the cigar offered to him. 'I was foolish enough to be too far forward of my lines on an inspection and had underestimated the cunning of your band of thieves. So here I am, a prisoner of your British allies.'

Patrick held out a light for Kurt who lit his cigar, sucked in the smoke and blew it out into the chill of the late afternoon.

'I am pleased to see that you are still alive, my friend,' Patrick said. 'I know that my Aunt Penelope must be relieved to know that you are now out of harm's way.'

'I suppose that you are right,' Kurt sighed as Patrick led them on a slow stroll through what was left of the garden of the French manor. The two MPs trailed a discreet distance behind.

'You know,' Kurt said, pausing to gaze across the fields divided by quaint stone walls, 'you and I have been pitted against each other as far back as Fromelles. Our intelligence service has been very good at keeping a dossier on your career. I have often thought of you on your side of the line.'

Learning his distant cousin had been aware of his military movements, Patrick had a painful thought. Possibly his eldest son had been providing the information. But he dismissed the idea. It was too horrible to think that his own flesh and blood could be capable of such a treacherous deed. George might be ruthless in his ambition to swell the family coffers but he was not a traitor.

'You look as if you could do with a hearty meal,' Patrick said. 'I have ordered a special dinner tonight of Yorkshire pudding to mark your company with myself and my officers.'

'I have always liked your English pudding,' Kurt replied, placing his foot on a low, stone wall. 'I am afraid that you must know the British naval blockade is having an effect on the Fatherland. Many women and children will die of hunger and that must play on your conscience, my friend.'

'You have had no conscience using your zeppelin dirigibles to bomb innocent women and children in London,' Patrick countered.

'We should not argue about the morality of what we do,' Kurt said, placating him. 'We are, after all, simple soldiers who do the bidding of our political masters.' On that point they both agreed and Kurt shifted the conversation. 'Tell me, how is my cousin Alex? Intelligence informed me that he has been sent to the front.'

'Alex was killed a few weeks ago on the Ypres front.'

'I am sorry. I did not know. Please accept my condolences. He was a fine man and a good officer, as I recall from when we were at your regimental ball in Sydney back in '14.'

'Thank you for your kind words of condolence,' Patrick replied, looking out across the fields to the horizon where he saw the flashes light up the darkening sky. Seconds later, he heard the booming and recognised the sound of long-range German artillery.

Kurt stood up straight to view the horizon. With little time to react, both men heard the distinctive sound of large artillery shells hurtling through the darkening sky in their direction. The first one slammed into the ground and exploded in a great geyser of smoke, earth and fire in the field they had been gazing at. The next four rounds exploded in a cluster just short of the manor. Patrick spun around to shout but before the words could leave his mouth another round blasted rock and shrapnel a few feet from where he and Kurt stood. Kurt was flung through the air by the blast and fell heavily ten yards away. Winded, he fought for breath, his ears ringing.

The shelling had ceased for now and Kurt guessed that his heavy guns were carrying out a registration mission. As he sat up to examine himself for injuries he saw Patrick lying face down in a pool of blood twenty paces from where he sat. One of the two MPs guarding him had been blown into bloody scraps from a direct hit and it seemed that Patrick had taken metal pieces from the exploding shell. Kurt scrambled to his feet.

'Patrick!' he yelled. He could barely hear his own voice as the blast had left him with a severe ringing in his ears. Already officers were spilling from the manor to race towards their brigadier.

Kurt rolled Patrick onto his back and groaned. Tiny wisps of smoke drifted from what was left of his chest and stomach. A large piece of red hot metal had all but ripped Patrick apart. Kurt could see that his cousin was still alive, but had little to no hope of surviving the terrible wound inflicted by the shrapnel. Patrick opened his eyes, his face unmarked by the blast. He could not speak, however, and within moments the old soldier died. Kurt took Patrick's hand but felt himself being pulled back.

'Leave him alone, you bloody Hun,' the operations major snarled as he dropped to his knees beside Patrick. The major's tears flowed, knowing that his friend and respected commanding officer was dead. Wiping away the tears with the back of his jacket sleeve, the major rose to his feet. He glanced at the captured German officer and felt a twinge of guilt for his outburst when he saw in the German officer's face his own grief.

'I'm sorry, sir,' the Australian major said gently. 'The brigadier told me that you were related.'

'Yes,' Kurt replied, his ears still ringing. 'And now the war is over for us both on this day.'

'I am sure that the brigadier would have wanted you to stay and dine with us tonight,' the Australian major offered.

'Thank you, major,' Kurt replied, brushing down his uniform. 'We will have the opportunity to raise our glasses to toast the simple soldiers that we are on both sides. No toasts to Kings and Kaisers – just to the young men dying in this war.'

The last remaining thorn in his side had been removed, George gloated when the news was delivered that his father had fallen on the Western Front. He was careful to present a sombre face to all he knew, receiving condolences for the loss of the man Sydney knew and respected for his philanthropic services to the community. George decided that he should have a memorial service for both his father and his brother on the same day to save time and expense. He chose a chapel that he knew his father's militia unit used for services and the little church was packed out with senior military officers who knew Patrick and Alex. Giselle was unable to attend as she was already en route to Queensland but Louise placed two wreaths on the altar on her behalf.

With the service over George was pleased to be out of the church. Although he had played the grieving brother and son, he had allowed his wife to make all the arrangements for the service and the wake that would be held at their home. Louise had done a very good job but as George stepped into the bright sunshine he was startled to see Sean Duffy leaning on his cane and talking with Colonel John Hughes. The sight of Sean made George's skin crawl. How could Louise see anything in the cripple? Sean looked away from the British army officer, catching George's eye, and both men stared at each other across the church steps with mutual hatred. George broke first, glancing behind to reassure himself that Louise was still in the church.

When she came out a short time later George watched her reaction when she caught sight of her former lover. She paused for a moment but turned away to walk towards him. The solicitor meanwhile had returned his attention back to John Hughes, for whom George also had a great dislike. Hughes had once intimated that George was on the German payroll as an agent for their Fatherland. Although he had not been able to prove it, George feared him more than ever since his plan to have Karolina killed had failed. Now that she was under the protection of the Lutheran pastor there was little chance he could arrange to have her silenced forever.

'Did you invite that bastard?' George snarled quietly to Louise when she was close to him.

'Who do you mean? Colonel Hughes or Major Duffy? Major Duffy served under Patrick,' Louise replied. 'He had every right to be here today.'

'Did you invite him because of your feelings towards him?' George snapped.

'It is over between us,' Louise sighed sadly. 'You have won. You have me under your roof and now you have total control of the family's fortunes. I am surprised that you did not organise a celebratory party instead of a service to remember your father and brother.'

'What I strive for is to make the Macintosh family name the most powerful in Australia,' George answered. 'So that my son will one day inherit what is due to him.'

'Have you forgotten that Giselle has a son, too?' Louise said, bridling, causing a scowl to appear on her husband's face. 'He has an equal claim to Patrick's inheritance.'

'That brat will be satisfied just having a roof over his head, and an allowance to squander as he grows older,' George replied. 'My brother's blood was weak and that will probably be his son's inheritance.'

Louise looked away, hoping to catch sight of Sean, but he was already gone. She knew that he would not attend the wake although he was entitled to. Her body still ached for his strong arms holding her at night but she also knew her sacrifice might keep Sean safe from her husband's dangerous machinations – so long as she did not break her promise to never see Sean again.

She excused herself and went down to the car waiting for her, leaving George still standing at the bottom of the steps to the church. Jack Firth had informed him that the solicitor had employed a man to ask questions about a wide range of matters that touched on their business arrangement. Tiny threads could be woven into a strong thread, George thought. It was time to arrange for some more threads to be cut. It was time to meet with Jack Firth.

23

Sean's meeting with Colonel John Hughes at the memorial service had not been coincidental. Sean had telephoned the British officer, as Patrick had once mentioned that if anything were to happen to him then John Hughes could be trusted with any matters concerning the family. They had agreed to meet at the service.

When Sean brought up the subject of Giselle's eviction, the distinguished Englishman expressed his contempt for George. Then Sean had led the colonel to the subject of Karolina Schumann. This in turn led to the contact between the police inspector charged with her case and his dealings with George Macintosh. When Sean mentioned the link between the two men, John Hughes did not look surprised.

'Do you have anything else?' he asked Sean, who now realised that he had entered into that strange game men in intelligence tended to play. It was like a game of poker, and the British officer was asking Sean to show him his hand without revealing his own.

'As much as I dislike the man,' Sean replied, 'I doubt that he is of any interest to your intelligence chaps.'

'You might be surprised,' John Hughes answered, casting his eyes towards George who stood on the steps of the church watching them. 'I am not at liberty to discuss the matter any further but I can tell you that there are highly placed forces within the government who are actively discouraging any of our investigations into George's affairs. It seems that he wields a lot of power beyond even the national interest.'

'You mean that our government is prepared to turn a blind eye to a man who is possibly committing treason?' Sean asked, aghast at the inference.

'When it comes to political power,' John replied with a sigh, 'possible treason takes a second place to the funds he contributes to keep them in power. Politicians only see their seats being protected – not the country.'

Sean had been given just enough to proceed in another direction, having realised that the British officer was hinting that they might be able to work together to bring George down. 'I will keep in contact, Colonel,' he said, and the two men parted.

It was only a matter of days before Christmas when Sean was visited by Harry Griffith at his office. The former policeman entered the room with a triumphant smile and dropped a manila folder on Sean's desk. 'Old Jack is gonna have the worst Christmas of his life when he finds this file missing,' Harry chuckled. 'It cost a bit to have it lifted, but I think you might find it useful.'

Sean flipped open the folder and, as he read, his face broke into a smile. It was the file pertaining to Karolina Schumann and the covering letters indicating that she should be arrested, signed by Jack's superior officers. No doubt they would be interested in learning the subordinate inspector had been derelict in his duties.

But Sean's smile evaporated when he turned over a few more sheets of paper and saw George Macintosh's name appear along with attached notes about observations made of him by the police even before the outbreak of the war – notes describing his meetings with a well-known German agent and the passing of money between the two men.

'You don't know just how badly Christmas will go for Inspector Firth – or George Macintosh,' Sean said quietly. 'What you have brought me is worth its weight in gold.'

'I thought you might be pleased,' Harry said. 'I did not pay it much attention but I did see where that Schumann sheila and the Macintosh bloke's names cropped up. If you ask me, this Macintosh bloke is working for the Huns and should be hung for treason. It seems that his mate, Jack, has been sitting on the file and probably getting paid by Macintosh to keep it to himself.'

'You should have been a detective,' Sean said, reaching into his drawer.

'I preferred to be in uniform. Too much paperwork being a detective.'

Sean retrieved the brown envelope and added a few more pounds as a bonus. The file sitting on his desk was invaluable. He thanked Harry and wished him a merry Christmas. When he had left, Sean wondered about where he would go from here. It was obvious! Colonel Hughes would be in a position to act on the file and bring both men down. He reached for the telephone and put in a call. As Sean did not discuss the contents of the file over the phone, he made an appointment to visit the British officer at his home, as Hughes was currently attending a military conference.

The appointment made, Sean put the phone down and reflected on the file before him. No doubt Firth had not destroyed the file to ensure George kept paying him to remain silent. But he had been careless in keeping it in his office, albeit hidden. Sean smiled. He wished he could be in the office when Firth finally got around to looking for his precious pile of papers.

But Jack Firth did not rage when he found the file missing. To do so would have brought attention to himself. Instead, he sat sweating at his desk, considering all the possibilities. He already knew from rumours around the station that the former police officer Harry Griffith had been asking a lot of questions about him. He had already confronted Harry and been perceptive enough to recognise Harry was indeed working for Sean Duffy. The file had to be in Duffy's possession, he concluded, calmly realising that he would have to silence the lawyer or risk being charged with being an accessory to treason. The idea of swinging on the gallows held little appeal to a man now well-off, thanks to Macintosh's payments. He cursed himself for being foolish in leaving the incriminating file at his office; he had never suspected that anyone would be brave enough to rifle through his things. Duffy must have paid one of his staff a lot of money to do that, Jack thought. He would find out soon enough who had betrayed him and deal with that person later. In the meantime, Jack had formulated how Major Sean Duffy, MC, would appear in the obituaries of the morning papers after his tragic accident. It would be a story of little interest, lost in the news from the war where hundreds of Australians were dying each week. Jack Firth knew Sean's daily routine – and there was one time during the day that the solicitor who had to rely on his walking stick was extremely vulnerable.

★

359

It was Friday afternoon and the clerks watched the hands of the big clock in the main office tick towards 5pm. When it did, they would disappear to their homes, while the solicitors of the firm would gather for a beer at a hotel nearby and celebrate the end of the week. But this afternoon Sean excused himself from the company of his learned friends. He had an appointment with Colonel John Hughes. Sean placed the incriminating files into a leather satchel and bid a good weekend to his clerk, hobbling out onto the city streets smelling of horse dung and petrol fumes exacerbated by the heat of a Sydney summer. Sean looked up at the sky. From the dark clouds gathering, he suspected the city was about to be cooled by a southerly buster, a fierce storm that would bring relief to the sweltering conditions.

He made his way to an electric tram and was helped aboard by a sympathetic man who had the sad smile and faraway look of a former soldier. Sean took the tram to Central Station and made his way to the suburban train platform. As he was still suffering the effects of the previous evening, which he'd spent getting drunk in an attempt to avoid the nightmares of exploding artillery shells and bodies being torn to bloody pieces, he failed to notice the man following him. Sean paid his fare and walked stiffly to the platform, where he sat on a bench until he saw the smoke heralding his train's approach.

Sean walked on unsteady legs to the edge of the concrete platform, crowded with workers eager to return to their homes in the suburbs. The train was braking to a stop when Sean felt the leather satchel being yanked from his hand. He attempted to swing around to defend himself and saw with horror the grim-faced image of Jack Firth snarling at him.

As the satchel was yanked clear, Sean felt himself toppling backwards onto the track. He was vaguely aware that someone had screamed but he knew nothing else until he slammed backwards across the steel tracks. Winded, he could not move and when he turned his head saw the great steam engine only a matter of yards away. Helpless, he braced himself and shut his eyes.

Jack Firth ducked his head and walked away through the crowd of horrified onlookers. He had guessed that few would have paid much attention to him. They would be more absorbed in watching the train approach. When Jack reached the end of the platform he glanced back. Satisfied that he had got away with murder, Jack strolled into the great foyer of Central Station, passing newsboys selling the papers proclaiming stalemate in the war that had no end. Only when he was on the street outside did he allow himself to open and inspect the contents of the satchel. As he had suspected, the incriminating evidence was inside. He would take steps to ensure that they never left his possession again. He knew just how close he had come to being revealed as a traitor.

Sean felt strong hands grip him under the arms and haul him from the track just as the steam engine ran over his legs. He screamed although he had felt no pain.

'Bloody close, Major,' the voice gasped in his ear. 'The engine got your legs.'

Sean felt himself being lifted into a sitting position. The screaming he could hear was from members of the public on the other side of the engine who had witnessed him fall to what would surely be his inevitable death.

'It got my legs,' Sean echoed, looking down at his artificial limbs, now crushed to useless metal and wood.

'Got your legs all right,' Harry said and broke into a chuckle. 'You will have to get some new ones.'

In the wonderful euphoria of still being alive, Sean smiled, then broke into laughter, no doubt confusing those on the platform who presumed that the man who had bravely flung himself onto the tracks in an attempt to rescue the disabled man had gone mad. Within a minute the two men were joined by a couple of railway porters who were shaking their heads at Sean's luck.

Not until he was lifted onto the railway platform and sat down on the concrete, did Sean realise that he was trembling uncontrollably.

'Firth got the file back,' he said quietly to Harry, who had remained close at Sean's side.

'The bastard tried to kill you,' Harry said. 'We have him.'

Sean shook his head, 'Unfortunately he will slip out of any accusation I make. I doubt that anyone here actually saw our struggle and, even if they did, Firth would make sure they did not give evidence. I know how he works and I am afraid that your word would not be good enough against him. This time he gets away with it but our fight has only started.'

Harry stood to allow two policemen who had appeared to speak with Sean. He informed them that he had slipped. They took notes and arranged for an ambulance to convey him to the nearest hospital for an examination although other than a sprained back and severe bruising, Sean had escaped serious injury.

'I have to ask,' he said, turning to Harry. 'How is it that you were there to rescue me?'

'I guess you can say that I was just keeping an eye out for you,' Harry replied self-consciously. 'Like we did for each other at the front.'

★

Sean extended his hand and clasped Harry's. No words were needed. As he was carried away on a stretcher he reflected sadly that any real chance of bringing George and the corrupt policeman to justice had just been snatched from his hand. He could tell John Hughes what he had read in the file – but without the file itself, he had no evidence.

George Macintosh felt his bowels turn to mush and desperately fought not to void them. He had returned from a satisfying day at his office where a board meeting of directors had congratulated him on his undisputed leadership of the family enterprises, while at the same time commiserating on the death of his esteemed father. It was this acknowledgment by some of the city's best known businessmen that established George as a ruler of a vast financial empire with tentacles that spread to almost every part of Asia and Europe.

But now he was standing in the foyer of his own home looking down the barrel of the old service pistol that his father had carried in his earlier days fighting the enemies of Queen Victoria. It was normally kept in his office, a gift from his father many years earlier to protect the house.

'You tried to murder him,' Louise said, holding the pistol with both hands and pointing it directly at George's face. 'You knew I loved him and even though I promised to never see Sean again you still tried to kill him.'

George was stunned. He had not had a chance to read the morning paper that day and was ignorant of the news.

'Duffy,' he blurted. 'I don't know what you are talking about.' He hoped his voice would not crack. From the expression in his wife's eyes she was ready to pull the trigger without considering the consequences of her actions. 'I swear on the life of our son,' he pleaded. 'I do not know what you are talking about.' For once he was telling the truth and it galled him that his wife did not believe him.

'It was in the paper this morning,' Louise spat. 'Major Sean Duffy, hero of Gallipoli and the Western Front, fell under a train at Central Station yesterday afternoon. Sean would not have fallen under a train unless he was pushed.'

'Firth,' George said in a whisper, considering him to be the only man other than himself who would have a motive to kill Duffy. 'You should put the gun down,' he said. 'Or you might accidentally pull the trigger, and what would our son do for a mother should you be hanged for murder?'

'Our son,' Louise repeated. 'That is the first time I have ever heard you refer to Donald as our son.'

George attempted to take a step forward but Louise stiffened. He immediately resisted any urge to overpower her. 'You must understand that all I have done is in the interests of you and our son,' George said. 'I may appear to be cold and calculating, but that is the way of business. My father and brother were weak men who did not understand the commercial world as I do, and if the companies had been left to them we would have been in the work house for the destitute before long. I have a dream that one day our son will take over from me and be seen as a man among men. You are his mother. Surely you have our son's best interests at heart. I swear that I knew nothing of Major Duffy's accident until now.'

Louise watched her husband's face very closely and listened carefully to the tone in his voice. She knew him well enough to know when he was lying, and for once she suspected that he was telling the truth.

'Do you know who might have wanted to kill Sean?' she asked.

'No,' George lied, careful to mask his expression. After

all, he had considered disposing of the Sydney solicitor. 'I am sorry that you think I might have tried to kill Major Duffy,' George added.

'I know that you are lying about being sorry,' Louise said, letting the revolver swing at her side. 'But, strangely, I do believe that you did not know of the attempt on his life.'

The sudden release from the threat of death brought a wave of euphoria over George. He stepped forward to put his arms around his wife. Louise stiffened, but did not fight him.

'You are an absolute bastard,' Louise said. 'But you are the father of my son.'

'Our son,' George corrected. 'We could have a good life together if you try.'

Louise felt spent. She no longer had the will to resist her husband. All she had to do was pretend that she was a loyal and loving wife in front of his friends and colleagues and, in turn, she would have Donald to herself.

Angus, Giselle and David had first travelled by steam train north and then taken a Cobb & Co coach to a depot in central Queensland, before being picked up by an employee of the Glen View station in a buggy. The last leg of the journey took a full dusty day before they finally reached the property at sunset.

Giselle had heard much about the station from Alex, who had once told her that when he was a boy he had spent a short time living there with his mysterious grandfather Michael Duffy. Alex had always spoken fondly about Glen View and Giselle thought it would be a good place for her son to grow up, considering his father had loved this land so much.

As Angus helped Giselle and her son from the buggy, a short, stocky, balding man in his middle years strode out from the house and introduced himself as the manager, Hector MacManus. He welcomed his three new residents and gruffly explained that they would live in the house with him. He was a widower and said that he looked forward to a future of good European-style cooking as his Aboriginal cook, a young girl, was having problems serving up much more than boiled beef. From his handshake Angus sized up the station manager as a good but gruff man, and was quick to notice the trace of his Scottish accent.

'You would be from Glasgow way,' Angus said, releasing his grip as he towered over the shorter man.

'That I would be, sergeant major,' he said with a wry grin. 'I have already heard about you from Mr Patrick Duffy and of how you and he soldiered together against the heathen fuzzy wuzzies. I was once a member of the Black Watch regiment.'

Immediately the two old soldiers found common ground and chatted about campaigns they had fought and exotic places they had taken leave, careful in the company of Giselle and her son not to allude to the brothels they had visited.

'But I must get you all settled. We can talk about your jobs here over a haunch of boiled beef – the last I hope to see in a long time,' Hector said, leading the way.

The house was made of mud brick, with a corrugated iron roof, wide verandahs and a simple, wire-fenced yard to keep out the kangaroos and wallabies of the surrounding plains. Suddenly Giselle felt the full weight of just how isolated her life was to become, living on the central plains of Queensland where she would be the only European female for many hundreds of miles, in a world of tough stockmen and nomadic Aboriginals who drifted to the station from other parts of the vast lands. She was given a relatively large room to share with her son, and the employee who had picked them up from the depot placed her large suitcase in a corner of the room.

'Welcome to Glen View, Mrs,' he said. 'The boys and I are looking forward to some good home cooking for a change.'

Giselle thanked him and he departed, leaving her with David in the silence of her new world. Despite all that Alex had said about the wonders of living in the country, Giselle found that she was sitting on the rickety bed and sobbing. She missed her mother and few friends in Sydney. But mostly she missed Alex. David clung to her hand, frightened. Giselle saw that her emotional state had caused her son to be fearful. Wiping away the tears with the back of her hand, she attempted to smile. 'Come, my little man,' she said in German. 'We must eat and learn to accept this place as our new home.'

After dinner, Hector invited his new guests to take tea on the verandah. Giselle now understood the magic Alex had known living on the property. She stared up at the night sky in its full glory of countless stars, twinkling over the silent plains. Hector noticed that the beauty of the evening had captivated her.

'The blackfellas around here used to say that the stars were the souls of the ancestors looking down on the earth,' he said, plugging his pipe with tobacco. 'We still have one old blackfella who lives in a cave not too far from here, called Wallarie,' Hector continued, scratching a match to light his pipe. 'I was told that he is the last of his tribe.'

'I have heard of this man called Wallarie,' Giselle replied. 'My husband told me that he is an almost mythical figure, with ancient powers to turn himself into a young man or eagle when it suited him.'

Hector puffed on the pipe. 'The old bugger spends a bit of time sitting there under the bumbil tree, the one growing just outside the fence, from when the pastor and his Mrs used to run the mission station for the blackfellas,' he said. 'But he's no magic man – just an old blackfella who has outlived all his family and has everyone fooled with his stories.'

'There'd be magic people in the Highlands, when I was a wee lad,' Angus said, breaking into the conversation. 'Magic things that only the old ones living in the glens knew from the time before the priests came to force them to flee to the shadow world.'

'That's the trouble with you heathen Highlanders,' Hector chuckled. 'You spent so much time away from the civilisation of the low lands that you really believed in those things.'

'Patrick, God rest his soul, used to say that while Wallarie lived, there would always be a curse on his family,' Angus continued. 'Given that he, little Nellie and Alexander are now all gone from this world, it may be possible that the family is indeed under an ancient curse.'

Giselle clasped David close to her as he sat at her feet playing with a short length of rope. 'I hope that all this conversation about curses is merely talk to frighten children,' she said. 'My son carries the blood of his father, and if there is a curse then surely he must also inherit that.'

'Oh, I am sorry Mrs Macintosh,' Hector hurried to apologise. 'The talk of Wallarie and the curse is nothing more than that. Just idle banter by the blackfellas and my stockmen, because they have nothing else to talk about out here.'

'Will it be possible to meet this strange man you speak of?' Giselle asked.

Hector took a breath and sighed, tapping his pipe on the arm of his chair. 'Funny thing,' he said. 'No-one around here has seen hide nor hair of the old fella for some months now. It is as if he has just up and disappeared. Maybe even gone out into the bush to die and join his ancestors up in the sky. My blackfella employees – and even my white stockmen – feel uneasy about his absence. They have some strange idea that if Wallarie is not to be found a terrible thing will happen here. But, as I say, it is all just idle talk.'

Giselle could see that her son had tired of the adult conversation and was ready to sleep. She bid the men a good night and took David to their room, leaving the two old soldiers on the verandah.

The moon rose over the plains, dimming the stars. The mournful cry of a curlew broke the silence, joined by others calling across the scrub.

'The blackfellas say that is the sound of the dead,' Hector said. 'It certainly fits in with the stories the stockmen have passed down over time about this place being cursed.'

'So you believe in the stories?' Angus asked.

'It is a queer thing,' Hector said. 'But every manager who has been here tells of how old Wallarie once said that there is an evil in the blood of the Macintosh family that can only be exorcised by the death of the Macintosh family itself and the returning of the land to the Darambal people. But it is just one of those stories that gets bigger with the telling.'

'Have you ever met your boss, George Macintosh?' Angus asked.

'Once, when I was in Sydney for an interview,' Hector replied. 'I didn't like the man from the moment I met him, but his father approved my position here. There was something about his son that made my skin crawl.'

Angus did not comment but puffed on his own pipe, listening to the tormented cries of the bush curlews and watching the plain light up under the full moon. The land reminded him of the places in Africa where he and Patrick had fought, shoulder to shoulder with rifle and bayonet.

'Well,' Hector said, tapping his pipe out for the last time. 'Not much chance of George Macintosh ever visiting Glen View so it's unlikely he'll meet a sticky fate at the hands of a blackfella curse. I will bid you a good night, Angus, and see you before first light for breakfast.'

Angus lingered, taking in the view the moon afforded him of his new home. He had been so much a part of the family since Patrick had recruited him from the slums of Glasgow, where he probably would have died from the drink had not Patrick saved him. Angus had lived through a time when the best of the family had died, leaving the most evil to rule. He wondered about the Aboriginal curse. David was also a Macintosh – as was George's son, Donald. Were they to be included in this ongoing drama stemming from this harsh land?

'Och, man!' he softly chided himself. He had only been on the property a few hours and already he was becoming one with the world around him of scrub and red dust. It was bad enough that he believed in the spirits of the old ones of the Highlands, let alone in heathen ghosts as well.

In her room, Giselle's attention was drawn back to the night sky. Through a window she found herself searching for the biggest and brightest star. Surely it would be her husband looking down on them.

After a couple of weeks Giselle was warming to station life. She was in a strange position, neither guest nor employee, and fully realised that Alex's brother had sent her to Glen View to get her and David as far from civilisation as possible. She also understood that while her son lived he was a rival to his cousin, young Donald, for the inheritance of the Macintosh empire.

Giselle soon befriended the young Aboriginal girl, and taught her how to prepare a greater variety of dishes than boiled beef and damper bread. And Giselle found herself as the resident medical practitioner, stitching wounds, soothing burns and setting broken limbs. It was as if she were back on her father's plantation in New Guinea. The work of healing gave her great satisfaction although she still mourned the lost opportunity of studying medicine.

Each day, David toddled in the yard, playing with the Aboriginal children of the men who worked alongside the Europeans. Giselle and Angus laughed when on the verandah one night David spoke to them and Hector MacManus in the language of his playmates.

'He's a bonnie young lad,' Hector said, plugging his pipe. 'He will make a fine bushman, and maybe eventually manage Glen View when I am gone.'

Giselle had come to like this tough former Scot who ruled with a friendly, fair and firm hand over both Aboriginal and European stockmen and their families. The demand for beef for the war effort ensured good prices for the cattle the men mustered and for her part Giselle quickly earned the man's respect for her competency in this land that was still a frontier.

One evening while only Giselle and Hector were on the verandah he slipped into a reflective mood. When Giselle gently prompted him as to his thoughts, Hector told her how he had been married when he first took up his management of the property.

'The poor lassie had a fatal fall from her horse after a visit to the cave,' he said softly. 'The blackfellas said that she went inside to explore but no woman is to step inside the sacred place of the blackfellas. They said that death would come to any woman who did so, but her fall from the horse was just a bloody accident. That was three years ago.'

'I am sorry,' Giselle answered. 'I understand you must still be grieving.'

'That you do, lassie,' Hector replied. 'Just don't be tempted to go where my wife did.'

His comment struck a chord with Giselle and she took it to heart. Man did not know all that lay beyond death, and possibly the ancient people who had lived so long with nature might have insights beyond European understanding.

Angus had settled into his role as the gardener. He had little understanding of horticulture but the resident Chinese gardener, using a few words of broken English, taught him the business of growing cabbages, lettuces and other vegetables.

The arrival of mail was the most anticipated day of the month. The postman rode by with his saddle bags full of newspapers, letters and parcels for the isolated property and would stay overnight, providing as much local information as he could to his hospitable hosts. In the morning he would leave with a hangover.

Angus and Hector had become firm friends and as the weeks turned into months Giselle found time had little meaning anymore. Life on the property assumed its own cycle and she was wonderfully surprised when she walked out onto the verandah early one morning to take in the peace of the rising sun. Hector was standing in the yard, holding the reins of a fine-looking mare.

'Happy birthday, Mrs Macintosh,' he said, beaming. 'I have a present for you.'

Giselle was stunned. She had forgotten! She gazed in rapture at the generous gift.

'How did you know it was my birthday?' she asked, stepping from the verandah.

'It was on the station records,' Hector said. 'And I'd be getting a mount for young David on his birthday. About time the future manager of Glen View learned to ride.'

Giselle stroked the mare's nose.

That evening Giselle was treated to a camp dinner, with all the station staff gathering around a half beast roasting on a spit. Sitting under the night sky as the soft, red embers rose in the clear, star-filled heaven, Giselle felt at home. She now understood Alex's fond memories of Glen View. She did not miss the crowded city streets of Sydney – or the frivolous social life. Here she was with nature, surrounded by men who appreciated her skills as a cook and healer. David was growing into a strong, sturdy boy in the healthy clear air and the plagues of flies, heat and occasional dust storms were simply taken in their stride.

According to the calendar on the back of the kitchen door it was now 1918. The war dragged on without any sign of it ending. Giselle had satisfied herself that she had no urgent duties to attend to, and informed Hector that she intended to go for a ride on her mare, which she had named Valkerie, to see the sacred hill. She also told him she wished to do so alone and explore some of the country around the creek she had heard was not far from the sacred hill.

'Be careful, Mrs Macintosh,' he said, frowning. 'There are still one or two wild blackfellas who come through this way. And remember my warning about the cave.'

With what he had said echoing in her head, Giselle dressed in jodhpurs and rode out, carrying extra water canteens. She had been given a map of the property and followed the directions until she came across the craggy red hill that rose like an island in a sea of stunted scrub. It was certainly an eerie place, Giselle thought uneasily as she felt the sun beating down on her in the middle part of the day.

She sensed that she was not alone and when she turned her attention on the surrounding bush she saw a man standing there, armed with spears and half naked. He had a long, dark bushy beard and his chest was covered in welts. He was a young man, and Giselle remembered the warning.

But the man, only fifty paces away, made no threatening move towards her although the mare under her shifted. Their eyes locked and Giselle could swear that he was talking to her without words she could hear on the hot, still air. He was telling her that all would be well and that soon they would be coming for both of them. When Giselle focused on the young man in the shimmering heat haze between them, she became aware that he was not young at all, but very old.

Valkerie shifted under her, snorting in confusion at what she sensed but could not see. For a moment Giselle's attention was distracted from the man as she fought to keep control of her mount, and when she looked up he was gone. Suddenly Giselle's horse reared. A huge wedge-tailed eagle rose with a slow flapping into the sky. Giselle brought the mare under control. She wanted to call out to the Aboriginal man but felt foolish. Had she seen a mirage that had set off her imagination? The eagle took a course westwards. It was a magnificent bird and Giselle admired its beauty.

That evening at the dinner table she mentioned the young Aboriginal she had seen who suddenly turned into an old man and how he had simply disappeared.

'Did you see an eagle?' Hector asked hesitantly.

'I did, Mr MacManus!' Giselle exclaimed.

'Then you saw Wallarie.'

Angus helped himself to more peas from the ceramic pot in the middle of the table and grinned. 'So you, as a low-lander, believe in the spirits?'

Hector squirmed. 'It's just that the local blackfellas say Wallarie appears as a young warrior, then flies away on the wings of an eagle,' he replied. 'You must have got a touch of the sun on your ride, or have heard the story from the men around here.'

Giselle did not argue that she had not heard any such tale, but the words she heard still echoed in her mind . . . *they will come for us both.*

24

Jerusalem had fallen before Christmas 1917, with the Australian Flying Corps following the advance of Allenby's mounted army, providing vital support. Captain Matthew Duffy had been able to secure leave from his squadron to visit the ancient city and had been accompanied by Saul Rosenblum, who had a good knowledge of the backstreets and byways from previous visits.

Saul revelled in the capture of this holiest of holy places, sacred to the three religions that dominated the Western and Middle Eastern worlds.

'The Syrian's place is just down here,' he said.

The two men passed between the stone walls of tenement-style houses that overlooked a shaded alley. They reached a narrow door; a small verandah with a pot plant perched above. When Saul knocked, a young man answered through a small sliding window in the thick, wooden door.

Saul spoke to the man in his fractured Arabic and the young man bade them enter.

Matthew was surprised how spacious the building was inside. It extended to a small but pretty open space between the buildings towering on either side. Persian carpets covered the stone floor and the beautifully crafted furniture indicated that this was the home of a well-off man. They waited while the young man went to fetch his master.

'You are the father of Benjamin,' a balding, bespectacled man wearing a red fez hat and goatee beard said, entering the room holding a long cigarette holder between his fingers. 'I am Dr Shariz.' He spoke perfect, unaccented English and Matthew was pleased.

'I wish to thank you, doctor,' Saul said. 'For saving my son's life.'

'He is well, then?' the doctor asked. Saul replied that he was.

'What do you know of an American woman, Miss Joanne Barrington?' Matthew asked without any preamble.

'You must be Captain Duffy. Miss Barrington spoke much about you,' the Syrian said, turning his attention to Matthew.

'I am, doctor,' Matthew replied, extending his hand. 'I was informed a few months ago that Miss Barrington had been taken by the Turks and handed over to the Germans to be sent to Berlin.'

'Ah, yes, that was their plan,' the doctor replied, indicating to the men to take a seat. 'May I offer you coffee and dates?' he asked. He spoke in Arabic and when the young man hovering in the background disappeared from the room the doctor took a chair opposite the two guests. 'I have sent my servant away as I wish to speak with you in private about Miss Barrington. She was not sent to Berlin.'

Matthew felt a cold sweat and had trouble finding his tongue. 'What has happened to her?' he heard himself asking.

The Syrian leaned forward to speak. 'Miss Barrington is most probably back in America with her father by now.'

His words swept away Matthew's fears. 'How is that possible?' he gasped.

Shariz lay back against the cushions, a secretive smile on his face. He took a puff from his cigarette. 'I was able to convince the local commander here that Miss Barrington would be worth a lot more for a ransom than she was to the Germans for interrogation. The commander is a practical man and arranged through the Red Cross to have her fate put in the hands of a Swiss banker, who, in turn, arranged for a large sum of money to be transferred to Istanbul. The commandant is an honourable man and so, shortly afterwards, the American woman was smuggled aboard a neutral ship which would take her home to her father.'

Matthew looked at Saul. He felt he could hug him in his joy at the news that Joanne was most probably enjoying the Christmas season with her family in America. All that mattered was that she was safe, and if he survived the war he would go in search of her.

'There is something else that I think you should know,' Shariz said as the servant re-entered the room, carrying a silver salver upon which were tiny cups, a plate of dates and a large, silver coffee pot. He placed the tray on a small, low set table and retreated after the doctor spoke to him.

'Gentleman, please help yourself,' he continued. 'Ah, yes, something else you should know . . . Miss Barrington was under my roof for two months before being smuggled from the country. In that time we learned she was with child and she informed me that you are the father, Captain Duffy.'

It took some seconds for the news to sink in. Matthew was about to ask how this could be so when he remembered the night before the attack on the Arab village. He was shaken from his silence by a slap on the back from Saul.

'Congratulations, Matthew, you sly dog,' he said, a broad grin splitting his bearded face. 'A father, eh.'

Matthew did not reply but looked to Shariz, who also smiled.

'I can assure you, Captain Duffy, that when she left me Miss Barrington's pregnancy was proceeding as expected,' he said. 'If all goes well, you will be a father in around three months' time.'

'I have to find Joanne,' Matthew finally spoke.

'I am afraid that will not be possible for the foreseeable future,' Saul cautioned. 'We have not yet brought the Ottomans to the table to sign their defeat. I don't think your country will stop the war for you to find your Miss Barrington until the Turks are defeated.'

Matthew felt his elation rush from him like a breath exhaled. Saul was right. The best he could do was write to Joanne in America and tell her that he would be coming for her when the war was over. He would be able to obtain the address of her father's residence through the Red Cross. So, there would be a grandson or granddaughter for his mother to hold, Matthew thought. For a moment he found himself reflecting on the irony of life. His own father had been an American citizen and if his child was born in the United States, he or she would also be an American citizen. He did not care whether his child was a boy or girl. All he cared about was that Joanne was in good health and so, too, was the child she carried.

Now all he had to do was stay alive.

★

Corporal Tom Duffy sat on a low stone fence in the village square and stared at the old, Gothic-style church with its gargoyles and angels around the arch above the wide wooden doors. It was cold but he did not feel the chill anymore. Villagers hurried to get inside their little houses or shops, seeing the darkening sky as a prelude to heavy, sleeting rain. Unlike his comrades who were inside the taverns drinking wine while on leave from the front, Tom preferred to roam the town and surrounding peaceful countryside, a landscape so different to the vast and lonely plains of the Gulf country where he had grown up.

'You should get in from the cold,' a female voice said in heavily accented English.

Tom turned to see the pale cherubic face of a young woman with large brown eyes and short dark hair, about eighteen years of age. She wore the dress of a farm girl and carried a large basket filled with duck eggs.

Tom pushed himself off the stone fence. 'May I help you, mademoiselle?' he asked, reaching for the basket. She did not resist his gesture and thanked him.

'My name is Tom Duffy,' he said by way of introduction.

The girl smiled at him, her eyes emitting a warmth that shone through from her soul. Tom felt himself drifting into that warmth and wondered if there could be any other woman as beautiful as this young French girl.

'You are an Australian,' she said, staring at the slouch hat that marked him as a digger. 'My people say that the Australians are very brave but that they steal things,' she giggled. 'You will not steal my eggs, no?'

'No.' Tom smiled. 'Where are you taking them?'

'To the tavern where your friends drink,' she replied, falling into step beside him. 'Why is it that you do not drink with them?'

'How is it that you speak such good English?' he countered.

She blushed. 'I learn from my cousin who live in England many years. One day I will be teacher of children.'

'A school teacher,' Tom said. 'But you look like you have come from a farm.'

'My parents have farm a half kilometre from town,' she replied as they walked as slowly as Tom could to prolong the time in her company. 'I finish school this year and now wish to learn to teach children, too.'

'You could teach a lot of Aussies how to speak English,' he said with a wry smile. The young woman looked at him blankly and Tom shook his head. 'That is a joke,' he said, his smile widening. 'I suppose that you are all getting ready for Christmas this time of year.'

The girl looked away before turning back to Tom. 'My brother, he was killed this year,' she said sadly. 'My parents do not want to, how you say, celebrate Christmas.'

'I am sorry for your loss,' Tom replied as they reached the tavern. They could hear the laughter of drunken men and the voice of a woman attempting to be heard over the merriment as her drunken audience shouted lewd suggestions at her.

'Place must be full of Poms,' Tom said. 'An Aussie would let the singer have a go.'

Once again the girl looked at Tom blankly. He smiled, shaking his head. 'I think you should learn how we speak in Australia,' he said. 'Much better than learning English. I will escort you inside to make sure that you are not molested.'

'What is molested?' she asked.

'What I will not have to explain if I go with you inside.'

While the girl spoke with the tavern keeper, all around them soldiers from the Empire tried to temporarily forget

381

that Christmas was coming and they would not be at home to share it with their loved ones. Cheap, red wine helped kill the homesickness and dampen the fear of what lay ahead for 1918. When the young French girl had concluded her dealings, Tom insisted on escorting her outside. When they were in the street, he handed the empty basket to her. 'I do not know your name,' he said.

'Does that matter, Tom Duffy?' she asked, pulling a scarf over her head.

'It does if I am to see you again,' he replied. 'I have four more days until I return to the battalion.'

The girl stared at him. 'You will be here for Christmas Day?' she asked.

'It seems so,' he replied. 'I am due back the day after.'

'Then you should be the guest of my family,' she said with a warm, inviting smile. 'Just ask the people where the Joubert farm is,' she continued. 'I am Juliet and you have been a true gentleman, Tom Duffy. Thank you.'

She walked quickly away, hoping to miss the rain that was threatening the little village. Tom stood in the street, watching until she disappeared into the green fields behind the village common. When the rain began to fall he decided to seek shelter inside the tavern.

That night, as he lay in his flea-infested bed in the town's stables that were being used to billet soldiers on leave from the front, he found it difficult to get to sleep. It was not the biting fleas that kept him awake – he had long grown used to the lice that infested the soldier's clothing on the front – but the image of Juliet's beautiful face swimming before him. She had not seemed to notice that he was of mixed race and, if she did, she did not seem to care. The French seemed less discriminating to people of colour. He had seen regiments of North Africans, men as black as the night, who had been treated respectfully by those Frenchmen with whom they served on the front. Maybe Juliet thought all Australians were tanned and had his facial features. Whatever it was, Tom was sure she had shown an interest in him. He hoped so.

Tom met Juliet and her family at the church for mass on Christmas morning. He was introduced to her parents, whose formal stiffness suggested a wariness about the strange man who obviously had a romantic interest in their youngest daughter. Tom soon learned that Juliet's two older sisters had married local farmers and one had already been widowed by the war. Neither parent spoke English, so Juliet translated. A couple of times on the walk back from the church to the Joubert farm house, Tom noticed Juliet exchanging annoyed words with her parents. They had glanced at the young Australian soldier over their shoulders but otherwise acted in a courteous manner towards him. They knew of the fierce reputation the Australians had established for themselves on the battlefields of France and Flanders, and the reputation for reckless courage did not bode well with parents who had already lost a son to the war.

Inside the farm house Tom could feel the warmth of the open fireplace and smell the delicious aroma of a roasting goose in an oven. On the mantelpiece was the framed photo of a young man in uniform. Tom was struck by how much he looked like himself. Even Juliet's mother had glanced at him with a curious expression on her face whenever she thought he was not looking at her. Tom tried to be as unobtrusive as possible and when they all sat down for the Christmas lunch bowed his head as Mr Joubert said grace.

When lunch was over Juliet sat at an old piano in the corner of the small but cosy living room. Tom was pleasantly surprised that she could both play with an expert touch and sing with a beautiful voice. Her sad songs alone enchanted him and he knew that he was falling in love with this enigmatic young French woman. He sat on a sofa as her parents joined in the singing. When their song finished, Mr Joubert raised his glass of brandy towards the photograph of his son. 'Vive la France,' he said.

Tom echoed his words – the few he knew in French.

That afternoon, aided by the brandy, Mr Joubert softened his attitude to the young Australian soldier and, through Juliet, asked him many questions about his life in Australia. Attempting to identify with his host, Tom said he too was a kind of farmer of livestock, which endeared him a little to Juliet's father.

When the Frenchman asked Tom how many cattle he had, Tom extrapolated to what he expected to own when he returned to Queensland. 'Around 3000 head,' he said.

Mr Joubert looked at Tom in disbelief. 'My father has said that a man with that many cattle would have to be the richest man in the world.'

Tom broke into a broad smile. 'I hope to be, Mr Joubert,' he replied.

The day went too quickly and soon it was growing dark. It would be cold walking back to his billet but he was to be on parade early next morning before being transported back to his battalion at the front. The men were engaged in patrols into no-man's-land, attempting to take prisoners for the intelligence people while the Germans carried out similar patrols. It was dangerous work and Tom dreaded returning now that he had found something far more valuable than the bags of diamonds.

He stood on the doorstep, bidding his hosts goodbye. Juliet watched him with sorrowful eyes. They had not had the chance to be alone in the house but Tom could see from her snatched looks that her interest in him was more than just that of a friend. How badly he had wanted to touch her hand and kiss her face.

'You will write to me,' she said, her breath meeting his and her large eyes fixing his own.

'Every chance I get,' Tom replied, forcing himself not to embrace her, as Mrs Joubert stood behind her daughter in the doorway.

'I will wait at the post office every day,' Juliet replied. Suddenly she stepped forward and kissed him on the cheek, despite her mother's gasp of disapproval. When she stepped back, Tom walked away into the cold night, the feel of her lips still warm on his cheek. He did not turn back. To see her face would have been more than he could bear knowing that he was going back to a war with no end.

But between missions of prisoner snatching patrols and lying out in no-man's-land sniping unsuspecting German soldiers, he did write. By the time 1918 arrived Tom Duffy was yet to face the worst weeks of his life on the Western Front. He treasured the most beautiful words he had ever read in his life, in the fine copperplate handwriting of his beloved French farmer's daughter. He would fight to stay alive and take home the diamond of his life – Juliet.

25

At Glen View the bite of the summer was going from the land. Soon the cold would come, bringing early morning dew onto the vegetable garden.

Giselle kneeled over the row of newly planted potatoes and pulled at the weeds. Beside her, the Chinese gardener worked diligently to keep his precious plants alive, watering them from a battered can. The heat was losing its potency as the day drew to a close and Giselle could hear the happy laughter of her son, who was playing with two little Aboriginal boys of his own age. The floppy straw hat she wore shaded her vision but she heard Angus call.

'Mrs Macintosh, we appear to have visitors comin'.'

Giselle straightened her back and gazed across the plains. A small plume of dust was spreading on a light breeze in the distance and, from the way it rose, it was obvious that whoever was coming was in a horse-drawn buggy. It was unusual for visitors to come to the station and Giselle kept the dust in sight until she could actually see the outline of the buggy with its driver and passenger.

'Who do you think it is?' she called to Angus, who from the verandah had a better view.

'I don't know,' he replied, shading his eyes.

After some minutes Giselle could see that the driver was a man dressed in black and his passenger a woman in a long flowing dress. Even before she could clearly see their features, Giselle knew who they were. She ran to the gate, flung it open and ran up the dusty track towards the buggy.

'Mama!' she screamed, her floppy hat falling from her head.

The driver flicked the horse with his small whip, speeding it towards the station house and came to a stop beside Giselle. Karolina leaped from the buggy into her daughter's embrace, holding tight as if planning to never let go. Both women sobbed with joy as Pastor Karl von Fellmann, the reins in his hands, looked down on the scene with a smile. Angus strode up to meet the visitors and, as Karl dismounted, took control of the horse. He held out his hand.

'You must be the pastor,' he said. 'Welcome back to Glen View.'

'And you must be Mr Angus MacDonald whom I have heard so much about from Giselle's letters to her mother,' Karl said, brushing away as much dust as he could from his coat. 'I have finally returned home,' he added.

When the joyous outpourings of welcome were over, Giselle led her mother by the hand towards the verandah from where young David had stared at the spectacle of his mother weeping and laughing at the same time. He shyly approached Karolina, leaving his companions to watch the meeting with curiosity. Karolina crouched down as the little boy accepted her embrace as she hugged him to her.

'Oh, my little man, you have grown so much since I last held you,' she said. 'You are so strong and healthy.'

'Ah, Mrs Schumann, Pastor, I see that you have arrived safe and well,' Hector said, emerging from the house. 'I pray that your journey here went well.'

'You knew!' Giselle said, turning on the station manager.

He grinned back at her. 'I'm afraid so, lassie,' he replied. 'But I was sworn to keep it a secret until the pastor and your mother arrived. It's good to have you back, Karl.'

The Lutheran minister thrust out his hand. 'Is Wallarie still here?' he asked.

'Haven't seen the old bugger in months,' Hector replied, slapping Karl on the back. 'But Mrs Macintosh reckons she saw him a few weeks back out in the bush.'

'That is good,' Karl replied. 'I fear for my old friend's health.'

'Wallarie will outlive all of us,' Hector said, turning to call for a housemaid to assist with the luggage from the buggy. 'You have arrived just in time for a dinner prepared under the supervision of Mrs Macintosh, so I can promise that you will eat well.'

That night Karolina and Karl shared stories of the world beyond the vast horizons of Glen View.

'Mr Duffy, the solicitor, was able to secure our release,' Karolina said in a sombre tone. 'He is a good man and has friends in the military who helped us put forward our case. Colonel Hughes, Patrick's friend and yours, argued that we would not be a threat to their security if we were to promise to remain on Glen View. That was not difficult, as I have committed myself to assist Karl in his work with the Aboriginal people of his congregation.'

Giselle looked at her mother in surprise and then at Karl, whose expression gave away nothing. For a moment

Giselle experienced a small shock at what she concluded had occurred between her mother and the Christian minister. Her mother was such a devout follower of her Jewish religion and yet it appeared she would be living with a Christian.

Karolina noticed the look on her daughter's face. 'Oh, dear, don't make any assumptions,' she said reassuringly. 'Karl is a dear friend.'

'Oh, mother, I was not thinking . . .'

'Yes, you were,' her mother gently chided. 'But for now the most important thing is that we are all together again and a family once more. God has been kind to me.'

That night was one of the best in Giselle's memory for a long time. She had lost her beloved husband, but her mother had returned to her in a land she was growing to love for its strange spirituality, one that only those who lived on the vast, semi-arid plains could understand. Here, she knew, her son would grow strong, and one day challenge for his rightful place in the leadership of the Macintosh dynasty.

After everyone had retired for the night Giselle gently woke her son and took him by the hand. Still drugged with sleep, David rubbed his eyes. She led him to the front yard and there, in the chill of the night, spoke softly to him.

'This land will make you strong, my little man,' she said, staring up into the night sky. In the distance a dingo howled to its mate and the curlews fell silent. 'You have the spirit of your father and must make him proud as he watches over us from above. You are all that I love and will always love.'

David did not understand the words his mother spoke but was transfixed by a terrifying sight in the dark beyond the old bumbil tree. There was a man he had never seen before and he was watching David with great interest. David clung to his mother's hand tightly. He wanted to tell her about the scary man watching them but she did not appear to see him. Then the strange black man suddenly smiled and David relaxed his grip. He felt safe, as if this man was talking to him.

Sensing her son's agitation, Giselle looked down at him. 'David?' she queried.

The boy slowly pointed into the dark.

'I don't see anything,' Giselle frowned, peering in the direction of her son's outstretched hand. Then suddenly she gasped. 'You see him!' Her frown turned into a smile. 'He is the good spirit of this land, although I know that only you can see him now,' she added. 'His name is Wallarie and he will always be here to look over those who come to his lands.'

David still did not understand his mother's strange explanation but sensed her inner peace. It would be many years before this moment would come back to him in a dream.

EPILOGUE

Glen View
Lutheran Mission Station
1934

The tall, broad-shouldered young man stood respect-fully waiting for the old Aboriginal to speak again. The sun was low on the horizon and the heat of the day disappearing. In a short time a soft, orange glow would herald the appearance of the stars in the moonless night.

Wallarie tapped his pipe against the hardwood club beside him and turned his head towards the orange ball hovering over the plains.

'You still here?' he asked, knowing full well that he had entranced this young man with his story. 'The bumbil tree I sit under was young when I was young,' he sighed. 'It will still be here when you and I have become one with the sky above.'

Wallarie sensed that the young man was reluctant to leave him, and the woman who had stood behind the young man earlier in the afternoon was long gone from their presence.

'You said it was 1918 when it all happened,' the young man said. 'That was the year the Great War ended. I was only three years old.'

Wallarie turned to the young man who had squatted with his back towards the west.

'I have more tobacco to give to you if you tell me what happened that year to change everything.'

'The ancestor spirits were angry and sent the death that took away many people,' Wallarie said. 'The Great War between the whitefellas you speak of ended for all except Tom Duffy. He went to a place of great cold to fight more whitefellas. He was a great warrior. But I am tired and the mother of your mother is in the house. You should go to her.'

The young man rose to his feet, frustrated that the story had come to an end for the day. Wallarie was little more than a charlatan, he scoffed to himself as he walked to the verandah. He was just an old man spinning stories as incredible as those he told about the young man's own ancestors. Tales of his magic were little more than the imagination of poorly educated European stockmen and the nomadic Aboriginals who had taken up residence on the Glen View lands, working beside the European cattlemen for flour, sugar and tea.

The young man's grandmother stepped from the house to inform him that dinner would be served shortly. 'Oh, look at that!' she gasped. 'Is it not beautiful?'

The young man turned to see what had attracted her attention and caught sight of a great wedge-tailed eagle soaring skywards above the bumbil tree. He suddenly felt fearful. Wallarie was no longer sitting cross-legged under the tree. He had simply disappeared. But the young man reassured himself that this was nothing more than a coincidence.

As he returned to the house the eagle flapped its wide wings and flew towards the dying sun. The young man froze in his tracks. Had he imagined or actually heard the old Aboriginal's voice? *'You come back tomorrow. I will tell you what happened in your year of 1918.'*

AUTHOR NOTES

From the Sudan campaign of 1885 to the time of writing, the official death toll of Australians who have died for their country totals 102,814.

During World War One alone we lost 61,513 of the above figure, and that does not take into account those returning men who died some years later as a direct result of their wounds. That is why, even today, on 11 November each year, we pause to reflect on The Great War of 1914–19 and its impact on our young nation.

The terrible loss of life between those years must be seen in the context of our small population at the time; there were very few homes that did not mourn the loss of a beloved member who had volunteered to go overseas to fight for King and Empire. I have reflected this in the deaths of three central characters in this family saga.

I did not intend to write a military history of the battles

Australians fought as this has been done in a very readable style by Les Carlyon in his magnificent *The Great War* (Pan Macmillan, Sydney, 2006). I would strongly recommend that it be read to gain an understanding of the historically significant role our forces played in changing the course of history in the early part of the 20th century.

Many years ago, while I was an infantry officer with the Army Reserve 1/19 Battalion of the Royal New South Wales Regiment, I had the fortune to dine with veterans of our unit from World War One in the officers' mess. In discussions with a Lewis gunner and the battalion's adjutant, I asked if the places they had fought at had a great meaning to them at the time they took part in the major battles. They replied that, during the fighting, their only concern was to stay alive in the tiny piece of battlefield they occupied, and that grand strategy had little interest to them. Many former veterans of any war would tell you the same thing – that their main concern at the time is that little piece of ground they occupy. For it is on that section of a battlefield that they either live or die. So this novel concerns a little piece of battlefield and excludes the tactics and planning of politicians and generals.

I remember a story that the old Lewis gunner told me that night at the dinner table. He had received shrapnel wounds to the lower part of his body at Mont St Quentin. As a result of his wounds a certain part of his anatomy was put in plaster and he was then granted medical leave in Paris. He turned to me with a sad expression, saying, 'What bloody good was leave to me in Paris with that kind of wound?' Sixty-five years later the story proved to be funny to the listener – but not at the time to a young, red-blooded Aussie digger in the fleshpot of France. I have mentioned Private Dan Frogan in passing and wanted to make a note that his grandson of the same name lives in the Clarence Valley and has become something of a sporting legend achieving legendary feats not unlike those accomplished by his grandfather.

Needless to say the story has not ended. In the next instalment of the saga I will take the reader to 1918. In that year it could go either way as to who would win the terrible war as the events of the Russian revolution released German troops from the Eastern Front to the Western Front. In that year too Aussie diggers fought their most important battles, turning the tide against Germany for the final victory. We will see that story through the experiences of Sergeant Tom Duffy, and we will see the family story continue through the eyes of those still left alive in their struggle for control of sacred land and a family fortune.

The year 1918 also saw a horrific pandemic come to the world. It caused more deaths in a matter of weeks than all the years of battlefield casualties combined. It was a year that changed the course of history in ways that we have lived with although not knowing the reasons why.

ACKNOWLEDGMENTS

A few readers have contacted me to say that they enjoy reading the acknowledgments because it is like an author's newsletter. I guess in many ways I could also call this section my annual report to readers.

To start with I would like to thank my publisher, Cate Paterson, for her ongoing support, and congratulate Cate on her new position as head of the publishing department at Pan Macmillan. Fortunately, James Fraser, whose position Cate has gone into, will still be around so that I can shout him a cold ale when I am in Sydney. Over the years, James has always been one of my strongest supporters and I want to thank him for that.

When it comes to the hard miles developing a novel, Catherine Day works just as hard as I do on the manuscript and my heartfelt thanks to Catherine for her wonderful style of editing.

In the publicity department I have lost my dear friend Jane Novak to fresh fields but would like to acknowledge all those years we spent on the road, putting our livers at risk with the many functions we attended from one end of Australia to the other. So now a welcome to Louise Cornegé, who has joined Pan Macmillan, and a promise I will ensure her liver does not suffer as did Jane's and mine.

A special thank you to my old friend and agent, Geoffrey Radford, for his ongoing support. As each year passes I appreciate his efforts even more.

To the three men working on the *Frontier* project – Irvin Rockman, CBE, and Rod and Brett Hardy – my very special thanks for all the truly professional work that has gone into developing the concept for television. It will only be a matter of time.

Congratulations to Kevin Jones, OAM, for receiving overdue recognition this year with his award in the Australia Day honours list. Needless to say, Maureen and family also deserve to wear the medal for all their support of Kevin's hours away from home while serving the community.

Congratulations also go to my old mate Larry Gilles for becoming an Aussie citizen. He is the only Yank I know who puts half a jar of vegemite on his toast and on those grounds alone I think the government decided to grant him citizenship.

I would like to thank a wonderful young lady, Kristie Hilderbrand, for setting up a Facebook website for my readers. Kristie has provided a means for me to keep readers up to date with news, photos and prizes.

For the day-to-day support that I get from those around me I thank Jan Dean and her sister, Eve Hunt, Mick and Andrea Prowse, Fran MacGuire, Dr Louis Trichard and his wife, Christine, and John and Isabel Millington.

On a sadder note I wish to express my condolences to Col Bambrick's family for his passing late last year. Col was a reader who served his country as a national serviceman in Vietnam.

For my old mate John Blackler, APM, and his wonderful wife, Judy, my thanks for all the research material you have sent. John is one of the most prominent former policemen whose academic and practical work has added so much to the field of criminology.

A special thank you to an Australian icon, Kay Cottee, AO, for her compassionate care of my dear sister, Kerry McKee, whose health has deteriorated. Kay still has her love for the sea with her vital work in marine rescue.

And last but not least, a mention of author colleagues Dave Sabben, MG, Tony Park, Steve Horne and Simon Higgins; a thank you for your friendship and many shared bottles of red wine.

For Naomi, these acknowledgments and the books I write would not exist without your love and support.

Postscript

As many of my friends have been recognised by Australia for their service above and beyond what is required, I am providing this explanation to those not familiar with post-nominals.

CBE Commander of the Order of the British Empire. For Irvin's services to the Australian community.

MG Medal for Gallantry. For Dave's service as a platoon commander during the battle of Long Tan. He is also an author.

AO Officer of the Order of Australia. Kay was the first woman to complete a solo, non-stop circumnavigation of the world. She is also an author.

APM Australian Police Medal. Awarded to John for his considerable and distinguished service to the NSW Police. He is also an author.

OAM Medal of the Order of Australia. For Kevin's long and important voluntary service to many communities that he has lived in over the years.

Peter Watt
Cry of the Curlew

I will tell you a story about two whitefella families who believed in the ancestor spirits. One family was called Macintosh and the other family was called Duffy . . .

Squatter Donald Macintosh little realises what chain of events he is setting in motion when he orders the violent dispersal of the Nerambura tribe on his property, Glen View. Unwitting witnesses to the barbaric exercise are bullock teamsters Patrick Duffy and his son Tom.

Meanwhile, in thriving Sydney Town, Michael Duffy and Fiona Macintosh are completely unaware of the cataclysmic events overtaking their fathers in the colony of Queensland. They have caught each other's eye during an outing to Manly Village. A storm during the ferry trip home is but a small portent of what is to follow . . . From this day forward, the Duffys and the Macintoshes are inextricably linked. Their paths cross in love, death and revenge as both families fight to tame the wild frontier of Australia's north country.

Spanning the middle years of the nineteenth century, *Cry of the Curlew* is a groundbreaking novel of Australian history. Confronting, erotic, graphic but above all a compelling adventure, Peter Watt is an exceptional talent.

Peter Watt
Shadow of the Osprey

On a Yankee clipper bound for Sydney harbour the mysterious
Michael O'Flynn is watched closely by a man working undercover
for Her Majesty's government. O'Flynn has a dangerous mission to
undertake . . . and old scores to settle.

Twelve years have passed since the murderous event which
inextricably linked the destinies of two families, the Macintoshes and
the Duffys. The curse which lingers after the violent 1862 dispersal
of the Nerambura tribe has created passions which divide them in
hate and join them in forbidden love.

Shadow of the Osprey, the sequel to the bestselling *Cry of the
Curlew*, is a riveting tale that reaches from the boardrooms and
backstreets of Sydney to beyond the rugged Queensland frontier
and the dangerous waters of the Coral Sea. Powerful and brilliantly
told, *Shadow of the Osprey* confirms the exceptional talent of master
storyteller Peter Watt.

Peter Watt
Flight of the Eagle

No-one is left untouched by the dreadful curse which haunts
two families, inextricably linking them together in love, death and
revenge.

Captain Patrick Duffy is a man divided between the family of his
father, Irish Catholic soldier of fortune Michael Duffy and his adoring,
scheming maternal grandmother, Enid Macintosh. Visiting the village
of his Irish forbears on a quest to uncover the secrets surrounding
his birth, he is beguiled by the beautiful, mysterious Catherine
Fitzgerald.

On the rugged Queensland frontier Native Mounted Police trooper
Peter Duffy is torn between his duty, the blood of his mother's
people – the Nerambura tribe – and a predestined deadly duel with
Gordon James, the love of his sister Sarah.

From the battlefields of the Sudan, to colonial Sydney and the
Queensland outback, *Flight of the Eagle* is a stunning addition to
the series featuring the bestselling *Cry of the Curlew* and *Shadow
of the Osprey,* with master storyteller Peter Watt at the height of his
powers.

Peter Watt
To Chase the Storm

When Major Patrick Duffy's beautiful wife Catherine leaves him
for another, returning to her native Ireland, Patrick's broken heart
propels him out of the Sydney Macintosh home and into yet another
bloody war. However the battlefields of Africa hold more than
nightmarish terrors and unspeakable conditions for Patrick – they
bring him in contact with one he thought long dead and lost to him.

Back in Australia, the mysterious Michael O'Flynn mentors Patrick's
youngest son, Alex, and at his grandmother's request takes him on a
journey to their Queensland property, Glen View. But will the terrible
curse that has inextricably linked the Duffys and Macintoshes for
generations ensure that no true happiness can ever come to them?
So much seems to depend on Wallarie, the last warrior of the
Nerambura tribe, whose mere name evokes a legend approaching
myth.

Through the dawn of a new century in a now federated nation, *To
Chase the Storm* charts an explosive tale of love and loss, from
South Africa to Palestine, from Townsville to the green hills of
Ireland, and to the more sinister politics that lurk behind them. By
public demand, master storyteller Peter Watt returns to his much-
loved series following on from the bestselling *Cry of the Curlew*,
Shadow of the Osprey and *Flight of the Eagle*.

Peter Watt
To Touch the Clouds

*They had all forgotten the curse . . . except one . . . until it touched
them. I will tell you of those times when the whitefella touched the
clouds and lightning came down on the earth for many years.*

In 1914, the storm clouds of war are gathering. Matthew Duffy and
his cousin Alexander Macintosh are sent by Colonel Patrick Duffy to
conduct reconnaissance on German-controlled New Guinea. At the
same time, Alexander's sister, Fenella, is making a name for herself
in the burgeoning Australian film industry.

But someone close to them has an agenda of his own – someone
who would betray not only his family but his country to satisfy
his greed and lust for power. As the world teeters on the brink of
conflict, one family is plunged into a nightmare of murder, drugs,
treachery and treason.

To Touch the Clouds is a powerful continuation of Peter Watt's
much-loved saga of the Duffy and Macintosh clan, begun in *The Cry
of the Curlew*.

PHOTO: DEAN MARTIN